The Alien Code

THE ALIEN CODE

Aliens disclose contact
and expose the true nature of the Greys

Mathieu Hamaekers

1	2	1	2	1	2	1	2	1	2	1	2
2	1	2	1	2	1	2	1	2	1	2	1
1	2	1	2	1	2	1	2	1	2	1	2
2	1	2	1	2	1	2	1	2	1	2	1
1	2	1	2	1	2	1	2	1	2	1	2
2	1	2	1	2	1	2	1	2	1	2	1
1	2	1	2	1	2	1	2	1	2	1	2
2	1	2	1	2	1	2	1	2	1	2	1
1	2	1	2	1	2	1	2	1	2	1	2
2	1	2	1	2	1	2	1	2	1	2	1
1	2	1	2	1	2	1	2	1	2	1	2
2	1	2	1	2	1	2	1	2	1	2	1

For more information about the author and internet links, used in the book, surf to:

http://www.thealiencode.net

or

http://www.thealiencode.info

First print

© 2008 English translation
Translation: Mathieu Hamaekers
Cover design: Mathieu Hamaekers
Design of all illustrations: Mathieu Hamaekers
ISBN/EAN 90-902311-7-X
NUR 305
D/2009/Mathieu Hamaekers, publisher.

For the sake of humanity

Prologue
27/2/2007

Ramon is sitting quietly in his computer room in front of the two computer screens, normally filled with magical 3D drawings. But now the situation is different. With hesitation, the first letters appear on the screen. In his mind, conflicting arguments cause hesitation.

Come on, Ramon, let's do the job. There is only one way to know whether the information you had to cope with last year, has any significance. You have to write the damn book.

But, I don't like to write. Give me a pencil or a 3D drawing program. But writing! Jesus, no! If anybody would have told me some months ago that I would write a book, I would have laughed in his face.

But you can't refuse to write this book. Imagine that everything Teimon told is true. Imagine that it really is true.

Wrinkles of deep concern appear on his forehead. The consequences would be too severe to imagine.

On the other hand, if it is all just imagination, I will find out soon enough. It is not because the information can be true that it is also true.

Shit! Why is there always doubt? But what the heck! I doubt therefore I am. To be honest, I hope it is all just a strange twist of my own imagination. Misinterpretation of the circumstances. I prefer to be called a fool than to discover that all the information of Teimon's SOS messages is true.

In his mind, Ramon remembers crystal clear how it all began.

No, no, I have to write it down. And I have to write precisely how the information was revealed. Otherwise I will not find the courage to put this strange story into words.

Again some words appear on the computer screen.

But… I have so much other things to do. I really don't have the time.

Come on, Ramon. Don't look for excuses. We went there time and again. You have to do it. Teimon's message is too important.

Ok, ok. I give myself a year to do the job. That must be feasible. All the other projects I'm working on will have to wait.

Come on, Ramon. Stop your doubting mind. In the end, it will work out well. It always does.

But I don't have all the information yet. There is a lot more to come. Ok, Teimon said that synchronicity will help me all the way. I can't wait until I know the whole story.

Ramon feels he has to start writing now. He must not hesitate another day. The existence of "The Alien Code" has to be revealed.

Again some words appear on the screen but his mind is still not focused. Because he studied at the mystery school, he could deal with all the strange things that had happened in the last months. People having contact with or even abducted by aliens, telepathic contact with beings from other worlds, alien signals from space. These phenomena were as normal for Ramon as making coffee. But the timing was his main concern.

He looks at the pile of notes beside his keyboard.

Enough, Ramon! Please, don't hesitate any longer. The book must be written. Before it is too late. Before somebody prevents it from being written. You have to take your responsibility. The dice are thrown…

Except for the sound of the keyboard, it is extremely silent in his WebCom, most of the time filled with drum 'n' base vibrations. Glad that he finally made a decision, Ramon starts to put the bizarre adventure into words, respecting the cry for help from his good friend Teimon.

1899 Nicolas Tesla receives rhythmic signals from outer space on his home made radio wave receiver. His conclusion: they have to be signals of intelligent life elsewhere in the solar system.

1908 June 30th at 7:17 p.m. in the Tunguska region, a powerful explosion takes place with a force equivalent to 60 A-bombs. Probably caused by an unknown type of meteorite.

1909 A regiment of the US Cavalries hunts down a group of criminals in New Mexico. During this action, they discover a cave system, hiding metallic horseshoe shaped crafts. During this discovery they are confronted with small grey demons.

1915 The federal agency NACA is founded. Its task is to stimulate the aviation industry. In general the founders believe in the future of this industry. Meanwhile, the First World War rages in Europe.

1927 On July 5th, a group of scientists led by Johannes Winkler, establish the VfR, "Verein für Raumschiffahrt", Society for Space Travel. Two key members are Werner von Braun and Hermann Oberth.

1929 Hubble discovers that the universe is in constant expansion and is filled with billions of galaxies like our own Milky Way. Every galaxy contains hundreds of billions of star systems like our own solar system.

1930 One of the first modern, convincing UFO sightings is reported by Clyde Tombaugh, the astronomer who discovered Pluto. He saw six illuminated elliptic objects in the sky.

1930 On April 4th, the AIS, the "American Interplanetary Society" is established with the same goal as the VfR in Germany. To develop rocket technology and to promote and stimulate space exploration. Beside scientists, some members of the group were famous science fiction writers. In 1934, this society gets a new name. The "American Rocket Society", ARS.

193? A UFO crashes at an unknown spot on Earth, probably in the USA. The three cosmonauts are dead. This is the most secret crash in history. The bodies were probably kept hidden in one of the cellars of the Capitol in Washington D. C.

1933 In Great Britain, the BIS is established, the British Interplanetary Society. A lot of famous science fiction writers were members. For instance Arthur C. Clarke, writer of "2001 A

Space Odyssey". In Russia the GRID foundation had the same interest as the VfR, the AIS and the BIS: building a rocket.

1933 In Germany, Adolph Hitler, leader of the Nazi party, comes in power. His logo is the well known Shiva swastika of the Hindu religion. Shiva is the deity or goddess of destruction. That's why the rotation of the swastika is counter clockwise.

1938 On October 30th, a radio show called "The War of the Worlds" by Orson Wells, creates panic in several cities in America. Listeners think the show is for real.

1940 The beginning of the Second World War. Hitler manages with the help of the SS to kill millions of Jews in concentration camps, by exposing them to gas in big shower rooms, then burn the dead bodies and mix the ashes in the asphalt for roads. This most evil crime against humanity ever was possible by hiding everything in the utmost secrecy. Most German citizens were not aware of this most horrible conspiracy of the 20th century.

1942 Los Angeles experiences a frightening night a few weeks after Pearl Harbor, when an Unidentified Flying Object flies slowly over the city. Hundreds of anti-missile rockets are fired from the ground and from airplanes but the airship doesn't suffer any damage and just follows its way.

1947 On July 8th, an Unidentified Flying Object crashes in the vicinity of Roswell, New Mexico. In the first press relays, the military spokesman admits that an alien spacecraft has crashed. But a day later, everything is denied. The free press is not allowed until the entire terrain is extensively cleaned by military personnel. Only the photographer "James Bond" is allowed to make some photos of the debris, found on the terrain.

1947 By signing the National Security Act on July 26th, eighteen days after the Roswell incident, the American president Truman founded the NSC, the National Security Council. The NSC founded in its turn the CIA, the Central Intelligence Agency.

1948 Project SIGN is started on January 2nd. Their first conclusion that some UFOs are of alien origin is rejected by the top of the military and project SIGN is aborted. Project GRUDGE takes over the task to investigate UFOs.

1952 The year with the most UFO sightings. In the USA alone some 30,000 witnesses declare to have seen UFOs.

10

1952 The most provoking sighting of a UFO happened in Washington D. C. above the Capitol. Some sources declare that president Truman ordered the military to shoot. The UFOs defended themselves.

1954 President Eisenhower has a secret meeting with EBE's, Extra-Terrestrial Biological Entities. EBE is the new name for the grey demons in the beginning of the century.

1955 The U. S. Air Force present "Project Bluebook" to the press on October 14th. Astronomer Allen Hynek is a major player in this document about UFOs.

1957 On October 1st, President Eisenhower restructures the NACA and establishes NASA (National Aeronautics and Space Administration). The NASA organization in its turn establishes an agency where Werner von Braun, an ex-NAZI, starts working to develop the Apollo rocket.

1957 Russia brings its first satellite into space: the Sputnik.

1961 On May 25th, President Kennedy makes his plans public to bring a man to the moon before 1970 and bring him safely back to Earth. The race to the moon between the USA and Russia has begun.

1963 On November 22nd, President Kennedy, the great visionary of the Apollo project, is killed in public. The whole world is in mourning.

1968 On April 6th is the premiere of the movie, "2001 A space Odyssey" by Stanley Kubrick, written by Arthur C. Clarke. In the movie Dr. Heywood R. Floyd explains in short the reason for secrecy because they have found proof of extra-terrestrial presence on the moon. He also explains the method to preserve secrecy until humanity is ready.

1969 Neil Armstrong is the first human being to put his foot on the moon on July 20th at 10.56 p. m. during the Apollo 11 mission. "A small step for man, a giant leap for mankind." Apollo 12, 14, 15, 16, and 17 make the Apollo missions the greatest adventure of mankind.

1977 Two satellites, Voyager 1 and 2, start their great odyssey into the solar system. They will give humanity the first detailed pictures of Jupiter, Saturn, Uranus and Neptune.

1981 The Colombia, the first space shuttle, leaves Earth on April 12th. It is the first spaceship that can come back to Earth and land on its own.

1986 Space shuttle Challenger explodes a few minutes after take off on January 28th and seven astronauts die in this tragic event. One of them, Christa McAuliffe, was very famous and loved by the people.

2001 On May 9th, the Disclosure Project gives a press conference under the guidance of Steven Greer in the National Press Club in Washington D. C. A few dozen witnesses tell their story to the press. They declare that the UFO phenomenon is real and that they were confronted with these phenomena in their work environment. They all state that they want to repeat their testimony under oath for the National Congress.

2001 On September 9th, two Japanese tourists make a helicopter trip and shoot a video of a flying saucer appearing behind the World Trade Center in New York.

2001 In the morning of September 11th, the World Trade Center in New York is hit by two airplanes and a few hours later the towers collapse like a cardboard house. The legend of the tower of Babel in modern times. A few months later, the second part of the movie The Lord of the Rings goes in premiere. Name of this movie: The Two Towers.

A penetrating, almost painful pressure on the forehead makes it impossible for Mira to continue working. I have to lie down, she thinks. I can't work this way. Why won't they leave me alone? My pro bono clients will have to wait.

A meaningful gesture is enough to explain her assistant that everybody has to wait. Lena knows immediately what Mira wants to say. While she informs the clients, Mira leaves the room. As she stumbles upstairs to her sleeping room, she wonders who wants to come into contact. It can't be Teimon. No. Impossible. There is an information stop as long as the Greys are occupied with the transportation. So it must be the Greys. Who else? She falls down on her bed and the first virtual images penetrate her mind. She clearly sees three grey creatures appearing at her bed, as if out of nothing. The three creatures look at her with their big dark eyes.

Mira notices that the new one is bigger and is looking at her in a hypnotic way. First they suggest her that they know a better way to help her clients with their problems but Mira refuses, realizing that she must not pay them any attention. The large Grey is clearly annoyed, and without feelings or emotions he sends his thoughts to her mind. Mira senses the dominance of the monotone artificial sounds of his mental voice.

We want integration, orientation, adjustment, leadership, progress, clear objectives, consciousness and... propagation.

That's the wish of any dictator is Mira's immediate answer to the Grey's indoctrination and before the tall Grey can go any further, Mira gives a straight mental answer. I am not interested in what you want! Who do you think you are?

The large Grey can't handle this surprising reaction and in his confusion, his body seems to shrink before her eyes and what is left of him is a pitiful creature. His arms hang slack and his bowed back gives him the look of a burned out freak. The other two small Greys can't do anything and look paralyzed. As sudden as they appeared, they disappear but Mira doesn't let the tall Grey go.

A stream of images manifests in her mind and she realizes that she is looking through the eyes of the large Grey. She has him completely under control and she becomes aware of the place where the Greys live. He appears to be in a cylindrically shaped small room, perfectly designed as if it is made in one piece. Only two small vertical slits indicate there is a door. She feels that this room goes downwards. It must be an elevator of some kind. Softly the elevator stops and without sound the door opens.

In front of her she sees a large room with access to several hallways, perfectly shaped just like the elevator. She enters one of the corridors, lit with a soft bluish light. The corridor and the floor are very smooth. As in a nightmare, she goes deeper and deeper into the endless tunnel. The Grey seems to stops at one of the doors which opens automatically by splitting in two parts. The doors are perfectly rectangular and broader than normal doors. She enters a large white room.

There is nothing there except three beds. They look like a combination of the tables of a beauty shop and the chair of a dentist. Perfect designs, no sharp corners and super clean. On the left bed lies a man. He is in a kind of hypnotic sleep or under narcosis. Strange! He is wearing his normal clothes. As if he was directly transported from his garden to this room.

Beside the bed stands a technical devise on a small cupboard, all in white. The devise is connected with a computer. On top of the device a long flexible tube is connected. It splits in two and both ends are connected with the eyes of the man with the help of two lentil shaped connectors that are placed under the eyelids. The man is completely disconnected from his surroundings. It is really ghastly to see.

Mira comes closer and disconnects herself from the Grey to enter the mind of the guy on the table and for a while she experiences the brain manipulation of the man. Rapid light flashes dance in front of her eyes. Like a strange kaleidoscope, she sees the most complex light patterns combined with a strange fluctuating sound, like of a group of birds at a distance. As an ultra fast accelerated movie, Mira realizes that this man is reprogrammed. No, this is not a good word. He is made attainable for the Greys. He becomes mentally one of them!

Mira is shocked. Oh no, this is real. I know enough. I have to get out of here! And still in distress she gradually disconnects

14

mentally from the man on the bed and comes out of her trance state. Still a bit dizzy, she gets out of bed and takes a deep breath. How long was I gone? I have to go back to my clients. Gradually she comes back to herself. Deeply moved by this horrible experience, she goes downstairs where some people are still waiting for a treatment of her healing hands. Nobody knows what she experienced. The pressure on her forehead is still there and with an "excuse me a moment" she goes nervously to her small computer room.

Come on Mira, you have to control yourself. I hope he is behind his computer. He has to know what has happened to me. She tries to focus on the keyboard and shortly after, a message leaves her laptop. Some miles to the northeast, a message enters a computer with a customized sound. Hasty foot steps enter a strange, surrealistic computer room.

Can I come over? Urgent!

- 2 -
10/8/2006
A few months earlier

I quit, Ramon, really... I just don't see the significance any longer, says a disappointed voice at the other end of the line.

Yes, I understand you very well, Marika, but don't get so excited about it. Ramon tries to calm down Marika's frustrations about the whole situation.

You must understand, Marika. The secret service can't just tell you that your information is correct. The entire investigation has to stay secret... Yes... yes I know Marika... it is all wrong, but... I can't change that situation... Yes... but just listen a second, Marika! It becomes silent on the other side of the phone.

Marika, you know that I know how important it is that a psychic can check the visions he gets, by going to the place where everything has happened. In this way he can compare his visions with reality. This would improve significantly the interpretation of his or her paranormal impressions. That's the way it should be. I know. But you can't expect that the secret service just takes you to the place of the action so that you can check it all out. It's just not the way the secret service works.

I know Ramon, says Marika clearly disappointed. But I become so frustrated. You know how much time end effort it takes to get a clear vision. It's not fair that I'm not informed how real the information is.

You are very right, Marika. It must be very frustrating. I promise you that I will contact Stan. I will explain the situation to him. And don't misunderstand me. You are right. He must understand that this is no way to work together. I will call him immediately and will inform you as soon as possible. That's a promise, Marika. Ok?

Ok, Ramon. The voice of Marika sounds a bit less furious.

But tell him that I will stop doing this, if I can't get any decent response. Bye Ramon! And with a click of the mouse, the connection is broken.

Ramon goes back to the kitchen, just in time to save the potatoes of a cruel burning experience. While cleaning the mess, he thinks it over.

Of course, Marika has a point. I have to speak Stan about her complaints. It would be a shame if she would stop. And I know her. If she gets angry, she will stop. You can do whatever you want, once her mind is set, it's for ever. I must call Stan immediately. Where is my mobile phone?

The smell of the freshly cooked potatoes makes him hesitate. Eat or call? Call! He quickly removes the kettle with the potatoes. A bit irritated, he finds his cell phone between some books and papers.

Great invention, these cellular phones! But the batteries are always empty, the memory is always full and you never find the damn thing. Quickly his fingers scroll through the phone list and with a click, the technical imitation of telepathy finds the mobile of Stan, wherever he is. While the mobile is in search for the right connection, Ramon remembers just in time his daily job.

"Days of Our Lives" is the favorite soap of Joy and while she has to study, he records the soap on video every day. Always everything simultaneously, he thinks. The ring tone is still busy and with his free hand, he puts the videotape in the recorder. The moment he pushes the recording button, he hears the calm voice of Stan.

16

Hello… Ramon. Stan here! What's up?

Mister The Flaming! I'm glad to hear your voice. I hope I am not disturbing?

No problem, Ramon. What can I do for you?

Well… I wonder, can you find some time to come over? I would like to talk you about…

I will be at your house in about… half an hour. See you soon.

Thanks, Stan.

Stan is a man who doesn't need many words. And he is always correct. He knows it is important when Ramon calls him. The video is running and Ramon smiles. Just in time!

Okay, that's that. And what must I do now? Oh yes. Stan will be here soon. First things first, I have to clean up this mess in the kitchen, make coffee and… not to forget, serve some cake. Ramon's freshly grinded coffee makes speaking so much easier. While he starts cleaning, he remembers all the exciting adventures with Marika. Besides Mira, she was the most gifted visionary person he had ever known.

After his study of parapsychology and comparative religion, Ramon realized very quickly that he wouldn't have a professional future as a parapsychologist in his country. He still remembers a talk with a university professor.

Parapsychology, sir? We Belgians are too sober to take that subject seriously.

Too sober? Too sober! It makes him mad, remembering this stupid answer. That's probably also the reason why there are three hundred thousand alcoholics in our country. And the biggest brewery is located in the biggest university city of Belgium.

But what the heck! Thank God, in The Netherlands there is a Parapsychological Institute. Parapsychology was an official human science at the University of Utrecht.

If only the people knew how many hypersensitive people get the wrong treatment in psychiatric clinics! But what to do? Ramon's parapsychology, professor H. van Praag, always stressed the main task of parapsychologists: to learn how to make distinction between paranoid schizophrenic patients and paranormal people. Poor people they are, if they are misunderstood and misdiagnosed. Paranormal people have to be treated as students, not patients.

This was the reason why Ramon always made time for these exceptional people and to guide and educate them in their special talents. Marika was indeed very sensitive and specially gifted to see danger if the lives of innocent peoples were at risk.

The problem was to get this information to the right persons at the right place. Ramon remembers the possible prevention of a second bomb attack at the Olympic Games in Montreal.

Sir, his contact had said during their last conversation, how does she know all this hidden information? We have to know the identity of this person. And that was the breaking point.

Sorry sir, was the response of Ramon without hesitation. The secrecy of my source is holy.

Then I'm afraid we have to say goodbye, was the response and Ramon never heard of this guy again. Still, the situation was disappointing, although it was the first confirmation that her information was clearly useful. Like all the genuinely psychic people, she was afraid to become known for her paranormal abilities. This attitude is common among psychics. They want to be appreciated as normal people and don't consider themselves different from other people. They just have a gift. That's all. End of story. No nonsense about supernatural energies or spiritual contact or whatever.

Ramon never knew anybody as gifted as Marika, except Mira. It's really a pity that the scientific attitude against these people is so unprofessional.

While thinking Ramon pours the hot water over the freshly grinded coffee.

But what can you do? Our scientific world-view is based on empiric proof and a strong materialistic empirical world-view has discriminated any tendency to incorporate the world of feelings and inner experiences in the field of science. Let alone the higher feelings or religious experiences. It all made Ramon a bit sarcastic.

It's all in the mind and the mind is just an organ like the stomach. No, no. Feelings are out of time. There are only emotions and behavior. All the rest is part of a romantic period in science history. We now live in the times of common sense.

What a pity! They don't even know the real meaning of the

phrase "common sense". Aristotle saw it as a mental ability to explain how it was possible that people and in fact all living creatures were able to communicate with one another. He believed there was a sense organ responsible to understand one another and to prevent confusion in the communication.

The people have forgotten the meaning of the words they speak. It's a shame. The smell of fresh hot coffee tickles the nose of Ramon. Hmmm, now that's real coffee, the only legal drug in the world. He brings the coffee to the reception room where his paintings of the eight chakras decorate the walls. When he sees the Ohm sign, he remembers the time of the crimes of the "Ohm" sect in Japan. Marika was at her best in those days. It was the first time Ramon witnessed the special gift of "remote viewing". She knew everything that would happen several days in advance. When the leader of the group was finally arrested, she told Ramon something very strange. She said that the guy took a drug, bringing him in a state of mind that enabled him to live in a mental state, almost completely disconnected from his body. But he was still able to have contact with some important members of the group.

Ramon was shocked that one man could discredit one of the most important sounds of Indian and Tibetan religion, the holy "Ohm" sound. It was comparable to what the Nazis did with the Hindu swastika symbol. Imagine that somebody starts a religious group and calls it "Amen". And after a while, he starts killing people at random. I don't think that the Holy Church could laugh with this negative association.

The question was: Why was he doing it? Who benefits from such a terrible crime? Are the holy symbols of old religions targeted, to give them a bad name? In favor of new cults? It wouldn't surprise Ramon a bit.

Anyhow, it would be a shame if Marika would stop using her gifts to prevent these crimes. It was an honor for a parapsychologist to work with such a gifted person as Marika.

Ramon checks whether everything is present for his special visitor: coffee, milk, cake, sugar, an ashtray and his notebook.

As he looks at his notes and reads the parts of the last visit of Mira, Ramon wonders what adventures are waiting with his new paranormal student. He has not known Mira very long, but one thing was clear: she had a special telepathic ability.

He remembers her first visit very well. Mira is a very beautiful woman. Long golden blond hair with an almost aristocratic appearance, like a Madonna by the famous painter Jan Van Eyck, Ramon's all time favorite painter.

Mira told Ramon how strange it was to be able to read the mind of her colleagues and especially her business partners. For her type of work, this gift was definitely an advantage. But in her personal life this "mind reading ability" prevented her to have a real love relation because she detected every game the guys wanted to play with her, without them realizing it.

But that wasn't the real reason for her to visit Ramon. For some weeks now, she sees a purple light glittering pattern around herself. Very beautiful but also a bit frightening. She didn't have a clue what it could mean. First she thought there was something wrong with her eyes. But no, there was nothing wrong with her big deep blue eyes.

Suddenly a loud ring tone sounds and brings Ramon back to reality. Stan is here! He quickly opens the front door and a gentleman greets Ramon in his typical educated style.

Ramon, glad to see you. How are you?

Mister The Flaming! I'm fine, thank you.

Stan for friends, Ramon.

Yes… Stan. Please, come in.

Stan knows the way.

I don't have much time, Ramon. I'm on call 24 hours. It's again one of those times.

No problem, Stan. We can handle this quickly. But I hope you have some time to taste my coffee.

Why do you think I came in person, my dear friend?

Both laugh and in no time, two completely different people of completely different worlds start a conversation.

- 3 -
11/8/2006

With a monotone voice, a correctly speaking GPS voice comes through the speakers. Next traffic lights to the right!

It is a tradition for Rich to bring Ramon back home after a night of intense debate and enjoying the good things of life. Rich is Ramon's best friend. They became good friends at the mystery school, 30 years ago in the old-fashioned but still very friendly country of Luxemburg.

Not that anything unusual happened at the mystery school like the name could suggest. The only difference with a normal university was the basic principle "In Omnibus Omnia", meaning that all knowledge could be united in one global concept of reality. That everything is interconnected with everything. The word "mystery" means the "unity of what seems to be separated". Everything is one. The oneness of differentiation.

Rich only studied a few years at this mystery school. But their friendship never ended.

Where is the time, Rich? Do you know that we have known each other for already thirty years? Funny stories come to his mind and make him realize how different the world was in those hippy days of love and peace.

Yes Ramon, those were the days, my friend. I wouldn't have missed that experience for the world. But what would our Wise Teacher have thought of your situation with Marika?

That, I do not know, Rich. But what I do know is that the situation is frustrating. Especially if you want to do scientific work. I can't make a decent report of the paranormal experiences of Marika. Because I don't know what will happen with the information. But what can you do? I'm not a member of the secret service. That's the last thing I want to be, you know. It is all so strange. On the one hand, science has never been so defensive against anything paranormal. But on the other hand, movies and TV series are filled with paranormal people and paranormal happenings.

That's a fact, Ramon. Seen from a sociological point of view, people are in the middle of a schizophrenic input of information. But what worries me the most is that the paranormal is gradually moved to the world of fantasy and illusion. For young people, movies are just entertainment. They don't take it seriously.

I agree with you, Rich. Especially if you know that a lot of movies are based on real facts and happenings. By making a movie of these phenomena, the science behind it will never be taken seriously. Take for instance all the visions of Marika. It is unbelievable what she sometimes knows in advance. But I will never be able to prove it black on white. I don't get feedback of the people who use the information. It isn't fair, Rich.

I understand your frustration, Ramon. But the fact that Stan accepts the information and makes time for it, says a lot about the value of the information. Don't you agree?

Absolutely, Rich! You haven't lost touch with your analytic mind.

Thanks, Ramon. Glad to see that we still are on the same wavelength.

Ramon laughs.

Absolutely, Rich. We haven't change a bit. I told Stan exactly the same thing.

And? What was his response?

Always the same, Rich. It is impossible to give concrete feedback, because of the secrecy concerning the investigation.

My response was simple. Stan, I said: if we know what is right and what is wrong, Marika could improve her abilities.

Sorry to interrupt you, Ramon, but are you sure that Stan knows the Observational Theory of Biermann?

Oh yes. I explained this remarkable theory several times. But you know, secret is secret. End of story. Don't get me wrong, Rich. I understand his position very well. But I also understand the complaints of Marika. Anyway, I hope our last conversation can make a difference. He told me he would see what he could do.

Don't worry, Ramon. You have to understand his position. He is just a small part of a broad network of services. He has to stick to the rules. It must be a dilemma for such a man, you know. Anyhow, it's not your problem, Ramon. It's just the system.

You're right, Rich. I can't help it. But I am glad I could talk it over with you. I'm on my own, you know.

For a moment it is silent in the car but the always friendly GPS voice breaks the silence: Second road to the right.

The blue street lamps of Ramon's village mark the end of the trip.

Back home, Ramon. Isn't our GPS lady a wonderful invention?

Yes Rich, who could have thought ten years ago, this would become a gadget in every car? Shall I quickly make some coffee?

Of course Ramon, we have to stick to certain traditions, don't you think?

And with a perfect bow, Rich parks his car exactly right on Ramon's parking space.

It's a deal, Rich.

A bit clumsy, Ramon gets out of the car and stretches his legs. While Rich closes the doors, Ramon goes to his small garden at the back of his house. Surprised he looks around, seeing lemon bottles spread through the garden. As he sees the surprised face of Rich, looking at this surreal composition of empty bottles, Ramon brakes out in laughter.

What does this mean, Ramon?

Oh nothing, Rich. I know who made this Arte Povera composition. It must be the work of Reg. Young artists have a strange sense of humor these days. He just wanted to let me know that he was here. Reg is a good guy, you know.

Still laughing, they both enter the house and Ramon immediately starts the coffee ritual. He activates the water heater and grinds the coffee beans. Thousands of aromas fill the kitchen while Rich finds himself a chair.

I really enjoyed our discussions last night, Rich. Living alone has its disadvantages, you know. But lest I forget, shall I show you that movie about the Illuminati?

No Ramon, I can't stay that long. Please, another time. I have to get back to my wife. She wants to visit her family.

That's a pity, Rich. Another time then. It isn't urgent. But really, you have to see it. It is unbelievable what happens behind the screens of secrecy. Not that I am really interested in the occult. But I have one paranormal student who is very into this kind of information.

Oh yes. You told me about him last night. Ury, if I remember well?

Yes, Ury. A few days ago he visited me late at night. What he told me gave me cold shivers.

Rich looks surprised at Ramon. Ramon is not easily shocked.

Tell me something more, Ramon. You make me curious.

Well, it is a long story, Rich. I have known Ury for a long time. Ury is a very exceptional guy. He is incredible intelligent. Do you know what he is doing for a living?

No idea, Ramon.

He has worked for years on a laser beam weapon for a company.

You're kidding!

No, no. And, you know, he never had an official education. He is a true autodidact. His father didn't allow him to go to school. He preferred to give his son classes at home. Perfectly legal here in Belgium, you know. His dad always said: on public schools, they teach you a lot… but they break your will… and I will not allow that they do this to my son! In recent years, Ury has mastered homeopathy and painting techniques of the middle ages. He wants to know the alchemistic tricks of the great Flemish masters. But that's not the reason I came to know him. From a young age he has been in contact with a mental guide.

A mental guide? What's that, Ramon? A kind of spirit?

Ramon produces a smile.

Well yes, something like that. But first let me give you some coffee.

Two mugs are filled and for a moment, the taste of this remarkable alchemistic invention gets all attention.

Hmmm… good coffee, Ramon. It makes you realize there is life before death. So, Ury is visited by a spirit. But isn't it better to call it an archetype of his own higher consciousness? You know, Jung!

I see what you mean, Rich. But it is not really the same. Archetypes are rather static images or idealistic concepts. Like the ideal concept of "mother" or "father". But this guide is very independent and he speaks with him. They even have discussions. It's more as if he has telepathic contact with somebody or something. The spiritual guide helps him with his scientific research and even with his problems in life. Sorry Rich, I am a bad host. Some cake?

Hmmm, please. Ok, I get the picture, Ramon. But what does this spirit look like? Is he seeing him in real, in his room?

No, no. He sees him in his imagination. It's as if he thinks of him and then he is there. But he sees him clearly, as if in a dream-like state, although he is awake. He can be with him while working. He looks like a monk from the middle ages. He comes and goes and is very friendly. Really strange! Anyway, the important thing is that this guide very recently gave him information about two, to me unknown, secret societies. Both groups have twelve members. One group is called the "Guardians". The other group is called the 'Warriors".

I have never heard of such groups, Ramon. Who and what are they?

Ury doesn't have a clue either, Rich. But gradually, his guide revealed more information about these secret groups. Ury was very unsure about this information and hesitated to tell me about it.

Hesitated? Why?

Yes Rich, he really was afraid to talk about it. You have to realize that he is a very strict scientific guy. He really thought he was becoming schizophrenic, but he couldn't hide it from me. You have to understand, Rich. It was a difficult step for him to take. Nobody wants to be called a fool or crazy. You would be surprised, Rich. Paranormal topics were discussed very openly at our mystery school but it is still taboo for most people. Especially if you work in a very high-tech environment. But he trusted me. And that's good. Ha, ha, now I remember. We call this entity "Merly".

You mean Merly, like Merlin the magician and counselor of King Arthur and the twelve Knights of the Round Table?

Ha, ha, well yes, Rich. Why not? Merly talked about the twelve Warriors and twelve Guardians so the link was easily made.

But with King Arthur included, there were thirteen, Ramon, not twelve, were there not?

I knew that you would come up with that, Rich. Yes, yes, laugh all you want, but listen. Merly told Ury that an extra Warrior is now being prepared to join this secret club of twelve.

You mean that the twelve Warriors will get a king or emperor?

That could indeed be the case, Rich. That would make sense, wouldn't it? I make notes of everything Ury tells me. First the Warriors were called the "Thirteen", but gradually Merly gave a better picture of this group and called them the Warriors. They are very powerful and as a group they are one of the most powerful organizations in the world.

But Ramon, if they are so powerful, they should be famous. Do they have an official name?

Well, that's the strange thing. It is possible that this name is only used inside their own secret society. Or maybe it is just a nickname that Merly uses. Anyhow, you don't find the name on the web. But you know me, Rich. I surfed a lot at random and I found a lot of sites that could point to the existence of the Warriors, based on what Ury told me about them. And I found one group that definitely could have a link with the Warriors, "The Illuminati". That's the reason why I wanted you to see the documentary of the Illuminati. There are thirteen Illuminati fractions or families.

I see what you mean, Ramon. But I never heard of that group. Who are these Illuminati?

I didn't know anything about them either. But in searching for traces about the Warriors or Guardians, I found by accident a site discussing this group, which is hidden in secrecy, and is called the Illuminati. The resemblance between what I read about the Illuminati and what Merly told about the Warriors was so striking, that they had to have a link with one another.

I see, Ramon. What's with the name? Are these Illuminati enlightened people like the saints in Hinduism?

No, on the contrary! But they are not stupid. That's for sure. The organization goes far back to the period of Enlightenment in Western Europe. I guess that is the reason why they used that name for the group. The founder Adam Weishaupt was born in a wealthy family. He got his education by the Jesuits but could not agree with their world-view. He founded the "Ordo Perfectibilis" on May 1st 1776, together with Adolph Baron von Knigge. Later, they changed the name in "Ordo Illuminati Bavarensis". Weishaupt became also a member of the Free Masons in 1777. In general, you can say that they had very strong liberal ideas and the group was very successful. Around 1785, the Illuminati as well as the Free Masons and other secret societies became forbidden organizations. They were seen as a threat to the aristocracy in Europe and the Roman Catholic Church. Once Napoleon came in power, the Ordo Illuminati Bavarensis was completely dismantled. But it is strange to read that afterwards, the organization found new ground, especially in the USA. If I have to believe what is published on the web, the group became very powerful in the twentieth century. The top of the organization would exist of thirteen chosen ones. These individuals have the highest degree of secret knowledge and power. They have really worldly power, Rich. That's why I think they could be the Warriors. They influence the world via the secret societies. In Europe we know secret societies like the Free Masons and the Wicca's. But the Illuminati are generally unknown.

During Ury's last visit, the name Illuminati fell during the conversation about the Warriors and it shocked Ury quite a bit. He immediately received a strange message from Merly. **"Illuminati eliminate Illuminati"**. So the Warriors and the Illuminati have to be separate groups.

That's very strange indeed, Ramon. It sounds to me like there is an internal war between the different members of the group.

That's my idea too, Rich. And you have to understand, most members of secret societies haven't got a clue what happens at the top of their society. If I am to believe some articles, most known secret societies are portals to the Illuminati. They are completely ignorant of the reality of the Illuminati. The secrecy of the existence of the Illuminati is the main reason why the Illuminati are so powerful. Wait a second, Rich. I will draw you a simple model to show you how the group is structured.

A model! That is always enlightening, dear Ramon.

Quickly, Ramon draws a triangle on a sheet of paper. Look, Rich. The pyramid is divided in two. A flat pyramid and a triangle on top of it. As Ramon draws an eye in the triangle, he smiles.

Do you remember this triangular symbol, Rich?

How could I forget it, Ramon? That triangle was hanging at the wall of every classroom in our Catholic school. It was the symbol of the all seeing eye of God. And under this triangle was written: God sees you. They both have to laugh with the old-fashioned persuasion tricks of the Catholic Church.

But listen, Rich. This model is also an important logo in the secret societies. You can even find this logo on the one dollar bill. The basis of the pyramid represents worldly power. The thirteen levels of the pyramid represent the levels of the secret hierarchy.

So, if I understand you well, the basis of the pyramid represents worldly power, but at the same time the pyramid represents the secret levels to get access to the top of the Illuminati. Then, the triangle could be the place of the thirteen Illuminati.

That's definitely a way to look at it, Rich. And the highest level of the flat pyramid could represent the Warriors. Don't forget, there are still twelve of them, not thirteen. It is possible that the thirteen Illuminati have the highest degree, ruling over the Warriors and in this way have control over the entire flat pyramid. The Warriors would in this case be the key figures of the power structure of the flat pyramid.

That makes sense Ramon, but how must I understand this? How can a handful of people have so much power in the world? There are so many countries, so many different cultures. I really don't get it.

That's what I ask myself too, Rich. Merly explained that the Warriors have families in different cultures. The Illuminati belong more to the western civilizations as far as I know. I don't see how else the Warriors could have control over other cultures. But you are right again, Rich. I don't know how both groups work together. I'm just guessing. It is just a model, you know.

According to Merly, the Warriors were originally controlled by twelve Guardians, who were controlled by God. So, if we use the model of the flat pyramid again, the top triangle was originally the seat of the twelve Guardians. And the eye was indeed the eye of God as the invisible thirteenth member, so to speak.

That's interesting, Ramon. In this case, the Guardians were probably the highest priests in the different cultures in the past.

That could indeed be the case, Rich. Merly says, the problem these days is that the place of the Guardians is taken over by the Illuminati. They consider themselves to be Gods or God. And if the Illuminati eliminate Illuminati, it could very well be that the different Illuminati fractions are in conflict with one another. And that would be a very dangerous situation for the world, Rich. I guess Merly wants to warn us for this, one way or the other.

And what about the thirteenth Warrior? Who could that be?

No idea, Rich. The thirteenth is generally the king of kings. The tradition of the teacher with twelve pupils is very old. Arthur was the king of twelve knights, Merlyn was probably the high priest

28

of a circle of twelve priests. Maybe the highest level in an organization has always twelve members, lead by one chairman.

Well Ramon, maybe the Illuminati have decided to choose an extra person to unite the twelve Warriors. If the thirteen Illuminati are in a struggle for power, the winner needs a Warrior to rule over the other Warriors. Like a supreme ruler. But it is all so vague. The problem is always the same with secret organizations. How do you check it?

You are right, Rich. The web is a nice gadget. But it is filled with a lot of "information pollution" these days. Our Wise Teacher always warned us for the growing information pollution. Check your sources, he always said. Don't just believe everything anybody says. Do your homework.

Yes, Ramon. He made a very prophetic point there. When he was still alive, there was no World Wide Web. Information pollution these days is as dangerous as environmental pollution. People don't know anymore what is right or wrong. But Ramon, it is nice to know all this. But what is Merly expecting from you?

You tell me, Rich! I have no idea why this information comes to me. I can only guess. The only thing I can do, is find clues of everything what Ury tells me. Believe me, Rich. I don't believe anything just like that. That makes Marika's information so interesting. I can really do something with it. It is clean-cut information about a specific event. But I really don't know what to do with this information of Ury, except check it out.

I would take it with a serious amount of skepticism, Ramon because…

Before Rich can finish his sentence, Mira rushes into Ramon kitchen.

- 4 -
11/8/2006

Mira is clearly upset. While gasping for breath, she sees that Ramon is not alone.

Oh, I'm sorry Ramon. I didn't know you had a visitor. I will come back some other time.

No Mira, please… Relax. There is no reason to go. Rich is a very good friend. Wait, I will get you a chair.

Thanks, Ramon. But if you want, I will come back later.

Rich understands there is something clearly wrong.

I think you both need some privacy, Ramon.

No, sir. That's really not necessary. You don't need to leave for me! You are a good friend of Ramon, aren't you?

That's right, Mira. This is Rich, my best friend. You know, I told you about our adventures in the mystery school.

Nice to meet you, Rich. Ramon told me a lot about you. Excuse me, for my state of mind. I'm normally a very calm person.

Quick as always, Ramon prepares a mug of coffee.

Here you are, Mira, drink this and you will feel better in no time. Milk and sugar as usual.

Rich looks at the clock and realizes he has to go anyway.

Sorry friends, but I really have to go. My wife waits for me and with Ramon I always lose track of time. I really can't stay any longer. Nice to have met you, Mira. The description of Ramon was clearly not exaggerated.

I really hope to see you again some time in better circumstances, Mira replies.

And while she enjoys the warm mug, full of fluid life force, Ramon accompanies Rich to the car.

Rich, you really don't need to go, you know.

Of course not, Ramon. But I really have to. You know my wife likes punctuality and I think Mira needs some privacy with you. Something strange must have happened. If it is really important, just let me know and we will talk it over. Rich gets into the car, activates the GPS and smiles to Ramon.

What have you told her about me, Ramon? She was so polite.

Nothing but good things, replies Ramon with a big smile. You are a very important person, Rich. Don't deny that. Give my regards to your wife, please.

With a big smile, he starts the car. And the friendly GPS voice tells him immediately which direction he has to turn. Both laugh when they hear the voice of this futuristic gadget of modern technology, the beginning of Artificial Intelligence. While Rich follows the advice of his electronic guide, Ramon waves his dear friend goodbye. Back in the kitchen Mira has calmed down.

Feeling better, Mira? I was really worried, you know.

30

Yes, Ramon. Thanks. Sorry for the inconvenience.

No problem at all, Mira. But tell me, what freaked you out like that?

With hesitation, she starts to speak.

You know, Ramon. Those purple lights showed up again. And then, and then… Oh, it was so strange. My heart was pounding and my breath was out of control, and… I was sweating! I thought I was having a heart attack. I ran out of my house and I had only one thing in mind. I have to go to Ramon. And here I am.

But Mira, I still don't understand. Wait. I will take some coffee. Tell me step by step what happened.

Ramon takes his notebook and sits down. Swiftly, he reads through his notes from a couple of days ago. He reads aloud what Mira told him in confidence.

Date: 8/8/2006. Night time. Full moon. The bedroom of Mira is filled with a haze of purple light. Suddenly, a skull appears in the center. It was not a normal skull.

Question 1: Can you describe the skull in more detail?

It's a purple skull. The strange sculpture came forward and was hanging in front of me. It was so real… as if I could touch it. The skull appeared to be made of a special kind of glass. No, it was not glass. It was too clear and transparent. I think it was very pure, shining crystal. Almost like a diamond.

Question 2: Were you afraid?

No, it wasn't a nasty experience at all. It was beautiful to look at.

Question 3: What do you think it is? Or, what does it mean? What is it used for? Reading this, Ramon realizes that in fact he didn't know what to ask.

I have no idea. But I have the feeling that the skull contains information or something alike. And, oh yes, afterwards, I saw a sign.

Question 4: A sign? Can you describe it? Any idea of the meaning?

It was a "**W**" shape. But more of a curved style. But I have no clue what it means.

End of the notes.

Ok Mira, I'm back on track. Sorry, but Rich's red wine was really superb. I'm still in a state of recovery.

The gentlemen had fun, while I was working! Nice Ramon, very nice!

Ha, ha. Yes Mira. It was fun. Drinking with Rich is fun. Believe me. But don't distract me now. So, you have seen the skull again, haven't you?

He sees that Mira feels uneasy to talk about it.

Don't make fun of me, Ramon!

Absolutely not, Mira. I wouldn't dare.

Ramon understands very well why she hesitates to talk about her experiences. She is still afraid that she suffers from paranoid schizophrenia and that it is all just imagination. Ramon has tried to explain her over and over again that it isn't the case with her at all. But she doesn't need much to doubt herself.

Tell me, Mira. What was it that freaked you out?

Ok, Ramon. Firstly, it was the same experience over again. My whole room became purple and there was the crystal skull, but… How shall I describe it? The skull was brighter and inside the skull, I saw a cube kind of structure, composed of square facets, put together in a strange way. Then I thought: Ramon will surely know what it is.

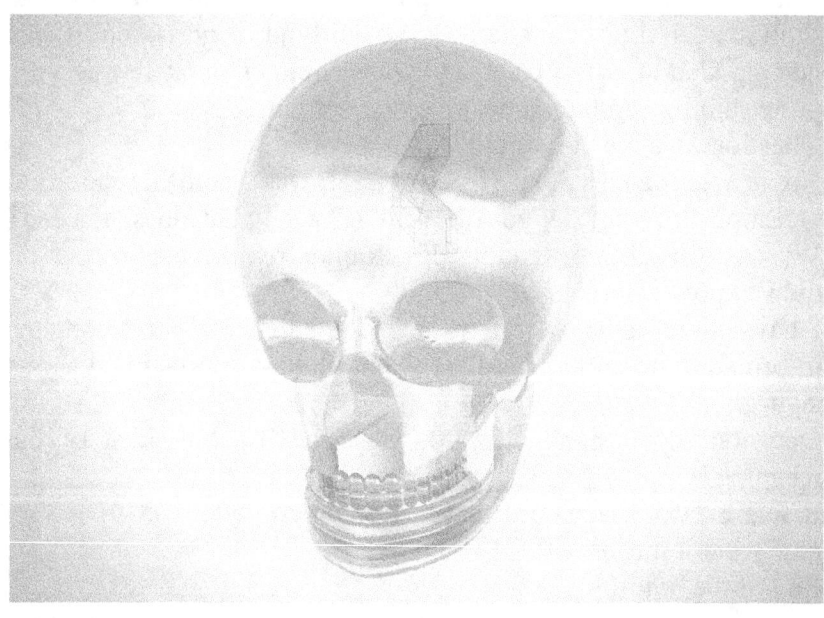

A network of squares, Mira? Are you sure?

Mira has his full attention now. The cube is the central shape in Ramon's artistic oeuvre. He even lived in a cube for several years during his studies at the mystery school. He was convinced that the cube had not revealed all its secrets, on an artistic as well as on a scientific level. But a cube structure in a crystal skull? That was new to Ramon.

Can you be a bit more specific, Mira? Can you make a drawing of what you saw?

He immediately gives Mira pencil and paper.

A drawing? Me? But I can't draw, Ramon!

But Ramon doesn't take no for an answer.

Come on, Mira. Give it a try!

A bit clumsy, Mira sketches a kind of network of more or less square figures.

Look, Ramon. You see what I mean? First you have one square and behind it another one, but a little bit slantwise, and then the next one and again another one. Does it make any sense?

Not really, Mira. He looks doubtful at the drawing.

It reminds me of sketches by Kandinsky, Mira. Rather abstract. But I think I know what you mean, although I can't make anything of it. But anyhow, you see such a structure in the purple skull?

Yes, Ramon, in the middle region of the brain.

Ramon hasn't a clue what to think but he makes notes anyway. You never know.

Let me think, Mira. Was the skull massive?

Her body language tells him that she sees the skull again in detail in her imagination.

I think so, Ramon. It looks a solid sculpture to me.

And have you any idea about the function of this structure?

No idea, Ramon. No idea at all.

Let me put the question differently, Mira. What is your impression when you concentrate on this structure?

For a moment Mira looks very deep into her mind.

I see it clearly now, Ramon. Strange! I have the feeling it is a kind of transmitter.

A transmitter? Ramon is very surprised by this answer. A transmitter of what?

A transmitter of information, I guess. You know, like the antenna of an old TV.

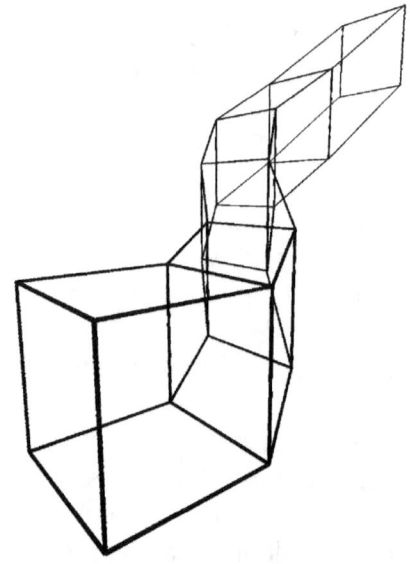

Aha… An antenna to receive information. But information about what?

No idea, Ramon. No idea.

Strange! It is the only thing Ramon can say while he puts the drawing in his notebook.

Strange it is indeed, Ramon. But, well, it is just a feeling, but I have the impression that this is the beginning of something very important. But don't ask me what.

We will figure it out together, Mira, whatever it is. I promise you I will look on the web. Maybe I can find something on the web about this mysterious skull. But what I wanted to ask: do you have the feeling that this skull really exists? Or is it just a personal archetype?

Mira looks very serious.

I'm convinced this skull really exists, Ramon. But I have no idea where it could be.

Then I have only one question, Mira. What scared you so much? Come on. Tell me! Don't be afraid!

Before the skull disappeared, that cube structure started to vibrate. Very strange, Ramon. And then… I had the feeling that... as if I was falling into that structure. It was so real. Purple lights were flashing all around me. And then...

Yes, and then...?

I heard a voice saying: **"I greet you"**. The face of Mira gets a reddish colour of excitement, as if she relives the whole experience.

Don't be ashamed, Mira. It's okay. So the voice said: "I greet you". Nothing else, Mira? Just "I greet you"?

Yes. That was it. It took me by surprise, Ramon. My heart started to pound and before I knew what happened, the skull was gone. I didn't expect this at all, Ramon. The rest you know by now.

Ramon completes his notes, wondering what it all means. But it gives him an undefined sense of importance.

I think you are right, Mira. It is the beginning of something, whatever it is. I will consult the web tonight. Don't worry, Mira. Whatever it is, we will figure it out together.

So, enough of all the paranormal stuff. Let's do something normal, Mira. A glass of red wine?

The best idea I heard in days, Ramon. I hardly take any free time to relax, you know.

In no time Ramon finds his way to the cellar. Yes, there it is! A bottle from the year 2000. A year before the world came under the spell of the World Trade Center disaster. Back in the kitchen, the bottle is opened, glasses served and after a clinging sound of the crystal glasses, both singles enjoy the wonderful taste of red wine.

It's already dark as Ramon waves Mira goodbye while her car disappears in the dark. I can't make a living with parapsychology in this country, thinks Ramon. But I wouldn't like to miss the discussions with all my paranormal students. If people just knew what topics are discussed in my small kitchen, they would be amazed. A bit dizzy of the wine, Ramon goes back inside and takes a seat in front of the dark computer screens. With a move of the mouse the two screens come back to life.

Crystal skulls? Hmm. Let's see what Google has to say. With sleepy eyes he types the words: "crystal skulls". Ramon looks for his spectacles.

Ramon, old boy, you shouldn't drink that much anymore. What? As he looks at the screen again, he sees numerous links to "crystal skulls". A bit shocked about his ignorance of this subject he starts to surf.

Several hours and cups of coffee later, he has read the most diverse theories about the mysterious crystal skulls. Mira, I have news for you! Point one. Crystal skulls really exist. Point two. They have been found! Not one but several ones. All made of different types of hard crystal. The oldest one is probably several thousands of years old and made of very pure quarts crystal.

Point three. Nobody knows how people could make such magnificent sculptures without the proper tools. And they are found in different sizes, different colors and different shapes.

But then again, a purple one wasn't mentioned. Typical Mira! A few moments ago, I wasn't aware of the existence of crystal skulls. And now, they not only exist, but they have been circulating already for years in certain New Age organizations. Some sites show nine skulls while others claim to know there are twelve crystals but some are still to be found. Several books are written about these strange artifacts of the past. Remarkable is their cross-cultural appearance. They have been found in different regions of the world. It seems that all shamanistic cultures were interested in making skulls out of crystal for one reason or the other. Some authors defend the theory that these skulls enable shamans to communicate with the world of spirits or even with the gods. But as always in this kind of matters, nobody really knows for sure of course. Strange that nobody speaks of a purple crystal skull?

Too tired to think Ramon unplugs his WebCom system with a few clicks and goes to bed. Tomorrow is another day and in no time he falls in a deep sleep.

- 5 -
12/8/2006

The next day, Ramon can hardly motivate himself to start working. Two days of drinking wine is a bit too much of the good things of life. Only an overdose of coffee convinces him to get on track again. A drawing must be ready for a cultural event. During the coffee break, he googles the web to find more information about the crystal skulls and to find videos about secret societies and related topics. It is his favorite pastime for the moment. Ury's contacts with Merly about the Warriors brought this new interest into Ramon's life. Some weeks ago he found a lecture of David Icke. Ramon was too educated to just believe all the stuff Icke told but he admired his struggle in trying to construct a total picture about the secret societies and their immense power. Whatever you think about this British gentleman, his lectures are entertaining, to say the least. That some people can change in reptiles was just a bit too farfetched.

Ramon's professor in parapsychology would quote the famous writer Goethe in this respect: "Wo endet die Wahrheit und wo fängt die Dichtung an?" Where does truth end and where does fabrication begin? But Icke's general picture of all the secret societies fascinated Ramon. Time flies by and it is late in the evening when Ramon takes a break in his little backyard after a simple meal.

Before he knows, he falls asleep. When Mira arrives and sees him lying knocked-out in his chair, she smiles. Poor boy! He can't handle long days and short nights anymore. Carefully she tries to wake him up.

Ramon. Ramon! Are you asleep?

Surprised, Ramon comes to his senses.

Mira? You here? Sorry Mira, I didn't hear you coming. I was daydreaming.

Ha, ha, yes. I believe you were and with a smile she takes a seat.

Still struggling with your last alchemistic experience, Ramon?

Together, they start laughing.

You win, Mira. Two days of drinking wine is too much. But you know, sometimes I really need a break. Where shall we begin? Coffee?

That would be nice, Ramon.

Some moments later they can smell the scent of coffee filling the kitchen. While serving the delicious fluid, Ramon tells Mira everything he found on the web about the mysterious crystal skulls.

So, if I understand you well, crystal skulls really exist?

To my own surprise, Mira, they do.

So I'm not crazy?

Of course not, Mira! You are just exceptional. That's all. But tell me. What brings you here? New impressions?

Mira blushes. She can't lie to Ramon and gradually she starts to talk.

Where shall I start? Before I fell asleep yesterday night, the same thing happened again. My whole room started to twinkle in purple light and there it was again, the crystal skull appeared out of nothing, even more shining. And then that square structure started to tremble again en some force pulled me into that structure and before I knew, I heard a voice. But it was another voice than last time. I could understand this voice better and he told me… two proverbs.

Two proverbs? A different voice? Ramon doesn't have a clue where she's heading at.

Well yes. Two proverbs. At least, that's what I think they are. Ramon, don't laugh!

No, no, I wouldn't dare, Mira. But wait a second. I take my notebook. In a hurry, Ramon takes his writing materials. Now tell me, what are the two proverbs? Not too quick, please.

1.000 **The chameleon changes colour, but keeps its disposition.**

I got it, Mira. And the second one?

1.001 **If the green frog yells and the yellow frog croaks, the red fox watches.**

Ramon writes it down and looks surprised at Mira.

I don't know these proverbs, Mira. Have you any idea what they mean?

Mira shakes her head.

I haven't a clue, Ramon.

Well, that makes two of us. A croaking frog, I can live with that, but a yelling frog? I have never heard of a yelling frog, have you?

Mira sees that Ramon has a difficult time not to burst out laughing.

You are making fun of me, Ramon. Admit it!

No, no Mira. I am not, really not! It only sounds funny, don't you think. Yelling frogs?

Yes, yes, I hear you. Mister Ramon thinks it sounds funny.

Well, you have to admit Mira, it does sound funny and Ramon

38

starts laughing, seeing the face of Mira.

Mira can't help herself either and seconds later, both laugh loudly. Crystal skulls and yelling frogs. My god. Laughing keeps on going for several minutes until they finally get a grip on themselves.

Oh… Jesus. Ha, ha, ha. You know, Mira, I hope the meaning will become clear in its own time. Ha, ha, ha. I will check it out on the web.

I hope it will, Ramon. Tears of laughter drop out of her eyes.

Don't worry, Mira. By the way, what do you think about people that can change into reptiles?

Again both start laughing.

I'm not joking, Mira! Ha, ha, ha.

No, no, of course not, says Mira, with a pain in her stomach of laughing. Ramon explains the theory of Icke. Some Babylonian myths tell the story of people coming from the stars, called Anunnaki. These Anunnaki had contact with the rulers of that culture. They were pictured as having reptilian heads and they gave the Babylonians the knowledge of the stars as well as mathematics and geometry. And now it comes, Mira. Icke stated that it is written that these star people created hybrid human beings by marrying the daughters of man.

In the mean time, without Ramon noticing, Mira sees the surroundings of his backyard changing into purple light flashes. The skull appears and in no time she tunnels through the square matrix into the unknown.

Ramon… Ramon… Wait a minute, please.

Sorry Mira, am I boring you with my talk?

No, no, Ramon. It's not that! But I hear that voice again.

Ramon is immediately serious when he realizes that Mira has contact with the source, whatever the source is.

Mira makes a gesture to write everything down.

1.002 **In ancient times there was contact with extra-terrestrial people.**

1.003 **Some people inherited a gene, not from this world. It has nothing to do with reptiles.**

1.004 **It's a gene, belonging to people from another world. Their body features were a bit different than the people of Earth, but they were real people. No reptiles or reptile**

people.
1.005 **These hybrid people have certain body characteristics, but they are hardly visible.**

While Ramon writes everything down, he's a bit confused to say the least. It is as if the voice had listened to their talk just minutes before. Mira gradually comes back to her senses and an uneasy feeling overpowers her.

Ramon, what is happening to me? Am I becoming schizophrenic?

But Mira! No! Absolutely not!

Because, if I am, you have to be honest with me, Ramon.

No Mira, this has nothing to do with being mad. I admit. It is unusual but I need time to figure out what is happening to you. The information is not odd at all. This kind of information has been circulating since the mid-sixties you know. Von Dänicken was the first to go public with this kind of ideas. Nowadays, Zecharia Sitchin writes one book after the other about the alien connection. So, this information is definitely not crazy. These ideas are still not proven, but that's another matter. It's not that everything these guys write is correct. But the general idea of alien contact is not at all stupid. But I have another question, Mira. Where is that information coming from? You know you are telepathically gifted. I wonder who is on the other side of the line.

Don't ask me, Ramon. It was not the same voice that gave me the proverbs last night. I'm sure of that. It was the same voice that said, "I greet you". First I clearly saw the skull and then I heard the voice. But Ramon, you're not going to tell me that this is normal.

Well no Mira, this is clearly paranormal. Not that I have all the answers. But maybe there is a link with something I read on the web yesterday. It's possible that the contact is the same as the contact the shamans had in antiquity. They called the source of information they came into contact with via the skulls, the Gods, whatever these Gods were. Maybe they were Aliens, maybe spirits of the Akasha. I don't know. But don't worry, Mira. We will figure it out.

I really hope so, Ramon. But imagine that this would happen at my work!

I don't think that will happen, Mira. In such a business environment, it will not happen. I think that I triggered your contact by talking about the reptiles, remember. I even had the impression that it was a reaction to what I told you. But nobody tells such stories at your work, I guess.

Ha, ha. No, Ramon. They only have numbers in their mind. Money, money. A smile appears on Mira's face and her skin regains her normal color. I'm going home, Ramon. I'm tired and at five a clock I have to be back on my feet.

Good idea, Mira. You know where to find me. If there is anything, just give me a sign. I always make time for you.

Promised?

Promised, Mira.

Thanks, Ramon.

The last sunlight gives the clouds a purple red color as Mira's car disappears into the night. As a parapsychologist, Ramon can stomach a lot, but what Mira just experienced is completely new to him. Crystal skulls, proverbs, and contact with God knows what. What is going on? A quick check on the web doesn't give any results. The proverbs are unknown. A bit confused Ramon decides to finish the 3D drawings and in no time he's lost in the virtual reality. It's deep into the night before he switches from the artificial world of modern technology to the wonderful world of dreams.

- 6 -
13/8/2006

Could it be that alien contact took place in antiquity? The strange messages of Mira brought Ramon back to the sixties when these ideas were openly discussed in the hippy culture. Ramon was a real fan of these revolutionary alien contact theories. The idea that extra-terrestrials visited our planet fascinated the young Ramon. But at the same time, he was always very skeptical about so called "empirical proof". And his considerable knowledge about astronomy made it clear that interstellar travel was not a simple task. Even with the speed of light, it took four years to travel to Alpha Centauri, the nearest star in our galaxy. And even if this was technically possible, proof of life on one of the planets of this star was still a big question. Nevertheless Ramon was convinced that our Earth was not the only planet where evolution of life took place.

But even then, evolution of life on Earth needed three billion years to finally create a living human creature. Humans have evolved only in the last five million years. So the chance that two different human evolutions in two separate star systems would meet in the same period was statistically rather low. One can compare it with winning the lottery. The chance to win is very minor. On the other hand, somebody always wins. So, it is possible. The same thing you can say about life itself. It's not evident, but it's possible. Look around you. On planet Earth it succeeded!

Between his design work Ramon surfed the web to check the more recent theories about alien life and possible contact. He surfs regularly to the site Niburu because it is one of the only sites in the Dutch language which publishes UFO news.

The name Niburu in itself had a link with Zecharia Sitchin. It was the name of the planet of the Anunnaki. Zecharia defends the theory that these beings came to Earth with the help of this planet. He wrote in one of his books that this planet encircled the sun every 3,600 years. Sitchin defended the idea that Niburu will be back in the near future. Ramon was shocked when he heard about this theory for the first time. How is it possible that people believe this nonsense? People are warm for lies and cold for the truth, his Wise Teacher always stressed, quoting Pascal, the famous French mathematician. Sitchin's books were a great success. The author based his ideas on old manuscripts. These manuscripts itself were very interesting. Relics and myths of an old culture are one thing. But to translate them in the right way is a very difficult task. Professionals had a hard time explaining to fans of Sitchin's books the linguistic misinterpretations of his popular translation of the old Babylonian language.

Ramon was not at all a specialist in old languages, but he was astonished about the way the word "planet" was interpreted. Before you start spreading catastrophe theories, the least you could do is to understand what the word "planet" referred to in those days, more than 5000 years ago. In our modern world, most people know that planets are worlds like our own Earth. Since Columbus, we know that the Earth is round. And since Copernicus we also know that all the planets have their own orbit around the sun. Everybody has seen beautiful pictures of Mars, Venus and Mercury and also from the gas giants Jupiter, Saturn, Uranus and Neptune.

But in antiquity, nobody knew anything close to what we know today about the planets. Surely, they knew the sun, the moon and the stars. And they also saw that some stars behaved differently than most other stars. They were called planets.

Most people seem to forget that in antiquity, the Earth was considered to be flat. The Earth was not considered to be a planet. Earth was the result of God's creation. It was the Garden of Eden. The lights in the sky belonged to the heavens. The Earth was considered to be at rest while the sun, the moon, the stars were rotating around the Earth once every day. Since Copernicus, we know that these movements of the celestial lights are not real. They are an optical effect caused by the fact that the Earth rotates around its axis every day. But in antiquity, people only believed what they saw and in general, right they were!

To people in antiquity, planets were a special kind of star. Be honest. If you see Venus in the sky, it is hard to distinguish Venus from a star. Maybe it is brighter, but at first sight, it is just one of the stars. But if you look very carefully to Venus you can see a few things that make Venus different from the surrounding stars. All stars twinkle, but planets do not. They give a constant light. And that is not the only difference. Planets have a property that makes them really special. The meaning of the word planet was originally "wandering star". And that's not without reason. All the stars have a fixed place, relative to one another. The constellations always look exactly the same. But the planets move in a different way. To the observers in antiquity, it was as if the planets were wandering, each of them in their own way. Each planet had its own behavior, independent of the collective movement of the twinkling stars. That was the reason why planets had an important place in astrology.

So, if the word "planet" was used in old manuscripts, the writers didn't associate this word with something as big as the Earth. What then was the planet Niburu in these old manuscripts referring to? Definitely not something like our own Earth! But what else? Ramon starts to meditate on that question.

If the Anunnaki came with a planet to Earth, it was more likely that the manuscripts were a very old report of a close encounter of the third kind, of a UFO.

Allen Hynek used a model of six different kinds of UFO sightings, starting with moving lights in the night sky up to close encounters of the third kind. The most commonly observed UFOs are just moving lights in the sky. So, imagine just for a moment that some observer in antiquity saw a UFO during the night. The first thing that would come to his mind would be: a wandering star, a planet! What else could he think? Because the light would move differently than the stars! So that would explain the name. A UFO would be an unknown planet in their language.

But imagine for a second that that UFO would land on the ground! I guess they would think that the planet they saw would land on Earth. For those people, it would be the only way to explain and understand what they saw. They had no clue what else to think. They had no idea what a real planet looked like. Imagine that after landing, people came out of that thing of light, that "planet". Those observers would think that these people would be god-like creatures, living in or on that planet. And it would be plausible that they thought that the Gods came to earth and that they eventually would come back after leaving, just as it was written. If such an event took place, the report of those old manuscripts would be realistic and correct!

While Ramon considered this explanation, he immediately saw a connection with another completely different problem that occupied him since his study. Ado, a good friend at the mystery school, was the only one who he could consult about this sudden insight. Ado is an expert on the Thora and the Talmud. Ado has the same habit as Ramon: working late at night. A click in the Skype list and immediately, Ramon hears his educated voice.

Ado, Brussels. What can I do for you?

I know you're a busy man, Ado. Do you have a few minutes?

For you, I always make time, dear friend. It is still early in the night.

Well then, Ado. You know that in Genesis the heavenly lights are mentioned.

Yes, chapter one, verse 14 to 18, is his educated response. It's commonly known, I hope.

Well then, Ado. Or Wise Teacher pointed to the fact that the sun, moon and the stars in this myth, were not considered to be gods.

Absolutely, Ramon. In Genesis, the heavenly bodies were not considered to be gods. They were just lights, to guide the people at night. Our Wise Teacher also pointed out that this myth was much older than the other myths about creation. In later myths, the sun, the moon, the stars and the planets became gods.

So you agree that apparently they changed their mind. Do you remember the lecture of the Dutch nuclear physicist, Prof. Jacob Kistemaker?

Absolutely, Ramon. How could I forget him? He made perfectly clear that as a scientist he was astonished that Genesis was the oldest myth but at the same time the most modern one. If you substitute the days of creation with periods, the genesis story follows the same order as the evolution theory by Darwin and even the cosmology of the Big Bang theory: first the space-time and then the four forces of nature, creating light and matter eventually. And on Earth, first all the minerals are created, then the plants, the animals and only at the end, the human being. And as you will remember, the paradise story is about the beginning of human culture, especially creating a language.

Exactly, Ado. Well, don't laugh, but could it be that the idea that the planets and stars are Gods could have been triggered by a close encounter with a UFO?

Ramon tells him in short his personal interpretation of the Babylonian myth.

Very interesting, is Ado's first reaction. Your idea is very logical. That would be reasonable taken into account what you told me about the Anunnaki. If they thought that the UFO was a planet, it could be that they thought afterwards that all the planets were the same thing as the UFO they saw, populated by god-like beings. It could be a good explanation why the older myths didn't give stars the status of Gods. I must admit, it is an exotic theory, Ramon. But it is at least a logical one. Don't forget that the American Indians thought that white people were Gods.

Cultural advantage does strange things with the mind of people when they are confronted with things they don't understand. You must not ask how strong the mental impact would be when people of antiquity would come into contact with highly technical people. The greater the difference, the greater the impact and the confusion. But Ramon, do you have a new hobby? I thought you were only living for art?

Ramon laughs. He could talk for hours with Ado about alien theories when they were still students. For Ado, it was sometimes too much.

I will explain it later, Ado. It is a long story.

It was nice to hear you, Ramon. I really hope to see you soon.

I do too, Ado. Thanks for your comment. Bye.

A pleasure to be of help, dear friend. Bye.

While Ado returns to his Talmudic study, Ramon thinks everything over. So I could be right? Ado says my hypothesis is logical, and that means a lot. Could this myth really be a transcript of a close encounter? It would only be natural to misinterpret the context of the visitors of other worlds. When Christians visited for the first time the Chinese temples they were convinced that the Chinese worshipped the devil. Just because the dragon was a central symbol in Chinese culture. For the Chinese, the dragons were the vehicles of the Gods. Not some evil concept of aggressive dragons like in western myths and legends. My grandfather was right after all. The whole world is one big misunderstanding. If you see how people react on UFOs these days, it's hard to imagine the impact they could have had on people of antiquity. Glad to have solved this riddle, he makes some notes. Only one question remained. The myth also mentions catastrophic floods in the same period. What could be the cause of those events?

But of course! How can you forget! Don't forget your lectures geology, Ramon. The end of the last minor ice age was some 12,000 years ago. From that period on, the ice sheets started melting. The sea level was rising dramatically. Most people seem to forget that the sea level had risen hundred and twenty-five meters in seven thousand years. And that is a lot! All over the world, the people, living on the coasts had to move, generation after generation, to be safe for the rising water. Every century one and a half meter! Until the rising came to a hold some five to

46

six thousand years ago, in the same period of the Babylonian manuscripts.

Constant floods were happening all over the world for seven thousand years. It was a riddle to Ramon why historians had problems with the fact that stories about catastrophic floods were written down in myths all over the world. Specialization in science has its disadvantages. That was the main reason why the mystery school was founded in the first place. Planets that would pass Earth very closely had nothing whatsoever to do with the floods. It just became a bit warmer on mother Earth. When even most people in present days don't understand the real reasons of the floods, you can imagine what prehistoric people might have been thinking. But it would be reasonable to assume that extra-terrestrials who happened to be in the vicinity in that particular period would give the people of our world a helping hand after millennia of struggle to survive in the ever changing environment by the melting of the ice causing the sea to rise.

Again late at night, before Ramon falls asleep, he can't help laughing as he thinks how astonished people in prehistoric time must have reacted to interplanetary tourists and how the alien visitors had to struggle to explain our ancestors who they were and where they came from.

- 7 -
14/8/2006

For a couple of days there is no sign of Mira, but then a message enters his computer, just when he is taking a break after a whole day of painting.

"Can you make time tonight?"

"I always make time" is his short return.

"See you soon." is the short replay of Mira.

Through the window Ramon sees the twelve painted wooden plates drying in the sun. They are the basis for twelve sculptures. The burning sun does its work well and the paint dries fast. He goes outside for a last check. When these panels are ready, the real work can start. He checks thoroughly whether he has done his work well. The fine dust of polishing is all over his body and

Ramon yearns for a good shower. It's a relief to feel the jets of water flow over his body.

A while later Ramon enjoys a hot cup of coffee, cleaning his throat from the fine dust. Twelve impossible sculptures! That's his job for the coming months. His exhibition "Alien" has to be a new milestone in his artistic oeuvre. Since Ury's information about the Warriors, the number twelve has gotten a new meaning. It's easy to divide a circle in twelve. Twelve can be divided by six, four, tree, two. Twelve art works is just enough to fill the exhibition room. Together with the already finished sculpture, it is just enough. It is twelve years ago that the sculpture, named Unity, got a stand in the center of his village.

Time to bring something new. He studies the first sketches carefully. He will have to take care of a general color balance. The wooden panels will have to be a neutral grey. When the coffee pot is completely empty, he knows it's time for the third layer of paint. The sun has done its work well. If he starts now, everything will be done before Mira arrives. A few hours later Ramon does the dishes, glad that he finished the job. Suddenly, he senses that Mira comes into the kitchen, silently like she always does. As if he has eyes on his back, he surprises Mira at her own game.

Hello Mira, everything ok?

How do you know it is me, Ramon?

Who else could it be, Mira?

A smile appears on his face. But at the same time, Ramon senses from her voice that she is in an altered state of consciousness or trance for the friends.

Ramon, says Mira with a trembling voice, I'm not going crazy, am I?

You're not, Mira. Crazy people don't ask themselves this question. Please, take a seat and relax. Tell me, what is going on? No, wait! First, I will make some fresh coffee.

As fast as he can, Ramon cleans a few mugs and puts the water heater on. Moments later, the aromas of coffee fill his little kitchen.

Coffee coming up! Now tell me, what's on your mind?

Ramon's optimistic style brings a smile to her face.

All right. Take pen and paper. I think you need to write this down.

In a hurry, Ramon takes his writing materials and in a blink of an eye, he is sitting in the kitchen, wondering what he has to write down. Is it again information of the purple one?

Mira's voice is deep and Ramon observes her carefully to learn more about the effect on her body while she is in contact with the purple skull.

How long have you been having contact, Mira?

Since last night, Ramon. It was so alien, you know. First I was looking at the skull, the internal matrix started to tremble and before I knew I was gone and there was that voice again.

And? Has this voice revealed its identity?

First listen, Ramon. Lest I forget all, I think it is very important that you write it down literally, as I say it. And with earnestness and carefulness, not at all typical for her, she starts to spell the message she memorized in her mind.

1.006 **To the people of the planet Geya.**

This is a message via the purple gateway of Orion.

To the one that speaks without sound.

Geya, Mira? It sounds like the Greek word "gaia" meaning "earth".

Please, Ramon. Don't interrupt me now. First take notes. Keep your questions for later. And slowly she continues translating the message.

1.007 **We are positioned at 10,000 light years. We have tried several times to come into contact with the people of Geya, by sending signals in the binary code.**

1.008 **But the signals are wrongly interpreted... or not at all. But nothing has been done with the signals!**

1.009 **Now I see zeros and lines on squares. No idea what it means.**

It is silent in the kitchen except for the sound of Ramon's pen. Once finished, he looks up to Mira.

That's it?

That's it, Ramon.

She looks at Ramon to see his reaction. But Ramon's attention is all on his notes. He reads his notes aloud to check whether he wrote it down correctly.

Yes. That's it, Ramon.

Half dazed, Mira rolls a cigarette.

What does this all mean, Ramon? I don't understand, you now.

Ramon feels she is questioning her state of mind, worried that this might be the final proof that she's really crazy.

Well Mira, there is only one way to find out. We have to try to understand what it means. If we can answer that question, I can answer yours. While he tries to reassure Mira, Ramon thinks within himself: There you are, Ramon. Parapsychologist, educated by the best teachers, years of studying, even the ufologist Allen Hynek was one of my teachers... And I don't have a word to say for myself.

Let's start with a question, Mira. Is this again information from the purple skull?

No, no Ramon. This information is not from the purple skull. It came to me "via" the purple skull. The information is not from the skull itself. I think, my first feelings were right, Ramon. This skull is a kind of antenna, an amplifier to improve the clarity of telepathic messages over very large distances.

She is surprised to hear herself explaining what the purple skull is all about.

Ramon writes it down and reads the notes again with growing

50

astonishment.

How do you know?

Look, Ramon! Mira yells, look… I'm bleeding! I have a wound on my head, just like yesterday.

With concern, Ramon sees indeed a watery red spot on top of her head and he immediately gives her a paper handkerchief.

Don't be so worried, Ramon, she says when she sees the concerned expression on his face. It doesn't hurt. It is just irritating and it itches after it stops bleeding.

Ramon takes a deep breath. So much the better, Mira. It is not something that happens every day, you know. Is it okay if we read the text again? You know, to be sure I understand it right. Or is it too much for you now?

Go ahead, Ramon. I still have contact with the skull. I feel a pulsating pressure on my forehead. Maybe some coffee will help me. Would you believe I worked all day in this condition? I feel exhausted.

I believe you, Mira. A fresh mug of hot coffee will do us both good.

In no time, fresh Arabica beans are transformed in a lovely dark brown liquid full of aroma and taste.

You can ask questions, Ramon. Maybe the pressure goes away, as soon as the information is clear.

That's a good idea, Mira. Where shall I start? Have you any idea what or who sends this information?

No, Ramon. He will reveal his identity later. Now it is important to understand the information. Ask any question but you have to understand:

1.010 **There is much more information to come, but not at the moment. It's too dangerous now.**

Too dangerous? I don't understand. What is dangerous?

I can't answer your question, Ramon. He says it will soon become clear.

Okay! Ramon serves the coffee and starts to analyze the information.

"To the one that can speak without sound". That clearly points at you Mira or anybody who is telepathically gifted. Telepathy is speaking without sound! And if this source is 10,000 light years away, we have to consider the possibility that the source has to be located on another planet somewhere. 10,000 light years isn't exactly close by, you know, Mira.

If you say so, Ramon.

So, it's possible your contact is extra-terrestrial?

Extra-terrestrial? You mean I have contact with an alien?

Ramon laughs at Mira's reaction.

Well yes. Who else? I don't think you find people from Earth at such a far distance, don't you think? But don't worry, Mira. It's just a possibility.

But something else now. I would be surprised if they would speak our language.

That's why this contact is so exhausting for me, Ramon. I hear a voice speaking in a different language, but I understand the meaning as if it is my own.

Fantastic, Mira. Really, you surprise me.

Fantastic? You call this fantastic? I call this freaky!

Ramon laughs again.

Let me explain why I find this contact amazing.

While both enjoy the hot coffee, Ramon tells Mira about his fascination for the Apollo project when he was young. The Apollo space program of NASA and astronomy were his favorite topics when he was a young boy. He explains how worried he was about the fate of the astronauts when they would travel into deep space. The farther they travel the more difficult it would be to stay in contact with the home base on Earth.

If you land on Mars, it takes five to six minutes before anyone hears you on the other side of the line. That was the reason why Ramon became interested in parapsychology in the first place. He once read an article, stating that telepathy didn't need time to send a message. Telepathy happens in the "now time" and doesn't need time to travel over large distances. He immediately concluded that this could be the solution to stay in contact during interstellar travel. Of course, it were only theories, circulating in books on parapsychology. But nevertheless, Ramon found it to be an intriguing idea. And now, with the help of a crystal skull, that very idea could be put in practice and happening before his very eyes.

Don't you find this intriguing, Mira? So, if the source is 10,000 light years away, only telepathy can make that contact possible.

52

For you get answers to your questions, otherwise I can't explain this immediate response.

But Ramon, isn't it too soon to come to conclusions? Do you really believe I have contact with an alien?

I don't believe that, Mira. I suppose that. It's just a first guess. But it is a better explanation than contact with spirits or gods, don't you think? For the moment, it seems to me a reasonable explanation. There are other options of course. But let's try to understand what the information tells us. As long as there are no contradictions, I want to take it seriously.

I don't doubt that the information is sent right this very moment, Ramon.

What makes you so sure, Mira?

The source says so.

Ramon has forgotten that Mira is still in contact.

Sorry, Mira. I have to get used to this situation, you know. Can you ask your source about the signals he mentioned? It looks to me that a technical signal is sent. Maybe I don't understand but radio signals travel with the speed of light. So the signals need 10,000 years to arrive here. How can that be?

Immediately the source gives Ramon an answer via Mira.

1.011 **The signals are sent via the gateway of Orion.**

The gateway of Orion? But what can this gateway be, Mira?

I haven't a clue either, Ramon. I only know they used another way to send a message to Earth. But how they did it? Don't ask me.

Okay. So, suppose they have sent signals and that the signals have been received here on Earth? But by whom? I surf regularly to the SETI site. Do you know that organization? They scan the sky for alien signals. But I never heard they received intelligent signals. Although... I remember they discovered pulsars by accident. But that was in the eighties if I remember well. Pulsars are...

Spare me the details, Ramon. I believe you. Point is that the source tells me that signals have been sent. I can't tell you any more.

Sorry, Mira. Don't get me wrong. You know me. I'm just thinking aloud. Another question then. Those zeros and lines on the square frames? Can you describe more in detail what you saw? You saw them as images, didn't you?

Mira immediately enters a deep mental state and her eyes are completely turned inside her mind. Yes. I see the images again, Ramon.

1.012 **I see square planes... and they are divided in a square frame.**

The zeros and lines are placed inside the square frame like a crossword puzzle.

Swiftly, Ramon sketches a square frame between his notes. Any notion what this raster represents, Mira?

No, Ramon, but that will become clear in the coming days. I have the strong feeling that much more information will come. Her voice is deep and serious.

Ramon is excited and worried at the same time. He doesn't know what to make of it.

We will see what the future brings, Mira. For the moment I can only make notes and try to understand.

Suddenly, Mira jumps from her chair. My God... I have to go, Ramon. I have to feed my animals. Especially the deer. It can't wait. When I'm too late, they will be mad at me for days, you know.

Ramon is glad that Mira hasn't lost contact with reality and accompanies her to the car. Gracefully she enters her car. I will come back tomorrow, after my pro bono work, if it's not too late. She closes the door but opens the window fast.

Jesus! It's a greenhouse in here. I hope I can sleep tonight. My attic is even worse. I could hardly sleep yesterday, so hot! Bye!

Before Ramon can react, her car disappears into the early night. He waves but no response of Mira. Gone with the wind she is. Well yes, that's Mira alright. First she quickly brings you news from an alien and then she has to feed her animals. And her contact, whatever or whoever "it" or "he" or "she" is has to wait too. I hope the alien has a sense of humor. Ramon takes his notes in the kitchen and sits down in his garden chair, enjoying the hot air. Step by step he reads his notes again.

"To the people of the planet Geya. This is a message via the purple gateway of Orion." It sounds a bit cliché but also very official. It is directed to all mankind. Great, thinks Ramon. But why sending this information to the middle of nowhere. Well yes, Mira is a powerful telepathic person.

But this binary code in a square matrix. It reminds me of the movie Contact. Could it really be true? Or is it just a daydream of Mira? A mix of fragments of different movies. Ramon doubts. No. It would be my first thought with anybody but not with Mira. Ramon knows she has to be taken seriously. There is only one way to unravel this strange event. I have to see what the future brings. Time will tell. But I have no time now. I have to work.

With a mug filled with fluid brown work power, Ramon goes to his WebCom. I have to finish this drawing as soon as possible. Ramon gives his mice a nudge and a second later the screens flash on. Still five posters to go. Come on, Ramon, let's do it. When they are finished I'm free to start making the sculptures. They are waiting.

Until late in the night he works to finish the last drawings. But in his mind, Mira's information doesn't let go. While working on the last poster, he wonders what his professor parapsychology Van Praag would think of all this. He organized the first UFO conference in Luxembourg. He will never forget the event. It was in 1977. He was a man with a lot of courage. He was also the director of the mystery school. Founded on 11/11/1976 at eleven o'clock. For him, no subject was taboo. He was a very serious scientist, but he had no problem whatsoever with the paranormal, mysticism or spiritual matters. After his studies, Ramon wanted to use everything he learned in his own way and to spread the word via his artwork.

While thinking, Mira's sketch of the square matrix catches his attention again. What could be the significance of this? Codes and riddles were his favorite hobby, especially geometry riddles. He solved the problem of impossible figures in 3D when he was twenty-three years old. As a minimal artist, Ramon understood the importance of the basic symbols of human culture, namely the point and the line, the square and the circle, the cube and the sphere. Ramon's holy mission was to discover unknown properties of these basic figures with the help of his artwork. One statement of his Wise Teacher he would never forget. "If you can break the code of a culture, you can develop a new culture." Same goes for art.

Indeed, very simple ancient symbols were the basis of some most complex philosophies. Take Confucianism. This philosophy was based on two symbols: lines and broken lines. Could these square matrices have something to do with the I Tjing? Since Mao Tse Tung's Cultural Revolution, Confucianism, Shintoism and Taoism were suppressed philosophies for a long time. But just like Qin Shi Huangdi, the first Emperor of China, Mao was the only one in possession of the I Tjing, his Wise Teacher said once. This fact alone shows the importance and the hidden meaning and knowledge of this remarkable book. That is, if you know how to use it. The I Tjing was the bible of Confucianism. But nobody has ever broken the code of the I Tjing. Emperor Fu Hsi, the inventor of this simple line system, was the Henri Poincaré of ancient China. Even today, Bill Gates protects the mother code of his worldwide spread Windows system. So, nothing new under the sun!

While thinking, Ramon finished his last drawing and saves it to his hard disc. Thank God, it's done. He looks at the clock: quarter to three. Pfff, again that late. As he reaches to unplug the computer, a sound of an incoming e-mail catches his attention.

From Mira, at this time of night? He opens the message. Some extra information!

1.013 **We are Human. We left the "ego" stage.**

1.014 **But we are confronted with other evolutions! Giant block-cultures dominate. Only in our minds, we are free.**

1.015 **Thoughts are our only way to communicate. On physical level, others have complete control over everything that happens.**

1.016 **The signals have to be decoded or Geya will face the same fate.**

I send it in case I forget. I'm exhausted. See you tomorrow. Mira. In a hurry, Ramon writes everything in his notebook. "Giant block cultures?" "The same destiny?" It sounds more like a cry for help! A kind of cosmic SOS.

"We are human". So they are people just like us. "We left the "ego stage". Wow! They could be a kind of mystic civilisation. Something like an advanced Tibetan culture. "We are confronted with other evolutions!" What could that mean? And "giant block cultures dominate!" That could mean that Belgium is not alone in this respect. Ramon starts to laugh in the middle of the night.

56

When Ramon is tired, a good laugh is never far away. Ramon, you never take anything seriously, is a common reaction of even his best friends.

Ramon dries the tears in his eyes. **"Only in our minds, we are free"**. Isn't that the grief of every poet? And just for a moment Ramon remembers the poetry of Jotie T'Hooft. He knew him only a short time before he died.

Whatever this is, it really is a cry for help... and a warning! **On physical level, "others" have complete control**. Who are those "others". Those block cultures maybe? It is as if they live under a kind of cruel dictatorship, whoever the source of this message is. But what kind of message is carried in the signals? And how am I supposed to figure all this out? With more questions than answers, Ramon writes a message for himself on the small black board in the kitchen. And minutes later he falls in a restless sleep, wondering what the heck is going on.

- 8 -
10/4/2007

Okay. For the time being, I leave the text like it is. And with a click Ramon saves the file "The Alien Code 04". While writing, he remembered vividly the first odd experiences he had with Mira. Already eight months have passed and still no traces on the web about alien signals. Not even on the hardcore UFO sites.

Hmm, fifty pages done. My God, I still have a long way to go. If it wasn't for all these pro bono jobs, I would have been halfway by now. Come on, Ramon. Complaining doesn't help a bit.

The sharp sunlight shines through the windows and hurts his eyes.

I have to go to the garden. The plants need water or they won't survive.

It's been abnormally hot for weeks now. Summer in the springtime! Officially there is still nothing wrong with our climate. Will Al Gore succeed to wake up the world with his video and book "An Inconvenient Truth"? He really hopes so. "The club of Rome" was ridiculed in the seventies. They had the same message.

Meditating about the ins and outs of climatic change, Ramon makes it to his garden on his bike. It's burning hot in his small garden of Eden. Luckily, the nights are still long or the grass would already be burned. In a hurry Ramon makes his tour with the water can and the seven beds with vegetables look much better after a shower. Ramon used an Indian mandala as a blueprint for his garden. The biggest square is the basis of the design. The square is marked with fruit trees. Inside the square he spread the bushes and the flowers in an orderly fashion. He left four openings to enter the circle. In India they are the four gateways to enter the world. These gateways were marked with purple lilac trees. Inside the circle of plants, eight round beds were placed. Only the bed at the east gateway was covered with tiles. Ramon built a garden house in the center. The house had a square base, and vertically, the shape was based on a regular triangle. All together, the place radiated a special atmosphere.

Land Art was for Ramon serious business. It was a famous art style in the sixties. Christo became internationally renowned with his enormous land art projects. But most artists went undercover. As a young artist, Ramon was convinced that land art could be put into practice everywhere. When Ramon reads about the discovery of a new crop circle, he always has to smile. Give it to 'em, guys!

After a small pause in the garden, Ramon goes home. The open air has given him new energy and with a mug of good coffee, he finds new courage to continue his lonely adventure. After opening the file "The code 04", he's right back in the middle of his story. With the help of his notes, the past comes to life and gradually he's sinking back into the story.

He suddenly remembers that only a year ago, he decided to write a small article about the UFO problem from a philosophical point of view. At first, Unidentified Flying Objects were not that much seen by people. UFO was a military term. UFOs were objects seen by radar. Any unidentified object in the air is a UFO. Everybody is aware of the reality of airplanes to spy. In the period of the cold war and the threat of an atomic war in the fifties and sixties, UFOs seen by American radars were in general Russian airplanes. They were spying, whatever the mission was. UFOs were primarily considered hostile and were carefully observed and followed by radar. But some UFOs were neither from the USA nor from the USSR. And these UFOs were a real danger to world safety and peace. They were real objects and no optical illusions. A well known ufologist, Robert O. Dean brought a lot of information out in public about these genuine UFOs. These "not from Earth" UFOs were an ever growing problem in the fifties and sixties, probably due to an ever growing radar park all over the world and later in space. Some UFOs had mind blowing speeds. Thirty to sixty-thousand miles an hour was not exceptional. And even at this speed, these UFOs could turn in angles of ninety degrees without changing speed.

Such maneuvers were technically impossible for airplanes. Anyhow, human beings could never survive such maneuvers; they would be killed on the spot. In those days, more and more civilian witnesses declared to have seen a UFO. In the 1960s alone, 30,000 sightings were reported. In general, these witnesses were ridiculed for what they pretended to have seen. Pictures of UFOs couldn't impress skeptics either. UFO's do not exist! End of story. They were optical illusions, weather balloons, strange clouds and so on.

But however severely critics denigrated UFO witnesses, the UFO phenomenon did not go away. On the contrary! The fact that UFO's were associated with alien visitors, made it easy to ridicule anybody that came forward with a story. Aliens? Come on! Out of the question! Impossible! Not even worth considering!

In his article, Ramon wanted to show the link between UFO sightings and observations of meteorites and comets in the middle ages. These now commonly known phenomena were not accepted as real phenomena in those days. The reason to deny their existence was rather simple. God created Heaven and Earth. Heaven was perfect and Earth was imperfect. Everybody could experience the latter every day: sickness, suffering and death and so on. Heaven was perfect and by Heaven they meant the sky and the night sky. Heaven couldn't change because it was perfect. Earth was in constant changing mode. The seasons, ebb and flood of the sea and so on. All these changes lead to imperfection. Change was considered a sign of imperfection and negative.

The conclusion was simple. Meteorites, named "falling stars" or comets could not exist. It was impossible to suddenly see lights in heaven. Because that was impossible in a perfect, never changing Heaven. There were only stars and planets. God had created these lights. There was no place for other lights. Because that would suggest that Heaven was not perfect. And that was impossible of course. After all, God Himself was living in Heaven, so Heaven had to be perfect. So people who saw falling stars or comets had to be wrong. Or worse! These people had seen signs, created by the devil. The devil was the incarnation of evil. And of course, he would try to convince people that Heaven was not perfect. Eyewitnesses of comets risked to be accused of having contact with the devil when they said they saw a meteorite falling on to the ground.

The idea that these lights were rocks was even more outrageous. How could stones fall from the sky? That was absolutely ridiculous. Come on! It becomes even more confusing if you know that in de Ka'ba, the big cube shaped temple in the center of the Holy Mosque of Mecca, the holiest of the holy, a big black meteorite is preserved. It was the only image of God which Mohammed didn't remove from this old temple when he conquered Mecca in 622. It must be a very old meteorite. In the year Ramon wrote the article, an impact crater was found in Jordan. Some eight thousand years ago, a relatively large meteor of ten to fifteen meter must have crashed there. Maybe the black stone was a part of that meteorite. What would the witnesses of this event make of it? They must have believed that this stone was a gift from the gods in heaven.

In the middle ages, you had better keep quiet if you saw moving lights at night. The conclusion was very simple. The world-view in those days didn't allow falling stars to exist. If you saw changing lights at night, you were seduced by the devil or worse, worshipping the devil. Whatever the accusation was, it wasn't healthy for you.

The skeptics of those days were not amused. Those people had a strong believe in the religiously inspired world-view of those days. It was their job to make sure that everybody was faithful to that world-view. The punishments were severe for the heretics who believed they really saw something changing in the night sky.

Luckily, those days are over. Or are they? We perceive the world totally different. But if people nowadays see UFOs making strange maneuvers and move with incredible speed, they have a problem. Why? For the same reason as middle age observers of meteorites! Okay, they are not put on a stake. But they are ridiculed in the press, and their mental sanity is questioned. Like in the middle ages, they get a stigma, based on our scientific world-view. And why? Because what they see is impossible, based on what our scientific world-view prescribes. Nevertheless, every philosopher knows that a world-view is only a temporary attempt to explain the world we live in. This view is handy for the time being and a gift of human intellect. But it is not the truth and nothing but the truth. It is a tool for the human intellect to get grip on reality.

And these tools have to change in the wonderful adventure of the mind we call science. The world we live in is so much more complex than the human mind can grasp. So regularly, our world-view has to change, to get closer to reality. If that happens, we have a paradigm shift, a change of our world-view. Allen Hynek gave a lecture at our mystery school in 1980 and taught us that our science needed a new physics if we wanted to understand the UFO phenomenon. But the scientific attitude against UFOs has not changed very much in the last sixty years. At universities ufology is still not accepted as a science, neither is parapsychology, by the way.

UFO sightings aren't even mentioned in the free press anymore. But like meteorites keep on falling and comets keep on coming back, UFOs keep on flying through our skies and keep showing up on our radars. Ramon was always convinced that most UFOs were unknown natural phenomena, though he didn't neglect the theory that some UFOs are of extra-terrestrial origin. For Ramon, it could even be reasonable that alien UFOs are based on a technology of the natural UFOs. Think for a minute. In our time almost everything works with electricity. Electricity is as old as the Earth itself. Humans were confronted with this wonderful natural force in lightning, produced by thunder storms. Who has no admiration or even fear for lightning? So it wouldn't be crazy at all to assume that the physics involved in natural UFOs could be the basis for new insights and technology. Nature has invented every physical thing from the beginning of times. The phenomena are there, waiting for us to be studied and eventually used.

It wouldn't surprise Ramon a bit if non-earthly civilizations had figured out the physics of natural UFOs long ago and use it in their technology. For natural UFOs are likely to occur on all planets. Nature is the same everywhere. This credo of Newton is the basis of physics. We can do fantastic things with our technology. But Ramon was convinced that thousand years from now, our technology would be as old-fashioned to the people of the future as the technology of the middle ages is to us.

To think that alien contact is not possible is a gigantic overestimation of our own level of scientific knowledge. It's a shame that skeptics treat witnesses of UFOs the way they do. Their behavior can sometimes be compared to the inquisitors of the middle ages. Not that you have to believe everything just like that. But you have to have a critical, open mind. But criticism must be based on scientific proof and not based on common opinion. Questioning the mental health of people that have witnessed a UFO sighting has nothing to do with science. Furthermore, there is something that critics seem to forget. They pretend to base their reasoning on the scientific world-view. But that is not the case. Allen Hynek was a serious scientist and a professor in astronomy. Skeptics use a popularization of the scientific world-view. We tend to forget that the real scientific world-view is a gigantic complex domain, called science. Even the greatest philosophers of our time have a hard time digesting the rapid changes in science. Let alone translating this rapid evolution to the people in a kind of global world-view. Mishio Kaku, Stephen Hawking and Roger Penrose and some others have done a very good job, though.

That was also the reason why Ramon accepted the invitation of Teimon to write a book. It was a challenge to turn the recent UFO debate inside out and upside down, to study everything and keep what is worthwhile. It is late, very late when Ramon closes everything down and falls asleep.

The lasts drops of the first, full-size coffee pot fall into Ramon's mug. With sleep still in his eyes, he sees the cryptic message to himself. Mira... Information. With disbelief, he reads the notes of yesterday night. It looks so official, so polite.

We are Human. We left the 'ego' stage.

That's interesting. His thoughts go to the wise words of his Teacher. If you want to become enlightened, you need to leave the egocentric stage behind and become a personality. In Buddhism and Hinduism the ego is seen as the greatest obstacle to develop the deeper layers of one's own personality. He named Martin Luther King as a good example of a great personality. He spoke out against racism and believed in a multicultural society. Hitler on the other hand was a perfect example of somebody with a lack of personality. He compensated his inferiority complex with large manifestations, propagated racism and manipulated his own people with lies. So, it could be that Mira's contact is a member of a civilization that has left the stage of egocentrism and egoism. That would be great of course.

We are confronted with other evolutions.

Other evolutions? Where is the source referring to?

On the physical level, others have complete control. The block cultures dominate.

It really looks as if they are in trouble.

Thoughts are our only way to communicate. The signals have to be decoded or Geya will face the same fate.

So not only are they in trouble but we face the same danger. Ramon realizes he has to take this information seriously. Contact with aliens is one thing. But this sounds as if the source, alien or not, wants to warn us for something. For some kind of danger, whatever it might be. Freaky, to say the least! But what must he do with all this information? The sound of the church bells brings Ramon back to reality.

Eleven o'clock. Damn! I have to start working. Everything has to be finished before tomorrow. And then... bye everybody...

Ramon is off to enjoy a music festival. It's his only holiday in the year. It is a relief as he puts the last board, decorated with a print of the poster, against the wall. Relieved, he fills his mug with some cold coffee and goes to his WebCom. With a few clicks he opens his mail box and reads all the breaking news of science and astronomy. While looking at some beautiful images of the Orion nebula, he hears a car stopping at the back of his house. Seconds later, he hears a familiar voice in the kitchen.

Ramon… Ramon? Are you home?

I'm here, Mira. Take a seat, I come in a minute.

Ramon smiles as he enters the kitchen and sees the beautiful lady with in the background the painting "Remember Golgotha and Auschwitz".

Coffee, Mira? I see you need one as much as I do.

Yes please, Ramon. Sorry but I am a bit later than I thought.

Tired, she takes a seat in the first chair at hand.

If I don't do everything myself at work, I'm in trouble, you know.

I know exactly what you mean, Mira.

I haven't had any sleep last night, Ramon, looking at the mountain of dishes on the sink, waiting for a hot shower. Bachelors, she muses.

Sorry Mira, for the mess in the kitchen. The coffee will be ready in a few minutes. No sleep, you say? Do you mean you had contact again?

Yes, Ramon. All night long I had contact with the purple skull. And always that pressure on my head. It's so alien, you know. The strange thing is that I am not really tired. My body is, but not my mind.

Well, if the Kundalini energy rises to the sixth or seventh level, you hardly need any sleep, Mira.

That may be so, Ramon, but don't think I am enjoying it. The pressure on my head was sometimes unbearable. And the images and the impressions kept on coming. And before I forget, this information I got yesterday. I wrote it down for you.

1.017 **Block cultures give disinformation and infiltrate the population**.

1.018 **First they give power. Then they take over. I will be back.**

1.019 **I salute you. Aodin.**

Ramon glues the paper into his notebook.

64

Aodin?

Yes. Aodin is his name.

Aodin. That's a strange name. And who is he?

Well, that's the person who gives the information!

That's clear, Mira. But I mean, is he a real living person like us?

Oh yes. I'm sure of that.

So, no archetype, no phantom or a spirit?

No, no Ramon. He is definitely a living person. I haven't seen him, but the contact feels real, as real as contact with human beings.

And this Aodin is located at 10,000 light years?

That's what he says. And oh yes, Aodin is a man. It's not a woman. He says that you can ask questions, Ramon. I can still come into contact with him.

Are you kidding me, Mira?

Mira enjoys the surprised look on Ramon's face.

I'm not kidding, Ramon. But you have to ask questions about the information you already have written down. And keep it short, because it is extremely tiresome.

Ramon takes his writing materials while questioning his sanity. Could Mira really have contact with an alien? And how does this telepathic contact work?

Mira, don't you think I first have to ask something about…

With a gesture, Mira asks him to be quiet. Surrounded by a nebula of purple light she's staring at the vibrating matrix inside the purple skull that appears to her and some moments later, Mira starts to speak with a slow, deep voice.

1.020 **The key of the translation of the signals is in the names… in the names I will receive.**

1.021 **Only a few people on Geya can have contact with us.**

1.022 **A man can reach a woman, a woman can reach a man.**

Ramon takes notes while questioning how Aodin knows what he wanted to ask. He remembers the books of Alexandra David-Néel. She was the first woman to enter Tibet in the beginning of the twentieth century. During her travels in this vast country, she met tulkus. They are a kind of monks who master the technique of telepathy. They still play an important role to protect the Dalai Lama. Mira seems to have a similar talent. And it seems to work better if the contact is between a man and a woman. It's all nice to know. But experiencing telepathic transmissions in your own kitchen is very odd. But Mira doesn't give Ramon much time to think.

1.023 Teimon salutes you to let you know: you look like us.

1.024 On Geya, the process of duality is starting right now. Try to understand and you will find the key.

1.025 Physical power and mental strength. These are the two powers involved in the process of duality.

1.026 The previous contacts were physical power. Follow the mental path. The key is...

Mira stops abruptly. I think this will not be for today, Ramon.

What do you mean, Mira? Is the contact broken again?

Yes, says Mira, relieved that the session is over.

Look, Ramon, I'm bleeding again on my head.

A red spot is clearly visible. With a handkerchief she softly cleans the wound.

I didn't break the contact, Ramon. Teimon suddenly said: I come back when the danger has past. And before I knew it, he was gone.

How strange, Mira. This is the second time that they talk about some danger. What the heck can this danger be? He fills the mugs with the rest of the coffee and reads the notes to be sure he hasn't forgotten anything.

Mira? Teimon? Is he somebody else than... Aodin?

Yes, she whispers. I could clearly feel the difference, Ramon. It was not only the sound. It felt differently. Or am I imagining it all, Ramon?

No, no Mira. It's also new to me, you know, but you are not crazy. This is serious information. What it all means isn't clear to me either. You know how I think about telepathy.

Most paranormal people receive information from the Akasha. This ability is well known in Hindu literature. Akasha is the fifth element in the ancient Hindu world-view. You can compare the Akasha with memory. The memory contains everything you have learned in your life. The Hindus also believe that the universe has a similar memory of its own. It contains information of everything that has happened.

To Hindus, a human is a micro cosmos and the universe is seen as the macro cosmos. And both are one! Some humans have the

66

gift to see into the universal memory. That's how I explain the gift of clairvoyance of paranormal people. They can see the past and the present, but the future is much more difficult. The future is still not fully written down in the Akasha. And that's a good thing. You can compare it with the weather report. The further you look into the future, the more difficult it becomes to get it right.

That's perfectly clear for me, Ramon. But what is telepathy?

Well, if you have telepathic contact with another person, you just make a phone call. The difference is that you don't use a mechanical device, like a phone or a cellular phone. In fact, if you think about it, telepathy is really not that special. You just use a part of your brain that has the ability to make contact. The Tibetans have known for centuries how to develop this ability. For them it was a necessity to survive in the extreme environment of the Himalayas and to keep in contact during the long winters. The difference between telepathy and clairvoyance is not always that clear. But what you are experiencing is clearly telepathy. Obviously, it is a special kind of telepathy. I must admit that the crystal skull is new to me. It could indeed be that the crystal skull functions as a common focus point for those who have contact. It could very well be an amplifier like you said.

It was my first impression, Ramon. And it must be a sender and a receiver because we can talk and ask questions. That cube matrix is crucial, Ramon. I always have to travel through it to have contact.

You are right, Mira. We must stick to that explanation unless we see contradictions.

Glad that he made a first step in explaining what happens, he turns back to the notes. This Aodin contacted you first, I suppose?

Absolutely, Ramon. I don't do anything. Suddenly he's there, whether I like it or not.

Unbelievable, Mira. I have to be cautious about what I say, but if everything I think is true, it could be that you have contact with a human of another world. Do you realize that?

Mira shakes her entire body.

Jesus, Ramon. If you put it like that, it gives me the creeps, you know. But why me?

Well, only a few people have this gift, Mira. Aodin himself said so. For one reason or the other, they came into contact with you. And they are males and you are a woman. But we can only guess why they took you! Maybe they just like you, says Ramon with a smile.

The expression on her face tells him that she doesn't like it a bit.

Listen, Mira. I honestly have no clue what they expect from us, or why we get involved. But we will figure it out. As we always do.

I really hope so, Ramon. But in the mean time, I have to bear that pressure on my head. It's not funny, you know!

I believe you, Mira. I wouldn't like to be in your shoes. But when you arrived, you said that the information kept coming all night long. What was that all about?

Oh, all kinds of things. It's kind of personal, you know. If you don't mind, I'd rather not talk about it.

Her facial expressions tell the rest. Private is private. She probably means that she's not ready to talk about it.

Mira, I give you a good advice. Go home and try to have a good sleep. I'm going to a music festival tomorrow. So I will turn in early too.

But what must I do if I receive more information, Ramon?

Write it all down, Mira. I think I know why you have so much pressure on your head.

Oh yes? I'm listening!

If you have telepathic contact, you have to "pick up the phone". Otherwise they keep trying to come into contact. So if you feel pressure, get some privacy and write it down. I'm sure the pressure will go away.

Now that you mention it, Ramon, after I told you everything, the pressure indeed faded away. It is as if I have to tell it to you. But it isn't always easy to get some privacy at work. But thanks for the advice. Although, I hope they leave me alone tonight.

I hope so too, Mira. But just in case. If there is something important, text me a message and I will see what I can do, okay?

A bit languidly, she walks with Ramon to her car.

Ramon? Promise me to tell nobody about all this.

Promised, Mira. I wouldn't know where to begin. Would you?

With a smile on her face she gets in the car. Have fun on the festival. Don't stay up too late, you know.

Ramon waves while the red lights of her car disappear in the night. Back in the kitchen, Ramon smiles at the sight of the mountain of dishes and in a hurry, he washes up everything of the last days. As he hears his stomach growl, Ramon realizes, he has not eaten all day. After a short meal, he meditates a last time about the information that Mira received. Teimon and Aodin? Now I have two aliens in stead of one. He shakes his head, wondering why this is all happening.

The duality on Geya has started now! And the key is…

What key? Ramon is too tired to think it over. In bed, he sets the alarm clock. What did Teimon mean with "the previous contacts"? Does he mean the first contacts with Mira? Or what? Tired of working and the excitement of the information, he falls in a deep sleep.

- 10 -
26/8/2006

The evening falls as the video "The Secret NASA Transmissions" comes to an end. Ramon is deeply impressed by this remarkable video about "natural UFOs" filmed in space. He starts cutting the vegetables for his soup. As the soup starts to boil, the smell of the flavor turns his kitchen into heaven on earth. He checks whether the varnish is dry. In the paint room, a long table is filled with 800 small cubes, waiting for the next treatment. Four sides done, two to go, muses Ramon. In a quarter of an hour, he turns the cubes on the rhythm of the music with the help of a simple tool. He gathers them in eight blocks of hundred cubes, paints them and takes care they are all separated for drying.

While daydreaming about the music festival, he repeats this ritual six times a day. Still several weeks to go and the 24,000 thousand cubes are ready to be used for his cube sculptures. After he came back from the festival he used the time while the cubes were drying to consume an overdose of UFO files and videos.

Gradually, he discovers that in recent years, several whistleblowers put themselves in the frontline. Colonel Phillip Corso is already a legend in the UFO community. In 1997, Ramon heard for the first time of this old military gentleman. He remembered it very well because it was the first time he had access to the World Wide Web. One of the first words he entered in the search engine was UFO. Just out of curiosity. In the seventies, he read several books about UFOs. In those days it was a very mysterious phenomenon. Jacques Vallée, Allen Hynek and John Keel were his favorite authors. Newspapers regularly reported UFO sightings and it intrigued the young Ramon beyond words.

He remembered being very surprised how many UFO sites existed on the web. A short document about Colonel Philip Corso's dead was one of his first clicks. But he had no time to go into the UFO subject. He had a hard time developing an artistic game with wooden cubes. Kubido it was called.

But now, thanks to Google and YouTube, a lot of information was published on the web. Corso's book "The Day after Roswell" had sent a shockwave through the UFO community. He was a high ranked military colonel and worked closely with president Eisenhower. Corso confirmed that in Roswell an alien spacecraft had crashed and that the passengers were all dead. The passengers of the craft were only one meter in height, had big heads and bigger eyes than humans. Their skin color was a pastel grey. Later their nickname became "the Grey". What really shocked the readers of Corso's book was his statement that pieces of the wreckage were first studied by the military industrial complex and later given to the biggest companies of the USA for further research. Microchip technology would even be a direct result of this back-engineering. Corso stated also that the passengers were in his view not real people but a kind of biological robots and part of the spaceship.

Of course, skeptics were all over him, but his story introduced a complete new concept in ufology: the influence of alien technology on our society. But he never said a word about alien signals.

Another whistleblower was Dan Burisch. Three interviews of him were published on the web on the site Camelot Project.

First of all Dan Burisch stated that he had worked in Area 51 as a biologist. He was involved in the biological and medical research of an alien that was kept there under special conditions. Burisch named the creature J Rod. Burisch said that he had telepathic contact with an alien named "J Rod". The alien told him that he was from the future. And not only that, he told him that there were three types of grey aliens and that they all came from a different time in the future, but also from a different timeline. The grey type from timeline 1 came from 24,000 years in the future. These were the ones that crashed in Roswell. They are the most humane Greys.

The J Rod type belonged to timeline 2 and came from 44,000 years into the future and the third Grey type was from timeline 3 and from 54,000 years in the future. And they all came to the same period in the past, meaning now, to warn humanity for a coming natural catastrophe that would happen in the coming years. J Rod stated that the three Grey type creatures are future descendants of the human race. Depending on the actions of the humans in the coming years, the catastrophe could be minor or major. The catastrophe would come anyhow. But our actions would determine which of the three timelines would be our future. In the best case scenario, the future of the humans would be the Grey type of 24,000. If the catastrophe would be worse, then the future of the humans would result in the Grey type of 44,000 years. And in the worst case scenario the fate of the humans would be timeline three, resulting in the Grey type of 54,000 years into the future. They were the most cruel Grey type, lacking any form of compassion and responsible for the abductions of numerous humans and animals.

To prevent the worst case scenario, drastic measures had to be taken. J Rod suggested that there were alien technology "star gates" on Earth. There are natural star gates but also artificial ones. And J Rod suggested that the artificial star gates had to be destroyed. The catastrophe would have galactic proportions. It would be a kind of energy release from the galactic center that would spread shockwaves through the Milky Way via natural star gates, with devastating consequences. That event would be inevitable. But the artificial star gates, brought to Earth in the past, had to be destroyed. If that would be done, the catastrophe would be less destructive because artificial star gates would increase the level of destruction significantly.

Dan Burisch even stated that the destruction of the star gates was the real reason for the war in Iraq. Iraq allegedly possessed several star gates, received from an alien race millennia ago. That was the reason why so many museums were robbed, shortly after the occupation of Iraq.

Ramon didn't know what to think of the testimony of Dan Burisch. In the three interviews, he also spoke about the looking glass technology that enabled you to look into the future. Burisch even said that he helped J Rod to escape, when they were on a top secret mission in the Cheops pyramid in Egypt.

For Ramon, this story was rather unbelievable. Especially the theory about the origin of the aliens was in Ramon's eyes nothing more than a complex "Back to the Future" story. A good idea? Definitely! But true? Come on!

The problem that Ramon had with Burisch was his appearance. He was very convincing and was clearly an educated and decent ethical and sensitive person. Not a profile for a deceiver. What struck Ramon even more was that the people who interviewed him, didn't ask any questions about the link of his story with the movie "Back to the Future" by Steven Spielberg.

For Ramon, this was the end of the Dan Burisch story and he concentrated his research on anything that was published about the grey beings, Colonel P. Corso referred to.

The Greys, the name of the best known alien species, were already discussed by abductees in the sixties. Abductees are people that claim to be abducted by aliens. The most common alien type that was described by these abductees was a small creature with a light grey skin. The first famous abduction case in the media was the case of the married couple, Betty and Barney Hill in 1961. From that period, the image of the Greys became the most common image of aliens.

While working on the cubes, Ramon had time to listen to all the interviews on the Camelot website. And gradually he became acquainted with some important whistleblowers in the UFO community.

It is again late in the evening as Ramon enjoys a cup of coffee while the cubes are drying. No trace from Mira since the music festival. It worries him, especially because of her sudden contact of possibly alien origin. The words of Teimon and Aodin made a deep impression on him. The web wasn't very helpful in solving the puzzle of statements. But he realized the importance of correct interpretation.

"Wo endet die Wahrheit und wo fängt die Dichtung an?" As no other, Professor Tenhaeff could interpret the impressions of the psychics he worked with. He argued that if you have a good psychological profile of the psychic and you ask the right questions, you can distillate much more correct information from their paranormal impressions. But you always have to be cautious. An inexperienced parapsychologist can misinterpret impressions, resulting in wrong conclusions. That's what Germans call "Dichtung". Especially when a psychic has a vision of a future event. A good advice is to let the information speak for itself. First you need to have all the information by the psychic. Then interpretation is allowed. Then you have to wait until the event actually happens. Only then you can make judgments about the significance of the vision. "First you need to know the truth. After that, you can approve or disapprove" was a statement of his Latin teacher. Only much later, he started to understand the deeper meaning of his words.

In the background, the radio plays "Nights of Cydonia". Ramon quickly turns up the volume and on the rhythm of the music he hops back to the kitchen. Immediately, he's back in the atmosphere of the festival. And with good memories in his mind, he makes a fresh dose of coffee. What could be wrong with Mira, he wonders. Ramon contacted her after the festival. I will come tomorrow, she promised. But the rest was silence. The sound of an incoming e-mail is hardly detectable because of the loud music. Surprised, he sees that it is a message of Mira! Speaking of the devil!

Are you home, Ramon? Can I come over?

Why not? The coffee is ready, is Ramon's reply.

As she enters the kitchen, the smell of fresh coffee brings a smile to her face.

Hm… just in time, is the first thing she says.

Mira! Please, take a seat. You look well.

Thanks, Ramon.

With a simple gesture, she throws her long blond hair backwards and her deep blue eyes seem to look into eternity. Ramon, you don't believe how glad I am to have found the courage to come over. All day long I have had that pressure on my head. It was unbearable sometimes. I think Teimon wants to send information. Last week, the pressure was hardly detectable. But I was just not in the mood to open my mind for him. I still have a hard time to accept the reality of this contact and I just didn't have the time.

So you didn't pick up the telepathic cellular phone, Ramon replies. Mira, Mira, what must the aliens be thinking of us. That we are impolite or what? Both have to laugh with the situation.

Anyhow, Mira, now you're here and that's what counts.

After the coffee ritual, Ramon takes his writing materials and takes a seat.

Let's see. Where were we? Ramon looks at his notes.

Oh yes. Follow the mental path. The key is… And then, the contact was broken.

With doubt in her heart her dark blue eyes look straight into Ramon's eyes.

First, I have to tell you something important, Ramon. You know that I am very skeptic about it all. But perhaps, there is more going on than my personal imagination.

Ramon keeps quiet and gives her the time to find the right words. The contact was indeed broken, but while driving home, Teimon was back online. I didn't want to disturb you on the music festival, so I decided to wait. You must not forget that I have a hard time accepting the reality of the purple skull. Especially when you will hear what Teimon revealed to me. I was really convinced that I was going crazy but after a while, I accepted the consequences and decided to accept the contacts again. I'm surer of myself now.

Nervously, she rolls a cigarette.

Believe me, Mira. I realize, the purple skull must give you a hard time, especially because you have to endure the physical effects. But now, you have made me curious. What made you so upset? I don't understand.

Well then, write it down, Ramon, and you will see for yourself. I have memorized everything word for word.

1.027 The "key" you have to find, is the translation of the code. The code of the signals and its meaning will make your mental strength even stronger.

That was the ceremonious part, Ramon. It was as if Teimon chose every word carefully. He clearly doesn't want misunderstandings. After the introduction, he sent me lots of images. And that's what freaked me out.

1.028 I saw images of aliens. They are clearly creatures from some other planet or something like that. I saw scenes of things that those creatures did on our planet, a long time ago. I was shocked to see how those aliens performed DNA experiments on some humans, millennia ago.

Aliens? Do you mean you saw Aliens who were doing experiments on humans?

Yes, Ramon. But the intentions were not wrong. Just keep your questions to yourself for a while, Ramon. There is more to come.

1.029 The intention was to add a small part of their genetic make-up to the human DNA of a select group of people. It would create a small change in their brain, to be inherited genetically by their children. The chosen ones would automatically have a telepathic ability from birth.

Like a new kind of sense organ?

Yes, Ramon. That's the way you could describe it. But unexpectedly, something went wrong.

Ramon is all attention. What was that, Mira?

1.030 If the person with the extra gene is a woman, she can handle the extra sense easily. She won't misuse the gift. But if it is a man, he generally uses the extra ability to enlarge his power over others.

The feminists would like to hear you talking, Mira.

Mira smiles. I just tell you what Teimon told me, Ramon. And he is a man! Anyhow, after that, contact was broken again. I came home and immediately went to bed. But then, something else happened. I was lying in bed and suddenly, I heard a kind of clicking sound in my head. A strange sound. And then… I saw two small grey creatures in front of me.

Mira, don't tell me that you were abducted by Greys, is all Ramon can think while writing the words down.

Nervously, she rolls a new cigarette.

And then … What happened, Mira? Ramon notices that she is extremely nervous.

Nothing, Ramon.

Nothing? So, they just took a look at you and gone they were?

Yes, Ramon. They were looking at me and then they were gone, just like they came.

It's clear that she has a hard time to remember the Grey experience all over again. Ramon senses the tension and the only thing he can think of is a simple question.

Eh… some more coffee, Mira?

Yes, Ramon, please.

She feels that Ramon has his doubts. I can't tell him everything, she thinks. Not now!

While fulfilling the holy coffee ritual, Ramon contemplates it all. Mira, if I understand well, most telepathic people could be ancestors of those genetically changed people? Or am I wrong?

No, no, Ramon. That's not the case. Everybody can develop a telepathic ability. If he has the right teacher. But genetically changed people don't need years of yoga exercises. They have it from birth.

That's strange, Mira. It's the same information as the info the first contact gave you. Do you remember?

Now that you mention it, Ramon, I remember it. You were talking about the reptile people, weren't you? And then I heard that voice. But that was somebody else. It was neither Teimon nor Aodin.

At the same moment, Mira sees the kitchen turning purple again. She can't reject the call for contact any longer. The skull looks at her and the purple matrix opens the cosmic gateway.

Ramon, I have contact again, says Mira with a deep voice.

Just a second, Mira.

The coffee is ready. In a hurry, he serves the coffee and sees her eyes stare.

You can ask questions about the information I received, Ramon.

76

Ramon is nervous and doesn't know where to begin.

Eh... I salute you, Teimon.

Mira looks surprised.

We had better be polite, don't you think?

Teimon, tell me. What exactly do you mean with a block culture? Because I don't...

1.031 **Block cultures are groups of highly organized beings you call Greys. They are the same aliens as the ones that were found in Roswell.**

Roswell! Ramon immediately thinks of Colonel Corso.

So Mira, if I understand Teimon well, these block cultures are groups of alien creatures, called Greys?

Yes, that's what Teimon says.

Okay. And why are they called "block cultures"?

1.032 **The Greys have no individuality. They can only function in groups.**

1.033 **They have the ability to mentally link up to one another in a group.**

So, these grey beings function only as a group. Ramon is thinking aloud. They have group individuality. But what kind of beings are these Greys? Are they further evolved than us humans? Are they from the future? Ramon is curious what the answer will be.

1.034 **The Greys are genetically manipulated creatures.**

1.035 **They communicate exclusively telepathically.**

1.036 **The Greys don't procreate. They are clones.**

While making notes, Ramon realizes how exceptional this communication is. What a situation! I am taking notes of an interview of an alien being with the help of a telepathically gifted woman! At the same time I get first hand information about other aliens, the Greys! Can it be crazier?

One more question, Ramon and then I have to stop, says Mira with a deep voice. The pressure is too severe.

Ramon has so many questions. Okay Mira, that's a start. Let's see. Do you have problems with those block cultures? I mean... Are they the new evolution you mentioned? Quickly he looks at his notes of the previous session: on physical level "others" are in control. Are you talking about the same Grey block cultures? Ramon doesn't know how to put the question right. Mira translates the question as well as she can and after a silence, the answer comes out of her mouth.

1.037 **The Grey block cultures have our world under control with physical force.**

1.038 **Also the Earth is in great danger. You have to act quickly or humanity will undergo the same fate as our world.**

Ramon is speechless. Again this warning that the Earth is in danger. It sounds so convincing. Mira sees he's a bit confused and signals Ramon to keep on writing.

1.039 **The key of the code has a connection with the wound that cures itself.**

1.040 **It is this energy that is needed to translate the code. I salute you.**

Suddenly, Mira looks up. That's strange, Ramon. Before he broke the contact, he sent me some pictures.

Okay. Describe what you saw as well as you can, Mira.

I see a cube. It's the first stage of a kind of stairs. No wait Ramon… It is no stairs. It's the first cube of the structure of the square matrix in the purple skull.

Ramon writes it down but doesn't understand a thing.

That's strange, Ramon. The contact is broken and the pressure is gone. And now I need to go to the… Mira runs to the toilet.

That is the only disadvantage of coffee, says Ramon smiling. He reads the notes and shakes his head. Who will believe what's happening here? Anyhow, I start to understand a bit more about the previous information. Maybe, it will help me to get a better understanding of what is happening in the UFO community.

Mira comes back and looks reborn.

Just in time, she says with her normal voice. Ramon, do you have any wine in the house?

Wine? Now? Ramon starts to laugh. That's typical Mira. With a smile, he enters the cellar. What a woman! The witches of the middle ages are minor, compared to her. He takes a looks around and yells "Red or white, Mira?"

"White" is her response.

Some time later, they both enjoy a fresh glass of white wine and the first stress of the shocking information fades away.

You know, Ramon, scientists always laugh with alchemists, but if you give them a bottle of good wine, they never complain.

Right you are, Mira. Wine and beer are both inventions of alchemists.

Shall we take a look at the download, Mira?

Download, Ramon? What do you mean?

Well, the information of Teimon. If you compare telepathy with a mental internet connection, you have downloaded the information, have you not?

Oh, is that what you mean. I thought you were already drunk…

Not yet, Mira, not yet. Let's see. You know, based on this information, Colonel Corso was right. He never believed that the passengers of the Roswell craft were normal humans.

Who is Colonel Corso? Never heard of him, Ramon.

In short, Ramon tells her what he knows about Colonel Corso.

And if I have to believe Teimon, then the Greys are very dangerous creatures, Mira. God knows what is happening behind the screens of secrecy. I wonder what Dan Burisch would have to say about Teimon's information.

Dan Burisch? Never heard of him either.

Ramon tells Mira about Dan's experiences with the Grey creature and his theory of their origin.

This guy isn't telling the truth or he is just fooled by that J Rod creature, Ramon.

That is the least you can say, Mira. Although, he looks a serious man if you see him on video. He sounds sincere. But I didn't believe a word he was saying.

But another thing, Ramon. What could Teimon mean with the wound that heals itself?

Ramon looks at her head. Did the bleeding stop?

I don't feel anything anymore. Take a look.

I see nothing, Mira. It is as if nothing happened.

Strange, don't you think? Any idea what it could be, Ramon?

Well, it could be that it is a reaction of the skin when the seventh chakra is active. Maybe that's the energy that makes telepathic contact with Teimon possible. Hindus believe that paranormal abilities are caused by Kundalini energy. Harish Johari taught me a lot about that topic. This energy moves through a channel or nadi, called "the brahmanadi". A nadi can be compared to the meridians of acupuncture. But nadis, flow inside the body and the Brahmanadi flows parallel with the spinal cord and vanishes into the seventh chakra, close to the top of the head. I don't know much about it, Mira. It's possible that this energy has to flow to the top of your head to enable you to have contact with Teimon via the purple skull. The Tibetans know a great deal about this. I remember that a student of Harish Johari once told us that when the seventh chakra is activated, a kind of fluid is released on top of the head. Some monks even consume this fluid.

You don't mean that, Ramon!

Really, that's what he told us. That fluid would activate the pituitary gland or something like that.

Okay then, Ramon. Next time you may try it. She starts giggling.

No thanks, Mira. I prefer coffee or wine. I'm sorry, lady, I see that I'm a bad host.

The glasses are filled again and with a toast they continue the conversation.

What a situation, Mira. So, these Greys have no individuality. Let's meditate about this. If they have no individuality, then they have no conscience. If they have no conscience, they have no ethics. That could explain why they abduct people. Ethical people don't do things like that. Aliens too should behave decently, don't you think? Did you know that "you shall not kill" also means "you shall not abduct people"?

No, I didn't know that, Ramon. But it sounds reasonable.

You must surely know the story of Troy?

Sure, Ramon. The story about Helena who was abducted by Paris. Who doesn't know that story? I saw the movie. Very romantic!

Yes, very romantic, Mira. But in fact, one abduction caused the death of thousands of people and forty years of war. I think that those who died during that war had another opinion about this romance. But yes, people are people. Let's turn back to the notes. I wonder what Professor Penrose would think of those clones.

Penrose? I heard of that man. He knows a lot about impossible figures, doesn't he?

That's him, Mira. But he is also the head of the Mathematical Institute of the University of Oxford.

He wrote a book about artificial intelligence, "The Emperor's New Mind". He discussed the question whether robots could have a consciousness. He stated that this could only be proven when we could teleport people.

Come on Ramon. Teleportation! That's just fantasy!

Oh no, Mira. Once it will very well be possible. But wait. I will explain. The last wine flows in the two glasses. Where was I? Oh yes, teleportation. If you want to teleport a human being, you have to copy the body and send all the particles to another location. There, you have to assemble all the particles again, in the same order of course.

If you say so, Ramon, says Mira smiling.

Let me finish, Mira. There is a problem. The original body is still on the first location after teleportation. The question is: must you destroy it? If the copy has the same consciousness as the original human, the answer is "yes".

Mira looks with disbelief and Ramon starts laughing out loud.

Well yes, Mira. Think about it. Otherwise, there would be two Miras. And one is more than enough. No? Don't forget. It would be very dangerous to send the original directly. If the transmission goes wrong, you would be turned into dust. The point is that this experiment could prove that consciousness is a part of matter or indeed something else. Because if consciousness is something else, different from matter... like a soul, it would not be teleported. You got it? And if the copy would have consciousness, then that would mean that consciousness is directly linked with matter. And that would mean that robots and computers can develop consciousness too. So, if the Greys are biological clones, they could have consciousness but not necessarily self-consciousness. No individuality.

But Ramon, now wait a minute. Even animals have consciousness and individuality. I don't understand why those Grey clones can't have individuality, if they are living creatures. Could it be that it is because they are not only cloned but also genetically changed?

I haven't thought about that, Mira. You amaze me, you know. We have to figure that one out, Mira.

Okay, Ramon. But now something else, please. I begin to understand why you like to go to Rich. Can we change the subject please? Do you know the joke of …

Till late at night, they laugh as Mira tells one joke after the other.

Ramon is still laughing when Mira has gone home and Ramon gets in bed and falls gradually asleep. He is still laughing as he remembers her face after telling her one particular joke.

A parapsychologist did research on a poltergeist. When he entered the room where the noise was heard, he asked: "Is there some-body in this room?" And the ghost said: "No, there is no-body in this room."

The vibrating noise of his mobile gets him out of sleep mode. A text message? This late? With a few clicks, the message appears on the screen.

Are you home tomorrow? Urgent! Ury.

With a short 'no problem" the message is replied and Ramon falls in a deep sleep.

- 12 -
9/9/2006

Ramon closes the door while waving to Sana as she leaves on her bike. She came to get the poster for her party next month. With a big smile she waves back, glad she can start promoting the party just in time.

So, that's done. Time for an excursion on the web. The cubes are drying and with a mug of coffee, he takes a seat behind his digital drawing table. **The key of the code has a connection with the wound that cures itself.** All very well, but first we have to be sure somebody on Earth has received the signals.

It looks as if SETI hasn't a clue. One thing is for sure. If something has been published on the web, I will find it. You have to help me, says Ramon smiling to his two workstations. With an open but skeptical mind, he works himself through mountains of information until he finds a link to the Disclosure Project.

Never heard of this project! It seems serious enough. Steven Greer is a medical doctor. He gave a press conference on Mai 9th 2001. Some twenty people gave a brief speech about what they witnessed, related to UFOs, during their professional career. With growing astonishment, he listens to the most amazing stories. How is it possible that I don't know anything about this

82

conference? Ramon is sure this conference wasn't mentioned in the European press.

Especially the testimony of Sergeant Dr. Karl Wolf blows his mind. He was a precisions electronics photographic repairman, involved in the Lunar Orbiter project in the state of Virginia. He had a Top Secret Crypto Clearance and was responsible for the electronic equipment used for the montage of the pictures which were sent to Earth by the Orbiter satellites. In those days, he was asked to check the equipment. Somebody of the lab showed him pictures of a lunar base of unknown origin. He saw mushroom-like buildings, gigantic domes, towers of hundred of meters height and all kinds of artificial constructions.

This testimony comes as a real shock to Ramon. While varnishing the cubes, he is aware of the implications of such a discovery, if it is true. After giving the cubes some attention, he looks to the rest of the video. But not one word about signals. Who is that mister Steven Greer? He listens once again to the introduction. It's unbelievable what this person is telling the people of the media and the press. He speaks openly about secret projects of hundreds of billions of dollars. Greer reveals that in these black budget projects, crashed UFOs were back-engineered. It's clear that he knows more about the projects about which Phillip Corso was talking about five years earlier.

Greer even went so far to state that the USA was now in the possession of technology, comparable with real UFOs. He especially stressed the point that these new technologies could create free energy. Zero point energy, much cheaper and friendly for the environment. Greer believed that these black projects could mean the end of poverty in the whole world.

Great, if this all was true of course. Strange he never mentioned Colonel Corso. Ramon searches for "Corso" on YouTube and several videos immediately pop up. Ramon listens carefully to everything Corso has to say in several interviews.

It's already late as he meditates about what Greer had to say. How is it possible that the press hasn't mentioned this at all? That's the problem of internet. Everything is there. But the popular media ignore it. Especially UFO related information. The information is there, with free access, but nobody is paying attention. Only a small group of die hards try to keep up with the latest developments. But in general, the press is silent about anything related to the UFO subject.

But what Ramon can't understand is why the government has not reacted to Greer's accusations. Probably they don't want to make martyrs of these whistleblowers, nor give them extra attention in the press.

While cooking, Ramon thinks about Teimon's information. If he is really who he pretends to be, he must know things I can't find on the web. That's the only way to get proof that Teimon is not a fabrication of Mira's imagination. During web surfing, Ramon found different descriptions of the Greys. But nothing was mentioned about a lack of individuality. Although Steven Greer and others regularly used the term higher dimensional beings, who see the human species as a kind of intelligent predator and that the Grey want to help humans to evolve to a higher plan or something like that.

But if the Greys are clones, somebody had to create them. Except if they are aliens that stopped collectively to procreate naturally in a certain period of their evolution. Corso's viewpoint was simple. We don't know who they are or where they came from. For Dan Burisch, they came from the future. Maybe, Teimon could give a better explanation for the existence of the Greys. But whoever made them, what Teimon told about these creatures wasn't reassuring.

A few hours later Ramon enjoys his meal after programming the video for the late night movie. Suddenly, the bell rings. That must be Ury! He quickly opens the door. A slender man looks at him with a big smile and big clear eyes.

Hello Ramon, is there still life before death?

He shakes Ramon's hand and while joking as friends do, they go to the kitchen.

Nice of you to make time, Ramon and wearily he takes a seat. His bald head and unshaved chin give him the appearance of a skinhead. In spirit though, he has nothing in common with this extreme right winged group.

Have you eaten, Ury?

Yes, Ramon, thanks. Please, enjoy your dinner. Give me some brown magical fluid when you have finished. That will do. I just finished a work shift of forty-eight hours.

No, no, first things first my friend. In no time Ramon makes a full pot of hot coffee. While Ramon quickly finishes his late dinner, Ury enjoys the lovely mug filled with magical elixir.

What was the urgency, Ury? Has Merly been back on line?

Yes, Ramon. I had to come over, Ramon. You remember the previous message, that the Illuminati eliminate Illuminati?

How could I forget, Ury? I have done some extra research in between all my other research, but I'm not becoming any wiser of all the stuff I find on the web.

Well Roman, I think the Illuminati have a lot to do with the Warriors. Let me explain!

1.041 **Merly explained that the "Guardians" have lost control over the "Warriors" and are now under control of the Illuminati. They demand absolute obedience from the Warriors. At this very moment, the Illuminati fight one another for ultimate power with the help of the Warriors.**

Ramon writes it all down.

So they close ranks in their own groups, while fighting a battle for ultimate power? Nice. Really nice. Have you any more good news, Ury?

No, that's it, Ramon.

But Ury, you could have told all this on the phone?

Ury starts to blush.

Come on Ury, I'm waiting. There is more, isn't there?

Nervously, he plays with his mug and hesitatingly he reveals what is on his mind. Ramon, do you believe in aliens?

Ramon almost chokes in his coffee.

Well, Ury... I have never seen one myself.

He tries to hide his astonishment. But now that you mention the subject, I have read a lot about it in recent days. In short, Ramon tells the story of Colonel Corso.

You see, Ramon. That's synchronicity! Listen what Merly says.

1.042 **Merly states that the Illuminati are the hidden rulers of the world and some of them have contact with aliens. Then Merly mentioned that they have problems in preparing the thirteenth Warrior for his task.**

But wait a minute Ury. How did the Illuminati got into contact with these "aliens"?

1.043 **It is complicated, Ramon. Merly said that the aliens**

manipulate some Illuminati because they have penetrated the power structures of their Warrior. The method is simple. These aliens help them to develop advanced technology. But in doing that, they have also infiltrated secret military projects. Merly said that in fact, these aliens are dangerous. They want the world for themselves. And then Merly stated that these aliens have suggested the idea of the extra Warrior. But the aliens want to use this extra Warrior for their own gain. But neither the Illuminati nor the Warriors know that. They only see the ultimate power and don't realize the danger that threatens their own existence.

Does this make any sense to you, Ramon? Do you think that these aliens are the Greys that Corso talks about?

It's possible, Ury. I don't know! But it could very well be the case.

Do you think I am going crazy, Ramon?

Of course not, Ury. Crazy people never think they are crazy!

Ury smiles.

I'm not so sure Ramon. Could it be that the strong electro-magnetic fields in the lab I'm working in, have an influence on my brain?

It could be, but I don't think so, Ury. I have known you for so many years. I would have noticed this a long time ago, don't you think.

Well listen, Ramon, the strangest thing that Merly told me – and I had to tell you this as soon as possible – was: "Ramon knows the code". I really don't know what to think. Do you?

No, Ury. Not really.

Not really? What do you mean? I know you, Ramon. You know more, don't you?

Now it's Ramon who's blushing. He can't lie to his dear friend. He admits that one of his students has come forward with information about aliens.

But I can't tell you who it is, Ury. You know, it's my holy duty to respect the privacy of my "students".

Of course, Ramon, I respect that. So I'm not the only one with this kind of information.

Ramon shakes his head.

No, Ury. And I'm worried. If this is true, it's bad news for the

86

world. The Illuminati are very powerful people. So if some of the Illuminati are indirectly manipulated by the Greys, then something is very wrong, dear friend. One could compare it with "The Lord of the Rings". But this time it is for real.

For a while, it is silent in the kitchen.

Do you really think that this is for real, Ramon?

I can't prove it, Ury, but I promise you, I will go to the bottom of this. You are the second person that talks about "the code". To me, this is no coincidence, because you and the other person don't know each other.

And those aliens, Ramon, any idea who they are?

Well, some websites only stress the evil actions of them. They see them as manipulative creatures. While on other sites, they are compared to peace seeking angels. But I think that Corso was the closest to the truth. You know, Ury, I will send you some links. You can read it for yourself.

Please do, Ramon! I really want to know more about it.

One thing I know for sure, Ury. Nobody really knows who they are or where they come from. Has Merly told you more about their nature?

No, Ramon. I told you everything. He looks at his watch. I'm sorry, Ramon but I have to go. I have to get up early tomorrow. I really need some sleep.

Sure Ury, thanks for the information.

Glad to be of help, Ramon.

Walking to the front door, he sees the cubes.

Nice work, Ramon. When is the next exhibition?

That's a good question. No idea, Ury. I hope within a year. But who knows. It will be ready when it's ready, you know.

Ury smiles.

Keep me informed, young man. Take care.

Sleep well, Ury. Get home safely.

The streetlights shine on the face of Ury as he enters the car. He looks like an overworked Buddhist monk. But then again, Ury is more interested in Hinduism. He waves and disappears into the night. While closing the door, Ramon sees the dust bins of the neighbors. Oh yes. I mustn't forget to put mine out. The aliens will not help me with that. He walks to the backyard, pulls the dust bin from under the wooden stairs and rolls it to the street.

Suddenly a voice says: "Is he gone, Ramon?"

Mira, you here? Gee, you almost gave me a heart attack, you know.

Mira laughs. Don't tell me you thought I was an alien?

No, no, I thought you were Mira.

Both have a good laugh.

Sorry to surprise you at this hour, Ramon. I heard you had a visitor, so I took a walk to the river. The Maas is beautiful with full moon, you know. Do you have a few minutes?

I always make time for you, Mira. Let me guess? The skull showed up again?

Yes, Ramon. I have information. A lot!

Please go inside, Mira. I will be there in a minute.

While Ramon brings the dust bin to the street, Mira takes a seat in the kitchen. She sees the mug of Ury and takes it in her hands.

Is your visitor somebody like me, she asks Ramon, when he enters the kitchen. Do I know him?

I don't think so, Mira.

He is lonely sometimes, isn't he?

Ramon takes the empty mug out of her hands.

Mira, don't do that. Don't be so curious.

No, no, she says with a shy smile. I wouldn't dare.

She knows that Ramon never talks to others about his students.

Sorry, Ramon. You know me.

Forget it, Mira. Some coffee?

Yes, please. I have good news for you, Ramon.

She hangs her black overcoat on the hat rack. You have to make me a hat rack like this, Ramon. This thing has so much space.

If I find the time, Mira. But tell me. What is the good news?

You won't believe it, Ramon, but I know the meaning of the signals.

What? Seriously? Just like that?

Well, not just like that. But now I know.

She lights a cigarette and looks Ramon straight in his eyes.

Do you remember the last images I saw? You know, first a purple cube, then a stairway and then the purple matrix of the skull?

Yes Mira, vividly! But wait a second. The coffee is almost ready.

While Ramon makes his famous fluid life force, he is very

excited about what Mira has to tell. He serves the mugs and takes his notes.

You don't believe what kind of confusion I went through yesterday night. But finally, Teimon could explain it to me.

Okay Mira, I'm ready. Please, tell me everything.

1.044 Those squares with the symbols that Aodin talked about in the beginning, are star maps, Ramon.

Star maps? Ramon is shocked. That was the last thing he expected.

Listen, Ramon. I hope I can explain it. You know I am not good at geometry.

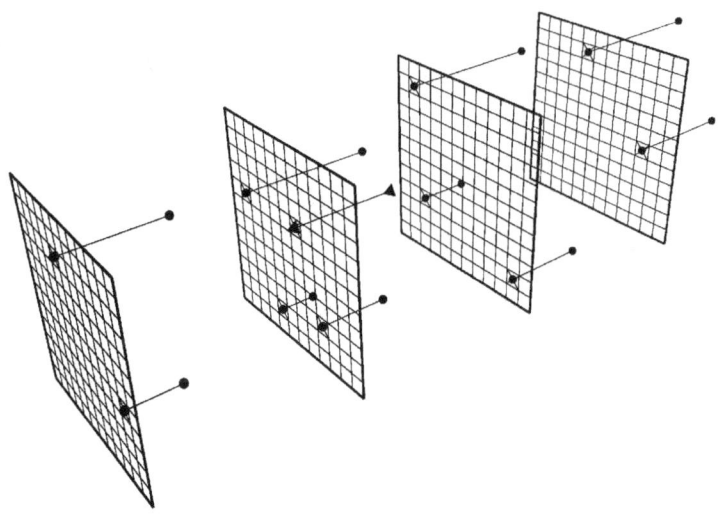

1.045 The front and back side of the cube I saw are the two first maps. The matrix in the purple skull is composed of a sequence of square maps behind one another. One way or the other, these squares contain the coordinates of the location of Teimon's home planet. And these coordinates are hidden in the signals that Aodin talked about.

1.046 The symbols on the squares are the stars, located between two maps.

Wait a minute, Mira. Explain that again. So, the squares with symbols are star maps and they have to be placed behind one another? He makes a quick sketch of squares.

Like this?

Yes, Ramon, something like that.

Okay! And?

1.047 Well, on every square, the stars in the space behind the square are projected.

Oh yes. Now I see. So the stars in the space between two maps are projected in line with the cube on the first square. Okay, now I understand. And in the small square where the star is projected, there is a symbol.

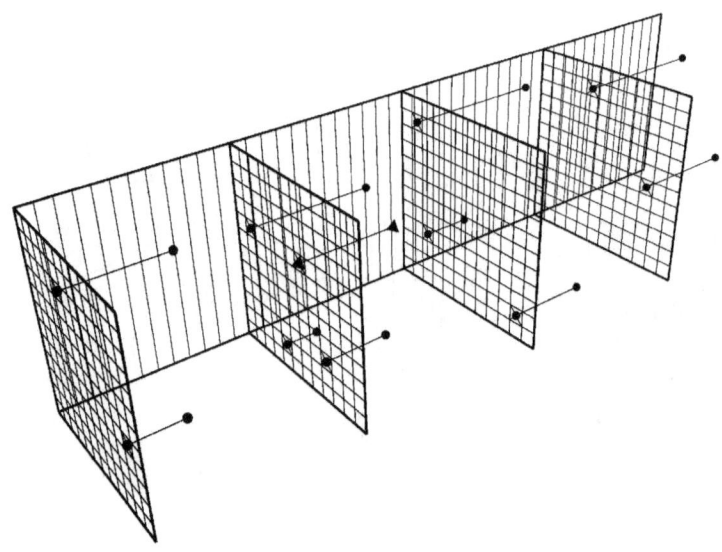

Exactly, Ramon. That's what I mean.

But Mira, that is just great, you know. But wait. What is the distance between the squares?

1.048 I think the distance in between the maps is like a cube. The space behind has the same size in-depth as the side of a map.

Wow, Mira. It looks to me to be a very practical system. So, they have divided the space in cubes, and project the stars on the front side of every cube?

Yes, Ramon. That's it, I think. Teimon had a hard time explaining it to me, you know. It really made me so confused.

90

I do believe that, Mira. No really, this is great. So, if I understand it well, the matrix of the skull is a kind of 3D map of a part of space?

Well, it is more of a simplification, Ramon.

1.049 Yes. But in the signals that were sent, we can find very detailed information of the total map.

Ramon can't believe his eyes when he looks at the sketch.

Wait, Mira. I want to know exactly. He draws a new sketch. So there is a beginning and an end, like Aodin said during the first contact.

1.050 Yes. The total map is the road from here to their planet through space. The beginning is our solar system. And the other end of the map ends in their star system.

Ramon is speechless.

Unbelievable, Mira. So the signals contain information about a certain number of square maps.

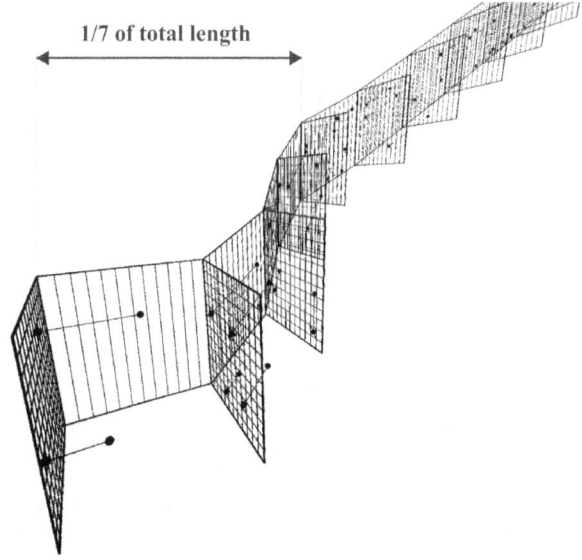

1/7 of total length

1.051 Yes. The maps have equal distances. But it is not like this drawing. There is a twist in it. It is not a straight line.

Ramon, do you remember the first sketch I made of the skull matrix. Well, there was a twist in it too, remember?

Why yes Mira, you're right! Ramon is silent. Suddenly, Mira is a space cartographer.

She looks at the sketch of Ramon. Look Ramon, if this is the entire length of the star map, the curve runs from the beginning to this point here.

So, one seventh, more or less. Thanks Mira, and he makes a new sketch.

Yes, like that Ramon.

Ramon can't believe it. Mira, do you realize that this is a very practical way to visualize a travel path through space? I can't imagine that this is just an invention of your imagination. Let's see. Has Teimon told you the size of these square maps?

Wait, I will ask him.

You mean, he's online at the moment?

Not yet, Ramon. I can reach him. I still have contact with the skull. The pressure is still there. As she speaks, the space around her is filled with a purple nebula and via the matrix of the purple skull, she gets into contact with Teimon. The question is translated and with a deep voice she translates the answer of Teimon.

1.052 **I salute you. The square maps are divided in smaller squares. Twelve on twelve squares for each map. Every map has 144 parts. The small intervals of the signal are the internal parts of the map.**

1.053 **There is one single symbol for all the stars.**

1.054 **There is another sign for space. Most parts are space.**

Ramon is fascinated by the efficiency of the map system. Simple and binary. Thank you, Teimon. So there are only two symbols?

1.055 **No, there is a third symbol, which locates every space station of the Greys. These space stations are controlled by the Greys. We used different frequencies in the signal to indicate the difference between space, stars and space stations. The whole map is just a technical drawing.**

With mixed feelings, Ramon writes this information down. Those Greys have space stations. Jesus, if this is true, we are dealing with powerful creatures. But I have to stay concentrated. I must see that I get as much information as possible before the contact is broken again. Just a technical drawing, says Teimon! But this is genius. Wait, Mira! What were the dimensions? In light years if possible.

1.056 Every segment of the square map is 12 on 12 light years.
Okay, that means 144 by 144 light years. That is reasonable. It's not too big to map a space path of 10,000 light years. So, the space between the maps is also 144 light years. And how many maps are there, Mira?

1.057 There are 72 square maps.
Wait a minute, Mira. I want to check it out. So the distance between the maps is 144 light years? So that is seventy-two times hundred forty-four makes … 10,368 light years, minus 144 is 10,224 light years.

That is close to ten thousand light years, is it not? Ramon can't believe his own calculations. Gee, Mira, this seems to be the first evidence that this is no illusion. I can't imagine you made this up, Mira. No way. We have to seriously consider Teimon to be a real person.

But Mira is absent. Her blue eyes stare inwards as if she sees something. Suddenly, she's back. Ramon!... I saw the place where the signals were received.

1.058 It is a place where different radars stand in line. I see it clearly. I would recognize the place if I see a picture.
Come Mira, I will show you the observatory of SETI. There are pictures on the web.

Seconds later, Mira looks to the pictures of SETI.

Yes Ramon. That's very similar. Or it looks very similar.

It's possible, Mira. Maybe SETI received signals, but they had to keep it quiet. But how am I going to prove that?

For a while, it's silent in the WebCom of Ramon. Too much excitement for one day. Together they go back to the kitchen.

Well Mira, now I know at least a place to send the information. SETI will surely be interested in this.

I think you had better wait, before you make that decision, Ramon. And a bit nervous, she takes some coffee and rolls a cigarette. This is not all, Ramon. After this map story, much more information came... about the Greys. Sit down and I will tell you everything I remember.

Quickly, Ramon serves what is left of the coffee and with the pen in his hand he wonders what Mira has to tell.

While she smokes a cigarette, she tells Ramon the rest of the information she received last night as vividly as she can.

After her pro bono activities she immediately went to her garret. Dizzy after a day long of introduction to star mapping, she falls exhausted on her bed. The full moon is visible through the window. The full moon period enhances her telepathic abilities. As she gradually relaxes, a purple nebula of light fills her bedroom and the purple skull appears in all its glory. As the purple matrix starts to vibrate, she tunnels through a gateway of square facets like a beam of lightning. First she sees the "W" symbol again and then she hears the familiar voice of Teimon.

1.059 I salute you. I will give you more information about the Greys. The Greys are the result of genetic engineering.

Mira notices a sense of shame in the voice of Teimon. He is clearly embarrassed by what he's going to tell.

1.060 Our ancestors are the makers of the Greys. The goal of that experiment was to create a biological robot with our own DNA which would be able to survive in space.

1.061 The body of natural beings, evolved on a planet, can not stand long exposure to space. A human body is not made for such a hostile environment. The experiment was a success, but these creatures had their own evolution.

Mira is shocked to hear that Teimon's ancestors were the makers of the Greys.

1.062 The Greys communicate from brain to brain. You call this telepathy. But in fact, the brains of the Greys are designed in such a way that they use telepathy like a cellular phone system. To them, it's a kind of a sense organ like the vocal chords.

1.063 They have no ears, but are still able to hear sounds through small openings, situated in the places of our ears. They do not have a real mouth either, because they don't speak with sound nor do they eat through their mouths. Only a small opening can be seen. They communicate exclusively telepathically.

1.064 Our genetic specialists made their brain in such a way

94

that the Greys could not develop an "ego" centre. They were and had to remain robots. So they could not develop psychic privacy like we can. Their brain can't develop an independent individuality because they are interlinked in a collective network. They have neither identity nor personality. Because their brains are interconnected telepathically, their information is shared in the group. You can compare it with computer networks.

Mira starts to understand what Teimon means. The Greys think and act in a kind of collective network. The difference is that everything works with telepathy.

At that moment, Mira comes back to herself and for a moment she's back in her room. The moon is still shining, but now much higher in the sky. How long was I gone, she questions herself. Her whole body is vibrating, indicating the contact is not over yet. A warm flow of energy runs upwards through her back, and again she tunnels through the purple veil of squares where Teimon waits for her.

1.065 **The Greys do have a kind of group identity. The smallest blocks consist of six Greys. Originally, our ancestors created one prototype. He became the Central of one complete block culture. This prototype was cloned six times. These six were cloned once again, making twelve Greys in total. These twelve were cloned again making 24. These 24 were cloned again. This procedure was repeated over and over again. Their entire block culture is mentally and physically structured this way.**

1.066 **But the basic blocks consists of six Greys. Each block has its own place, its own tasks and experiences. Each block differs mentally from the other. But in the overall Grey hierarchy, they are strictly ordered and mentally connected as one whole.**

1.067 **This block hierarchy, we call a block culture. The telepathic information is organized in the same way. So, a block culture is a very efficient organization. A Grey block culture is purely focused to grow.**

1.068 **The block cultures can travel over large distances in space, seeking new planets that could be of use to us. Because telepathy works instantly, without time interval, we could** stay in contact with them, wherever they were. If a block culture is big enough, he can split in two. In this way, a hierarchy of block cultures was created to analyze and explore the star systems, presented in the star map.

1.069 **Over time, the Grey block cultures went further through the Milky Way to reach Earth. With the help of the star map, they found Earth. They kept us informed what happened on Earth. There was plenty of food and energy. But something went wrong.**

Mira senses that Teimon has a hard time telling all this and she wonders what went wrong. It's silent for a while. With growing fear, she has to hear what the Greys did to his people.

1.070 **Some eighty years ago, the block culture of Earth came back to our planet. We knew they came back. But until then, we had the entire Grey industry under control. We didn't know that the Greys had changed. To explain this, I have to tell you how the Greys are cloned.**

1.071 **Their bodies grow in artificial wombs. They are containers filled with a kind of fluid. When they are fully grown, the body is separated from the container. So, they don't grow up with parents and don't have a childhood or youth.**

1.072 **Fully grown, their cerebral brain is generally speaking empty. All information they need to function in unity with their block is programmed into their brain with the help of a computer. After this procedure, they can immediately take up their place in the block. From the moment that they were created, we controlled the information that was downloaded into their brain. Everything happened under our supervision.**

1.073 **So we were not at all suspicious when they came back. But something unexpected had happened. They had evolved and had become a danger to our society. When they arrived, they infiltrated in the power centres of our society and took control of our world before we could react.**

1.074 **When we discovered their real intentions, it was too late. The elite of our world is now under control of one of their block cultures.**

1.075 **You have to understand. A block culture is very powerful. Even if a block culture is completely destroyed,**

96

another block culture can take its place. The information of a block culture is spread like a hologram over the other block cultures. Information does not get lost.

1.076 **Telepathic contact makes sure that every single Grey is like a part of the hologram. You have to understand! The brains of all the Greys are linked and are one big super brain, controlled by the Central Grey. The genius of this super brain is unimaginable.**

Mira opens her eyes. A morning concert by the birds gives her a hint of time. Her head is heavy and she feels exhausted. The pressure on her forehead is unbearable.

And I'm supposed to go to work in this state? But she doesn't get much time to think. A wave of energy rises through her spinal chord and once more she tunnels through the purple matrix.

- 14 -
8/9/2006

Only once more, Aodin sends to Teimon, or Mira won't survive.

Teimon's body lies on the ground, completely relaxed. His deep dark eyes are focused on a crystal matrix, placed in front of him. It looks like a copy of the matrix in the purple crystal skull on Earth. His thoughts fuse with the thoughts of Mira, while she sees herself lying in a purple nebula of lights. Again, Mira has to digest a large amount of information.

1.077 **At this moment, our leaders act as intermediary people between the block culture and our citizens. Our population has no clue. But gradually, they all become slaves and become plugged into the Grey hierarchy.**

1.078 **The Greys use our people like a herd of cattle to produce hormones and other bodily fluids, to fill their hormonal shortcomings.**

1.079 **The Greys don't have ethical feelings. Their desire to enlarge their block culture doesn't take into account ethical considerations. Before they changed, we were their conscience. The Grey clones have no individuality, no personality of their own. Everything they do is tuned to the survival of the block culture. As an individual, the Grey is** more or less empty. The commands for his actions always come from the collective mind. Their persona is the block they are part of.

While listening to this all, Mira asks herself who Teimon and Aodin are. They seem to be free of Grey interference. Teimon immediately senses the question.

1.080 **We are the Sheyan. We are members of a very old spiritual order. "Shey" means "to know", "An" means "experience". Through meditation and bodily techniques, we come into contact with our deeper inner self. We communicate telepathically with people on Earth via the crystal skulls.**

1.081 **The Greys know that we have developed instruments to communicate over long distances. In the far past, the crystal skulls were made by people of our order.**

1.082 **The skulls were used by our ancestors to stay in contact with our colonies that were spread over a large part of the Milky Way. We now have modern techniques, built with the help of the Greys. But the skulls are still in use for all kinds of reasons. The Greys have no access to the technology of the crystals.**

1.083 **The Greys are not able to find these crystal skulls themselves. Their brain doesn't allow that. But the monks of the order of the Sheyan are all in great danger. The Greys know that the Sheyan can send information. Some Sheyan have been arrested and even killed by their own people who are under Grey control. But we forgive them because they don't know what they are doing.**

For some moments, it is silent again. It feels as if Teimon cries. Mira is at the end of her strength and hopes this telepathic session will soon be over. With a last effort, she translates the words of Teimon.

1.084 **Only a few Sheyan are free. We found shelter in a secret network of underground caverns in the highlands. Every opposition under the population is immediately and ruthlessly oppressed.**

1.085 **Who revolts is locked up and disappears for ever. These captured rebels are used in underground compounds for experiments and the production of hormones.**

1.086 **The arrests appear to come from our own people. But they all are under control of the Greys and without knowing the entire population is manipulated.**

1.087 **All members of government of our world are manipulated by the Greys. First mentally and then physically. Mental manipulation happens telepathically. You call this process abduction. Once the Greys succeed, a kind of antenna is implanted in the person's body. What your people on Earth have to know is that, with an implant the Greys have complete control over the actions and the thought-processes of that person.**

1.088 **In this way every official on our home planet is controlled by one of the Grey blocks. The Greys are masters in manipulation. The Central Grey takes care of the central coordination in such a way that every official of our people does exactly what is necessary in the context of the general strategy of the Greys.**

1.089 **In this way, all people gradually become part of the Grey block culture. Only the thoughts sent by the Greys are executed by these abducted officials. Because the Greys only want one thing: complete control.**

1.090 **At this moment, on the surface our institutions are not changed. Nothing seems to be changed. But it is all just a masquerade. I stop now. We salute you. We will come back.**

Drops of blood seep on Mira's cushion.

Aodin gives Teimon a mental sign. He knows he has to stop immediately or it will be fatal for Mira. Gradually, Mira comes back to her senses. The light of the morning sun hurts her eyes. As if she has a serious hangover she gets out of her bed.

And now I am supposed to go to work, she sighs while taking a cold shower. She prepares herself for work and realizes the importance of Teimon's information. Ramon has to know this as soon as possible. But I must go to work. One thing is for sure. You're not imagining this, Mira. No way. This is really happening. Teimon and Aodin are real. Carefully she goes downstairs. "Why me?", she says loudly.

What do you mean, Mira? Is there something wrong? It is Sandra, the cleaning lady.

Oh nothing, Sandra. It's just one of those days.

Mira laughs as she remembers the face of Sandra. She's such a good person. If only she knew. Ramon is bewildered by everything Mira tells him.

My God! This is a worst case scenario, Mira. Tired of writing he really needs a drink. Coffee, Mira?

Yes Ramon, please. You know, although I haven't slept a minute, I don't feel tired at all, Ramon.

Unbelievable, these witches of modern times, he jokes.

Mira smiles but senses the worries of Ramon.

A terrible story, don't you think?

I'm speechless, Mira. Really!

Absorbed by the overdose of information, he makes a few mugs of fresh hot coffee.

If this is true, we will soon be in deep shit here on Earth. God knows what happens behind the veils of secrecy. But who is going to believe this story? He hears the video turn backwards automatically. At least one good thing happened tonight. Joy will be happy I didn't forget to tape the movie.

Mira, you will not believe it but I found the time to make waffles. Would you like one?

Yes please, and her hands disappear in the big waffle box.

I will not go into detail of everything you told, Mira. It is very clear, don't you think? I need time to fully absorb all you said. But I still have some questions. What do Teimon and Aodin look like?

Hmmm, these waffles are delicious, Ramon.

Take as many as you like, Mira.

Yes, I saw them, Ramon. Teimon sent me some impressions. But they were rather vague, as far as I can remember.

1.091 **They are dressed in a very surprising way, you know. They wear a kind of dressing jacket, made of a rough material. The caps are very large. And they look small compared to us. But I couldn't see their faces.**

Ramon is very surprised by this description. He remembers, that long ago, he wondered what alien beings would look like. Strange but true, he saw a kind of monk, exactly like Mira

100

described the Sheyan, walking in the mountains. This image made a deep impression and he never forgot it.

And how come, they are still not captured by the Greys?

I don't know, Ramon. I guess they escaped or could hide in time.

We have to know, Mira. It might be crucial to know. It is important to find out next time you have contact.

I will try, Ramon. But please, not at the moment! May I have one more waffle?

Please Mira, serve yourself. Oh yes. Lest I forget, how did the Greys invade their planet, Mira? What was the trick?

Very simple, Ramon.

1.092 **Before they realized what the intention of the Greys were, the Greys blackmailed some key figures of our society. They threatened them with mass extinction if the leaders didn't obey their requests.**

1.093 **And they have the means, you know. The leaders knew they were not bluffing. The Greys use fear as a weapon. If people are afraid, it makes it easy to take them over mentally. They use the same trick when they abduct somebody. The only way to defend yourself against abductions is to overcome your fear.**

So people, who are abducted, shouldn't be afraid of them?

Exactly, Ramon.

1.094 **If people see a UFO or are visited by grey creatures, they must show no fear or interest at all. You have to neglect them by all means. Act as if they are not there. The Greys have no answer against such behaviour. If you are afraid, they feel superior. If you neglect them, they can't mentally penetrate your mind.**

How do you know all this, Mira? Don't tell me you have contact again?

No, Ramon, the contact is broken. I don't know. I guess I get a lot of information I'm not aware of. It is as if I'm remembering it. It was a long night you know.

That would be great, Mira. I have so many questions. For example, Teimon told a lot about cloning. How do they eat? Without a mouth, I think this is difficult.

1.095 **As far as I know, they rub all kinds of fluids on their skin. I don't think they have a stomach.**

Freaky! And these fluids? Are they what Teimon refers to as human hormonal fluids?

Yes, that's what these fluids are. Personally, I think it is disgusting, Ramon.

But why do they need human hormones, Mira? I don't think that was the case when they were created?

1.096 **As far as I understand, their genetic make-up is disturbed by their evolution. Their gland system doesn't work properly anymore. So they can't make certain hormones themselves. To survive, they need an external source.**

It is all so weird, Ramon. Don't you think I'm going crazy?

That's just the point, Mira. It's too weird. If this was just imagination, there could not possibly be such detail. Patience, Mira. Read my lips. We will figure it out.

Can we stop now, Ramon? I feel again a pressure on my head.

Right away, Mira. I think this is enough for one day.

When Mira leaves Ramon a bit later, she is feeling well and full of energy again.

Try to get some sleep tonight, Mira. Take care!

But the noise of the car is too loud. She waves and in no time, her car disappears into the night. Back in the kitchen Ramon cleans the dishes. The weekend starts tomorrow. After cleaning the mess of a week, the kitchen looks as new. With the last coffee, Ramon goes online while meditating about everything he heard. So what Dan Burisch told about the feeding habits of the Grey is true after all. His description of the Greys is very similar to what Teimon says. It proves that he was really into contact with that J Rod. That part of his story is true. He only doesn't know they are not natural creatures. He just thinks they are from the future. Maybe he just told what the Grey creature told him. So the Greys must have been lying to him! Well, you can also lie telepathically. Paranormal abilities don't necessarily make you a better human being.

Till late in the night, Ramon surfs on the web and finds more and more viewpoints about the nature of the Greys. Some say the Greys are here to save the world from an ecological catastrophe. Others think the Greys want to protect the world from a nuclear threat.

If they would only know, Ramon says to himself with deep concern. What Teimon told Mira is explosive information in the UFO groups. As he walks upstairs, for a good sleep, he sees the moon high above the clouds. I hope Teimon leaves Mira alone tonight. Her health comes first.

As he lies down on the bed, the moonlight makes shadows on the wall. And what should I do with this information, he questions himself. Is our world really threatened by grey clones of alien origin? Deeply worried, he falls asleep.

- 16 -
10/9/2006

The Worldcube in Mira's bedroom is rotating slowly. The white light of the moon lightens the side of Europe in the darkness of Mira's bedroom. She can't sleep and looks at this strange work of art of Ramon. How can somebody get the idea to make such a thing? The Earth in the shape of a cube? Warm energy starts to flow from her feet to the top of her head. Oh no! Why can't they leave me alone for one night? I'm so tired. But the force is stronger and with tremendous speed she tunnels again through the purple matrix of the crystal skull. Teimon's voice is very clear tonight.

1.097 **I salute you. Sorry for the inconvenience, but it is urgent. The starting point of the star map is on the moon.**

1.098 **The Greys use these coordinates to travel between their space stations and the moon.**

Suddenly, she sees a gigantic construction in space and on the background a beautiful blue planet.

1.099 **This is a space ship of the block culture in the vicinity of Teimon's planet. It looks like a giant cube composed of four pyramids. Every pyramid is divided in four platforms and the top of the four pyramids is connected in the centre of the cube. In between the platforms, there is some space. The central part looks like a cube. Mira is impressed by the size of it all. The hierarchy of the block system is clearly visible in the space city. The central block of the block culture that lives in this space station must be located at the central cube**

where the pyramids come together.
Still under the impression of this mastodon, Teimon starts to talk
again. He feels that Mira is in optimal condition. There is a full
moon and she is easy to reach. The crystal matrix in front of him
glows in a purple light. The vibrating matrix makes contact with
the skull on Earth, telepathically linked with Mira.

1.100 **I know that Ramon has many questions. These are
some answers. We rarely travel into space. Space travel is not
good for humans.**
1.101 **The body of a human is evolved on a planet and
adjusted to the physics of that planet. Therefore the body of
a Grey is adjusted to the space environment so that they can
survive in space.**
1.102 **The Greys were the biological part of a highly
technological installation, for mining on other planets and
moons and to produce energy for our cities.**
1.103 **The Greys were not super humans. They were just very
practical and flexible biological robots.**

1.104 The Greys also had to help us to reach Earth.

1.105 In the beginning, everything worked smoothly. But our ancestors made a theoretical mistake. The people of the Earth need to know this.

- 17 -
11/9/2006

With a smile she looks at Ramon. She is sure he will be interested in this.

You know what his theoretical mistake was, Ramon?

No idea, Mira. Ramon is trying to write everything down. He was painting when she arrived and with paint on his hands he immediately started to note everything that Teimon told her last night. Mira was so excited to tell him everything that he decided to stop working and to listen to the good and bad news from the cosmos.

Well Mira, I'm listening. What was this terrible mistake?

1.106 Teimon told me that the genetic engineers had forgotten something very basic, namely the self-consciousness of matter. In the world-view of our ancestors, living tissue had no consciousness. But that was a very big mistake.

1.107 The Greys absorb substances through their skin. Skin cells react to exterior stimuli of substances and react accordingly. The skin is one big sense organ. The skin is the sense organ and basic for the development of emotions and feelings. The stimuli of the skin are individually recorded and saved in the memory of the brain. This was the beginning of their sense of individuality.

1.108 Every Grey feels his own skin individually and these sensations are not shared by the block he belongs to. During the clone evolution, this sense of individuality evolved gradually. Remarkably, these personal sensations didn't conflict with the block that the Grey belonged to.

Wait a minute, Ramon. Let me think. How did Teimon describe it?

1.109 We now have experimental proof that living matter always seeks self-consciousness. So even while our ancestors

prevented the cerebral brain to develop individuality by linking the Greys mentally in a collective block, the Greys developed a sense of individuality with the help of their sensitive skin.

Ramon is impressed. He immediately thinks of a statement by Jesus, in the gospel of Thomas: when the flesh is created by means of the soul or the spirit, then this is a miracle. But if the spirit or soul is created by means of the body, this would be a miracle of miracles. And he added: But I'm surprised how this great wealth (the spirit) lives in such poverty. Jesus was clearly more concerned about the state of mind of the people than about how the spirit came into being. Our biologists and genetic engineers are still in debate about how consciousness came into being. Is consciousness an aspect of an immortal soul or is self-consciousness just a by-product of the brain? And when did consciousness appear during evolution? Have only humans consciousness? Or do animals and plants have consciousness to?

These questions were discussed over and over again at the mystery school, Mira. But as I explained, as long as we can't make the test like Penrose suggested, we are not sure.

Maybe somebody will listen to what Teimon has to say.

But Mira, why didn't they know that? If this feeling of individuality was a long process, couldn't they see it coming?

Oh yes, Ramon. They knew it. But they were not suspicious. The latent sense of individuality didn't interfere with the block system. Everything seemed to be fine.

Suddenly, Mira gets nervous and she looks at the clock.

I have to go, Ramon. The animals you know. But can you roll me a cigarette? I'm out of tobacco.

Of course, Mira. And what do you think of a fresh hot coffee before you leave?

Well … okay then. But then I really have to go.

It's a deal, Mira. In a hurry, he heats the water, rolls a cigarette and then pours the boiling water on the freshly grinded coffee beans.

It's unbelievable how much is written about the Greys, Mira. Oh yes, lest I forget, I found a video about a Grey. You must see that before you leave.

Okay, why not. Do you have some more waffles, Ramon?

106

Yes Mira, plenty. Please, help yourself.

While she enjoys a delicious waffle, Ramon serves the coffee. He has the feeling that Mira is holding something back. He must convince her to speak out.

I am more and more convinced that Teimon's information is the missing link to understand the Greys, Mira. By the way, has Teimon told you anything more why the Greys became dangerous?

Well… yes Ramon. She enjoys the fact that it is Ramon who is asking the questions. But I'm sure you will declare me crazy when I tell you that.

But no Mira, how can you think that?

Okay then, I will explain it to you. But don't laugh.

No, no Mira, I wouldn't dare. Please tell me what you know.

Listen. You won't believe it.

1.110 **The escalation of the Greys started not that long ago. Teimon estimates that it must have been in the first half of the last century. They don't know the exact date. The Greys came by accident into contact with a toxic substance.**

They came into contact with a toxic substance? Here on Earth?

1.111 **Yes, here on Earth. The substance was from a cactus.**

A cactus? Really? What kind of cactus?

1.112 **It was a… Nevada cactus. Yes, I see the image Teimon sent me. A big cactus with beautiful red flowers.**

The Nevada cactus? Ramon is astonished. You won't believe it Mira, but … I was in the desert of Nevada today. I mean, I saw a few videos of Colonel Corso when he brought a visit to the Nevada desert where the Roswell incident took place. Come, I show you. Ramon takes the coffee mugs, Mira the waffle box and a few minutes later Ramon activates the video footage. On the video, you see Colonel Corso walking in the desert where the legendary crash of Roswell took place.

Stop, Ramon. There! Do you see that cactus? That's the one I saw.

Ramon is astonished. What kind of weird synchronicity is this, Mira? This is really too crazy, you know. Wait a minute! I have to show you the video of that Grey creature. The mouse pointer finds its way through the long list of favorites. The clip downloads and starts to play. The footage is only a few minutes long. It is a rather controversial video. It shows a Grey in detail. Just look at it. I get some more coffee.

While Ramon is in the kitchen, Mira looks at this macabre piece of footage. After a few minutes, the Grey creature seems to go into a state of shock, as if it is ill.

What do you think, Mira?

Mira is quiet and clearly impressed. A few people try to help the obviously sick creature.

1.113 He needs seaweed, says Mira with a sad voice. But he can't explain it to his contact person. He is not going to live very much longer.

Who are these bunglers? Mira shouts. Just stop this video, Ramon. I can't stand it. It makes me sick.

Ramon is surprised at her reaction. With a mix of annoyance and powerlessness, Mira returns to the kitchen. Ramon moves everything back and gives her the time to calm down.

Sorry that I react this way, Ramon, but I can't stand abuse of animals, or any living creature. Even if it is a Grey. If I see something like that, it makes me mad.

So you are sure that this footage is real?

Oh yes it's real. Definitely. But it makes me sick to look at it.

I understand you fully, Mira. Just forget it. Let's turn back to the Nevada cactus. Can you tell me what happened when they came into contact with that cactus?

Listen, Ramon. You will never believe what I'm going to tell you.

Try me, Ramon replies.

1.114 A few Greys came into contact with the juices of that cactus. Some hallucinogenic substances in that cactus gave them a kind of identity experience.

You're not going to tell me, these Greys came into contact with a kind of drug?

Well, that seems to be the case, Ramon. I only tell you what Teimon told me, you know.

Ramon is speechless again. Okay, and then? What happened then?

1.115 The Greys started to experiment more and more with these kinds of substances. That was when everything turned aggressive. This change in behaviour was what Teimon's

108

people couldn't perceive in advance. It never happened before they arrived on Earth.

Ramon writes and writes.

1.116 But that was not all. When the Greys came into contact with these substances the first time, it created a dangerous reaction in their block culture.

Mira takes her mug and awaits the reaction of Ramon.

I think I know what happened, Mira. The Greys are mentally connected with the other Greys of their block. So the entire block received telepathically the same mental awareness and passed it to the other blocks. In this way, the experience of one Grey could spread through the entire block culture.

Exactly, Ramon! You do understand me.

1.117 Indeed Ramon. The effect must have been so severe that the entire block culture got into a state of ecstasy resulting in a kind of collective religious experience. A kind of ego experience.

That's the reason why I was so angry when I saw that alien in the video, Ramon. Not only he, but the block he was linked with experienced the same feelings of sickness. They collectively shared the tests, performed on him. Mira takes a deep breath. And now I have to stop, Ramon. That's all I know. I feel sick and in saying that, she runs outside.

Ramon immediately follows her to check is everything is all right.

Are you okay, Mira?

Yes, Ramon. I'm feeling better already. I just needed some fresh air. But I'm relieved I told you everything. Again she takes some deep breaths. By the way, Ramon, do you have any wine in the house?

Wine? Now? What about the animals, Mira?

Oh, they have everything they need. I took care of them before I came. I was just so nervous to tell you all this.

I understand, Mira. Wait, I look for a bottle of wine. While walking downstairs, he shakes his head. Women! I will never understand them. They always have an escape route.

Look Mira, this is the last bottle of wine. A red one! With a big smile, he uncorks the bottle. Shall we stay outside, Mira? It is not cold.

That would be nice, Ramon.

So, that was the cause of the Greys turning violent.

Yes, Ramon. Isn't that an incredible story?

Indeed, Mira. It is beyond anything I could expect. And was that the end of the contact last night?

No, Ramon. Afterwards, Teimon told me some things about why the genetics of certain people in the past were changed.

Really? That's just great. Please tell me, Mira.

1.118 The Ancients added some genetic material of themselves to the human DNA. They did it by means of artificial insemination. Some selected women were chosen and they became pregnant.

Did Teimon use the word "Ancients"?

Yes, that was the word, Ramon. The Ancients did the genetic experiments.

1.119 The Ancients wanted to offer humanity the most precious gift imaginable: a part of their own evolution. For the universe is not always friendly towards life. Supernova can destroy hundreds of star systems in a few centuries.

1.120 It is the holy obligation of the Ancients to spread their genetics and to protect life from the destructive powers of the material world.

After that Teimon told me that my own ancestors were linked to one of these genetically altered people.

Ramon doesn't react but he sees that Mira has problems with this information.

Half an hour later, the two are chatting and laughing with a last glass of wine.

You know what I think, Mira? A slightly intoxicated Ramon says: I know how the Greys came into contact with the juices of the cactus. Maybe one managed to escape after they crashed in Roswell. Because there were five bodies found. And perhaps there were six of them. Maybe he used the juices to stay alive. Or maybe worse: when they crashed, one was catapulted out of the vehicle and fell with his butt on a cactus.

Mira bursts of laughter.

Ha, ha, I see it happening, Ramon. The entire block must have jumped straight up. Ha, ha, ha. And then, the shit hit the fan.

Ha, ha, ha. Oh my God. Just imagine, Mira. I see it already in the

110

newspapers. World threatened by aliens! They fell with their butts on a cactus!

Ha, ha, ha. Mira is slowly gliding out of her chair of sheer laughter. Obviously they both have their ways to handle stress. When she finally goes home after a last mug, Mira is back her old self.

Are you not afraid of police alcohol control, young lady?

Not at all, Ramon. I take the roads through the fields to get home.

Ramon is back on his own. A bit dizzy, he cleans everything. On the table, the flower of life is still visible. Nineteen red circles, made with his glass. Even if Ramon spills wine, he makes it a work of art. Still giggling, Ramon thinks back on the alien-cactus connection. It is not as silly as it sounds. Hallucinogens played an important role in shamanistic cultures. Maybe it was a kind of awakening experience for the Grey clones.

Mira is one of a kind. When she left, she felt as new. Unbelievable, the metamorphoses she can undergo in a few hours time. Ramon looks up and sees the full moon, shining in all its glory. The good old moon, symbol of the enlightened one in India, the God of evil in Mazdaism and a dead rock since Copernicus.

Suddenly he remembers the first things Mira told him. I forgot to ask her about the connection of the moon with the star map. That bloody wine is bad for my short-term memory. She was talking about the coordinates, extending from the moon. Quickly, he walks indoors and reads his notes.

Hardly readable of course. The starting point of the star map is on the moon. So the testimony of Dr. Karl Wolf of the Disclosure Project might be true! Wolf saw pictures of an alien base at the back side of the moon. I must know more of it.

Ramon realizes that if the star map is real, it's the only proof to make the information of Teimon credible. If that map is real, ufologists have to accept the value of Teimon's information. Ramon quickly looks again at the video of Karl Wolf on YouTube. The man looks so sincere. He has no website, never wrote a book. So he is not in it for the money. I hope Mira can use her talents to locate the place of this base. Still a bit dizzy, Ramon closes his WebCom and goes to bed. Could there really be an alien base on the moon? That would be fantastic. What would it look like? And if so, why is NASA silent about this breaking world news. Too tired to think, Ramon activates his alarm and gradually his thoughts fade away into the world of dreams.

- 18 -
12/9/2006

While enjoying the warm sunrays, Ramon is cycling to Mira's little farm. After reading the notes, early in the morning, he decided not to lose any time and to visit Mira at home. After a small text message announcing his visit, he collects all his astronomy books, jumps on his bike and starts peddling. Could it really be? A base on the moon? And this base is connected with the star map in one way or another? Could there be installations on the moon that make star travel possible? I hope Mira can help me.

As he thinks back on yesterday night's grey cactus connection, he laughs so loud that the cows look up, no doubt trying to figure out what this strange creature is all about. That cactus story will make history. Ramon admires the beautiful autumn colors of the leaves. He's glad to see Mira's farm in the distance.

The farm really fits the personality of Mira. Perfectly renovated and surrounded with unknown plants and flowers. Witches can't complain these days, he thinks smiling while ringing the bell. I hope she's home. She didn't answer my message, so I guess she is.

A smiling Mira opens the door. I can't believe you made it! On the bike?

Well, I don't like to cycle in a car, you know and while laughing they both get in. The veranda is full of light.

Can I get you something to drink, Ramon?

Well, coffee would be fine, Mira.

I thought so, Ramon. I hope you will like it.

All coffee is good, Mira. Thanks.

Meanwhile, Ramon puts all the old books of astronomy and the Apollo mission on the table.

112

Mira, I never thought these books could be of use to find an alien base on the moon. Ramon knows the books by heart and opens the maps of the two sides of the moon.

I read your message this morning, Ramon. You are lucky, I have a free day. It must be important to make this trip by bike.

Well, let's say I am eager to know, Mira.

With a hot mug in his hands he explains his visit.

I was reading the notes yesterday night. You remember telling me about the coordinates of the map? And that the map started on the moon? Teimon told you his ancestors created the Greys for space travel and space industry, yes? So I asked myself the question: could it be that they used the Greys to explore space. If the Greys found a livable planet, it is not unreasonable to assume that they built a kind of bases on the moon, so that later on the ancestors could use these bases after their long travel through space and find shelter on the hostile environment of the moon. But it is still not clear how it all fits together. Did the ancestors of Teimon use the Greys to find their way to Earth? Or was the Earth already known before they made the Greys? The idea to use robots to explore the universe is not new. NASA studied these ideas to go to Mars. But there is more, Mira.

Teimon told us that the Greys finally arrived at our solar system. With the help of several settlements on different planets and space stations, they could have built a kind of artificial interstellar space road from their planet to Earth. The coordinates of that road through space from beginning to end could be the star map. The star map extends over 10,000 light years. That's a long distance. Probably, the Greys use technology to travel very fast over long distances. Like "warp speed" in Star Trek. I think, in this technology, it is important to know exactly the coordinates from beginning to end.

So many questions, Ramon. Sorry but I can't give you answers I don't have. You have to ask Teimon. But Ramon, the light speed is the highest speed. How can they travel faster?

That's a good question Mira. I only know one real scientific explanation. The Einstein-Rosen Bridge. Einstein and Rosen developed this theory in the middle of the twentieth century. The idea is simple. Just make a four dimensional bridge between two points in space. The bridge is like a wormhole. If you travel through this bridge, you can enter at one point and pop up at another point in space in no time. In this way, it is possible to travel with multiple times the light speed via the fourth dimension.

Wait a minute, Ramon. You mean something like the technology of the television series Stargate? My nephew thinks it is a great show.

Yes Mira, that idea is based on the Einstein-Rosen Bridge. But in order to make such a space-time bridge it is important to know the beginning and end of your trip. God knows where you end up if the coordinates are not correct. Space is a big place you know. The slightest mistake and you will end up in some star system farther away.

So it isn't a crazy idea that Teimon's people could have sent a message? They could have sent the signal via such a space-time bridge.

Absolutely, Mira. Theoretically it's possible. Why not? But to come back to my earlier point, why would Teimon say that the coordinates start on the moon and end in the vicinity of his planet and not on Earth? If you think about it, the moon would be a perfect place for a base. There is no atmosphere and the conditions are almost like in space and there is hardly any gravity. There is enough material to build whatever. It is also a perfect environment to preserve a construction that can last for millennia. If you build something on the moon, it is there to stay a long time. There is no rain, no weather, no seasons and so on. And most importantly, a settlement or a base on the moon would also be a perfect place to hide this technology for humans. In this way they avoid interference with our own cultural evolution. That's why I brought these books, Mira. Do you want to try to see if you can locate a place where there could be a base on the moon maps?

I can try, Ramon.

Mira looks very concentrated at the maps. Suddenly, she points to a place on the front side of the moon.

There, there I see a point that lights up! And there I see another one. Ramon gives here some stickers and she glues them precisely on the points where she sees a light.

15.3°S / 60.0°E and another one not far from there at 33.0°S /

52.5°E.

Great, Mira. Thanks. And now look on the backside, Mira. Do you see something there?

She looks to an older drawing from the backside of the moon. The Spectrum Atlas may be old, but it still is a masterpiece by Patrick Moore. Without hesitation, she again points to two places.

12.3°N / 203.6°E and 42.2° / 172.4°E.

Look carefully again. Nothing more, Mira?

No, that's it, Ramon. And what do you want to do with it, Ramon? Go and take a look up there?

No, no Mira, ha, ha. But I will try to find high resolution pictures of these places. On the web, there are a lot of websites with lots of pictures of the moon. Maybe it can be useful to have an idea where to start looking. The moon is smaller than Earth but it is still a large place. Who knows?

The ringing of the doorbell abruptly ends the conversation. Who can that be? Mira looks at her watch. Is he already here?

Visitors, Mira? Then I won't keep you any longer.

But no, Ramon. You can stay. It's a colleague of me. He wants to discuss some things about a business meeting tomorrow.

No, Mira. I had better go home. My cubes await me. And I want to check this information out. Ramon leaves through the backdoor and as quickly as he can, he goes back home on his bike.

He realizes more and more that the star map is of utmost importance to interest anybody in what Teimon has to say. He remembers Teimon's saying about finding the key of the signals, that it will make the mental power stronger. Back in his WebCom, he surfs immediately to the Apollo Image Archive. He enters the coordinates that Mira gave and zooms in. The low resolution is annoying but at least he has some idea of the location. He makes backups of all the pictures. Fantasizing about the secrets hidden on the beautiful Luna, he continues varnishing his cubes until late at night.

While Ramon is busy with his cubes, 10,000 light years away, twelve silver colored discs fly soundless over a grotesque chain of mountains. It is night. Surrounded by a yellow orange glow, they are visible in sharp contrast with the dark sky. The waves of the endless turquoise blue sea bump continuously against the rocky coastline. Foggy white nebula clouds are lit by two moons. The biggest moon and its smaller satellite dominate the night sky. A small purple grey satellite appears at the horizon and gradually comes nearer. The greenish grey satellite of the large grey moon overlaps the big moon and its shadow on the surface of the large moon is an indication for the inhabitants of the planet that the conjunction of the three moons will happen in a few hours.

In a dark underground cavern, protected by the mountains, you can hardly distinguish two sitting figures. The dome-like vault resists the pressure of the rocks above. In the center of the vault is a large circular deep purple crystal disc. From the outside, it seems to be just a part of the rocks, but inside it's like a window. The stars in the sky are clearly visible. Only a dark purple glow lightens the faces of the two individuals. It's very cold. Their warm dressing jackets protect them from the cold. Like frozen, they sit still, waiting for the moment of the conjunction. Their deep dark eyes reflect the soft purple shine of the purple crystal matrix in front of them. With the large caps over their head, they look like monks of the middle ages. They look into each others eyes.

Still eleven days to go, Aodin thinks to Teimon.

Mentally, they share their sorrows.

The Greys are tracing us, thinks Aodin.

Yes, I feel them too, is the mental response. How long will we be safe here?

Just long enough to prepare ourselves, dear friend. The ones that could escape the terror of the Greys count on us. Their lives are at stake.

Patiently, they wait for the moment of conjunction. As soon as the three moons are on one line, a beam of purple light falls on

116

the purple matrix. They prepare themselves for the transmission. The crystal matrix starts to glow. It's contact time.

Teimon lies down and directs his mental state to the matrix. The purple crystal resonates only with the matrix of the purple crystal skull on Earth. The purple skull has the same proportions as their own head. The skulls of the Grey clones have another shape. That's a good thing. It makes it impossible for the Greys to detect the communication between Teimon and Mira. That's the reason why the Greys are not able to locate the purple skull.

But the Greys do know that some Sheyan have escaped. They know that the Sheyan are able to contact people on Earth and seek for help. Only the Sheyan are able to do this.

Teimon, Aodin and a few other members of the spiritual order managed to escape before everybody else was captured. To prevent detection Teimon and Aodin only communicate telepathically. But it's a question of time before they will be captured.

Meanwhile, Mira enjoys her free day. What a pity that Ramon left immediately. Her colleague didn't stay long. After feeding the animals, she decides to take a nap, enjoying the warmth of the sun.

As she relaxes, a warm flow of energy rises through her spinal cord. She recognizes the symptoms immediately. Teimon seeks contact! There goes my free afternoon! But she knows the importance of it all. The room starts to shine in purple light and the crystal skull appears in front of her eyes. She feels relaxed and without fear, she flows mentally through the vibrating purple matrix. The soft voice of Teimon sounds in her mind.

I salute you. Seven sessions will follow. Prepare yourself. Aodin will send extra knowledge. This is what you have to tell Ramon.

1.121 **Most people on Geya want wealth. The same goes for companies and countries. In itself, there is no harm in that. But some people want more. They want power and control.**

1.122 **Normally, we could defend ourselves against the Grey invasion, just by cutting of the food supply. But they got help from a secret organization on Geya.**

1.123 **This organization collaborates with them. They give the Greys the products they need in exchange for technology.**

Mira remembers the story of Colonel Corso. This man was telling the truth.

1.124 **It all started around 1933. The Greys made contact with some telepathically gifted people on Geya. We were not aware of that. Normally, contact with humans was only allowed with our permission.**

1.125 **In the same period, several carefully selected people were abducted. They were members of secret societies and they went on to become top people in those secret groups.**

1.126 **They didn't know that their ideas and thoughts were telepathically forced on them by the Greys. They thought that they were chosen ones.**

1.127 **This first Grey experiment to get Earth under their control went terribly wrong and the destruction on Geya was unseen in history. But this first experiment made the Greys stronger. They didn't care about the human suffering and developed a new strategy in another part of the world, again with the help of a secret order.**

1.128 **The most important members of the previous secret society managed to escape and regrouped in the western part of the world. After a period of integration, they again became high members of society. The Greys started abducting people from that secret order but also from the general population on a large scale. In this way, they infiltrated all vital institutions of that country.**

1.129 **We don't know much of what happened after 1933. What we know was sent by descendants of our own people.**

1.130 **These descendants live together with the humans. They know that we exist and are hardly distinguishable from real humans.**

1.131 **The newly established collaboration between the secret societies and the Greys is the same as the previous one: technology in exchange for food, but now on a larger scale.**

1.132 **The megalomania of the secret society is so severe that they don't see that the Greys just fool them. Some members have their doubts, but most members are convinced that they have everything under control.**

1.133 **What they don't understand is that they will be the first people to be eliminated as soon as the Greys take over.**

118

1.134 **Gradually, the Greys improved their manipulation techniques on humans and more and more people in central places became mental slaves of the Greys. The Greys are technologically superior but they need people for their hormones.**
1.135 **Ramon must write a book about the information that we share with you. Instructions for the book will follow.**
I salute you.

- 20 -
12/9/2006

Ramon is shocked when Mira tells him all these possible historical facts and has a hard time digesting all this. But when Ramon hears the proposal of Teimon, he looks puzzled at Mira.
Write a book? Me? But Mira, I'm not a writer!
I know, Ramon. But I am just telling you what Teimon told me.
I understand, Mira. But writing a book about all this? How am I supposed to do this? I have no time and I'm no writer!
Ramon, sorry to interrupt you but can I have some more coffee?
Yes of course, Mira. In silence, he serves the brown life-force while wondering what to think of Teimon's request.
Thanks, Ramon. She feels that Ramon is confused by Teimon's proposal.
It's not that I don't want to do it, Mira. But I have so much work. If I am to write a book, I might as well forget my next exhibition. And I need it. Financially, I live in a poor man's world, you know. I have to earn some money! On the other hand I realize that this information has to be revealed in one way or the other, especially, after what you told me today. He shakes his head. Teimon places me for a dilemma, Mira.
Ramon starts to laugh.
Why are you laughing, Ramon?
Well, I'm not going to weep, Mira. It is all so bizarre. If I understand it well, an alien asks me to forget my work and to write a book. You can hardly call this an every day situation, can you? Don't get me wrong, Mira. I want to do it. But apart from the fact that I'm not a writer, the timing is really bad. You know

what? Tell Teimon that I will think about it. Don't get me wrong. I do understand that a book would be a good way to put the information out in the open. SETI would be a possible candidate to just send the information. But if they received signals, why didn't they go public with it? So a book wouldn't be a bad idea at all to get the message out.

Mira doesn't say anything and observes Ramon discussing with himself. He's the only man she knows who can have an argument with himself.

You see Mira, publishing this information in a kind of a novel is like the horse of Troy. It could be read by a broad audience, not only by specialists. Considering the sensitive nature of the information it would be better if as many people as possible are informed about what Teimon has to tell. I don't think everybody is waiting to see this information become public. Especially not those people who are connected with secret societies and their Grey connection. If I have to believe what is published on the web, they do everything they can to keep the UFO files out of the public eye. I would say it is even dangerous to come out with this information. So, a book would be a good protection for us.

Ramon, look. I understand that there is some danger involved if you come in the open with this book. But most people will just read it as entertainment. And at the same time you reach a lot of people of the UFO community and people who are involved in hidden projects. If I think about it, it is in the first place an SOS message to everybody involved. I don't see why anybody could have a problem with the fact that you want to warn them for a possible alien danger. The way I understand it, nobody knows who the Greys are and who they are dealing with. The people involved are in fact in great danger, like Teimon says. So they deserve to be warned, whatever they have done behind the screens of secrecy.

You have a point, Mira. But writing a novel! Pfff. That is a hell of a job, you know. It takes at least a year. But let me first think about it. There is always a solution. Guido Gezelle once stated: before you do something, think ten times. And if you decide to do it, keep on thinking!

Ramon empties his mug and goes to his WebCom.

Let's change the subject, Mira. I want to show you something.

120

After finding the locations of the moon bases, I surfed a bit on the web and I found a strange site and a video clip. Ever heard of Serpo?

Never heard of, Ramon. Serpo, what's that?

You won't believe it, Mira. Normally, I would dump this story as pure nonsense. But after all the information of Teimon, it isn't that crazy after all.

Wait a minute, Ramon. If I have to stay longer, I will first get us something to eat. You like pizza?

Fine by me, Mira. I haven't eaten yet.

A while later, both sit in the WebCom with a glass of wine and a delicious piece of pizza, listening to the story of Bill Ryan. Bill Ryan is a ufologist and a while ago he received some e-mails from an unknown person. They told about a secret project during the sixties. The person asked Bill Ryan to make a website and to publish the information in the mail message on the web. Serpo became the name of the site. The information tells a story of an exchange program between Extra-terrestrial Biological Entities, EBE's, and a special team of astronauts. Twelve astronauts travelled with these EBE's to their home planet, named Serpo. They lived there for two years. Two astronauts didn't survive the trip. The most shocking was what happened with the body of the astronaut who died on the planet Serpo. These EBE's used his body for genetic experiments. Bill Ryan wasn't convinced that the story of this mister X was true. Maybe some parts were, but the rest was probably disinformation. At the end of the video, Ramon asks Mira what she thinks of it all.

I'm not sure, Ramon. Those genetic experiments can be real information. Because we have to assume these EBE's are the Grey clones. But the rest is fantasy, I think. I have the feeling that this story wants to inform the UFO community that these EBE's are not as friendly as one would wish. But as you know, the Greys are much more cruel than what they tell in this story. The question is: Who is the sender?

You are right, Mira. I personally think that this story comes from somebody who knows much more. Already in the beginning, some information was questionable. The planet Serpo was a planet of a double star, identified as Zeta Reticula. It's a double star system, some fourteen light years from here. The planet

Serpo would circulate around both stars, which is virtually impossible. When I read that, I knew something was wrong in this story. Every astronomer knows that this is impossible.

Indeed, Ramon. I think this story is just a fictitious background to discuss only one element: those genetic experiments.

I'm glad you share my opinion, Mira. By the way, do you have some more time?

It depends, Ramon, she jokes with a feminine undertone.

Well, I would like you to see the video of Dan Burisch. I haven't shown it to you yet. But now, I think it is time for you to hear the full story he told. It will not influence your thoughts anymore. Two hours? What do you think? Maybe some more information somewhere in the back of your memory will pop up. After some arguing, Ramon convinces her to stay and they both watch the footage with an extra bottle of wine and the last waffles.

That man knows a lot, she says. He is very intelligent, but he has been manipulated by that Grey. That's for sure. Those timelines Ramon, that's pure nonsense. Really, I'm sure of that.

And what do you think of the star gates and the looking glasses he talks about. Isn't this maybe part of the technology that enables the Greys to travel in time and look into the future?

No, Ramon. I feel there is something wrong. The whole idea of a catastrophic event in the near future doesn't make sense. I think the Greys fooled him and he believes them. It is understandable. Don't forget these Grey assholes are technologically advanced. They can tell you whatever they want. And who are we to doubt what they say? They are aliens, you know.

Ramon has to laugh with the way she reacts.

Mira, Greys have no…

Stop that, Ramon. No dirty language, please!

Sorry Mira, it must be the wine.

Suddenly, Mira becomes very silent and after a while she goes to the kitchen.

Come Ramon, I will tell you what came to my mind just now. I think it is information by Aodin. But please, come into the kitchen. I don't feel at ease near those computers.

Hours later they are still discussing the ins and outs of time travel. She has a hard time to convince Ramon that time travel is not possible. With theories about timelines, parallel universes,

122

time travel and wormholes Ramon defends the possibility of time travel. But Mira doesn't give up. She seems pretty sure of herself.

Time is not relative, Ramon. Our perception of time is relative but not time itself. Time has nothing to do with our perception or with relativity. You can compare it with perspective. The eyes see the world in perspective, but in reality, perspective doesn't exist. It only exists in our perception. We see a road coming to a point in the distance. But in reality, this is not the case. The same with wine... sorry... time. Time is the same in the entire universe. I know: the further we look the further back in time we go. But in reality these old regions didn't disappear. They still exist in the same timeframe as we. But we can't see what's happening there right now. Not with our technology.

There is only the "now" time, Aodin says. The whole of the universe is "in" the same time. If you travel through an Einstein-Rosen Bridge, the time is the same at both sides. The time it takes to travel through that bridge must be added to the moment you left. No matter how quick you travel, if you arrive it will be later than the moment you left. Even if you travel multiple times the speed of light, it will not change that fact. Time travel is not possible. What the Greys told Burisch is wrong. It's impossible to travel to the past or the future. But you can travel faster than light speed. That is definitely possible.

Then explain to me what Aodin suggested, Mira. For time travel is still a big question and a hot topic in physics.

Mira lights another cigarette.

Listen, Ramon! If you know how to connect two places in space, you can travel at high speed from one place to the other. For example: If Teimon has to travel from his planet to here, he needs some four years to get here when he uses the road of the star map.

Four years, Mira? Then they have to travel with 2,500 times the speed of light to get here that quick!

Indeed, Ramon. So, even at such a high speed it still takes a long time to get here. How big is the universe, Ramon?

Well Mira, at the moment, they estimate the size to be about 14 to 16 billion light years. Ramon is astonished: Mira talks as if in a somnambulistic state. It is as if she has been thinking all her life about these difficult topics in physics.

Okay then. Imagine you can travel with a billion times the speed of light. Then you still need fourteen years to get to the other side. Wherever that is. But even then, fourteen years would pass by. You would not travel back in time. Only with telepathy, you can communicate over long distances in the "now" time. While saying that, she puts her glass of wine on the table. And "now" I'm going home. Thanks, Ramon. The wine was good.

Mira looks determined. Ramon laughs about the way she ends her speech.

I completely agree, Mira. The wine was the best ever.

To be honest, Ramon, I was listening to myself, you know. Aodin has left some important information somewhere in my brain. I hope that what I said clarified some questions you may have.

Absolutely, Mira. I wrote everything down as well as I could.

Believe me Ramon, the theory of Dan Burisch is not true. If that is what the Grey told him, then that J Rod fooled him.

Convinced of everything she told, she goes to her car.

Jesus Ramon, to think that I have to go to work tomorrow morning! I hope that Teimon gives me some rest tonight. Don't forget to think about the book, Ramon. It's important. Her feminine body makes shadows on the wall and for a second, Ramon is in full admiration of the beauty of the female body. Agile as a cat, she jumps into her car.

I'm full of energy, Ramon. Can you believe that?

I believe you, Mira, but please drive carefully.

Don't worry, Ramon. Be happy. I'm in good hands. If I hear from Teimon, I let you know.

See you tomorrow, Mira.

The lights of Mira's car disappear into the night and Ramon goes back inside to clean up the mess in his kitchen.

So… no time travel! That is bad news for a lot of science fiction writers. Still something is not clear to me. If you want to make an Einstein Rosen bridge between two points in space, how can you bring two points in space together if they are thousands of light years separated from one another? I mean, at the same moment in time? I don't get it. Maybe with a kind of telepathic technology? To make a link between these distant points at the

124

same moment in time? God knows what is still to come.

But writing a book? My God! I have to wait and see. Imagine that the secret order that Teimon mentioned are the Illuminati or the Warriors. Could it really be that the Greys have infiltrated in the power structures of the world?

And what about the year 1933? Could it be that the Greys manipulated people in Europe? Was Teimon referring to the Second World War when he talked about the first contact of the Greys with humans? I must look for more evidence.

The moon is no longer full but its light still makes shadows on the walls as Ramon goes to his bedroom. Seeing the moon brings his thoughts back to the star map. The principle is clear. But in which direction is the map orientated? Nothing was said about that. Once in the room Ramon opens the window. With admiration he looks at the moon and a bit further, he sees the constellation of Orion. A powerful archetype from ancient times, especially in Egypt. Suddenly Ramon gets an idea. But of course! What was I thinking! The information comes from the gateway of Orion. Then that must be the direction because the signals traveled through the star gate of Orion. How could I forget?

Glad to have solved one of the puzzles of the star map, he falls asleep. The sounds of the church bells vibrate through the entire village. It's three a clock in the morning!

- 21 -
13/9/2006

Mira is relieved to feel the soft mattress of her bed. She took her time to get home and enjoyed the silence of the night. Still a bit dizzy of the wine, she's completely relaxed as purple lightning starts to surround her. There we go again, she thinks. In the distance, the night clock tolls three times. Once passed through the purple matrix, the familiar voice of Teimon sounds in her mind.

1.136 **I salute you, Mira. More answers on more questions of Ramon. Ten days from now, there will be a Grey transport to the moon.**

1.137 **The transport is organized with the coordinates of the star map. The inclination of the coordinates is 30°, based on the moon's equatorial plane. The transport is planned during new moon.**

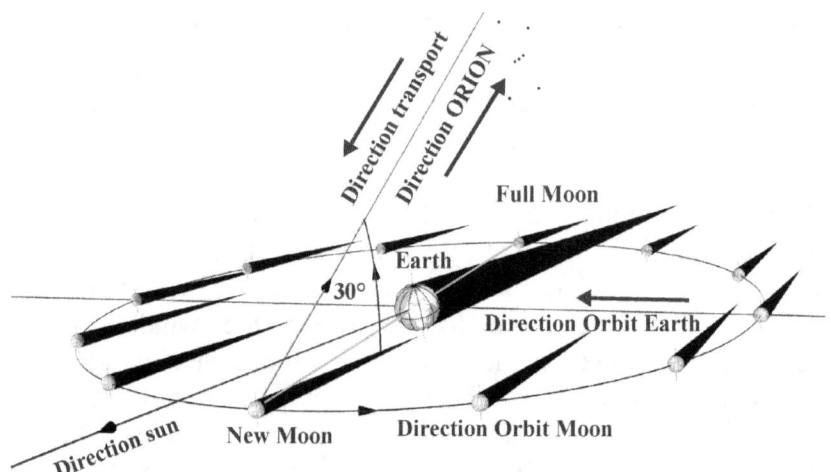

While she listens to Teimon, she suddenly seems to be in a kind of artificial planetarium. She sees clearly a 3D projection of the star map in the direction of Orion, starting from the moon. Suddenly, everything is gone. She gets a very uneasy feeling. Different images of people become visible.

1.138 **She sees an image of Hitler. Then she sees machines and explosions in the desert, followed by the image of an Asiatic man with penetrating eyes. On the background, red flags. Funny, she sees an old-timer of the Red Cross. Then, a map of Israel and the Suez Channel.**

These are images of the period in which the Greys became self-conscious.

Teimon gives her two dates. The year 1933 and 1939. We are not sure if the dates are correct. Ramon has to check them.

1.139 **The Greys are able to suggest. They can use their telepathic ability to suggest themselves in another shape than they are. People will see them in a different shape.**

1.140 They can even suggest complete surroundings. It depends how much blocks are used to create a suggestion.

1.141 The commands to suggest are agreed within a block. But the strategy of the suggestion comes from the general block culture.

1.142 The Greys are not able to create a complete new being with genetics. They can mix DNA with other genes but their genetic creations lack any resemblance with real humans.

1.143 The only drive of the Greys is their desire to become individuals. But they always operate and think in block.

1.144 They realize that they search something they don't have nor understand, namely individuality. Their search is like a bottomless thirst, impossible to quench.

For a moment, there is a break to give Mira the time to adjust. Teimon feels that the telepathic transmission between him and Mira becomes more fluent every day. He knows that he has to make use of the coming days. There is not much time left.

Aodin is sitting next to Teimon. He takes care that Teimon sends the information in the right order. He detects the questions that Ramon has during his discussions with Mira and sends additional information to Mira. He doesn't like it when they get drunk. It is to him as if they don't take it seriously. But he knows that humans have the strange habit to bring themselves sometimes into a state of drunkenness. He has studied all old chronicles about human behavior. It's just the way they are. After all, they are humans.

Teimon resumes his task hoping Ramon will get a complete picture of what is really happening on his own planet.

1.145 The Greys have no control over other alien civilizations, but they do control some humanoids.

1.146 Humanoids are genetic descendants of the first physical contact between humans and our ancestors. Long ago, a delegation of the ancestors of our people went to Earth. Their intention was to stay and to merge with the people of Earth, which is what they did.

1.147 The Greys can trace these humanoids and try to get them under control. They live among the people and are indistinguishable from humans. They look the same.

1.148 In general they are easy to reach with telepathy. The

Greys try to control them but as soon as they feel hesitation or suspicion, they immediately disconnect. The humanoids know that the Greys exist but they don't know that they have changed.

1.149 **The Greys don't want the humanoids to become suspicious. The humanoids don't have a clue about what's going on. Humanoids are very intelligent and have high functions in the public domain in many countries of your planet we call Geya.**

1.150 **The humanoids still think that the Greys act under our control. But that isn't the case. The humanoids are the first people that have to be warned, because they can easily disconnect themselves from the Greys. At this moment, they don't see the danger.**

1.151 **Any human who is under mental control of the Greys, becomes an extension of the Grey block. We call such a person a "Mental".**

1.152 **Many people become Mentals because of the fear they have when they come into contact with the Greys. Fear paralyzes them and breaks the resistance against the mental suggestions. Once you're a Mental, you become mentally linked with a block.**

1.153 **Once this is done, the mental is ready for the next stage: to transform him into a "Psy-mutant". A "mental" with an implant is a Psy-mutant. If that happens, you become a servant of a Grey block. These people are perfect to help execute the strategy of the Greys. They don't question the suggestions any longer.**

Aodin gives a sign and looks into Teimon's eyes. This will be delicate information. Mira feels hesitation. Soft pulsating sounds relieve the pressure on her head. Without resistance, the information flows into her mind.

1.154 **The Greys know that mythology is the basis of all religion. If you change the myths, you change the image of man, but also the image you have of the world and of God. The first experiment of the Greys failed. With the help of the entire bock culture, a new cult was created in the new world. The Greys call this cult the Sean Leyka.**

1.155 **The human founder of the Sean Leyka was a Mental**

128

and later became probably a Psy-Mutant. He was chosen by the most important members of a secret society. During several abductions, he was prepared by the Greys to create a new myth that had to be spread by the cult. He thought it was all his own idea, but in fact the Greys were behind his ideas. He created a mythology in which aliens play a crucial role. The sect operates in secrecy.

1.156 **The top of this cult are Mentals and some are even Psy-mutants. Not because they are abducted but because the rituals they use in this cult makes you open for mental suggestions in the same way the Greys operate. In a way, you can say that the members gradually become Mentals. But most members, if not all, haven't got a clue that they work for the Greys and spread their ideology in every layer of society. The intention of the Greys is to use the cult to spread their mythology all over the world. Hardly any member is aware of this hidden agenda of the Greys. So also the members of this cult must be warned with the book Ramon has to write.**

1.157 **Dan Burisch is a member of a group of people who are initiated in the alien reality. He is a good guy. But he is manipulated by the Greys. Some people of the group he is part of are Psy-mutants. He himself is a Mental or maybe even a Psy-mutant. He must be warned.**

1.158 **People have to understand: Mentals and Psy-mutants are victims. They don't know what is actually going on. In general, they have good intentions. But some became spellbound by the Greys. Particularly if their psychological make-up, their psychological profile has the tendency to control and suppress other people. People who like power over others. But whatever the reason! They have to be warned. We come back. We salute you.**

- 22 -
13/9/2006

Mira wants to continue but Ramon interrupts her in order to write everything down. After this marathon he looks surprised at

Mira.

Sean Leyka? Never heard of such a cult. Have you?

Me neither, Ramon.

Let me meditate about it all, Mira. It's one shock after the other. I have to admit it: Teimon is consistent in everything he says. I don't see contradictions. And I assure you, a lot of the information that Teimon told you is mentioned in one way or the other on the web. The difference is that on the web everything is fragmented.

One thing is clear. The image of these Greys becomes worse every day. If this is all true, the world is in great danger. Ramon fills the mugs one more time.

Mira, let's find out what Google has to say about the period 1933-1939. Maybe you recognize some of the pictures you saw.

It's the period of the great recession in America. Franklin Roosevelt was elected president of the USA in 1932. In 1933, Hitler became Reichskanselier in Germany. It was the beginning of the prosecution of the Jews by forcing them to live in ghettos.

Mira points Ramon to a small note below one of the topics on the popular search engine.

In the beginning, cars of the Red Cross were used to bring Jews to the ghettos.

I think that is what Teimon wanted to show me when I saw that funny car.

You are right, Mira. This can't be a coincidence. But do you really think that Hitler and the Nazi party had something to do with the Greys? I don't know much about it. I do know that Hitler became a member of a secret society. And that he created a new religion, based on old German myths of the pre-Christian period. After the war, a lot of Nazi scientists escaped to North and South America. Others, especially scientists were captured by the Russians and Americans to work for them. Some of them became top people. Werner von Braun was the most famous.

And look, Mira. You saw an Asiatic person with red flags in the background. In 1933, Mao Tse Tung published his book about the struggle of the different classes.

After the end of the virtual trip through history, Ramon looks into Mira's eyes, showing concern.

With those images, we are suddenly in the middle of our own

history, Mira. But I don't understand what the Nazis have to do with the UFO subject. Although, if I remember correctly... Do you know that American and English pilots observed strange flying lights, when they were bombarding Germany in World War Two? These lights got the nickname "Foo Fighters". By the way, it is nowadays the name of a damn good rock band. Nobody could ever find out what these bizarre flying objects were. In UFO literature, they are mentioned as the first registered UFOs. But if there is a link between UFOs and the Nazis, I will find it, Mira.

I don't know much about that period, Ramon. But the cruelty of the Nazi regime has a lot in common with what we know about the Greys. And the hierarchic system of the Nazi party had a lot of resemblance with the Grey hierarchy. So there could be some link with the Greys.

I agree, Mira, but before I blame the Greys of the devastation caused by World War II, I have to find more proof. But you have a point. The way a Grey block culture is structured makes it a perfect dictatorial organization. If the Greys abduct people and change them into Mentals and even Psy-mutants, we are facing an alien dictatorial and criminal organization. Just imagine for a minute that the top of the Nazis were Mentals or Psy-mutants. It would turn the history of the twentieth century inside out. But I have to give Teimon the benefit of the doubt. So I will do some research. Although, even if it would be true, it wouldn't change the responsibility of the members of the Nazi regime for what happened in the concentration camps.

Of course, Ramon. The Greys cannot get you that far, if your mental make-up is not open to such cruelties. On the other hand, I think that Teimon is right when he states that the Mentals at this moment are victims. Therefore, the book would give the Mentals a chance to know what is really happening and to refuse to participate any longer. At least then, they can't say: "We didn't know".

You again have a point, Mira. The book could help people, involved in secret Grey projects, to come into the open. Or to resist and to refuse to participate any longer. And not to forget, the book would be a great support for abducted people. For ignorance is the main source of their fear. Ignorance is the source of all suffering and evil. Buddhism is very clear on that point. So if Mentals and Psy-mutants are not aware of the Grey threat they are involved in, they have to be warned. Don't you think?

Absolutely, Ramon. If the Greys have plans to repeat the disaster that we call World War Two, a second holocaust could be prevented.

Believe me, Mira, if I have a slight feeling that there is something true in all that Teimon suggested yesterday, I feel I am under a moral obligation to write the book. I couldn't live with the idea that I could have saved lives if I would only have brought this information in the open. I don't care about the critics.

While meditating, Ramon fills the mugs with the rest of the coffee.

If we only had some solid proof, Mira, something concrete. But maybe crucial information is still to come. So far we only have this and he shows Mira his notebook.

I fully understand, Ramon. But imagine that it would all be fantasy. It would still be a good story, don't you think?

That's also true, Mira. It is indeed a fascinating story. If this is just a product of your imagination, you chose the wrong job, you know. If you see what is shown on television and in movies, this story would be a revelation. Still, I find it hard to believe it is just fantasy. Don't forget the signals and the star map. If that could be proven, we would have something concrete. By the way, if I would write a book, how must I write this story?

I don't now, Ramon. But one thing I know for sure. I want to stay anonymous. It's already difficult enough to do my job. If I would be associated with alien contact, I might as well move to another country.

Ramon starts laughing. That's typically Mira.

So you have telepathical contact with aliens, you tell me everything, but for the rest, you don't want to be involved. Ha, ha, ha. Yes, yes. And the critics will be all over me! Ha, ha, ha. Yes, I completely understand.

Both start laughing.

I'm just joking, Mira. You are right. It has to be written with care. For the moment, let's just wait and see. Who knows what Teimon will reveal in the days to come?

You're right, Ramon. As far as I understand, there is still much more to come. And lest I forget, do you remember the symbol I saw a couple of weeks ago? A kind of "W" shape?

Ramon quickly leafs through his notes. Yes, on august 8th 2006, you saw this symbol for the first time. Have you seen it again?

Yes. Just before Teimon stopped transmitting, I saw it again. This symbol has something to do with the entrance of a gateway.

A gateway? What kind of gateway?

I don't know, Ramon. But it is a symbol, indicating the place of a gateway.

Maybe it has something to do with coordinates of the star map?

I really don't know, Ramon.

Odd. Okay, I make a note of it. You never know.

Sorry Ramon, but I really have to go now. It's again two o'clock.

And before Ramon can react, she leaves the room in a hurry.

Mira waves as she sees Ramon waving while she drives away.

Why is he doing that? And as quickly as possible she drives home. While driving she feels the energy rising upwards and she is relieved when she arrives safely at her little farm. She feels the urge of contact and runs to her bedroom.

As soon as she lies down on her bed, her room immediately transforms in purple lights and the purple crystal takes her away for a rendezvous in the depths of interstellar space.

1.159 **I salute you. You have to realize, Mira. This contact is real. The people of Earth are in great danger.**

- 23 -
13/9/2006

1.160 **The name of our planet is Ter I. We call ourselves the "Ter I". But you may call us Téry. It's easier for you to pronounce.**

1.161 **At this very moment, a lot of people of your planet are implanted with a chip. Not by the Greys but by your own people. But this is still done on a small scale.**

1.162 **In general the official motivation to support implanting people is for all kinds of security reasons. If this idea becomes generally accepted, implants will be used for the** whole world population. This must be prevented because it would bring humanity in great danger.

1.163 Implants are the perfect tool for the Greys to get ultimate control. The Greys want control and they themselves started implanting abductees long before this technology was developed by your own people. The Greys did the same with my people, the Téry.

1.164 Almost all the Téry have implants now and they are all Psy-mutants. They are logged on to the network of the Grey block culture that rules our population. With the help of implants, the Téry became the slaves of the Greys and now they help them to expand their power over the entire population.

1.165 We, the Sheyan, are not implanted and that saved us. But the people of your planet are at great risk now. The plans to implant the whole world population are ready. This must be prevented by all means. Because the Greys can do much more with the implants than the people of the organizations who promote this implant business.

1.166 These organizations promote implants for location and identification and sociological statistic studies of the behaviour of humanity. But the Greys can use these same implants to link the people in their Grey matrix. The control by the Greys on humanity grows every day. If all the people of the world would become implanted, that would mean the end of humanity as you know it.

After this information, it's silent. Teimon remembers the terrible things that happened during the time of the "Great Reversal". The whole population changed over night. Aodin helps Teimon to focus again and to continue the transfer of information.

1.167 The implanted chip makes brain manipulation possible. In underground labs the Greys test how people react to this chip and the possibilities to increase the extent of manipulation.

1.168 In the underground facilities lots of people are implanted by contract. Also above the ground, implanting becomes a regular practice and is done voluntarily. In the army, in key companies, in prisons and all kinds of secret organizations, implanting is done for security reasons.

134

Soldiers, agents and important citizens wear an implant for their own protection, to trace them if necessary.

1.169 The micro chip has been tested on animals first and then on humans in controlled experiments. But now the test period is over. The most powerful people of your world want to implant all humans. This also happened on Ter I. The people rebelled against this practice, but after great struggle they finally surrendered.

1.170 The implants of the Greys are much more advanced than the human implants. In general, the implants of the Greys are located near the nerves, directly connected with the reptile brain. It enables the Greys, to control all the organic functions and the hormone production of the glands. For that reason, it's life-threatening to remove these Grey implants surgically.

1.171 The humans who supported the idea to develop implants are Psy-mutants themselves. They put the Grey suggestions into practice and belong to the top of the secret order and they often have connections with the Sean Leyka sect. It is important to inform them about the Grey intentions.

Mira is shocked to hear that the Grey have already penetrated our world to that extent but she hasn't much time to think.

1.172 In the last decennia, the efficiency of the human implant has been improved dramatically. This chip can be used for location but also has an effect on the hormone production of the glands.

1.173 But at this moment, the human implants can't be used for suggestion, like the implants of the Greys. But that's only a matter of time. We salute you. We come back.

Gradually, Mira finds herself back in her room and exhausted she falls into a deep sleep.

Teimon felt he had to stop. He comes out of his trance and thinks with Aodin about what to do. Aodin knows that the transmission has to be done step by step. This enables Ramon to gradually develop a total picture. Ramon knows the structure of the Akasha. He can handle it.

In his mind, Aodin sees a cube frame, subdivided in eight parts in the three directions. It's a 3D schedule of all information models, developed by humanity on Earth. For Ramon, it was just a conceptual artwork.

It would have been easier to use a model of twelve by twelve, Aodin thinks. But you can't have everything.

They both feel each other's worries.

I hope that Ramon will start working on the book as soon as possible. There is no time to lose, thinks Teimon.

Yes, but Ramon will make the right decision, is the answer from Aodin with an assuring expression on his face.

Both monks bow for one another and in silence they leave the purple room. They realize that the fate of their people is in their hands. Nothing may go wrong or all the people of Geya will soon live in a world, worse than hell.

In the meantime, twelve flying discs screen constantly the whole region for traces of the Sheyan. Teimon and Aodin feel their presence. The time comes nearer that they will have to make use of their last resource to escape the Grey threat. It's inevitable.

Via a natural underground corridor both enter a simple room with seven beds. Five other brothers are in a trance state to lock the Greys out. Teimon and Aodin bring themselves in the same state of trance, unreachable for the Grey mental power.

Next night, they wake up exact on time, do their daily rituals and hurry to the purple room, after eating some black grains, mixed with a honey-like substance. The three moons are in conjunction and the purple glow of the matrix lightens the whole room.

At the same moment, Mira feels it's time to lie down. She brought a quick visit to Ramon to tell him everything, but could resist his offer to drink another mug of his magical fluid. Tomorrow, she said. I must go, Ramon. Now! Don't ask me why!

Shining purple colors surround her on her mental trip and Teimon starts where he left off yesterday.

1.174 **I salute you. The book is your only way out. Ramon will understand it. It's the only way to inform the people world wide in a short time. Important is the therapeutic part. The humanoids, the Mentals and the Psy-mutants have to be warned. It will reduce the influence of the Greys.**

It's quiet again. Mira feels the seriousness in Teimon's silence.

1.175 **It's vital to prohibit implants. The humans have to**

136

refuse implantation. If you people of Geya allow implants, the Grey control of the world population is near.

1.176 This must not happen. The full truth has to be told. The book has to be written. If the people are warned, they can make their own decisions.

1.177 This is especially true for Mentals and Psy-mutants. Once the book is in circulation, hopefully they will realize there is something seriously wrong.

1.178 The recruiting of new members for the Sean Leyka sect is perfectly managed. They first attract important and famous people, well known in society. If they participate, common people will easy be persuaded to join the group.

1.179 For the leaders of the sect, it's just an efficient way of recruiting people. It's a general management practice for every large company. They don't know that they play into the hands of the Greys. They must be warned.

For a while it is quiet again. Aodin senses that Mira still doesn't understand why they have chosen her to release this terrible information and he uses Teimon to clear up this matter.

1.180 You are not the first person we made contact with, Mira. We contacted several people but they interpreted the information wrongly. Their minds were already polluted with superstition.

1.181 They became part of a sect or a secret society and came under control of the Greys. Now, they spread information in favour of the Greys. We are glad we found you, Mira. Together with Ramon, you translate the information in the right way. The book is crucial. Ramon will understand. Tell him everything. Don't hold back. He will understand. We salute you.

Exhausted, Mira tunnels back into her own reality and immediately falls a sleep.

- 24 -
15/9/2006

After a day long of varnishing cubes, Ramon has to hear the next cruel information about the Grey conspiracy. How the Greys have planted a web of control in our civilization and have increased their control day by day. Especially the urge to write the book weighs heavy on his conscience.

We have to meditate about the book, Mira. I think I found a solution.

While he makes some fresh elixir of the coffee gods, he explains his ideas.

Since last year, I have been preparing an art exhibition. Believe it or not Mira, but I wanted to call the exhibition "Alien". The twelve sculptures I want to exhibit are impossible triangles. These sculptures have something alien, something unreal. The book would fit remarkably well in this concept. You have to admit, Mira. A book dictated by a representative of an alien civilization is definitely an "alien" concept. "It's too crazy", as my dear friend Chel, God bless his soul, would say. The funny thing is that impossible figures are not impossible at all. So it leaves the question open if the book is a true story or not. It's almost an unearthly coincidence that it all fits together. So I have decided to accept the challenge.

Mira starts to smile. So, you mean you will write the book?

Yes. I will prepare myself, Mira. But how I have to do this in such a short time, you'd better not ask. But there is always a way.

I'm convinced of that, Ramon. As you say, you can "make" time. This is your chance to prove it.

Yes Mira, make fun of me. But anyway, let's drink a cup of coffee on my decision! The mugs are filled and while Mira enjoys the hot life forces of the brown fluid, Ramon reads the notes.

I still have more questions than answers, Mira. Yesterday I have searched the web to find more about those implants. Do you know how many sites discuss this topic? I'm astonished that this subject hasn't become a topic in the mainstream press. The company Verichip even makes publicity about these high-tech devices. The salesmen's arguments to promote implants are divers. One of the most important arguments is indeed safety. The threat of terrorism, kidnapping of children… You know. But to be honest, I have my doubts about these arguments as a means of protection. If a kidnapper knows that a child is implanted.

138

What will he do, do you think?

You tell me, Ramon.

Remove the damn thing of course. The situation of victims of terrorist kidnapping would even be worse, Mira. They would be mutilated immediately. And not with the best tools!

Mira looks terrified.

My God, Ramon! I never thought about that. Think of the cruelty, these children and soldiers will be exposed to if they wear an implant! Mutilation! My God! The sheer idea gives me the creeps.

Indeed Mira, and if you know that 85% of child abuse happens within the family, these implants don't offer any protection at all. Plus, research has proven that cancer cells grow around implants in ten percent of the cases.

Clearly worried that some organizations want to reduce people to products with a barcode, Ramon cuts a few slices of fresh cake.

Hmmm, Ramon. Thanks. I fully agree, Ramon, but spare me the details, please. I feel sick if I think what could happen to those people. I would never want to wear a chip, Ramon. It's like a tattoo. It disrespects the human body. Our body is beautiful like it is. I even have problems with religious circumcision, you know.

I fully agree, Mira. But the idea that you can be traced wherever you are is so unethical. Because who guarantees me that these technologies would never be misused. Imagine what happens if these technologies are used in a dictatorial regime to enlarge the control over the population. If Hitler had this technology, he would definitely have used it. We don't need the Grey threat to see the danger. No, humanity must never accept this idea. Nobody has the right to connect the human body to a technological matrix. The movie, "The Matrix" is much more realistic than we think.

And another thing is that organized crime will find a way to make copies of implants. The problem would be the same as with false passports. The world of crime always finds a solution for these control systems. The makers of this technology are unintentional criminals.

Yes, Ramon but don't forget, some of them are Psy-mutants. Teimon said that they are already implanted by the Greys.

That's true, Mira, I had almost forgotten that Teimon brought that matter into the discussion. Let's see. Yes, here it is. He also stated that a lot of people who work in those secret projects are implanted. That's a possibility. If they work in secret projects, their bosses would want to know where they are and what they do after working hours. It would be an extra control, in case they plan to desert, to get out or to leak information. Mira, what a situation!

Ramon sees it's already eleven a clock.

A day is nothing, is it?

Yes Ramon, a day flies by. But Ramon, if you have questions, please do ask. I'm still in contact with the skull. But not for too long, please.

In no time Mira gets into contact with Teimon. As if he was waiting.

I wrote some questions down, Mira. Let's see… Maybe it is a strange question. But how do Greys die?

1.182 **When a Grey dies, he starts to leak through the skin. You can compare it with sweating. The Greys feed themselves via the skin. When they die, they sweat themselves to death and the body dries out.**

They leak and die? Really? A smile appears on Ramon's face.

Like having a flat tire?

Mira is not amused.

Sorry Mira, I'm joking, and quickly he looks at his notes. Tell me, Mira. Can you tell me how Aodin sends information while you have contact with Teimon?

1.183 **I get this information from the same source as Edgar Cayce, the Akasha. But Cayce used another part of his brain to get access to this information. Aodin only needs to send me certain mental links that bring me into contact with the subject.**

With a shy smile she tells Ramon that Aodin is not happy that she is so critical about all the information. Ramon laughs.

Ha, ha. I understand very well, Mira. I don't know any person who is that critical about the information he receives. And now they are stuck with you. Ha, ha.

1.184 **Ramon, there will be an information stop in a few days. It has to do with the coming transportation of Greys. If you**

140

want to ask questions, you have to do it now.

Sorry, Mira. Information stop? Eh… Okay. Explain me later. I have enough questions. Let me start with this question. Is there still physical evidence of the Ancestors of Teimon on Earth? For that could be concrete evidence.

1.185 **On Antarctica, an ancient base was found. Those who found this evidence confused this base with the legend of Atlantis. In ancient times, it was a base of Teimon's ancestors.**

1.186 **The land of Antarctica was chosen so that the lives of the people on Earth would not be disturbed. The climate of Antarctica in those days could be compared to the climate on our planet Ter I.**

Atlantis on the South Pole? Have you heard about this myth, Mira?

Never heard of it, Ramon.

I do know that researchers situated Atlantis almost everywhere on Earth. The latest theory was from Marcel Mestdagh. He situated the center of Atlantis in Sens, somewhere in France. Personally, I think he discovered an old center of a Celtic metropolis, forgotten in time. Let's see if you can locate that place on Google Earth!

In no time, Ramon activates Google Earth and Mira starts to look at the surface while Ramon makes a fresh coffee.

But her attention goes more to the other computer screen. She sees a picture of a person on the SETI site.

Is this somebody of the SETI project, Ramon?

Yes, Mira. I was checking whether there was something new on the website. Do you know that the big boss of SETI, Dr. Bernard M. Oliver, died recently?

As Ramon enters the WebCom with two full mugs, Mira looks with sadness to the picture of the man.

1.187 **He knew too much, Ramon. He could no longer stand the pressure of secrecy. It became too much for his heart and became fatal.**

Do you really mean that, Mira? Do you think he knew something of the signals?

Yes, Ramon. I think he did. And he had to be quiet about it.

If that's true, it must have been really hard for him. SETI is known for its openness. If alien signals were received, it was their policy to immediately publish the data. But until now, the signals were all unknown natural phenomena. But imagine that SETI recently received genuine alien signals and was forced to be silent about it. Then it must be hard for those people to keep quiet. You can compare it with an artist who's not allowed to exhibit his artwork. You know what I will do, Mira? I will visit all UFO sites I know. There has to be a rumor about the signals somewhere.

I feel sorry for this man, Ramon. He reminds me of a Tibetan proverb. "If you can't say things, it will affect your heart." With concern in her eyes, she looks at Ramon. I suddenly get the feeling that it is all true, Ramon. The signals, the star map. It is all true. It's no fantasy.

Ramon has never seen Mira so serious.

Let's not rush to conclusions, Mira. First things first. I have to study the information and check everything on the web. Then write the book. And then we will see. The information of Teimon can change the classic world-view for good. Do you remember that I wrote the book "The Galactic World-view"? It proves that I have no problem with a paradigm shift. But we have to keep a critical mind. It will not be easy to present evidence for the alien reality. And I don't see how Teimon can give us hard evidence of the star map, without factual proof of the signals. But proof or no proof, If I am to write the book, I have to write it as it happened. How else can I identify myself with the whole story that happened to us? Before I forget to ask, Mira, why is there an information stop?

It's to protect me, Ramon. It has to do with the transports by the Greys. Maybe, the Greys can trace me or something like that. I don't understand it very well. Do you remember in the beginning, that sometimes Teimon or Aodin suddenly broke contact because there was danger?

Yes, now you mention it, Mira. Was that because the Greyq sensed something?

Indeed, Ramon. But I want to go home now. It's late again and I have to go to work tomorrow. I hope you find something on the web. Good luck!

And she immediately looks for her coat in the kitchen.

142

Wait, Mira. You have to show me the spot of Atlantis!

She looks a few seconds at the Google Earth map and points to a spot.

There, Ramon. There I see a point of light.

Ramon zooms in on the spot. Only snow, as far as one can see.

So it must be beneath the ice, Mira. I don't understand. I don't see any human activity there. But just in case, he places a pin on the spot as a reminder.

And now I'm off, Ramon. I have to sleep.

Sure Mira, good night. If there is information, you know where to find me.

Absolutely, Ramon.

She hurries to her car and Ramon is alone again. He immediately starts surfing on the web for clues of Atlantis in connection with Antarctica. South Pole, Atlantis... Search! Dozens of links appear on the search engine. Most convincing is the story of professor Charles Hapgood. It was he who found the map of "Piri Re'is". This map of 1513 was the ultimate proof that the coastline of the South Pole was known a long time ago. The real coastline of Antarctica is mapped only recently. The coast is covered with a thick layer of snow and ice and this conceals the real coastline. This made the map of 1513 a subject of much criticism. How could they know the real coastline in those days? It had to be a fraud. But officially ruins of Atlantis were not found. They could be covered with ice of course. But that proves nothing. The legendary researcher Hapgood even had contact with Einstein and stated that the South Pole was more or less free of ice 6,000 years ago.

Because interesting links are often hidden far back in the Google list, Ramon keeps on browsing when suddenly a link attracts his attention. A video about the Nazis and the South Pole. What's that? It's late but his curiosity is stronger and with a few clicks, he activates the video. It appears to be a movie of a battle between the USA and the Nazis, a year after World War Two! It's all in Russian but the footage speaks for itself. The video has been aired on Russian state television and that makes Ramon wonder. Is there a disclosure going on in Russia or what? So the relation between Nazis and UFOs isn't as foolish as I thought. I have to look deeper into this tomorrow. It's late but intuitively,

Ramon checks the disclosure site of Steven Greer to see if there is something new. The link "new audio tapes" offers some new interviews. Ramon can't believe his ears: in an interview Steven Greer states SETI has received alien signals three times.

Ramon is in a state of shock when he reads this and he remembers what Mira told a few hours ago about the person that had died. That can't be a coincidence. The interview is dated June 1st, 2006. That's not that long ago. He has to listen and with some cold coffee, he listens to what the man has to say. Greer states that a very important member of SETI told him that they had received signals. Ramon is shocked but also relieved. For the first time in weeks, finally somebody is talking about signals. What a situation! Nazis and UFOs, signals from the cosmos, Mira's contact with Teimon! Ramon is too tired to think. Tomorrow is another day and he closes his WebCom. As he sees the time, he rushes to his bed. The crescent moon shines high in the sky, surrounded by thin clouds. While he falls asleep almost immediately, it's almost midday at the backside of the moon.

- 25 -
17/9/2006

With sleep in his eyes and a mug full of coffee at hand, Ramon activates the computer early in the morning. The happy tunes of his chat program announce a mail message from Mira. Quickly Ramon looks for his spectacles and reads the message:

I have seen ugly images of an underground base.

1.188 **In Europe and America, underground settlements and compounds have been built.**

1.189 **Missing people are brought there and dissident people of secret projects.**

1.190 **A lamp, invented to replace sunlight, prevent people to suffer from winter depression.**

1.191 **The start of these underground projects was during the Cold War. Have to work now. Greetings. Mira.**

Before Ramon is fully awake, he is back in the secret human nightmare. Underground compounds? Now what!? With a full pot of coffee and a cigarette, Ramon opens Google and types the

144

key words "Underground bases" and hits the Enter key. Again, he is very surprised to see the number of links and he starts surfing. It's difficult to make a choice but a link to a video of Phil Schneider catches his eye. It is a video from 1995. He was a geologist, involved in building secret underground facilities.
Let's see what this man has to tell.
He prepares something to eat and with a third dose of coffee, he listens to a lecture of this remarkable man. Ramon is exposed to a mix of excitement and cruel feelings while listening to the story of this man. The underground projects he was involved in were primarily for protection in case of a nuclear war. At least, in the beginning. But the size and complexity of these projects became larger, spreading throughout the whole region of the USA and in most countries of the world.
In the mid-nineties, Phil spread a wave of disbelieve and astonishment through the UFO community. Million of years old specimens of ancient civilizations, personal contact with grey aliens, living in underground bases, small parts of the Roswell crash, gigantic underground compounds and tunnels, financed with black money. Even a small war with aliens in one of the underground bases, located in Dulce. Too crazy to believe!
But taking into account what Teimon has revealed, Ramon is flabbergasted by the things this man has to tell. He admires the courage of this man to tell all these things in those days. Nothing is easier than to deny anything Phil Schneider was saying. But imagine for a moment, this was all true. Then he was a very courageous man. He died in mysterious circumstances, after a dozen attacks on his life. How lonely he must have been in the moments of his death!
But he believed in his mission and lost his life to bring the truth in the open about these secret underground compounds and their use. Who believed the rumors during World War Two about concentration camps? Nobody! Who could believe that these perfectly dressed, civilized people who called themselves Nazis and listened to classical music, gassed thousands of people every day, men, women and children, burned their bodies and mixed their ashes in the concrete to make roads? Such a thing could not exist. Not in a civilized country as Germany. Impossible! No! But it was true. Only a few brave people risked their lives to

bring the truth in the open.

Could a similar conspiracy against humanity be happening at this very moment? Perhaps not to kill people but to experiment on them or to use them as slaves to develop new technological weapons and other devices without having to worry about ethics and human rights? And in collaboration with an alien race of clones? Impossible? Well no. Ramon remembered a statement of his Wise Teacher: If there ever comes a time that people think that the cruelties of World War Two can not happen anymore, that very moment they are already happening again. He warned his students to be watchful. Phil Schneider could be a psychopath, a sociopath or an anarchist, but during his lecture and from the way he talked, he appeared to be none of this. On the contrary, he appeared to be an honest man, even a bit naive. Ramon doesn't know what to think of it all. It's all so far away, so difficult to control. The concentration camps were in the open. But how can you prove the existence of secret underground facilities?

On the other hand, it would be a perfect location to create modern concentration camps, especially in a time of airplanes and satellites. Would Hitler live in these times, he would make his concentration camps underground. Even in his days, underground bunkers and factories were built for his secret projects.

Ramon reads the text of Mira again. A lamp for underground settlements and mining facilities. Mira always knows something more than the websites. If these settlements exist, you only have to know who makes and buys these lamps. It is an easy way to figure out who is interested in underground facilities. Who thinks of those details? Mira of course! Berlin was the place of the beginning of underground projects in Europe. Hitler had indeed an underground base there. He and his wife and his close staff committed suicide in it. And after World War Two, the Cold War between the USA and Russia started. And what else are shelters against a nuclear threat than underground facilities? The Cold War is over. So what's the function of these underground compounds now? I doubt they just let them fall apart. A nasty feeling gives Ramon the creeps. Could it be that a big part of what Phil Schneider told is true? It's all a bit too much for

146

Ramon and with a mug of coffee he goes outside for a while to get some fresh air.

He shakes his head. And I have to write this down in a book? He thinks back on the stories his parents and grandfather told about the war. The worst thing was that you couldn't trust anybody. At the same time, everything was based on trust. The world was divided in two sides. Could this happen again? To get the cruel message out of his mind, he goes to his paint room. The cubes seem to wait for him. But the lecture of Phil has shocked Ramon. The rest of the day he spends alternatively in his WebCom and in his garden. Late in the evening he enjoys a sober meal and tries to relax a bit in the heat of the late summer night. The music of Studio Brussels vibrates through his WebCom and he admires the first stars popping up in the sky.

Humans don't realize that we all live on a gigantic space ship that we call "Earth". Together with the moon and the rest of the solar system, we travel all together in this mysterious place called the "universe". As he hears on the news that politicians discuss the head shawl of Muslim women, he shakes his head again. Can you believe this? Millions of people starve to death and these so called politicians argue about a piece of cotton? They should be ashamed of themselves. When will they ever learn? Ramon remembers an Islam scholar from Cairo. He said that if people would become holy because they pray five times a day to their God, all the oil towers would be holy too, explaining to us that it's not the visual and symbolic aspect of a religion that makes a person holy, but the inner intentions. All the rest is tradition. But prohibiting the tradition of other cultures is the other extreme.

Jesus said a similar thing against the Pharisee who was praying in the open where everybody could see him. It is the inner state of mind that makes you holy. So symbols have no meaning on itself. A shawl is just a piece of cotton. It's a fashion, a custom. Nothing more. But it is an absurd kind of racism to turn wearing shawls into a problem. Some people are so narrow-minded these days. Haven't they learned anything from recent history? And meanwhile, secret organizations do business with alien clones. And why? For technology. For power and control!

It is the same old song over again. Ramon meditates for hours about the ins and outs of the book. The moon shines high in the sky as Ramon decides to go to bed.

Concerned about all the information he had to digest in the past weeks, he falls asleep.

- 26 -
27/5/2007

I need a shave, thinks Ramon when he sees his reflection in the mirror, trying to wake up, in his hands a mug full of warm brown morning glory. He activates his WebCom, switches on the radio and with some slices of bread and cheese he takes a seat in front of the screens. He scrolls with the mouse through the explorer of one screen and with the other mouse he opens the file "The Alien Code 06". Almost hundred pages! A good start, he thinks while searching in the long list of the UFO favorites folder of the internet browser on the other screen.

He remembers vaguely all the videos he saw last year and opens the Underground folder. He looks at all the links he collected about underground facilities. From a sociological point of view, it is a schizophrenic situation. The web is "the place to be", for this kind of information. But it is also the place of information pollution. All kinds of rumors about almost anything can be found on the web. But eventually, it is all just a virtual happening. Visitors on these sites are bombarded with all kinds of complot theories. Ramon has the strong impression that a lot of complot websites have become a profitable business. The only information Ramon wants to take seriously is the information of Teimon. At least he is sure that his information is not polluted or part of a hidden agenda.

With a click he opens the file of Richard Sauder, author of several books. Of all the links that Ramon found, he was the most credible person. He stressed the context of building these bases, namely the Cold War. Everybody over fifty must remember the building of concrete cellars in houses. It was a real rage in those days. In Switzerland, every new house had to have an atomic-proof cellar. But in general, all over the world nations built underground facilities for the political elite in case of a

148

nuclear war.

But after the nuclear threat, the building of underground facilities didn't stop. But has anybody ever seen pictures or drawings of these compounds? Just to have an idea of these compounds? Of course not. They are secret. Every body could see how President Bush was brought to an underground base during the 9/11 drama. But how big are these places? How many are there? Nobody knows except the military. Phil Schneider knew of some 150 underground bases in the USA alone. It is very likely that the USA spend a lot of money on these underground bases. The USA would be the first target in case of a nuclear war.

Steven Greer talked in front of the world press about secret projects during his introduction of the Disclosure Project in 2001. He pointed to president Eisenhower's farewell address to the nation in January 1961. The president told the nation about the danger of the ever growing power of the military industrial complex and that it wasn't in the best hands.

Ramon remembers the famous proverb of the great philosopher Heraclites: "War is the father of all things". In a way he was right. The most revolutionary inventions were developed in times of war. From the crossbow to the famous Stealth airplanes.

Take for instance the development of the atom bomb. During sixteen years a gigantic industrial complex had developed in secrecy, to make this most destructive bomb of all bombs. All in absolute secrecy. And that was sixty years ago. So, secret underground bases are not an impossibility. It is even very possible.

The development of the Apollo rocket during the moon race was a perfect demonstration of what the Cold War could bring us. History teaches that the world is always in a state of cold war between wars. The armies of the different nations are in a constant race to stay on top of one another. History teaches us that when a country becomes technologically inferior, sooner or later, he finds the enemy in his backyard. Think about what China did with Tibet or Germany with the countries of Western Europe. Or what the European countries did in Africa. Colonialism in general is the proof that war is never over. Even if there is no war. The technology keeps evolving and so the threat is always there.

Technologically, the USA have become a superpower. We only have to think back on the Gulf War and the recent war in Iraq. They were able to determine exactly how many days the war would take to do the job. Can you think of a better public demonstration to show your power? But don't underestimate the strength of China, Russia or Japan, to name a few.

But technological power is not enough to control a population, especially not after or in between wars. Could implants play a role to control the people better? Could implants become the next stage in mass manipulation? The next thing after the radio and the TV? Whatever the Greys want with the implants, the Warriors in the different countries of the world have their own agenda to get more control over their human territory. They probably need the implants so that the Illuminati can play their own games with more control than ever in human history. Maybe the Illuminati and the Warriors don't know that they play in the hands of the Greys. But that doesn't take away the fact that the Greys have become so dangerous by the desire of a small elite to get world power.

Ramon fills his mug once more. What a world! So, these underground facilities exist. That's for sure. But what is happening down there? Who is cleaning the rooms? Who is keeping the whole machinery rolling? They must need a lot of people to do that. And it must cost tons of money to keep these places livable, because there are no slaves anymore. Or am I wrong?

The Nazis had enough slaves. Hundreds of thousands of Jews had to work themselves to death. Agitated by all this, Ramon starts to clean the kitchen. The writing of the book doesn't leave much time to do anything else. After a few hours, everything looks decent again. As the alarm of his mobile goes of he runs to the WebCom to tape Days of our Lives. He wonders whether the script writers of that soap are familiar with the UFO files. It wouldn't surprise him a bit. Implants controlled by satellites and aliens who appear to be genetically manipulated humans. It can't be a coincidence.

Anyhow, he has to start working again. Moments later, Ramon's fingers fly over the keyboard with Studio Brussels in the background. The Foo Fighters have a new hit. Wonderful to be young in these times. Stockhausen and Philip Glass must have been surprised to see they had such an influence on the younger generation of musicians. Hours pass by and night falls.

Suddenly, Ramon hears somebody calling from the kitchen.

Ramon... Are you there? A beautiful young lady enters the WebCom.

Of course I'm here. Joy, what a surprise! I didn't expect you this late.

I always have volleyball training on Tuesdays, Ramon. You forget everything, don't you! With a smile she takes a seat behind the free computer. While she prints a document for school, she sees the file "The Alien Code 06" on the screen.

Are you making progress with the book, Ramon?

Oh yes Joy, every day a bit, you know. But it's still a long way to go.

Ramon is glad to see her and makes her a fresh mug of coffee. She never drinks coffee, but the coffee of Ramon, she can't refuse. For a while, Ramon forgets his problems. Joy saw the WebCom growing from one small computer to a multimedia studio. When she was young, Ramon noticed she had a very exceptional talent for strategic and IQ games. When she was ten years old, she already won every time at Invador of the Kubido game, the art game that Ramon designed at the end of last century. While Ramon cuts some fresh cake and tries to be a good host, Joy plays FreeCell, downloads at the same time some mp3's and tells Ramon about the examinations. With a hot mug in their hands, both talk as if they are alone in the world. Joy is of course curious about the book, especially since she is not allowed to read it. It's the first time Ramon seems to have a secret for her.

Tell me Ramon, how are the aliens doing in your book?

Oh, not bad, Ramon smiles. I'm still winning. I'm at page 150.

That many? I don't get it, Ramon. Who on earth writes a book about aliens? Can you earn any money with it?

Ramon laughs again. That's a good question, Joy. I hope I will. It depends how many people will buy it.

Well yes. But why are you writing a book when you don't know whether it is going to sell?

That's a difficult question, Joy. I have been asking myself that question all my life. I never earned much with my art either. But I do it because... I like to do it. I'm not in it for the money, you know.

Joy looks a bit helpless. Ramon sees the question marks on her forehead.

You know Joy, it was not my idea. I have to write the book.

Do you mean you have to write the book for somebody?

Yes, you can put it that way, yes.

Ah, but then you do it for an employer? But, then he has to pay you!

Ramon smiles. That could be, but I think it will not be easy for him to do that.

Joy is puzzled by that answer. But she has known Ramon for so long. He never does anything normal.

I will never understand you, Ramon. And she invites him to play a computer game.

Ha, ha. That makes two of us, Joy, and joking about old memories Ramon loses one game after the other. Joy leaves in a hurry to study and Ramon waves as she walks away.

I will come back tomorrow to get the videos, Ramon. Don't forget the movie tonight!

No, no, I won't forget. Good luck with your examination!

She waves once more and gone she is.

Back in his WebCom, he sees the empty mugs and the rest of the cake as silent witnesses of her unexpected visit. Where is the time she could hardly reach the keyboard? In no time she became a grown up, beautiful, young lady.

Before you know you become old and worn, my grandfather used to say. He was right. Come on, Ramon. Back to work. And with new courage Ramon starts to write again.

- 27 -
20/9/2006

The Skype phone rings through the WebCom and with tears in his eyes of cutting onions Ramon tries to find the mouse. Always when I'm busy, he thinks while he clicks on the green icon. Mira?

Can I come? Urgent!

At ten a clock in the morning? That's early! It's not her custom. After some rumbling sounds to connect the microphone, the confused voice of Mira sounds through the speakers.

Ramon... They were here!

What do you mean, Mira? Who are "they"?

The Greys, Ramon, the Greys were here.

The Greys? asks Ramon with growing concern.

Yes Ramon, the Greys were here. I was doing my usual work, you know... yesterday night... my pro bono work. And while I was working, I suddenly felt their presence. My clients didn't notice anything, but I saw them clearly. There were two small and one big Grey.

Calm down, Mira. Tell me everything step by step. But please, don't tell me they abducted you.

No, no. Listen. They just stood there and they were watching me. They observed what I was doing. It was as if they wanted to help me. In my thoughts, I heard them thinking. They made it clear to me that I would have better results if I would do it their way. Of course I let them know that I was not interested and neglected them completely. And the large Grey told me something. It was all telepathically. But it was totally different than with Teimon. You never believe what he told me, Ramon.

I'm listening, Mira.

1.192 **We want integration, orientation, adjustment, desire, consciousness and procreation.**

And then they were gone.

Gone? Just like that, Mira?

Yes. Just like that. Well... not really. I will explain it to you later. But afterwards, I felt really sick, no, not sick but dislocated.

Listen, Mira. Ramon is worried. Come over as soon as you can. Then we can talk it over. Just think for a moment, these are the guys who fell with their bottoms on a cactus!

Ha, ha, ha, don't worry, Ramon, I didn't have a problem with the fact that they were here.

But why then are you so upset, Mira?

Well, they appeared while I was working with people. Imagine, somebody would have noticed!

Ramon is relieved. A typical reaction by Mira.

I thought they had done something to you. But I understand. They have clearly no manners.

Don't make fun of the whole situation, Ramon. But I have to go. I have to go to work and I have visitors programmed. See you later. I will be fine. I will tell you the rest later.

The rest? Okay Mira, and if possible… stay away from the Greys if you can. Please?

But Mira has already disconnected. Ramon is suddenly awake. Luckily he has the book Abductions by John Mack freshly in his memory. I have to look at my notes of the book, before Mira comes. But now, back to the days of my own life. In a hurry, he cuts the rest of the vegetables and makes a pot extra strong coffee. The smell of the soup and the coffee gives Ramon the courage to start varnishing. As a robot, he starts the boring but necessary work. While painting, he suddenly remembers that Teimon warned us that the Greys would transport something. The reason why Teimon wanted an information stop was to protect Mira. So this visit of the Greys is no accident.

I hope the Greys don't suspect Mira is in contact with Teimon. It would be dangerous for her if the Greys would find out that Mira has contact with their greatest enemies. Because the Greys will do everything in their power to prevent that their true identity will be revealed. I wish my Wise Teacher was still alive. I really could use some good advice. Well then, I have to do it on my own. Luckily, the cubes are almost finished. As soon as I have done that job, I will start with the book.

Ramon works all through the day with an uneasy feeling. John Mack must have known that feeling to. Reading about abductions is one thing. But being confronted with it is another pair of shoes. During the drying periods, Ramon reads one article after the other about abductions. It's late when he finishes his daily job. Again eight hundred cubes. With a fresh cup of coffee, he meditates about everything he has read that day.

What annoys him the most is the unscientific discussion of the whole abduction matter. The discussion places two different approaches in a conflict model. The believers and the non-believers. But how can scientists use the word "believe" in a scientific discussion? This discussion seems to be held in a middle age fashion. In the middle ages, the Christian elite called

154

the non-Christians the heathens. Everybody who questioned the authority of the Christian church and its dogmas risked his neck. During the period of the inquisition, this contrast of opinions became a real danger for the heathens. How many scientists were killed for their scientific opinion? Take Pico Della Mirandello, Copernicus or Galileo Galileo. Some people were burned in public, just because they were non-believers. And every believer had to watch these severe persecutions. Even children!

Lucky for us, times have changed. In the case of abductions, there is only one thing "real" scientists can do. Study the cases of abduction. If a scientific elite judges from a theoretical point of view, without serious study, without taking into account the studies of ufologists about abduction cases, they make a serious scientific mistake, comparable with the church in the middle ages. Somebody who defends the alien hypothesis is judged before he can make a point.

But what can you do? Abductees often tell that they have telepathic contact with those aliens. And telepathy is scientifically non-existing. Parapsychology is not considered a science. If it was an official science, parapsychology would be on the schedule of every university. So, a scientific discussion about telepathy is rejected from the beginning. If telepathy doesn't exist, how can you have telepathic contact with aliens? So, if you are interested in parapsychology or in the alien hypothesis, you automatically become a "believer" because you study a topic that doesn't exist in science. And what science doesn't accept as real doesn't exist. End of discussion. Ramon can not comprehend that the majority of the scientists seem to forget that this is the same attitude as the theologians had in the middle ages.

In Holland there is much less of this narrow minded attitude towards paranormal phenomena. Professor Van Praag was convinced that most paranormal phenomena had to do with the difference between the left and right hemisphere of the brain. Further investigation of the communication between these two sides of the brain would bring light to the "how" and "what" of paranormal abilities. Basically, it's just a lack of knowledge that we can't understand telepathy and clairvoyance. Van Praag went as far as to announce the end of the parapsychology in 1986. And he had a good reason to do this. Per definition, parapsychology is the study of the confines of psychology, making it a specialization within regular psychology. Van Praag was very happy to announce that paranormal phenomena could soon become accepted as normal real phenomena. He also stated that the study of the right and left hemisphere of the brain would change psychology and pedagogy in the twenty-first century fundamentally. Yes, Ramon's professor of parapsychology was a real enfant terrible in the scientific community.

While thinking, Ramon remembers suddenly a discussion with Professor Tenhaeff. He was the predecessor of Van Praag. Ramon remembers an accidental meeting with him in the train station of Utrecht. The professor had to laugh when he saw this hippy student walking towards him. Eighty three years of age he was at that time, but still very clear minded. Ramon had a small discussion with him and the topic of ufology came up.

What are modern parapsychologists doing, Ramon? What have UFOs to do with parapsychology? UFOs are physical phenomena of unknown origin. They are not psychological phenomena. They are objects like air planes or boll lightning or something alike. So how could they be paranormal? Come on, Ramon. This is really proof of a low level of methodological insight!

Ramon agreed completely. Tenhaeff was really angry about this mix-up. As if parapsychology was a container for all the unexplained. UFOs could be a subject for paraphysics as long as they were not explained. But not for parapsychology.

But since Mira was confronted with alien contact, Ramon had to accept that the abduction phenomenon belongs to parapsychology as well as paraphysics. The UFOs and implants that the Greys use belong to paraphysics. The telepathic communication and suggestion belongs to parapsychology. But if you can use technical devices to improve telepathy it becomes para-psycho-physics. A kind of mix or fusion of the two specializations.

Professor Van Praag was convinced that advanced cultures could maybe develop telepathy and other paranormal abilities to replace technology. He stated that all the communication devices would once become obsolete because humanity would evolve

156

and paranormal abilities would gradually become the rule and not the exception. And probably, the Téry could be such a culture. The sound of Skype brings Ramon back to reality. It's a message of Mira!

Are you there?

Ramon replies: The coffee is ready.

I'm coming now.

Mira jumps in her car and drives to Ramon who cleans the kitchen in a hurry. As the aroma of the coffee tickles his nose, Mira enters the kitchen.

Oh great, Ramon. I see the coffee is ready. Nervously she takes a seat while she remembers the freaky confrontation with the Greys.

Just in time, Mira. As promised.

The mugs are filled and like a Japanese tea ceremony Ramon serves the coffee.

Ramon looks into her eyes.

So, now tell me everything, Mira? And also the rest?

Sitting in her typical posture, a cigarette in one hand and a mug of coffee in the other, Mira tells him everything she experienced and saw in the underground facilities of the Greys last night. Ramon listens with growing concern to her story while making notes. After she told him the whole story, she wonders how Ramon will react.

I was there, Ramon. And that person lying there couldn't do anything.

Ramon is stunned but also very worried. Contact with Greys is very dangerous. Especially if you take into consideration everything Teimon told about them. But he doesn't want to upset Mira, so he reads his notes again and starts asking questions.

If I understand you well, Mira, you say you first had telepathic contact with the large Grey. And then, you took control over him and … you could follow him? And in this way, you could enter one of the underground facilities. Am I correct?

Yes Ramon, that's the way it happened.

But Mira, you know how dangerous these Greys are!

I know, Ramon, but what can you do? Suddenly, they were there. I didn't invite them, you know. So what could I do? But I thought by myself, whatever you do with other people, that's your business. But you won't do that with me! When the tall Grey realized that he had no power over me, he wanted to get away. But then I seized the opportunity and took control of him.

Mira, Mira. So, in a way, I can conclude that you abducted a Grey! Both start laughing.

Well yes, Ramon. You could put it that way.

Ramon shakes his head. It becomes clear to him that one can better not underestimate the witches of today. They are the real Hells Angels!

I admire you, Mira. You're one of a kind.

Mira looks very proud when she hears him saying that.

What can I say, Mira. I'm glad that everything turned out well. But, tell me, those Greys behaved very strange when you took control. What do you think happened?

It was so alien, Ramon. It was as if he lost all structure in his body. His head, arms and legs lost their strength. I think they planned to abduct me, Ramon. But I knew that the whole experience was mental. I knew I was at home and in the same time mentally travelling with them.

Like a kind of out of the body experience?

Well yes. I suppose so!

Ramon feels that Mira enjoys her victory over the Greys.

So, if I understand you well, you took control over their block?

Yes, Ramon. And as soon they realized that, they tried to escape. And then, I seized the opportunity and followed them mentally. And before I knew, I was in their underground shelter.

Wow, Mira. I need some time to absorb this. And first of all I have to eat something. Would you like some soup? Freshly made!

Oh yes please, Ramon. I haven't eaten yet.

Then let's eat something first.

In no time, Ramon serves the soup and they both enjoy the first and oldest medicine in the world. Afterwards they enjoy the late summer evening.

Would you like a glass of wine, Ramon? A colleague gave me a bottle of red wine. The bottle is in the car, ready to be consumed.

Mira doesn't have to say that twice and a few moments later both enjoy a good glass of red wine with some bread and cheese. When the bottle is empty, the night falls over Ramon's village.

158

I still have some questions about your underground experience, Mira. Are you in the mood?

Why not, Ramon. If you make some coffee?

It only takes a word, and in a hurry Ramon goes through his daily ritual. With a mug in her hands, she's ready to answer some questions.

You want to know how this eye manipulation works, don't you, Ramon?

Well yes. How do you know? He sees Mira is smiling.

Never mind, Ramon. Listen. If the Greys put these lens shaped tools under your eyelids, you are completely disconnected from the world. You really enter a virtual reality. You don't have a clue where you are. And then you see all the flashes of light coming to you. You don't see real images, only light patterns. But these flashes of light have an influence on your brain, especially on the reptile part.

Interesting. You also told me that you heard questions in your mind. What kind of questions do you mean?

Well... for example: What are you doing on this planet? Isn't everything meaningless? Don't you think the world is bad? Why do people pollute the planet? That kind of questions.

Remarkable! Abductees tell the same things. There are differences but in general, this is a common practice. And what happened after the questions?

There was something really funny. Suddenly, I heard strange sounds. Like the sound of birds. You know, a combination of Donald Duck and the sound of swallows.

Mira starts laughing when she sees the face of Ramon. Yes, sorry Ramon, but I can't compare it with anything else.

Ramon starts giggling. Grey Donald Ducks? Now what?!

Ha, ha. I know it sounds silly. But it sounds better than you think. She bursts out with laughter as she sees his face. While the rest of the village is sleeping, they laugh with the whole situation. Tears fall on Ramon's notes.

Jesus, Mira. You can make somebody laugh. I hope the readers can laugh with it to, you know. Greys with the sound of Woody Woodpecker?

Ha, ha, ha. Mira has to stand straight of laughter. Ha, ha, ha. Laughing is good for the spirit, Ramon.

That's a fact, Mira. Ha, ha, ha.

Minutes later they have calmed down.

My God, Mira. My stomach still hurts. Ha, ha. Do you know that the "ha-ha" sound is more powerful than the "Ohm" sound? It simulates the seventh chakra.

I believe you, Ramon. My head is relieved of all pressure.

But I have to go now, Ramon and relieved that she told him the whole story, she goes to her car as she suddenly remembers something she saw on television.

Ramon, do you remember the proverbs that the unknown source gave me in the beginning.

Yes Mira, I do remember, as if it were yesterday.

Well, some shamanistic cultures in South America worship the green frog when their tribe is in danger. I don't know, but maybe it is an explanation.

It could be, Mira. If you take Teimon's message seriously, the whole world is in danger. But I don't think, it explains everything of the proverb. But it is a start. Thanks.

Mira, promise me to stay away from the Greys. Don't underestimate the power of their bock culture. But I think you did a brave thing, Mira. You have proven that the Greys can be overpowered. They are not gods. They have their weak spots and humans can defend themselves against them.

Thanks, Ramon. But I have to confess something. I couldn't do it earlier. I had already several visits of these Greys.

What? But Mira? Why didn't you tell me?

I didn't, dear Ramon. I thought, if I just neglect them, they will eventually go away. But they came back. Every time I was doing my pro bono activities. There were always two of them, but yesterday there were three. But now that I have abducted one of them, I think they will stay away. The transportations are done, Ramon.

Before Ramon can react, she drives away.

Mira, Mira. So that's probably the reason why Teimon sometimes breaks contact. As soon as he detects Greys in Mira's mental state, he disconnects! Because if the Greys suspect that Mira has contact with the Sheyan, they will do everything they can to use Mira to locate Teimon and Aodin. I hope the Greys will not be able to break Mira. For that would be a disaster.

160

Until late into the night, Ramon surfs on the web to read as much he can about recent abduction cases. In America, two million people suffer form abduction related mental disorders. It has already an official name. Abduction syndrome. As Ramon falls asleep, Mira has contact again.

- 28 -
20/9/2006

Teimon and Aodin look at each other. This is the last evening before they have to hide in the depth of their own mind. The Greys have come dangerously close to their hiding place and they have to block all external output. It is the only way. The Sheyan are happy that Mira kept the Greys at a distance when they came to visit her.

Gracefully, they enter the purple room. Teimon sits down by the shining purple star matrix. The two small moons align with the big moon and like a cosmic mandala they shine together. Their collective power sweeps the waves of the sea high against the rocky coast. The room glows in purple light. Teimon lies down and concentrates on the matrix. Meanwhile, Aodin keeps an eye on him.

Mira senses contact and immediately goes to her garret to be ready for the next information. She knows that she would get the last instructions before the information stop. Easily she follows the tunnel of the crystal skull and merges with the mind of Teimon.

I salute you, Mira. The Greys couldn't break you. Thank you for your courage. This is the last information we send before we have to silence our thoughts.

1.193 **The location of the crystal skull must never be revealed.**

1.194 **The Greys are not able to locate this skull on their own. They know that signals have been sent. They know that contact has been made with somebody who can reveal their identity. But they don't know who that somebody is.**

1.195 **The humans on Earth don't know who the Greys are. The Mentals and the Psy-mutants only know what the Greys** told them. Only the humanoids know of our existence but they think that the Greys still work for us. They don't see the danger.

1.196 **The Mentals and the Psy-mutants are strategically misinformed with lies. Ramon has to study the similarities of the Grey disinformation spread by their abductees and the Grey strategy will be unravelled. Compare everything you read with my information and you will see the pattern in their lies and in the disinformation spread via the media.**

1.197 **From the first contact on the Greys used images of fear about the future. Because of the Grey technological advantage and mental abilities, the government and the military that are aware of the alien presence, believed in general what the Greys say. Call them the "Initiated". But not every Initiated believes their stories.**

1.198 **Some initiated people are Mentals or even Psy-mutants. They are in general very motivated and have a lot of influence on the political leaders. The leaders of the greatest world powers on Earth fear for an apocalyptic picture of the near future. They themselves believe it is true. Some high placed Psy-mutants play a role in all of this.**

1.199 **The Greys use the superstition of existing religions. Belief in end times with a great fight between good and evil is common to all great religions. The Sean Leyka sect has to play that card. They spread the message that these prophecies will happen very soon. But that isn't the case at all. They just spread fear and fear plays into the hands of the Greys.**

1.200 **Remind Ramon that there are no different timelines, existing in the same time. There is only one reality. There is no time travel. It is an illusion, produced by the rational mind. The Greys use this illusion for a specific purpose. Ramon will figure it out.**

1.201 **The future is open. The future doesn't exist like the now-time. Only when the future passes the now-time, it will become the reality because it happens. Everything that happens, happens in the now time. After it happened, it will become the only real past. The past is closed.**

1.202 **Study all the stories of the Greys. Compare all these**

162

stories with what I told you and you will find out how the strategy of the Greys works.

For a moment, it's quiet. Teimon and Aodin look at one another and decide to close the session. The most important information has been sent, for the time being.

1.203 **We now have to rest in the highest. The transport of the Greys will start now. Look at the moon.**

1.204 **Mira, beware of the Greys. We will come back as soon as it is safe. We salute you.**

Mira comes back to her own reality and falls asleep immediately. Teimon and Aodin silently leave the purple room. The last glimpse of the moon conjunction fades away. They don't return to their usual room but follow a labyrinth of corridors until they arrive at a dark blue room. They enter it and see their five brothers are already in a deep trance. Without noise they lie down on their right side and in their minds they focus on a complex mandala. They focus on the centre and concentric rings start to move making the most beautiful patterns. Both feel the energy rising to the top of their head and a few minutes later, it looks as if they are in another world, mentally unreachable for the Greys. Their breathing is almost completely silent and their body temperature is very low. Only a smile on their faces indicates they are alive.

Meanwhile, silver lentil-shaped spaceships hang above their shelter. The instruments do not register any brain activity. The Grey minds can't sense any mental activity. The Sheyan went in hiding just in time. For the moment the Sheyan are safe. As the discs leave, the seven bodies are hidden in a mystical silence.

- 29 -
20/9/2006

The temperature at the back side of the moon is now at its peak and strange flashes of lightning appear high in the thin atmosphere of the moon. Twelve glowing alien discs come from different directions and move with incredible speed to a tower, rising high in the dark night sky on the front side of the moon. Gradually they create a large circle around the tower. Suddenly, with a powerful flash, a light beam comes out of the tower, directed to the constellation of Orion. Above the old base, once used by the ancestors of the Téry for mining and transport, the twelve discs start to pulsate. Out of nothing, a transparent object out of the direction of Orion approaches the centre of the circle of lights. As it reaches the middle, the transparent object lights up and a gigantic disc becomes visible, high above the surreal landscape of the moon that only the astronauts of the Apollo project saw with their own eyes.

The craft emits yellow orange light pulses. Suddenly the formation of discs moves away at high speed and disappears behind the horizon. They halt above a gigantic dome building at the backside of the moon. The roof reflects the sunlight of the midday sun on the moon. The dome is built over a perfectly round crater. The Grey colony on the moon prepares everything to welcome the leader of their bock culture. The top of the dome opens and the large disc descends through the opening into the depth of the moon followed by the twelve smaller metallic turquoise-colored crafts. They look like abstract insects, with a dark-glasslike cockpit. In a gigantic underground amphitheatre, the large craft comes to a stop above a circular platform, followed by the twelve smaller crafts. They stop and float simultaneously to the twelve corners of the platform, marked by symbols in an unknown language. Multiple symbols decorate the platform which seems to be made in one piece. Twelve gates open slowly and thousands of Greys enter the hall in formation.

Each group has a leader, walking in front of the group. The twelve Grey blocks slowly move to the central platform to welcome their great leader. They seem to know exactly how to walk. It looks like a military parade. Strange electronic sounds vibrate through the hall until the twelve groups come simultaneously at rest when their leaders reach the platform. Suddenly, a sharp light beam from under the central craft illuminates the platform. Thirteen figures appear in the beam of light. The one in the middle is the Central Grey, surrounded by twelve others, his first biological copies.

They look bigger than the Greys of the moon colony. They also have bigger skulls. They are the product of a new evolution in the clone technique. The twelve walk to their twelve counterparts

164

who are responsible for the different projects on the moon. Only one Grey remains in the center, silently. Everybody present looks with admiration to the Central Grey. The twelve look deep into the eyes of the leaders of the twelve blocks and telepathically they interchange information. The new strategies are downloaded and the information flows telepathically to everybody present in the hall. In no time, all the Greys know exactly what their task is for the coming period.

Soon after, they collectively make a bird-like sound, resounding louder and louder in the dome. It is as if they try to... sing. As if they are saying all together that the downloading has been a success. When the sound comes to a climax, the "Central" makes a sign and immediately there is a complete silence. A group of human-like individuals enters through one of the twelve gates. There is no expression on their faces. They all wear a basket with slices of red fruit. It looks like slices of a cactus. At the head of the group walks a young girl. She has human as well as Grey features. As if in a hypnotic state of mind, she walks up to the leader of the block culture. She doesn't dare to look at him and kneels. She gives him a piece of fruit. For a split second, she looks into his eyes and sees the reflection of herself in his big dark artificially implanted viewers. Afraid, she looks away and walks around the platform to give a piece of fruit to the twenty four commanders of the Grey colony. The other hybrid people spread to the different Grey blocks and every Grey gets a small piece of the forbidden fruit.

When everybody present has a piece, the hybrids withdraw from the hall like a group of freaks. All the Greys wait in silence. The leader rubs this piece of fruit over his long arms. It is stock-still in the dome. He seems to go into a kind of ecstasy and his body trembles all over. A sharp sound comes out of his hardly visible mouth, like the sound of a swarm of swallows. At that moment, the rest of the Greys rub the juice over their arms and they all go into in the same ecstatic state. They start to make the same peculiar sound and some of them start to... How to describe it? To laugh? In this bizarre collective state of mind, sounds in the back ground become louder and vibrate throughout the hall. Collectively, the Greys start to move their bodies and with elegant, jumpy kind of moves, they start to dance. In the mean

165

time, the leader steps with his block of twelve Greys to the same gate through which the humans left. Outside, dozens of discs fly around to protect the dome. No intruder will escape their detection system.

The sun burns high in the dark blue grey sky and the surface temperature is unbearable. Only at the horizon, thin fog-like clouds rise out of some deep craters to evaporate immediately in the sunlight and mix with the thin atmosphere of the moon. In the distance, a gigantic tower rises hundreds of meters above the grey surface of the moon and dominates the whole view. Enormous cigar shaped container ships are locked to an alien-looking disc shaped shed. Almost automatically, hundreds of containers float towards the shed and a gigantic lift brings them down to an underground laboratory. The transportation is a success. The Greys can speed up the production of clones. The great day comes nearer. The day that the Greys will succeed in their intention to recreate the planet Earth and to make it their own home.

- 30 -
23/9/2006

A few days pass by. Mira has given Ramon the latest information and now she is glad to be on her own for a while. Ramon spends all his free time on the cube job and on the study of every UFO case on the web. He takes the request of Teimon very seriously. His skeptical mind screens a lot of sites. He is surprised at his ignorance of some very important UFO events. For example the UFO observation above Los Angeles in 1942. He had seen a picture of this event but he thought that it was a picture of a movie.

But on the site of Rense much more background information of this historical event was given. Pearl Harbor happened two weeks before and brought the USA into World War Two. Everybody knows that, but this bizarre UFO encounter on 25 February 1942, five years before Roswell, is not mentioned in history books. UFO skeptics often say: Why do UFOs never show up in public. Well, it looked as if a genuine battle was

166

going on that night above Los Angeles. A battle against an unknown flying object, moving slowly above the city. And this thing was not of earthly origin. It was shot hundred of times from all sides, from the ground with anti-aircraft missiles and from the air. But the object had no problem whatsoever with the military reaction and just continued slowly its path, disappearing eventually to an unknown location. The guns had all the time to hit the thing, but they had no effect whatsoever. The message to the army must have been clear: We are technologically superior. By reading this, Ramon starts to understand why so many UFO communities exist in California. That region has a collective memory of that event. Thousands of people saw this battle and talked about it with their friends and children.

But also another article catches his attention. It states, President Eisenhower had a meeting with a small group of aliens in 1954. Ramon found a small video of Steve Wendell. He talked about this historic event. What surprised Ramon the most was Wendell's statement that these alien creatures showed everybody present at the meeting a kind of 3D video of the crucifixion of Jesus. Too crazy to be true, you would say. But thanks to the latest warnings of Teimon, Ramon found a first piece of evidence that the Greys use the religious feelings of humans to impress them.

Teimon told Mira that the Greys infiltrated secret organizations with the help of Psy-mutants. That they even can be found in the highest levels of governments. This is only possible if a selective group at the top of the political community is also involved in one way or the other and knows about it. But how can one be sure of this information? Ramon was well educated in the basic literature of ufology, but how can you check documents published on the web? Let alone get an overview of it all? The only thing Ramon could do was to take the information from Teimon seriously, checking everything and keeping everything that fitted with the story of Teimon.

Jacques Vallée proved decennia ago in his book "Invisible college" that some UFO communities of those days had connections with the Secret Services. Some agents even infiltrated the hippy communities and founded UFO sects. They spread the belief that aliens were real and dangerous. But their goal was primarily to convince these young, peaceful, naive people to be positive about the issue of weapons. For you had to be able to defend yourself against aggressive aliens. It was very clear that a lot of UFO stories were nothing more than professionally designed disinformation to make it almost impossible to distinguish between fake and fact. For every explanation there was a complete opposite explanation. Every serious story seems to trigger a counter story. This is definitely a clever way to discredit every story. It is even better than just to ridicule the story of a witness. Skeptics in general don't believe anything, making it a pro and contra game for the public. But if a UFO theory gets countered by another UFO theory, then you really confuse the audience.

Another thing caught the attention of Ramon. A lot of UFO organizations have professionally organized websites. There's nothing wrong about that but it is commercial to say the least and hardly of any scientific value, especially because these sites publish everything that is out of the ordinary. The UFO stories are just a small part of a list of topics. It's a lot of fun to surf on these sites. But nothing more than that.

However, there are also some serious sites. They give the real facts, do in-depth research and don't go along with all the superstition and questionable theories. Because the only people who have a real sense of what ufology is about are the people who personally witnessed a UFO or were confronted with them in their daily job. Military pilots, public airplane pilots, technicians of radar installations, et cetera. A fine example would be the persons who testified for the Disclosure Project.

And there was another kind of websites. Sites which look more cult-like. The "don't look for evidence any longer" sites. They just know it. They have the most fantastic names, like the Galactic Federation. They seem to have information from the aliens as if they are informed on a daily base and know exactly what's going on. Could these sites have a link with that mysterious cult, Sean Leyka? If such a religion or sect exists, they have to come in the open in one way or the other. For that reason alone, Ramon read a lot of genuine nonsense. He had to read it just to know what they are talking about. How else can one get an idea what goes on inside these groups? How they

168

think and what they believe.

But Ramon's main concern is to find all the different opinions and theories about the origin of the Greys. The most common theory is that the Greys are members of a highly evolved civilization. Ramon realizes that Teimon's story will be a real shock for a lot of people that share this perception of the Greys.

The same thing can be said about the theories that state that there are hundreds of different aliens. That Greys are just one of a multitude of alien species. Taking into account what Teimon said, they could all be mental projections of the Greys. Ramon is really glad that Teimon made that very clear. That piece of information alone will bring a lot of clarity in this chaos of theories and opinions.

For the basic intention of the book must be to bring some order into the chaos of theories, opinions and the tons of disinformation. That alone would make it worthwhile to write the book. And it would give the effort of Mira meaning. Ramon is concerned about the contact of his student with the Greys and feels very responsible for anything that can happen to Mira.

Tired of sitting in his WebCom, Ramon decides to go to his garden. He takes a poncho and runs outside to almost bump against Mira who enters the kitchen, silently as always. She smiles and looks as reborn. Ramon clearly notices that the information stop has done her well.

Time for coffee, Ramon? Or are you leaving?

I always make time for you, Mira. Please take a seat.

Glad that she recovered from the alien contacts, Ramon makes a full pot of brown liquid life force and some moments later they are chatting away while relaxing in the backyard.

I guess you haven't heard anything of Teimon any more, Mira?

Nothing, Ramon. No skull, no Teimon, nothing. It is as if nothing happened at all. As if everything was just a bad dream.

Ramon shows his notes.

It wasn't a dream, Mira. You see how important it is to write everything down. Maybe later, it can be of use for the study of the paranormal. Because whatever anybody will think of the book, these notes are real. No doubt about that.

It will support the parapsychological theory that telepathy is a real phenomenon. Your sessions prove that there is a sender and a receiver. Because that still isn't clear in the definition of telepathy. As far as I know, only Tibetan tulkus master this mental art of communication. Your contact with Teimon also proves that telepathy is reversible and that sender and receiver can switch. Because you can send questions and you will get answers.

I'm happy that you can do something with the information besides the content, Ramon. The only thing I can tell you is that it is very strenuous. Sometimes I was really exhausted.

Indeed, Mira. This kind of communication will not replace the telephone or the cellular phone. Before that is possible, we humans will have to evolve quite a bit. But the most important thing for parapsychology is that it is not your imagination and that telepathy is not something supernatural, that this ability is even genetically inherited. Don't forget that the Greys are just clones. And how can a purple crystal skull be an amplifier if telepathy would be supernatural? I personally think that telepathic people have not an extra but a more evolved common sense organ. Every human has this sense, but it is just not equally evolved in everybody. Very probably, the humanoids here on Earth inherited this genetic improvement. Maybe, that was also the reason why in antiquity, some people were genetically changed. Probably the Téry just wanted to improve this sense organ so that some people were able to stay in contact with them. Scientifically, this is a very important issue, Mira. Don't forget! Parapsychology wants to prove that there is a natural explanation for paranormal phenomena. Phenomena like telepathy exist but are not well understood, because we are scientifically unable to find the natural cause. The problem is that these paranormal abilities are still surrounded by an aureole of superstition. It is as difficult to fight against superstition as against scientific rejectionism.

Can I have some more coffee, Ramon? I feel sleepy.

Of course, Mira. Sorry, I'm a bad host.

The mugs are filled and with some cake they enjoy the sunset.

And how do you feel, Ramon? I can imagine that it is not easy for you either to digest everything that happened in the last month or so.

Well Mira, I have to admit it is a strange feeling to be almost

170

forced to enlarge your sense of reality. All the information of Teimon has changed my perception of the world in many ways. If Teimon's information is real, I have to accept that an alien civilization interacted with our own history. And still is interacting! But I must admit that there is still doubt in my mind. Although, I wouldn't be surprised at all if it would be true. I always was in favor of the idea that alien civilizations made contact with our planet. What's the big deal anyway? But if the facts are put right under your nose like your contact with Teimon does, it gives you an indefinable feeling. Like doubting your own doubts. Be sure and not sure. As if you are in the middle of a fantastic adventure but you don't know how it will end. I think that you feel the same way, Mira. No?

To be honest, I have not much time to be deeply involved, Ramon. That's your job. You know, I hardly remember what I told you. And I really don't want to think about it. I am afraid it would influence my translation of the information. That's the reason why I don't like to go on the web. I don't want to be influenced by information.

But Mira, don't you remember the information you told me?

I remember the essential things but all the details? No, I don't. And I have my doubts about the reality of it all. As long as I don't see Teimon standing before me, as long as I can't touch him, I will have second thoughts.

Ramon has to laugh.

I like that attitude, Mira. We mustn't take anything for granted and keep our minds open. That's also the reason why I search the web. I want to find any information to support the story of Teimon. But let me tell you this. Compared to the chaos on the web, Teimon's story is like the missing link that connects the dots. It won't be easy to write a book about this. It has to be written with respect for Teimon but also in a way that people will not panic. You can compare it with an orphan that grows up in another family. It is inevitable that the parents will have to tell that boy or girl that they are not his or her real parents. To tell the boy or girl the truth, is the same as writing this book and tell the people the truth. It will always be a shock. Because suddenly, the sense of reality changes. And the longer you wait, the…

…the longer it takes to pass the crisis and to go on with your life, continues Mira.

Exactly, Mira. Therefore, I think it is better to tell the truth as soon as the child can understand what the parents are talking about. Children are very flexible, much more so than adults. From a therapeutic point of view, the worst thing one can do is keep it secret. If the orphan finds out later in life by accident, he will feel betrayed. And that goes for any secret in general.

I agree with you, Ramon. It's better to be sad or mad for a while but to know the truth than to feel good with a lie, because the truth eventually will pop up.

Absolutely, Mira. And that's why it is so important what Teimon tells us. It will be an information shock. Not only to the common people but also to ufologists and especially to everybody involved in hidden or black projects. I mean the Mentals and the Psy-mutants, and not to forget the Initiated people. It is better that they know the truth than to keep it hidden from them. In the end, we have to face the truth in order to prevent that the Greys will endanger the whole world.

That's the reason why it is so important that we find hard evidence to prove that this information is real. I think that the credibility of Teimon's story stands or falls with the existence of the signals and the code of the star map. Only facts convince people. The famous sociologist Auguste Comte once said: If you find a fact, you have to take your hat off. Facts are rare, especially in the UFO business.

It is quiet again and Mira thinks back about her contact experiences with Teimon.

You know Ramon, if I have contact with Teimon, I hear him talking and see the images, but I am still conscious of where I am. I'm not gone to another place or something like that. It is not as if I don't exist. I can still think and be myself. Do you know what I mean?

Sure, Mira. In that respect, your experiences differ from those of Edgar Cayce. He didn't remember anything about his sessions. But that changed at the end of his life. He told a lot about Atlantis. Also about the pyramid of Cheops and the hidden archives of the pre-Egyptian culture and many more things.

Suddenly, Ramon thinks about his thesis for his mystery school. You know the real reason why I went to the mystery school?

172

No idea, Ramon. Tell me about it.

Well, when I studied at the art academy, I wanted to make a conceptual artwork. I wanted to design a concept that contained all the phenomena and ideas of the world in one global concept. And you know me. If I get an idea, I want to realize it, no matter what. And I did. I made this conceptual artwork in the context of my thesis for my master's degree at the mystery school. Originally, I wanted to make a book in the shape of a cube. I have to admit. It was not that practical, so it became a normal A4 format thesis. But the model of the Akasha Chronicle was a cube. It was a kind of a three-dimensional scheme in the shape of a cube.

My Wise Teacher knew how important art was for me. He stimulated all students to develop their rational mind but also their creativity. Even the lectures were given in a way to stimulate the left and right brain hemisphere. For example, one week we would have an astronomy class by Allen Hynek in the morning, but in the afternoon there was a creativity workshop by... Lisbeth Monath. Yes, that was her name. She was a well known artist in the USA. Funny that I remember her name now. Even Hynek himself participated in her lectures. A strange situation that was! I remember he enjoyed working with clay. I do remember his last lecture very well. It was dedicated to the UFO phenomenon. Hynek stressed the fact that to understand the physics of UFOs, we needed a new physics. What kind of theory it had to be, he didn't know either. But the physics, involved in the UFO sightings could not be solved with the physics he knew. That was in his eyes a fact.

It must have been very exciting for you all, Ramon. Did he talk about aliens?

Not that I can remember, no. He discussed the model of UFO sightings that he used in his book. The close encounters were the most exciting of course. And some witnesses saw little passengers in or around the landed disc. But he didn't discuss these beings in detail. But what shocked me the most was the way he introduced the lecture.

What do you mean, Ramon?

Well, he lectured a full week about astronomy and became very familiar with all of us through the week. He enjoyed participating in the creativity classes and you could talk about anything with him. But when he started his UFO lecture he became very serious.

He said: dear students, you may take notes for your own use, but when anybody of you goes to the press and publish the content of this lecture, I will deny everything.

You don't mean that. Why? Didn't he trust you?

I don't know, Mira. But it was very exceptional that a professor used such an introduction. He was a very open and gentle man. But that was what he said. Remarkable, isn't it? Nevertheless, in time I started to understand the reasons behind his behavior. Speaking about UFOs is a risk if you want to be taken seriously. You can easily be ridiculed and even lose your job as a professor. And probably, in this way he gave us a warning. As if to say, friends, what I'm going to tell you is delicate information. But by saying this, he also gave us a hint that the UFO phenomenon was real.

Allen Hynek was a good friend of Jacques Vallée. I read several books of Vallée. They were very well written. He had original ideas about the whole UFO subject. But what I…

Sorry to interrupt you, Ramon but I suddenly remember an image I saw yesterday. I don't think I told you. It wasn't from Teimon. That's for sure.

Ramon notices that she finds it difficult to go on.

Just tell me, Mira. You know me, I'm a big boy. I can handle it.

It was very horrible, Ramon. I saw images of a brain, connected to a kind of computer. It was the brain of a human and the brain was kept alive in one way or the other. It was really horrible. But then… it was as if I had contact with that brain. And the creepiest part was that this brain still had consciousness. The deceased individual and owner of that brain was still conscious of himself. And he was in a lot of pain. Not as much physical pain but the kind of pain of being locked, like being a prisoner in his own brain.

Ramon's body shakes.

Jesus, Mira. That's really disgusting. You mean that the brain is still conscious and experiences a kind of extreme claustrophobia?

Yes, you can compare it with that.

And do you think it was a kind of a scientific test?

174

Yes. It was in a medical environment. The brains were connected to a computer. It must be terrible, Ramon.

And the brain, Mira? Could it communicate with that computer?

No, not really. Not like talking. But there was an interchange of impulses.

If the brain can't absorb light impulses, the brain dies. The brain has to receive light, one way or the other.

I had so much compassion for that person, Ramon. It was terrible.

I can imagine, Mira. I really don't approve of this kind of experiments. Could it be that these experiments have a link with experiments in underground facilities?

No, not really. It is an experiment done in Europe. In Italy, I think. One of the people stopped working there. He could not handle it any longer. Do you think that these experiments are real, Ramon?

I have no idea, Mira. But these days, the weirdest experiments are done, you know. Experiments on animals to name one, but there is also the whole clone business. I'm not sure, but experiments on living brains of dead people, I don't think it would be legal. I wouldn't be surprised if it were true, though. The strange thing of it all is that biologists, who don't believe in a spiritual soul, have the idea that the soul is some effect of brain activity. So, the consequence of their own theory is that they must accept the fact that when a brain is kept alive, the consciousness of the brain must still be active. So they know that the person inside must be conscious. Maybe, that's the reason why that man who quit his job could not live with that idea. I don't think that such experiments would be accepted by an ethical commission. I remember that my Wise Teacher once made something clear in his typical way. He believed that organ transplantation would become a normal procedure in the future. But there was one organ that would cause problems: the brain. Not technically, but if person A gets the brain of person B, then that person B would in fact get the body of person A. That would cause a paradox in organ transplantation. I thought it was a funny remark. But now that I think about it... If you can put the brains of an old man in a young body, the old man gets a new, young body. Believe me Mira, if they can do it, it will become big

175

business.

I believe you, Ramon. There are enough old guys who would give anything to get a young body.

Ramon starts to laugh. And also a lot of old women, Mira. No doubt about that.

But, Ramon. Seriously, where was this image coming from? It was neither from Teimon nor Aodin. I'm sure of that.

Let me think, Mira. Maybe you had telepathic contact with that man of the experiment.

That could be right, Ramon. It was as if I communicated with that man and I saw all the experiments they did on him.

Now you mention it, Mira, it is possible that these experiments have a link with new developments in the implant business. Teimon told you that implants can't influence your personal thoughts. It could be that this is an experiment to look for methods to develop an implant that is able to interfere with your thoughts or to connect the brain with a computer.

Both sit quietly for a while.

Mira, do you want some more coffee?

No thanks, Ramon. I am going home. I want to relax a bit.

A good idea, Mira. Then I will continue my research on the web.

Like a silent shadow, dressed in a long black coat, she disappears into the night.

It is new moon and the stars are the only light in the dark sky.

- 31 -
8/10/2006

Two weeks pass by. Ramon enjoys his evening coffee and meditates about everything he has learned from the web these last days. His beard is a week old and the bags under his eyes show the long days and short nights. Day in day out he's watching videos, varnishing cubes, cooking and working in the garden. Fortunately, Joy visits him once in a while. Otherwise he would really lose touch with reality. Ramon's generation was the TV generation, but the young people of today are the computer generation. How wonderful to be young! For them, the world is still new and full of new possibilities.

176

Imagine we would really come into contact with people from another planet. The young ones wouldn't have any problem with that. Corso was right. Young people can handle it, he said in one of the interviews. Ramon fully agrees. You could compare it with the times of Columbus. Exploring new worlds and new cultures. Wouldn't that be great! The new generation grew up with computers and interact with these information machines via 3D games. From a young age, they watch movies and animation films filled with robots and aliens. And not to forget, with all kinds of stories where the paranormal is as normal as anything else. It has become clear to Ramon that there has been a cover-up of the UFO phenomena. But who are the Initiated who want to keep it silent? And why?

One of the reasons could be that they don't want to cause a panic in the world with the news that there is an alien presence in our solar system. Maybe. But Ramon is convinced that those who covered everything up were the ones who were panicking. Especially in the fifties, at the time of the Cold War. If President Eisenhower knew about aliens and UFOs, he must have informed the top of the political, military and religious institutions. Not only of his own country but also of the rest of the world. The same must have happened in other countries. Ramon wonders about their reaction when they received the good news that we are not alone in the universe. The first discussions must have been about the effect that this alien news would have on the most important institutions of the world.

But people didn't have any problem with the discovery of humans in America and Africa. They were people too and so, what's the big deal? Take Teimon and Aodin. They seem to be really good people. They admit the mistakes of their ancestors. They even bring their own lives in danger to warn us for the Greys. They don't want to dominate, like the Greys. So there can only be one explanation for the cover-up. The top of the world knew about the Grey presence and they were afraid of them. But why?

It would be understandable when our leaders were threatened in one way or the other. If the battle of LA was real, that could be seen as a violent act. If the military were threatened in any way, the cover-up was necessary to prevent the people of the world of knowing there is a real alien threat. That would make sense. Maybe the Greys did not allow the humans to make their presence public. That would fit their strategy and would buy them some time to prepare their strategy. On Ter I, everybody knew the Greys existed and who they were. But that isn't the case on Earth. Keeping their presence secret would be to the advantage of the Greys.

Ramon starts to meditate about the whole matter. If the Greys want to conquer the Earth, they need time to enlarge their block culture to do the job. And for that, they need lots of material. But what kind of materials? Teimon talked about the way the Greys clone themselves. They need special containers, filled with fluids and food. So water and hormones would be essential. Could that explain the cattle mutilations worldwide and UFO's seen above the sea and lakes? Not to forget, Mira mentioned that the Greys need seaweed in vast amounts.

Of course, Ramon was familiar with the experiments of some scientist to try to clone people. The time is near, humans can clone humans. Maybe they even want to design a Grey type of creature themselves, just like the ancestors of Teimon. Ramon had nothing against science but cloning techniques on animals and humans just didn't feel right. Especially if you know there are thousands of animal species exterminated every year. Just by pollution and aggressive agriculture. And what about the millions of people starving every year? Why not use science to solve that problem first? But no, it is all science for business. It's just criminal, Ramon shouts out loud and then he is very surprised to see Mira silently walking into the kitchen.

Have you got visitors, Ramon? And she looks around to see who is making Ramon angry.

Ramon starts to laugh seeing her surprised face.

No Mira, nobody is here. Sorry, I was just thinking out loud.

I hope you were not thinking of me!

No, no Mira. Don't worry.

Here Ramon! Maybe a good bottle of wine will change the mood of your thoughts.

That's a very good idea, Mira.

I don't know about you, Ramon but I really need a break. The whole day there has been pressure on my head. I had to come up

178

with a subterfuge to get a few hours free from work.

Is Teimon looking for contact, Mira? It's possible because I guess that the transportation business is over. Excited, he cleans the table and opens the bottle.

Shall I first make some good coffee, Mira? I don't want you to be drunk when you speak with Teimon.

Fine by me, Ramon. But hurry. I see purple light flashes all over the place. I can't suppress the contact any more.

Ramon hears that her voice is gradually changing. In a hurry, he serves two mugs and takes his writing material.

It would be great if we could know more about their planet, Mira. Teimon told us much about the Greys, but who are the Téry? We don't know anything about them.

Mira enters the purple matrix and in her mind she is light-years away.

Ask him yourself, Ramon. I have Teimon on line.

For Ramon it is still an alien feeling to talk with an alien.

So... I can ask questions, Mira?

Yes Ramon, says Mira in a deep voice. Just ask and I will translate.

Okay then. Are you all right, Teimon?

1.205 **I salute you. We are fine. The Greys could not find us. We are safe again for the time being.**

One particular question has been keeping Ramon's mind busy for weeks now. Can you tell me more about the way the Greys conquered your planet? How did they manage to escape your control system?

Mira quietly translates the question and then starts to talk.

1.206 **What happened on our planet is happening now on Geya, but on a larger scale.**

1.207 **The strategy of the Greys starts at the top of the institutions that govern your planet. First they force the political top to work with them. The Greys do this by demonstrating their power. But there is something else.**

1.208 **The Greys introduced a new way of doing business using the Mentals and Psy-mutants. Large scale competition replaced fair play in business. Hard competition creates monopolies. Once somebody has a monopoly, he creates congruence and shallowness in society.**

1.209 **This socio-economical process makes humans more uniform. This process happens on different levels at the same time. The various media take unwillingly care of the propaganda for this business style. It is not that the Greys do that. They just initiated the principle at the top of the business pyramid. The rest follows from there. Everybody follows the example of the top.**

Is Teimon referring to the shopping mall syndrome, Mira? You know, that everything looks alike.

1.210 **Yes. Everything becomes superficial. Individuality and uniqueness is discouraged. Because then you don't belong to a group. The Greys want to group everything. A lot is happening right under our nose but we don't see it.**

Can we do something about that?

1.211 **Humanity can still defy the Greys. But in order to achieve this, we need the people of the Earth. If there would come a counterculture against uniformity, the power of the Greys will be weakened. This would enable us on our planet to launch a counter attack.**

1.212 **If we, the Sheyan, would come in the open on Ter I, we would be killed immediately. The Greys have everything under control here.**

1.213 **That's the reason why we contacted you. We really need the help of the people on Earth.**

Ramon writes everything down and thinks about the next question.

Why did your ancestors alter the genetic make-up of some humans on Earth, Teimon?

1.214 **The intention of our ancestors was to change the genetic make-up of some people so that the human race would evolve a bit faster.**

1.215 **In this way, our mutual cultures would evolve more rapidly to the same level of culture and technology. This would make it easier for us to come to Earth and live together with the humans on planet Geya. A small colony of our ancestors lived with the people of Earth in the past. Mira is one of their descendants.**

1.216 **We apologize for the fact that the Greys changed their habits so drastically. It was not foreseen. But we should have**

180

been aware of it. We are responsible.

Ramon sees tears in Mira's eyes when Teimon tells her why she is different. It has been a big problem for her all her life.

Shall I stop, Mira? But Mira gives a sign, she wants to continue.

1.217 The Greys know a lot about social manipulation techniques. Everything happens with the idea that mass production will benefit everybody. But young people revolt against this evolution.

1.218 The indigo children and descendants of our own ancestors don't want to participate in this evolution of mass industry.

1.219 But they soon get problems, because the society discourages individuality.

Ramon writes as if his life depends on it. He fully agrees with this social diagnosis while he thinks about the next question. Why was there an information stop?

1.220 The Greys know that there is a spy on Geya. They know that somebody has broken through their security matrix. They know that somebody knows who they really are. But they don't know who it is.

1.221 That's why I stopped the telepathic communication with Mira. The Greys can trace telepathic messages like you can tap a phone call. But they can't trace telepathy via the purple skull.

1.222 My communication with Mira happens at a different level. The Greys know there is something happening, but they can't trace it. The sender and receiver are unknown. It has to stay that way. But to be sure, we disconnected and took precautions. We can not be too careful.

It is all so freaking real, Ramon thinks. What can I ask? Oh yes.

Can you tell me something about your planet? What does it look like?

Mira looks introvert and a lot of pictures come into her mind and she tries to describe them as well as she can.

1.223 I see a planet almost completely covered with water. The sea is everywhere but there is one large dry land, full of fjords. There is a lot of green forest. I see large forests everywhere with very high and mighty trees.

And do you see where the Téry live Mira? Can you see cities?

1.224 **Here and there I see large constructions, built on large towers, high above the sea of green forests. On the towers I see large glass domes-like structures, with in it a platform with strange looking buildings and gardens. I see dozens of these platforms, spread over a large area. All together, they form a city. They are connected with one another above the ground.**

Do you se other details, Mira?

Yes, I see so much, Ramon.

1.225 **There are no roads. All transport happens through the air. The landscape is not parcelled by roads like here on Earth.**

And the climate, Mira? What is the climate like?

1.226 **It's much colder than on Earth. That's why they built the domes. The weather doesn't change a lot. There are no real seasons.**

1.227 **Inside the domes, it is warmer and the air has all the gasses they need. Everything is heated with the light of the star of their star system.**

Oh, now I see animals.

Can you describe these animals, Mira?

1.228 **Some look like a kind of cow, like those that live in Tibet. They have very long hair. And I also see an animal with two short front legs and two large hind legs. Oh, now I see a large animal. Like a kind of elephant, but with small ears and without a trunk. The nose is like that of a beaver. It is a very intelligent animal.**

That's it, Ramon.

Okay then, Mira. Let's see. What can I ask? Teimon, have you evolved on that planet?

1.229 **No. Our ancestors evolved on another planet. Ter I is too cold for us. But originally, it was not the intention of our ancestors to stay here for ever.**

1.230 **Our ancestors were underway to create a new colony when they arrived on Ter I. When they continued their odyssey, they left a small colony behind on Ter I because there were not enough supplies to survive.**

1.231 **We call our ancestors the "Ancients". Our ancestors are a small colony of the Ancients that were left behind on**

182

Ter I. After the Ancients made sure that the colony could survive here, they went to Geya.

So the Ancients came to Earth? Now it is getting interesting, Ramon thinks. So the Téry are a colony of the Ancients, but the main group of the Ancients came to Earth.

1.232 Yes, on a regular basis the Ancients had contact with the humans on Geya. They educated the humans. Together with the human cultures of that time, they made "large constructions" all over the planet. The intention of the Ancients was to bring us to your planet, as soon as the humans were prepared to share their planet with us.

Large constructions? Pyramids you mean?

Mira confirms Ramon's remark and goes on.

Now I see a light source, Ramon. I don't know what it means. Then she hears Teimon say: Ramon needs hard evidence for the star map. What follows next is important to him.

1.233 You must understand. This is all part of our mythology. We don't know everything. It all happened so long ago that it became a myth for us too. But we have some knowledge what happened on Geya. We can only tell what we know from our own historical chronicles.

1.234 There is one pyramid on Earth that hides the knowledge of the star map. This pyramid is called Che Ops and is built in the direction of the code. Our myths say that this pyramid hides the star map that we recently sent to Geya.

Ramon is astonished when he hears this. If that is true, then we have the final proof that the contact of Mira is real. If the pyramid of Cheops has something to do with the star map, then that is really mind blowing news.

And where can we find this star map, Teimon?

1.235 To find the star map, you need to stand in the king's room. You have to push one stone in and pull one out. The stone on the left has to be pushed in while the stone on the right has to be pulled out.

Ramon wants to ask which stone but there is no time.

1.236 The intentions of the Ancients were good. You have to understand this. But it all happened a very long time ago. We don't know everything. It is so long ago. The Ancients came

to Geya and live on in your and our myths. They are the descendants of the oldest human civilization in our galaxy.

1.237 **The Ancients didn't stay a long time on Geya. The Ancients left the Earth, leaving a small colony behind, just like they did on Ter I. The people that stayed behind did this of their own free will.**

1.238 **The Ancients set a date when they would come back. The people on Earth called those who stayed behind the Wise People. They were just like our ancestors. They were direct descendants of the Ancients.**

1.239 **The humans were very impressed when they met the Ancients. And the leaders of the humans decided to allow the Wise Men to educate their own wise people, the shamans.**

1.240 **The Wise Men worked closely together with the shamans, the priests of the humans in those times. They were worshipped as gods.**

1.241 **The educational method of the Wise Men was based on the principle of Sheyan teachings, called Shey An: to learn by putting the knowledge into practice. Therefore the Wise Men taught the humans everything by making large monuments. For in order to make such monuments, you need rational knowledge, like geometry and mathematics and so on. But to mobilize a lot of people, you need social knowledge and a common language. You need an organization to manage everything and to learn to cooperate with one another.**

So the Wise Men educated the leading elite of the human cultures how to build the pyramids themselves?

1.242 **Yes. The Wise Men educated the intellectual elite of the existing cultures how to realize a large project. But the humans had to do it themselves. The Wise Men always started with the knowledge that was already available. The Wise Men showed every culture in their own way how to fuse their knowledge and intellect and techniques that already existed. The Egyptian people were masters in pottery. They were very good wood craftsmen.**

1.243 **The Wise Men educated the shamans, the intellectual elite who knew the stars rather well, to map the night sky in a way to better measure time. Measuring time is of utmost importance to organize.**

1.244 **But most things the people and the shamans had to learn themselves. The Wise Men were very cautious not to teach the people things that they could not understand. Otherwise the cultivation process would not last once they were back on their own.**

1.245 **The most important thing the Wise Men taught the people was the importance of ethical rules. The second thing was to fuse all the knowledge that existed into one general model. And the third thing was to put any knowledge into practice to see if it is right. With these three principles it became possible to give large communities a common goal without destroying the individuality of the humans.**

But couldn't we have learned this in our own in time, without the help of the Wise Men?

1.246 **Of course. But there was another reason. For thousands of years, the humans had to constantly move to other regions because of the rising water after the last ice age. You have no idea how much humanity had to suffer for millennia. The people on Geya had a difficult time to stay alive in the period of the rising of the sea.**

1.147 **Between the ice ages, there is only a relative short period of climatic stability during which people have the chance to develop.**

1.248 **The Ancients knew this. That's why the Wise Men stayed behind in the first place: to help the people to develop faster and to be ready for the next ice age.**

1.249 **This process took many centuries. Gradually, the Egyptian culture developed.**

1.250 **When the Ancients came back, centuries later, they saw the improvements that these clever people had made, under the guidance of the Wise Men. The Ancients decided to help them build a special symbol as a sign of their existence for the future generations.**

1.251 **The Giza complex was built with the help of the whole Egyptian culture. The Ancients decided to leave a special symbol inside this pyramid, as an undeniable proof for people to come that Earth was visited by an alien civilization.**

1.252 **Before the first contact with the Ancients, the humans believed that their spirit lived on in the afterlife. But the** humans could not understand space travel. So within their belief system, the Wise Men explained them why these pyramids had to be built in a certain way.

1.253 That's why the Ancients built the star map into the structure of the pyramid. The Ancients wanted to leave a symbol behind that could only be understood when the people would be evolved enough to understand the meaning of the structure.

1.254 So what the Ancients did was a kind of interplanetary development aid, to speed up the cultural development of the people of Geya. But at the same time, they wanted to bring the cultural level closer to their own level of development. In this way, the difference would not be too big when the Téry would be transported to Earth.

1.255 After the great pyramid was built, the Ancients left again. The Wise Men who wanted to stay were free to stay. They married humans and gradually their descendants became human.

Ramon has a hard time writing everything down. It is all so remarkable and intriguing. There are no words to describe what Ramon feels.

Do you have still questions, Ramon?

Questions? Of course, Mira! Wait. So, the descendants of the Wise Men are still here, living among us?

1.256 Yes. But Teimon doesn't know how many there are. They lost track of them. But their descendants are the humanoids. Some of them have contact with the Greys.

While Mira says these words, she stands up and nervously she looks for her coat.

Sorry Ramon, but I have to go now.

Her hands are trembling. She wants to be alone.

Ramon is hardly recovered from this information marathon but senses that she needs time to cope with the idea that she is a humanoid.

We will open the bottle of wine next time, Ramon. Okay?

No problem, Mira.

Nervously she empties her mug and leaves. Ramon goes after her but she is already starting the car.

Ramon, I see you tomorrow. I will explain.

And in no time she drives away and her car disappears into the night. It is understandable that she is upset. Imagine that somebody tells you that you have alien genes in your DNA. Worried, Ramon goes back to his kitchen and starts reading the notes. How will the new age people react on this information?

Ramon always had his doubts about alien contact. Not that he didn't see the possibility. The problem was that most authors saw alien contact as the main reason why humans became civilized and developed intelligence. Ramon didn't believe that. Humans are intelligent themselves. But the story of Teimon makes much more sense. The whole situation is much more complex. A true teacher teaches you what you already know. He only shows you the way to develop your knowledge, but you have to follow your own path by putting everything you learn into practice. The teacher helps you to discover your own intelligence. He stimulates you. He doesn't make you dependent of him. On the contrary. He makes you independent. He lets you free. He hopes you will finally become wiser than him and has no problem with that. Ramon takes his notes and goes outside to enjoy the rest of the evening. It is really hot outside.

What amazes Ramon the most is that the star map is hidden in the Cheops pyramid. Could that really be? Because that would be the end of all doubt. That would be genuine proof that aliens were here in the past. Is there a secret entrance in the room of the king? Can this room be opened by moving a few stones? He still can't believe it. Why then haven't they found it? Ramon reads all the notes several times. The ice ages, the Wise Men who stayed behind on Earth, the Téry who were left on a planet thousands of light years away, the Téry who intended to come to Earth, their planet with the cities on towers, the animals. So many different things in one session! It is impossible that Mira is making this up. Impossible!

Mira, Jesus. I hope she's OK.

A fresh wind announces the beginning of the night and Ramon decides to go to bed. He shuts down his WebCom and retires to bed.

So the people, who were once seen as gods are now in trouble and we have to help them. Things can change. But who will believe it? Who? And Mira? Is she really a humanoid? Gradually sleep takes his thoughts away.

- 32 -

Sorry I'm late Ramon. Forgive me that I walked away like that yesterday. But Teimon's explanation of my genetic origin made me mad, you know.

No problem, Mira. I understand how you must feel. I will make some coffee.

A good idea, Ramon. I brought something to eat. Do you want to join me?

With pleasure, Mira. I forgot to eat today. Can you believe that? But tell me. Why were you so agitated yesterday?

Well, isn't it clear by now? I am a humanoid myself, Ramon! The idea that I am a descendant of the ancients freaked me out. So I owe my paranormal abilities to an alien genetic experiment. My whole life, I want to be like everybody else. But it's clear now that this is impossible because in the past, aliens have manipulated one of my forefather's or rather foremother's genetic make-up.

Ramon doesn't know whether to laugh or cry.

Well Mira, I must admit, you do have an alien appearance.

Yes, yes, just make fun of me, Ramon. But I have to live with it.

Sorry, Mira. I'm just joking. I can imagine how choking this must be for you. It touches your very essence. Although, the most important thing is that you finally know the truth. When I think about it, Teimon already hinted at you being a humanoid. But so what? Whatever your genetic make-up is, what really matters is who you are as a person. Come on, let's eat a bit. The coffee is ready.

While they both enjoy their meal, Ramon tells her everything he found on the web and time passes by.

I hope Teimon will give us some more hints about the key that is hidden in the Cheops pyramid. I have surfed every free minute of the day. There are sites in abundance about newly discovered megalithic monuments. A Japanese diver even found megalithic compounds under water. That proves that the sea level was lower when that monument was built. It can be found on the site of The Morien Institute.

And of course, there are plenty of sites about the pyramids of Egypt. I wonder if there is a common aspect to all the pyramids in the world. Something that proves that the Ancients were behind these monuments.

Well, Ramon. Pyramids always have a pyramid shape, don't they?

Yes Mira, that's right. But it is not as simple as that. The general scientific opinion is that the pyramids visualize mountains. This theory suggests that prehistoric people believed that the Gods lived on top of the mountains. By building artificial mountains, pyramids, in the center of their villages, the people hoped that the Gods would come down from the mountains and would come to live on top of the pyramids.

You mean that the people built the pyramids as a house for the gods?

That is the common opinion, yes. It's not such a bad idea, Mira. You know, even churches and mosques are perceived as houses of God. And the pyramids were the oldest temples. Don't forget, building vertically is a rather modern thing. If you use stones to build a monument without cement, it's wise to build a pyramid. In that way you are sure that the building will not fall down.

But in a way you are right, Mira. I think it is strange that the pyramids always have a square basis. Okay, here in Western Europe, you find a lot of grave hills. They have a round base. But no pyramids exist with a pentagonal or hexagonal or octagonal base. Of course, the square may be the simplest figure. And the compass-card has four directions. But a lot of pyramids are not oriented to the wind directions, but to the direction where the sun comes up on midsummer. That goes especially for the pyramids of the Mayas and the Incas. The pyramids in Egypt on the other hand are mostly built to the four directions. Anyhow, the official standpoint is simple. Every culture had its own period of pyramid building separated from one another. And the pyramids have no common link. It would be great if Teimon could give us a hint, that can't be denied. For without proof, nobody will take this information seriously.

While Ramon serves the coffee, Mira sees the kitchen gradually filling up with purple light and via the crystal matrix of the purple skull she tunnels again into the unknown. Teimon screened the discussion between Mira and Ramon and decided to make contact again. Teimon understands that Ramon is not easily convinced.

You are so silent, Mira. Are you tired?

No Ramon, Teimon is on line. Take your writing materials. I guess the information will come soon. He will give some more details.

Her voice is deep and in a hurry. Ramon gets his notes. Excited, he waits until Mira translates the first information.

1.257 **The Ancients had three important contacts with Geya. Aodin studied the myths and found some information that will be of help.**

You mean the Ancients visited our planet three times?

Yes, Ramon.

1.258 **The first time was some 10,000 years ago. The Ancients had contact with a civilization in South America only. A second contact was 6,000 years ago. That was when they visited Egypt. And the third time was 4,000 years ago. The Easter Islands were visited.**

1.259 **Understand this well, Ramon. The monuments were built by the humans. The Ancients guided the people of Geya. The monuments were a gift to the people of Geya. The building of the pyramids happened mostly during the second contact.**

1.260 **But 4,000 years before that time, the Ancients had already made contact. The oldest gift of the Ancient to the people of Geya is the Purple Crystal Skull.**

1.261 **Because of this skull, the Shamans could stay in contact with the ancients.**

And Teimon, where are the Ancients now?

1.262 **That is a mystery to us too. The Ancients disappeared. Nobody knows where they are. We have had no contact with them since they made sure we could survive on Ter I.**

1.263 **Four thousand years have passed since then. We don't know where they went after their last visit on Ter I.**

But Teimon, didn't the Ancients have problems with space travel?

1.264 No, the Ancients can travel in space. They have the technology to travel in space without the physical problems humans have.

1.265 Because we were just a planetary colony, we had everything to survive on our planet but we didn't have the most advanced space technology that would enable us to travel in space without physical problems. It was our task to survive on this planet and to wait until they came to bring us to Geya.

1.266 Normally, we should have been brought to Geya a long time ago. That was the intention. We don't know what went wrong. That's the reason why we wanted to reach Earth on our own and made the Greys in the first place.

1.267 The task of the Greys was to try to figure out what happened with the Ancients. The Greys also built an interstellar road with artificial star gates to enable our people to reach Geya using our own less advanced technology.

Ramon looks startled at Mira. So the Téry had the intention to come to our planet Earth?

1.268 Yes. For on Geya, we might figure out where the Ancients went. We were sure that they left information about where they went in one way or the other. Together with the help of the humanoids, we hoped to find out what had happened with the Ancients.

This information goes far beyond Ramon's expectations. It is as if he is back in his mystery school. It was a fascinating time. Sometimes, when his Wise Teacher felt like it, he went to the student's room and like an old wise man in a fairytale, he would talk about mythological stories and their hidden codes.

Ramon, you are so silent. Are there no more questions?

Sorry Mira, I was just reminiscing.

Teimon, can you tell me more about the activities of the Wise Men? Mira immediately goes on.

1.269 The Wise Men lived in a settlement on Antarctica, built during the first contact. We don't know very much about that period. You must understand that to us it is just a myth.

1.270 The Wise Men were a select group of the Ancients. They were in close contact with the shamans of the different

cultures. Especially with the South American culture that had had contact with the Ancients.

1.271 **During the three contacts, the Ancients prepared everything to make it possible for the Téry and the humans to live together.**

1.272 **The first contact was primarily to show themselves to the people of the Earth, so that the humans knew that they existed. The Ancients had only physical contact with a South American civilization. They were the most evolved tribes on Earth in those days. A few monuments were built together. During that contact, the Ancients built a base on the South Pole. That continent was easy to reach in those days via large islands extending from the tip of South America because the sea level was more than hundred meters lower in that time.**

1.273 **The colony of Wise People that stayed behind extended this settlement on Antarctica during the long period between the first and second contact. Four thousand years passed by before the Ancients came back.**

And during the second contact, the Ancients came back and helped the Egyptians to build the pyramids? And they left the star map behind. Can you tell me more about that period?

1.274 **The second contact was used to spread the cultural code of the Ancients in a fragmented way over different cultures. The Ancients were cautious. This was done to prevent that one culture would dominate the others. Our chronicles mention that this period was also the period of the pyramids. In Egypt, the most important pyramids were built. The key to the star map was included in the Che Op pyramid.**

1.275 **The Ancients spread also six new crystal skulls over the world. All of a different colour. So in total there are seven crystal skulls on Geya. The shamans who were able to come into contact with the skulls could come into contact with the Wise Men and later with the Sheyan. The second period is also the period of the genetic marriage of a select group of humans with the ancients so that they were able to practice telepathy.**

1.276 **With the help of the crystal skulls the shamans of the different cultures could stay in contact and ask for support** from the Wise Men or the Sheyan in difficult times. Every culture with a crystal skull had to develop their part of the code in their culture. At first with the help of the Wise Men but later on their own.

1.277 **The purple skull is the most powerful skull. This skull has access to the other skulls. Only a few humanoids can have contact with this crystal. The shamans with access to the skulls were also able to have contact with one another. Cross cultural contact was possible via telepathy.**

1.278 **The last visit of the Ancients was on the Easter Islands. But the reason for that is not important now.**

1.279 **The most important thing for now is to find the star map. It will support your mental strength.**

1.280 **The reason for spreading the cultural code of the Ancients fragmented over different cultures is simple. The cultures had to work together to assemble the cultural code of the Ancients.**

1.281 **That is why it is so important to focus on finding the star map to begin with. For the discovery of the star map is the beginning of intercultural cohabitation on your planet. It will bring the mythology and the codes of the different religions together.**

Ramon writes as fast as he possibly can. For a while, it's silent in Ramon's kitchen. Only the drum and base beats of Studio Brussels sound softly on the background. Teimon gives Mira a small break. Aodin looks seriously into Teimon's eyes and gives permission to send the following information. They have waited with this information to give Ramon the time to put everything in a historical context.

1.282 **You have to understand. A lot of this knowledge is already known in some secret circles of the elite. The ruling top of the different cultures on Geya know of these contacts. The knowledge is passed over from generation to generation via the families of the genetically altered people. They know that they only have a part of the real code. To possess the complete code means to have all power. A lot of historical events but also events in recent history become clear if you know this.**

1.283 **The ancient people of the Himalaya received a skull**

from the Ancients. China didn't occupy Tibet only for enlargement of its territory. The leaders knew that Tibet had old manuscripts, connected with their crystal skull. If the Chinese could get their hands on the knowledge of these manuscripts, that would enlarge the knowledge and power of the Chinese. They would come closer to the complete code of the Ancients.

1.284 **The different skulls give access to different parts of the code. A small elite knows that he who brings the different skulls together can reconstruct the code of the Ancients.**

1.285 **That is why the purple skull is so important. It gives access to the other skulls. The Wise Men have hidden this skull on a location that nobody knows.**

Ramon is flabbergasted. Ramon knew that Mao was not as atheistic as he is portrayed in the history books. His Wise Teacher told his students that Mao Tse Tung consulted the I Tjing almost every day. In fact he could be compared to the first great Emperor of China. He didn't allow his own people to read the I Tjing and related books. He ordered to burn every copy so that he was the only one who could consult the I Tjing. In this way it was easier to keep control over that vast complex culture.

The I Tjing contains the wisdom for an emperor to rule a country. I Tjing means "Book of Change" and it contains the code of the Chinese culture. The Chinese sign is the chameleon. Mao did something similar as the first great emperor. He knew that the Tibetan culture had very old manuscripts and knowledge to improve the code of the I Tjing. It would enlarge his knowledge and power if he could get his hands on that knowledge. But the Dalai Lama brought that knowledge in safety and escaped to India. All these memories of his Wise Teacher are confusing Ramon. Was his Wise Teacher maybe a…

Ramon? Do you have other questions? I can't hold this contact much longer.

He sees that Mira is exhausted and decides it is enough for that day if Teimon agrees.

Mira asks and Teimon does so. He knows that Ramon has to think this all over.

1.286 **Tomorrow. Same time. I salute you.**

Both take a deep breath.

194

That was a marathon, Ramon. My throat is as dry as the Nevada desert.

I have a very good remedy, Mira. Shall I open the bottle of wine?

Good idea, Ramon. My head is almost exploding.

My head too, Mira, but not because of any pressure. I had so many recollections of my student time at the mystery school during the session. It is unbelievable how this is all linked with lectures of my Wise Teacher.

Moments later both glasses touch.

To Teimon, Ramon!

And to my Wise Teacher, Mira!

It is so strange that the information from Teimon about the codes is so similar to what I learned in the mystery school, you know. It is all so strange. I hope I don't need to accept that my Teacher was a descendant of the Wise Men that were left behind by the Ancients. It's all so mixed-up.

Ramon tells her about the search of the Uhr code and also the Uhr language, the unity behind the cultural codes on Earth.

So your teacher was telling the same thing about the codes as Teimon?

Not exactly, Mira. Not with crystal skulls and aliens visits. But he was convinced that all codes came from the same source. Some more wine, Mira?

Please, Ramon. The pressure on my head has almost gone.

Good for you. As long as a simple glass of wine takes care of that, you have no real problems. Most women get a headache of wine. Oh yes, before I forget, Mira. I hope Teimon tells us some more about himself tomorrow.

Just ask, Ramon. At this moment they are out of danger. The Greys are too occupied with that transport business.

That's a relief, Mira. I have so many questions.

Ramon shakes his head.

Mira, I hope you realize we are playing with fire now. If the Greys would know what is happening in this kitchen, we would be in danger until the book is written and published. And when the book is published, it is not over. A lot of information comes in conflict with other ideas that they have brought deliberately in circulation.

I think you are right, Ramon. But that is partially the intention of the book I think. The more criticism and discussions it will trigger, the more the book will be widely known. Are you sure that's what you want, Ramon? I wouldn't like to stand in your shoes.

I don't care about the criticism, Mira. If you realize what is at stake, it's worthwhile to take the risk. The Initiated must not shoot the pianist. I'm just a messenger. The rest is up to them. Don't forget. In this book, the true identity of the Greys will be revealed. And that will be a shock for anybody who is involved with the Greys. That's for sure.

Absolutely, Ramon. But it will also be a relief for lots of them. Then they finally know who they are dealing with. The truth is always the best medicine after all. I really hope that the signals and the star map exist.

That's my greatest concern, Mira. Imagine that these signals aren't real after all. That would be a joke, no. But I'm willing to take that risk.

You have to decide that for yourself, Ramon. You have to make up your own mind.

Don't worry about that, Mira. It is as Frans Masereel, a Belgian artist, once said: people think I am crazy. But I will prove that I am much crazier than they think.

Both start laughing and forget their worries. Ramon sees that the glasses are empty.

Sorry, Mira. Shall I finish the bottle?

Fine by me, Ramon. I have enough. I can hardly stand on my feet. I had better go now. It will be early morning tomorrow.

Ramon accompanies her to the car after a last coffee. How does she manage to keep on going, he thinks while waving her goodbye. The moon is in its third quarter and the satellite shines as a jewel in the night sky, surrounded by ever changing clouds that reflect the moonlight as silver velvet. The stars make the cosmic mandala complete.

While Ramon enjoys the late star night, Teimon and Aodin sense that the Greys are coming gradually closer in locating their hiding place. They have to move to the last shelter. Of the small group of refugees, only Teimon and Aodin are awake. The others have been in trance for months now. Contact with other groups of refugees is reduced to a minimum.

196

Ramon will write the book, thinks Aodin.

Then there is hope again, is Teimon's mental response. Will our brothers be ready for the long travel, Aodin?

They will be ready, Teimon.

Aodin realizes the importance of their mission. Aodin puts his arm reassuringly over Teimon's shoulders.

Everything is going to be alright, dear friend, is his reassuring mental message. Let us send as much information to Mira as possible, as long as we can. Both leave the purple room and disappear into the dark corridor: a middle age scene in an alien setting.

- 33 -
10/9/2006

Teimon, can you tell me something more about your own people? You know, what you look like, what your planet looks like? Things like that.

Ramon is glad that Mira is there on time and with the support of a mug of brown liquid, they immediately start the next session. In no time, Mira is ready for contact. Teimon immediately sends her a lot of impressions and Mira tries to describe what she sees.

1.287 **The Sheyan wear long coats with a large cap. They always wear them when they are outside or when they travel.**

1.288 **I see the large white domes they live in. These buildings existed already at the time the Téry were left behind on their planet Ter I. The Ancients have built them. Their society is rather uniform.**

Can you tell me what they look like, Mira?

1.289 **They have dark brown hair. There are more men than women in their society.**

Can you also describe their faces?

1.290 **They look like us. But their eyes are larger and have higher cheekbones. Also their skull is a bit different. Their heads are larger and are not round on top. They have a vertical point-like extension.**

1.291 **Their nose is long, but rather flat and smaller. Their mouth is fine-lined and much smaller than human mouths.**

They look very friendly and you can see that they are very intelligent. But although they are very intelligent and possess a high technology, they have a sober lifestyle.

Suddenly Ramon remembers a video he saw during the day and wants to ask the opinion of Teimon. He takes Mira to his WebCom and shows her a video, filmed by a space shuttle crew. You can clearly see strange transparent light bolls. Ramon is convinced that these are natural phenomena. They are definitely no solid space ships like real UFOs. But what are natural UFOs? Mira watches the video attentively.

Has Teimon any idea what they are, Mira?

1.292 **These energy bolls exist everywhere in the universe. They are no living beings. They are the result of natural energy processes. They feed themselves with energy. Like a magnet, they attract electro-magnetic energy from the surroundings. In this way, they get larger and bigger.**

1.293 **They feed on space lightning during storms. They can even penetrate the atmosphere and can be visible on the ground depending on the weather conditions. These energy bolls can split themselves and disappear and reappear in a different spot.**

1.294 **But they are no living organisms. Their electrical charge can be tapped like fuel at a petrol station. If they split themselves, the two parts can grow again. Space is filled with them. We often use them as a kind of fuel.**

Mira has to laugh if she sees the surprised face of Ramon.

So they are no higher dimensional beings like some people call them?

1.295 **No. They are manifestations of electrical energy. Like a ball-lightning, but then in space. These phenomena are not lead by information processes but exist on a pure physical level.**

Next question Ramon, says Mira a bit challenging.

She really enjoys the reaction of Ramon and starts rolling a cigarette. Ramon is surprised. The whole day long, he looked with astonishment to video clips, showing all kinds of images of these remarkable phenomena in space. A lot of new video footages were published on the web. Especially the footage of the Tetra project shows hundreds of these energy balls circling

198

around the Tetra after the project failed. He is surprised that Teimon confirms his idea that these are natural UFO phenomena.

1.296 **It is a physical phenomenon. But this phenomenon has to be studied closely. It is an important physical phenomenon because the knowledge behind this manifestation of energy is important for the development of the physical sciences on Earth.**

Ramon smiles. Just what he always thought! Scientists will be glad to hear this. They go back to the kitchen and as Ramon wants to ask some more details Mira interrupts him.

Ramon, wait. Teimon has something important to say.

1.297 **As you know, something went wrong in the thirties of the twentieth century around the year 1933. For the first time, the Greys did something on their own, without our approval. The Greys live in space. They were not made to live on a planet. They were not allowed to enter the atmosphere.**

1.298 **In that period for the first time there was violent contact with humans. There were sporadic contacts in the past between humans and Greys but always with mutual respect.**

1.299 **It happened first in America and then in Russia. From that time, we lost contact. The main power that the Greys had over humans was the psychological fear that the humans had for their strange appearance. That was a crucial advantage for the Greys on the Initiated humans.**

1.300 **When their contact became aggressive, an important man played a crucial role on the level of decision making. He was involved in law making. He had his own principles and his thinking was very linear. His opinion was to become defensive against the Greys. And he changed the existing policy against the Greys.**

1.301 **The highest religious institutions of the church were informed from the very beginning.**

Ramon and Mira are conscious of the delicate nature of this information. Ramon found a site, where the opinion of the Vatican about alien phenomena is discussed. But there is so much to find on the web. He hardly took notice of this site, because it was all in the Italian language. And how can you be sure of everything what is written on the web? Aodin senses the questions of Ramon and sends some extra information.

1.302 **A lot of revelations in the media are tests to see how people react on this kind of information, not so much to bring more openness in the UFO subject, for there is no official standpoint. Officially, UFOs and grey aliens don't exist.**

1.303 **Think about that! We salute you.**

That will keep Ramon busy for a while, thinks Aodin to Teimon. He has to understand that the highest people of the world institutions are informed about the alien reality. But I also trace the presence of the Greys, Teimon. We have to go undercover immediately. And as quickly as possible the Sheyan go down in the underground labyrinth and make themselves mentally unreachable for the Greys.

While Mira is returning to reality, Ramon starts to meditate about the latest information.

Teimon and Aodin are right, Mira. That childish nonsense of believers of non-believers! It is impossible that real research of UFOs can be done by amateurs as a hobby after their work. The military have radars all over the country and hundreds of military satellites in space. Get real! The airspace of the whole globe is surveyed by thousands of specialized radars. Anything that moves in the air, especially what is not identified, can be traced all the way. Come on! If one group knows about UFOs, it must be the military and more importantly, the space agencies. They have the technology to study the phenomena in-depth. They also do back-engineering of crashed UFOs. The military has always operated within strict secrecy. Not only for the research of UFOs. Nothing will come out if they don't want it to. And if the UFO phenomenon is real, the military has obviously informed the highest top of the political elite, the religious elite and even the industrial elite. Who else? And they won't tell unless they have no other choice.

The idea that our Earth is visited in the past by extra-terrestrials and still is, is a reality that they will hide as long as they think it is necessary. The consequences for our human society are as severe as in the days of the Copernican revolution at the end of the middle ages. The scientists who doubted the truth of the

200

geocentric world-view were demonized. Not because the elite of those days didn't believed them. But because their system of belief, the base of their control on the social institutions, was threatened.

The same is happening all over again with this UFO phenomenon. And all the scientific knowledge about the UFOs is kept secret. And to think that the game of hiding has been going on for more than seventy years now! Just think how much knowledge is hidden in secret projects and research groups! Think of the stories of Dan Burisch or Phil Schneider. And I found others: Bob Lazar and Karl Wolf and many more. And that's just the top of the iceberg.

Stimulated by Teimon's latest information Ramon goes on.

It's like the secret service, Mira. Everybody knows that this organization exists. But what they do, nobody knows. You can only guess. It is not without reason that Teimon had to contact us. Those secret UFO groups merely think they are dealing with humans of an alien civilization but in fact they are biological robots. With all their technological power they can't see the difference. But anyway, I'm glad that Teimon and Aodin found you, Mira. They don't want to contact people who work in secrecy. I think the reason for that is the fear that their knowledge can be misused. They want everybody to be informed. Not a small group of people that works for some country or other. And that's great! Shall we take a look on the web, Mira. Maybe we have more luck today with that magical date 1933. And who could that person be?

Mira looks at the clock.

Okay, but not too long, Ramon.

Minutes later they search the web together. Ramon just clicks at random.

Interesting! Clyde Tombaugh, the man who discovered Pluto, claimed he saw a UFO in 1930. But Mira doesn't react when she sees this picture.

No Ramon, he must have something to do with the law. I saw the image of him very clearly.

Another link was somebody from Rumania, an engineer for a German company who worked on the development of a kind of flying disc. Afterwards, he was only occupied with the healing water of the Hunsa's.

No, Ramon. No bell is ringing.

A lot of links follow, but nothing comes up.

I stop for today, Ramon. I'm too tired to look. I am going to sleep.

You just do that, Mira. I understand. You don't want to be influenced by anything on the web. Okay. I will do some research later. I will just put all possible links in one folder. But if that guy can be found on the web, I will find him.

Fine by me, Ramon.

She's almost ready to leave as she suddenly looks at Ramon.

You know what comes to my mind, Ramon?

No Mira, no idea. I'm not a telepathic.

I don't think this is information of Teimon. I think this is me thinking.

Tell me, Mira! Surprise me!

That crash of a UFO in Roswell. Well, I suddenly think that this may be a part of the Grey strategy. You know, the Greys can't think on their own.

Yes, Mira. The Central Grey gives orders and these orders are executed instantaneously by one of the blocks. What about it?

Well, maybe the Central could well have sacrificed a few discs to give the army the impression that they could fight back! And maybe the central brain just wanted the army to have some advanced technology but for a completely different reason than we would think.

Well yes… That could be possible, Mira. The Central must be a strategic master mind. He commands all the Greys of the block cultures. But he could invent a strategy spread over many decennia, as a kind of super chess player to infiltrate and invade a planet with Swiss clock precision.

I agree, Ramon. But not with the intention to destroy the planet but to submit the human population. They don't want to destroy the humans. They need us alive. The central brain had to know that the humans would back-engineer the crashed UFOs. And the country that studied the crashes would become technologically superior.

You have a point, Mira. There is more than one UFO crash reported over the years. There is even a UFO crash retrieval

202

conference every year in America. Maybe the Central Grey gave different countries a crashed UFO to see who can learn the most from it. To create a kind of technological race, comparable with the race for the nuclear bomb.

Exactly, Ramon. And the country that succeeds could become a super power. And which countries would be involved in this race?

Ramon doesn't need to think very long.

The USA, Russia and maybe China and Japan? And Europe?

Exactly, Ramon. And what kind of technology was Colonel Corso talking about?

Computer technology? That was the main success. So you think that the Greys gave their technology to several countries. Just to see who wins?

That's what I mean, Ramon.

But why would they do such a thing?

That's for you to figure out, Ramon. I'm going home now.

That is a very clever remark, Mira. I never really understood why suddenly so many UFOs crashed. Not that these UFOs can't have technical failures. Corso stated that the military used radars to take them down. They could send powerful electromagnetic beams to these space ships. And that was back in the fifties. In this way, the Greys could give the technocrats the impression that they could fight back. A good reason to put lots of money in secret projects.

Think about it, Ramon. There must be a clue. But it is just an idea of mine. Not of Teimon.

I won't forget that, Mira.

You will figure it out, Ramon.

By the shadows of the moonlight, Ramon sees her face and notices that she is very tired. Ramon waves, while she disappears into the night.

For a while, he enjoys the night sky and the pleasant coolness of the night. The waving habit of Ramon is an old tradition that he learned from his mother. She taught all her children to wave family and friends goodbye. You never now what is going to happen. Maybe it is the last time you see them. Anything can happen. The war had taught her not to take anything for granted. When his mother explained this to him Ramon realized as a young kid that people could die. And if something happens to one of them, at least you waved them goodbye. It gives you a good feeling. Back in the kitchen, he cleans the table and looks at the notes. Mira's remarks float within his mind. Could this trick of the crashes be done long before Roswell? There were already UFO sightings in Germany at the end of the nineteen-twenties. Could it be that the Germans had knowledge of a crashed UFO? And that the Nazis had knowledge about flying discs?

Ramon thinks back on the video of the Nazis and their base in Antarctica. Could it be that the Greys infiltrated the secret societies of the Nazis? And that the Nazis had knowledge of the settlement of the Ancients on Antarctica? If the Greys made the top members of this cruel organization into Mentals or even Psy-mutants, it could partly explain their extreme inhumane nature. Hitler's hate for the Jews was extreme. As if he wasn't human anymore.

Ramon shakes his head. This would be a dangerous conclusion. The last thing he wanted was to insult the Jews who suffered so much from this war. He remembers his Wise Teacher. How would he handle this problem? Leave this idea for now. But theoretically, it could be that the Greys had a hand in this cruel xenophobic group called the Nazis, with or without them being aware of it.

After that war, little was left of the positive image of the human species. How low can a man and people fall if they are filled with hate! Ramon gets a sick feeling about it all. If the Greys had a hand in that ink-black period of human history, it would not be unthinkable that something like that could happen again. That a group of fanatics want to repeat again what happened in that darkest period of human history. All the sites and videos about underground facilities come back to his mind. Not that he believes it all. But it all left a bitter aftertaste. He decides to let it go for that night and to go to bed. The fantastic information about the Ancients makes him forget all that.

I must not be taken away by freaky ideas before I have some real proof. I have to concentrate on the star map. First things first. And after a while, he falls asleep.

Why is it so dark in our barn, thinks Ramon while searching the exit of the room on his gut feeling. As if it is self-evident, Ramon walks through his parental house as if he was ten years old. It's evening and hot outside. The full moon appears above the trees and shines with a mysterious glow. Excited, Ramon walks into the garden as if he is searching something. But he doesn't know what exactly. He sees the small bench. He fell from it when he was seven years and broke his left arm in three places. His mother warned him to come out of the high trees, his favorite place to play when he was young. It gave her the creeps to see Ramon do all kind of acrobatic stunts. After that accident in a seemingly safe place, she never asked him to get out of the trees again. Strange! Didn't his father cut that old pear tree! Suddenly, Ramon sees his father standing against that old tree. He looks at Ramon with his typical smile, while enjoying a cigarette. The highest leaves of the fruit tree are full of fruits and while looking up, he thinks: if only I could fly. Then by itself Ramon starts to fly. It gives him such a wonderful feeling that he forgets everything and higher, always higher he flies, until he rises above the atmosphere and looks at the Earth below. How beautiful our planet is, he thinks and with enormous speed, he moves around his planet. Suddenly he stops over America and a strange force pushes him down. Before he knows, he enters a deep dark vertical tunnel.

Deep down, he stops as he sees a side-tunnel. It looks like an air shaft and in the far distance he hears voices and noises of machines. Curious, he enters the shaft and goes into a giant hall. An enormous machine is drilling its way into the rocky underground as if it is butter. Ramon sees different tunnels, starting from that hall and it looks like a kind of railway. The sound of the machine is deafening and Ramon wants to leave, but a long corridor in soft blue light gets his attention. Wondering, he enters the corridor and at the end, there is again a large hall. Personnel, dressed in a military kind of dresses, are busy, as if it is a large reception place of a military base. A large elevator seems to be the entrance to lower levels. As the elevator is empty, Ramon gets into the elevator and down he goes.

Soundless the doors go open on the second level. He sees a hall with several long corridors. It is like a copy of the first floor. But the people that he sees are dressed differently. Large mainframes and computers are visible but the door closes again while the elevator goes further down to the third level. As he enters the large central hall, he sees lots of people in white coats, walking in and out of the long blue lit corridors. Ramon floats out of the elevator and enters a corridor and sees a large hall through an open side door. People dressed in white seem to work together with little grey beings on a large disc in the middle of the large room. It seems to be a kind of aircraft. But quickly he's pulled back to the elevator and down he goes again. As he enters the fourth level, he floats around through the corridors and enters one of the rooms. Strange futuristic apparatus are against the walls and in the middle humans and Greys lie on tables, with long tube-like cables connected to their eyes. Everything is made of a super clean white material. The rooms are lit with the same blue color as the corridors. Ramon gets scared and he wants to leave the place immediately.

Intuitively, he knows that they change people here. They become mentally connected with the Greys. They are mentally transformed to become linked with a Grey block. I have to get out of here, is the only thing that Ramon can think and he floats back to the elevator. Ramon doesn't want to go deeper, but down he goes in this freaky compound and the doors open at the fifth level. He sees numerous little grey creatures walking in and out the side rooms of the long corridors. As if they are living there. With their big eyes and their thin bodies, they look like large living dolls. Where the hell am I, Ramon wonders. What is this place? He doesn't leave the elevator and the doors close again. He wants to get out. He pushes the up symbol but nothing happens. The elevator brings him deeper in this freaky place. As the doors open again he sees the corridors, lit with dark blue light and cautiously he enters the hall. He sees a group of Greys leaving a side room of one of the corridors and he can't help to look inside. Horrified he sees long rows of cages. In it are the strangest creatures: dogs with bird-like heads, human-like bodies with reptilian heads, fastened by chains, staring blankly and lifeless. Bodies of grey creatures with insect or human heads and abnormally large red eyes, moving nervously in their senseless situation. As a living painting of Jeroen Bosch, Ramon sees the one horrifying creature after the other. This absurd result of demonic genetic experiments makes him sick. He wants to get away here, away from this sick place of cruel intellect and he floats back to the lift. But he can't stop the elevator. Then the door opens on the lowest floor.

Only a few Greys walk around and a force pulls him into one of the numerous rooms. Again the same kind of cages but now filled with humans. In every cage a man, a woman or a child is locked. Completely apathetic and drugged, most of them chained like animals. In shock, Ramon sees these helpless humans. They look terribly sick, they are naked and numb. They stare as in a catatonic shock. As if they have given up all hope. A few Greys enter the room and go to a woman to give here some kind of serum. She groans and here red eyes show fear while she starts to scream for help. But nobody hears her. Ramon wants to help her and she looks at him. With powerlessness in her eyes, her arms reach for Ramon. He suddenly awakens from this terrible nightmare.

Shocked by the terrible images, he gets out of bed and opens the window to get some fresh air. The moon stands low in the west and the first birds start their morning concert. The videos and articles about these underground facilities have made a deep impression on his mind. He decides to go down and have a cup of coffee and a cigarette.

If that isn't hell, I don't know what is. How severely must the people in the concentration camps of the Nazis have suffered! What a shame, what a shame for humanity. People nowadays are afraid of vampires, ghosts or demons, with the help of movies. But didn't a study of Paris couturiers prove that the most dangerous people are the ones, dressed in perfect suits and with perfect haircuts? Were the Nazis not perfectly dressed gentlemen, perfectly mannered? Didn't they want to create a kind of superhuman? Based on the ideas of the - for the most part wrongly quoted - philosopher Nietzsche? Were they not doing experiments on twins in those concentration camps, often chosen by doctor Mengele himself? Only to get more insight in the relations between chromosomes and the human mind? Didn't they select people with blue eyes and blond hair to make an offspring of children for the new race? Could it be that such disgusting experiments are still going on in underground bunkers? Far away from the human eye? Far away from any control, maybe even with the help of these grey clones? Or are these experiments done by the grey clones for their own research? For their own strategic plans to get more knowledge of the human body?

Could this really be true? Of course it is possible!

- 35 -
12/10/2006

Hello Ramon! says an unexpected visitor.

Completely surprised, Ramon looks up from an article about alien abductions.

And, young man, says a smiling Ury. Everything all right?

Ramon is pleased with his sudden appearance at this late hour. Unexpected but always open for a deep discussion.

You look well, my dear friend!

Thanks, Ury. You know, the best friend of Hendrik Ibsen said the same thing when he was very sick. And do you know how Ibsen reacted?

No idea, Ramon.

He said: "On the contrary, dear friend", and he died.

Both have a good laugh while taking a seat in the kitchen.

And Ury, any news from Merly?

Yes, Ramon says Ury with a cheerful but tired voice. He was there again.

Coffee?

Why do you think I came? But wait, Ramon. I have a tasty present for you and he shows a bottle of Bordeaux of 2001.

Good idea, Ury. I guess it is going to be a late night!

And both go to the kitchen and enjoy the taste of that devastating year.

You are not serious, Ury, says Ramon an hour later, while enjoying the last drops of wine.

I am, Ramon. The fine hairs on the angels of Van Eyck's painting were done with the help of a substance to embalm dead bodies. It was put on the painting and a line of oil paint would roll up in a thin line.

Wow, that's clever. You know, I never understood how he did it, Ury. Some specialists say he used very thin brushes, but that doesn't work, you now.

Ha, ha, yes, yes Ramon. Those guys knew what they were doing. Those masters were true professionals. They had a lot of knowledge of alchemy long before it became the science of chemistry. They knew all kind of substances to make sure the paintings could stand the deterioration by time. We call these masters alchemists, but believe me, they knew very well what they were doing. By the way, a good wine, is it not?

Absolutely, Ury. Really a good choice. But let me take my writing materials. I have to write down what you said about the Illuminati.

A bit awkward, Ramon searches for his notes and puts the water heater on.

A cup of coffee will help us clear our minds, Ury.

With fresh coffee they both start to meditate.

The first thing you told me were the names of two members of the Illuminati. A computer giant and the owner of a large shipping company, no?

That's what Merly says, yes. The computer guy uses something in his chip that is back-engineered from alien technology. But don't tell anybody about it. I'm not sure that the names are correct.

That's a promise, Ury. You know me. My lips are sealed. At the moment, I'm only interested in the general concept of the Warriors and the Guardians. I don't find anything on the web about the Guardians. What I would like to know is how the Illuminati and the Warriors are linked together.

I can only say what Merly told me, Ramon. Merly only talks in general terms. It is clear that every Illuminati fraction controls a Warrior. The Illuminati don't do anything themselves. The Warriors are the ones that have to execute their orders.

I understand, Ury. But there are thirteen Illuminati and only twelve Warriors! How can that be?

Well, I guess that the thirteenth Illuminatus is just a kind of chairman with no real power.

Okay, Ury. That makes sense. Please repeat once more what Merly told you about the Warriors.

He told me so much, Ramon. But I will try to summarize. Originally, the Warriors were the kings and emperors of the world. But gradually, the ancient power structures changed. When the royal leaders lost power, their torch of power went partly underground. In every world continent, this process was different. But everywhere, secret societies were founded and they gradually got more power. These secret societies spread their tentacles in every level of society. Gradually, society came under control of a hidden cabal with a lot of financial power. They are in fact more powerful now than the Warriors in the past. But the Illuminati finally conquered the Warriors through their control of the currencies.

Merly could be right, Ury. There are two things going on here: money and power. Let's meditate on that. The Warriors have the power, the Illuminati the money. Originally, the foundation of the Illuminati in the eighteenth century was a positive development, you know. Don't forget, it was the age of Enlightenment.

Don't tell me, Ramon. I still feel Emanuel Kant in my stomach. Die Critic der Reinen Vernunft. What can I know? What should I do? What may I hope?

Ha, ha, ha, Ury, you have a good memory. Anyway, the name of the Illuminati was clearly based on that period of philosophy or was it the other way around? Who knows? Their goal was to stimulate social progress by developing a new economical model.

Oh yes? I didn't know that, Ramon. Tell me more.

I don't know the details, Ury. But as far as I understand, the most important Illuminati were descendants of wealthy banker families and often of royal descent. To stimulate the first industrial revolution, the new companies needed large amounts of capital. By inventing the system of paper money, the first large companies could get a loan from banks. The companies could repay the debt with interest over a long period of time. And by paying the workers with their money, the companies

210

brought the paper money of those banks in circulation. The companies had no problem to pay interest. The gold, the value of the money, was kept in security by the banks. The interest made industrial growth possible and the banks richer. The industrials believed in the future of technological development. The Illuminati were convinced that the world would become a better place. In a short time, barter disappeared. Progress brought more wealth for everybody. Especially the new promised land America was for these European bankers a new challenge. It was the land of the golden future and a perfect place to test this new way of economical thinking. Ury, do you know that interest on a loan is still forbidden in some parts of the world?

Yes. I know, Ramon. In the Islamic countries, it's still seen as a sin to ask interest. That is one of the reasons why they invest more and more in the west. For the interest, you know. Ha, ha …

Ha, ha. Correct, Ury. It proves that economy is not a boring mathematical model. Economy is in fact a social science. The economical model is a mathematical translation of the behavior of people. But economy has to take into account the ideas of a society. What the people think about what is important in life. Every culture has its own norms and values and life styles. So they also have a different economy. But with the help of the success of the technological revolution and nowadays the globalization, every part of the world uses a money system.

So the money system, invented by the Illuminati, has conquered the world. It's because they invented the paper money system that they have that much influence in the world. If I have to believe some articles on the web about the Illuminati, the dollar was the final victory of the Illuminati in America. Via their banks this fraction of the Illuminati control and produce the dollar. So the nation state America is not the owner of the dollar but loans the dollars from a private bank.

Are you serious, Ramon?

Well, it is a complicated story but it seems that the USA has to pay a kind of interest on every dollar they loan from the bank that produces the dollar. And that is definitely more than the printing costs of the paper money. That's for sure.

So, this bank has a kind of copyright on the dollar? My God Ramon, that's big business.

That's a good way to describe it, Ury. If you see the dollar as a kind of logo, the buyer needs to pay the designer who has the copyright. Since 1913, if I remember well.

But Ramon, these Illuminati must have gathered a gigantic fortune. No wonder they can control the Warriors.

Well yes, Ury. Merly could be right. It could be that the other currencies in the world are basically created in the same way as the dollar. So in a way, those in control of the money could be the Illuminati. Every currency could be controlled by a fraction of the Illuminati. They could be like a big family, spread over the world. That's why I don't understand why they fight one another. They have everything they desire. What is Merly's explanation of that?

If I must believe Merly, the Illuminati became lazy. The new generation inherited a fortune. Money and power are not really interesting any longer. The new game is ultimate power. The central theme in the internal conflicts of the Illuminati is about the way they can get this ultimate power. Maybe that's where the Warriors come into the game. Maybe, the Warriors have to put the Illuminati's wishes into practice. Some Illuminati behave like real despots within their own matrix of power. They want world power and use the means they have to reach their goal with the help of the Warriors.

Merly could be right, Ury. Some websites suspect that at least one fraction of the Illuminati has such plans. The craziest scenarios and speculations are discussed. But I think nobody really knows what they plan. But if we have to take the message of Merly seriously that the Illuminati eliminate Illuminati, then it is clear that not every member of that secret cabal agrees to the strategy to follow. Then the big question is: what is the discussion about? For example, imagine for a moment that the Illuminati of the new world want world control. I don't get it. America already is world power number one. What do the Illuminati want more?

Well Ramon, first of all, it is not America that wants that, Ramon. Most Americans don't have a clue what is happening above their heads. America is just the basis for the Illuminati. But maybe they want world power just for the power. You know: why was Cesar conquering Europe? For power. What else?

212

Absolutely, Ury. So if I understand what Merly is saying, the Warriors have to fulfill the goals of the Illuminati. If necessary by war. So it is not unthinkable that one the Illuminati families wants technological, economical, political, mental or even religious world power. And in order to do that, they have to eliminate the others with the help of the Warrior under their control?

Indeed, Ramon. Merly said that there is one group of Illuminati who wants to be on top of the world. They want one world, one socio-cultural control system and one ruler. Not on the surface, but in secrecy. They want the world. Maybe with different provinces, but with only one supreme power on top of their pyramid of secrecy. Don't forget. They possess the most advanced weapons. Maybe with the help of aliens they see possibilities to overrule the other Illuminati fractions.

There is nothing new under the sun, Ury. I guess the only thing that can bring about that kind of control is to have one world currency. That could generate tremendous amounts of money for those who control that currency. You know, colonialism always existed. Countries become larger and larger. History books are full of these dynamics of power games between cultures. In the end, the final step is world power. People in general are not aware of these games that are still going on and happening before their eyes.

But one thing is for sure, Ramon. Not everybody of the Illuminati agrees about the strategy to get control over the world. Only one Illuminati fraction wants to eliminate the others who refuse to cooperate with its plans. They are very serious about that. No doubt about that. But what these plans are, Merly didn't tell.

We have to meditate about that, Ury. Just suppose that the Warriors are the executers of the Illuminati orders. Then the Warrior of the most powerful Illuminati fraction has to defy the Warriors of the other Illuminati families, with or without war. If they want to prevent a war, then that would mean that all the Illuminati fractions have to agree with a new level of power. I guess that not all the Illuminati families will agree with that, Ury. Maybe, the cruel content of these plans is the reason for the internal struggle?

I don't know, Ramon. You could be right. Merly promised to give me more information. But now, I really have to go. Good luck with your projects and thanks for the coffee, Ramon.

Ury, I thank you for the good wine and the information.

It was my pleasure, Ramon. Bye.

As he gets into his car, Ury makes the peace sign with his fingers and drives away. Ramon responds in the same way. Those were the days, thinks Ramon. Everything changes so rapidly. He sees the lights of Ury's car disappear into the night while waving. Ramon closes the door behind him while the church bell chimes three times. Already three o'clock? In no time he gets in his bed. He catches a glimpse of the moon.

If Merly is right then one fraction of the Illuminati wants the same as the Greys. Teimon said that on the surface nothing is changed on Ter I. The Greys work in secrecy and gradually transform the society into their matrix of control. They can shake hands with the Illuminati who want world power. Maybe they did just that! Or is this merely a coincidence or what? But soon sleep takes his mind to the world of dreams.

- 36 -
14/10/2006

Ramon returns from the garden and puts his bike in the backyard of his house. It's already dark early and it feels great to be back home. Quickly he closes the door behind him.

Good evening, sounds a familiar voice in the kitchen.

Mira? You here? That's just great. I wondered where you were.

The kitchen table is filled with food.

I had not eaten yet, so I went shopping and came directly to your place. Will you join me, Ramon? There is plenty of food.

Of course, Mira. I will make some coffee.

Immediately, Ramon starts his daily ritual.

So, Mira, is everything okay at work?

Some big deal is within reach.

Good for you. By the way, nothing heard from Teimon?

No, Ramon. It is quiet in the cosmos. But there was some other information coming through, maybe from Aodin. I don't know.

214

Small details, but nothing important I guess.

What kind of details?

Ramon serves the coffee.

1.304 **Believe it or not but it seems a kind of antenna exists that can be implanted in a tooth. This antenna is made for important people.**

She looks at Ramon to see how he reacts.

Don't look like that, Ramon. I too think it is crazy. But this antenna would already be in use for a long time. And it is not an implant of the Greys.

1.305 **A lot of important public people make use of this antenna.**

And what is the use of this antenna? I hope it is not a radio or something like that.

No, no, it is nothing like that, Ramon. This antenna can regulate the mood of the person that wears it.

Okay. I want to believe you, Mira. But how does it work?

1.306 **The antenna is connected with some glands via the nerve of the tooth. It works like an insulin pump. It makes automatic calculations and reacts to keep the balance.**

Ramon sets the table for dinner. It looks inviting.

I have never heard of such a thing, Mira. But I have to admit that a lot of world leaders act as if they don't feel emotions. Their act is rather disappointing I would say. And you think balancing emotions can be achieved with such a pump antenna?

Well yes. That's what the information told me.

Not such a bad idea. Not everybody in high places has done yoga or theatre. Come to think of it: the previous Pope did some acting when he was young and president Reagan was an actor too. I suppose they did not need that kind of toy. Actors are used to handle stress. But first things first, Mira. Enjoy your dinner.

Both start to eat and taste all the good things of life. An hour later, strengthened by the food, they relax and talk at random with a fresh mug of coffee.

I'm relieved that I have finished the cubes, Mira. All twenty-five thousand of them!

That's great, Ramon. Then you can start on the book.

Well, not really Mira. Some days ago, somebody asked me to make a 3D model of a building complex. And you know me. I couldn't refuse.

And it is again a pro bono job, is it not?

Yes, Mira. But it is for a good cause. It will be used in education. This kind of organizations don't have the money.

I really don't understand you, Ramon. You need the money!

You're right, Mira. It is to give children a better idea of orientation and to better understand the dimensions of space. Don't panic! Meanwhile, I will continue my research. I will listen to all the new videos and radio interviews while working. And I will make a list of everything I read. I think it is important that the readers know where to find the web information I use. I will make a website just for that purpose. So they can decide for themselves what to believe and what not. They must be able to make up their own minds. They should not believe me on my word alone. I would hate that. They must use their own minds.

You know what is so strange about these abduction cases, Mira? Most victims finally become sympathetic towards the Greys. It can be compared with children who are kidnapped and become sympathetic towards the kidnappers. This type of reaction, you also find with children who are abused by their parents. They defend their parents and blame themselves. They see the abuse as a punishment for bad behavior. It's very difficult to treat these children. Because if you can't trust your parents, why should you trust your therapists.

I understand what you mean, Ramon. But we had better not underestimate the Greys.

What do you mean, Mira? Don't tell me you had encounters with the Greys again?

No, no, Ramon. But other details came to my mind. Especially when I work pro bono, information just comes to me. I think it is information from Aodin. A lot had to do with the concept of time.

Ramon immediately takes his writing materials.

Tell me everything, Mira.

Do you remember Dan Burisch? The one who claimed he had contact with that J Rod character? The back to the future guy and all his talk about timelines?

Sure, Mira. In his view, the Greys come from the future to warn us for an upcoming galactic disaster.

216

Indeed. According to Aodin, this J Rod, this Grey just fooled Dan Burisch for a specific reason. So the story that Dan Burisch tells is really the story that J Rod told him. And Dan is convinced that it is true, because he became friends with this J Rod.

But why, Mira? Why tell such a lie? There must be more to it than that?

For several reasons, Ramon. But the overall reason is to create fear! The people who know about the alien presence, the Initiated, can be people from all levels of society. They can be from the world of finance, the government or the military. It could be scientists or business people. In most cases they are also members of some or other secret society. If the Initiated, who are surrounded by Mentals or Psy-mutants, believe the stories the Greys stored in them by abductions, they must think that the Greys are invincible. You must not forget that the Initiated decide how to handle the alien problem and make policies based on what they know. If they think that the Greys can travel in the past and the future then they can not make any strategy. They probably think that the Greys know every step they will take, because they come from the future. Every step would be an open book to the Greys, because the Greys know the future.

So how can the Initiated design strategies to fight them if they think that the story of Dan Burisch is really the truth? This story is a kind of intellectual blackmail from the part of the Greys. They use fear as a weapon to abduct people. But they also use fear by spreading this kind of lies about their technical capabilities and their knowledge about our catastrophic future. Because they pretend that our future is their past. They pretend they are our descendants in the future.

I fully agree with this point of view, Mira. If time travel is impossible, then this story is the perfect lie. Burisch stated that there are three timelines. Whatever the Initiated would decide to do, they would always end up in one of these three timelines. But if the Initiated would know that it is all a lie, then the fear factor would go away. Remember, Teimon said that the Greys used fear and threats to manipulate the leaders of the Téry. So it is definitely possible that the Greys used this lie of time travel since the beginning of their contact with humanity. I remember a video I saw of Stevens Wendelle. He stated that during the first meeting with President Eisenhower and the Greys, the Greys showed a kind of 3D video depicting the crucifixion of Jesus Christ. This meeting was in 1954.

Come on, Ramon. Did he really tell that?

Absolutely, Mira. My first reaction was the same as yours. Ridiculous! But maybe it makes sense. For by doing that the Greys are suggesting that they were witnesses of this event, two thousand years ago. Maybe they even pretended that they were there with a UFO, later known as the star of Bethlehem, suggesting, they could travel in time. That would fit to the story of Dan Burisch.

Jesus, Ramon. It must have been a shock for the Initiated who were present at that meeting.

Indeed, Mira. The question is: how did the Greys get these images? Could it be that the Greys were really there 2,000 years ago? Then they could have made pictures of that event. Teimon told us that the Téry colony was left behind 4,000 years ago. So the Greys could have reached Earth in those days. We must ask Teimon about this when he makes contact again. But just suppose that the story of Wendelle is true. Then the Greys suggested several things at the same time. They prove that they can travel in time and they suggest that their stories about the coming galactic catastrophic events may be true. The central brain of the Greys could indeed be able to invent such a story to take advantage of the superstitious nature of us humans. I told you that Dan Burisch's story is based on Back to the Future. But maybe this movie was based on rumors, circulating within the circle of the Initiated. In a way, this movie made the idea that time travel is possible acceptable for the general public.

You are right, Ramon. But what I don't get is: how is it possible that these Initiated people were fooled. I suppose they are all intelligent people.

Superstition, Mira. First of all, "aliens" said all these things. That is absolutely an advantage of the Greys. You know that all revelation religions believe in stories about the end times. Eschatology is the collective scientific name for it. You know, the stories how the world will come to an end. Especially Judaism, Islam and Christianity believe in a cruel apocalyptic vision about the end times. Do you remember how many stories about the end times were spread in the period of the new millennium? The millennium bug, to name one. But dozens of movies were made about catastrophic events. Finally, nothing happened, except the destruction of the World Trade Center in 2001 on 9/11. But you can hardly call that a natural disaster.

But now, a new hype is in the making. The year 2012. If you believe all the stories, it will be the moment of the great transformation. And again, the most absurd catastrophic events are prophesied. All the catastrophic ideas about this period have an unconscious effect on those who believe in apocalyptic end times. Even atheists don't escape the fear for these unexpected events. A lot of these prophecies are all based on possible natural events. Like meteorites that threaten the world, super tsunamis, super volcanoes, super earthquakes, disastrous climatic changes, galactic catastrophic events. Things that theoretically can happen. You don't need to be religious to believe these stories. How many times have I heard the saying on National Geography: It is not a question if it can happen, but when it will happen? Such statements are maybe true but make people nervous and fearful. The story of J Rod is only confirming some of these modern New Age prophecies.

I agree, Ramon. And we must not forget that the Greys are all telepathically interconnected. The Central Grey determines what they do. Everything that J Rod suggested to Dan Burisch was determined by the block he belongs to. And they have fantastic technology. They use their "alien image" to convince the Initiated and the abductees. If aliens tell us these things, who are we to doubt their predictions? So what Aodin says about time travel is important. Because if you know time travel is not possible, it breaks the power of suggestion of the Grey predictions. I can only repeat it.

1.307 **Time travel is not possible. The whole universe only exists in the same time.**

1.308 **We can travel over large distances in a short time. But the future doesn't exist as a reality. Nobody can come from that non-existing future.**

1.309 **We don't need to be afraid for the catastrophic predictions of the Greys. Their only intention is to trigger the unconscious fear of superstition.**

1.310 **Their lies are now spread by Mentals and Psy-mutants. It fits their strategy.**

Okay, Mira. You have convinced me. But what is the strategy behind these lies?

I don't know, Ramon. God knows what they really want. But like Teimon said, they want to control the Earth like they control Ter I. They want complete control.

The question is how they want to do that, Mira? We know that these lies about our future play a part in the strategy of the Greys. We know that the Mentals and the Psy-mutants infiltrated all the institutions of our world. But there are still a lot of missing links. But about one thing I am rather sure. Dan Burisch is a Mental. He was abducted when he was very young. So they could have prepared him for his task, without him being conscious of it. I hope he was not implanted. But he clearly suffers form an abduction trauma. He sympathizes with his kidnappers. J Rod could manipulate him to spread the timeline rumors in the UFO community. The Greys know that superstition will do the rest.

They are clever, Ramon. J Rod had all the time in the world to manipulate him.

Indeed, Mira. Dan developed friendly feelings for this creature. Burisch even helped this J Rod character to escape when they were in Egypt for a mission. They were in the pyramid of Cheops if I remember well. That is the place where the star map of the Ancients is hidden. By the way, what were they doing there anyway?

You tell me, Ramon. I can't put my finger on it. But I feel that all these details are interconnected in one way or another. The same goes for the crashes. It all belongs to one overall Grey strategy. The Central is a master in strategic thinking. And he has to be, if he wants to colonize our planet.

You're right, Mira. There must be a common factor in all these details. By the way, did the Greys have contact with you after that first contact?

Not really, Ramon.

What do you mean, Mira? Not really? Yes or no?

Well, I sense their presence sometimes. But they keep at a distance. It is more as if they observe me.

Mira! Be careful please. Those Greys take their time to discover your weak points.

No, no Ramon. They have to watch out for me, remember?

Yes I know, Mira. But keep them at a distance.

Don't worry, Ramon. I know what I am doing. They can't get to Teimon's information.

I hope so, Mira. I hope so. Just be cautious.

When Ramon waves Mira goodbye, he is feeling oppressed.

The Greys keep watching her. What do they have in mind? If they can't abduct her, there are maybe other ways to seek control. Mira can be so reckless. But what can I do? These modern witches are so damn self-confident. Which is a good thing of course.

While he cleans the kitchen, he thinks about everything Ury and Mira told him.

If there is one secret group that is informed about this, it must be the Illuminati. They would be perfect partners for the Greys. The new generation of Illuminati wants control, obedience and so on. They have the same wish list as the Greys. And not to forget, the deal with the Greys was simple: technology in exchange for food. Could it be that the Illuminati, who are suffering from a xenophobic pathology, possess Grey technology in their hidden power structures to conquer the planet? Maybe the Greys gave them something that makes them technologically superior. For it appears that this Illuminati fraction is very self-confident. The internal discussion within that secret group is not about the question if they can succeed, but about the way how to achieve their goal and when.

What makes it even more absurd is that this Illuminati fraction doesn't know they are fooled by the Greys. The Greys want world control themselves. The Illuminati are just useful idiots to help them come to power. That's an old trick. Desire for power is not improving common sense and intelligence. The Illuminati may have supreme power at this moment, but their desire for more power blinds the judgment to the dangers involved in making an alliance with the Greys. While Ramon goes to his bedroom, he remembers a simple story that his Wise Teacher once told.

A thief was walking around on a marketplace and there was somebody selling gold powder. The salesman was weighing the powder. Without thinking, the thief got to the guy, grabbed some gold powder and ran away. But the people on the marked saw him and caught him. When he was standing for the judge, the judge asked him: How could you steel gold powder in the middle of the day while everybody could see you? And the thief answered: I didn't see the people, your honor, I only saw the gold.

The Illuminati don't see the danger of the Greys. They only see world power.

Ramon looks through the window. It is again two a clock at night and the village looks deserted. The last leaves dance in the wind as if moved by an invisible power. The crescent moon stands above the horizon and the stars twinkle in the dark night sky.

Is the world really in danger? Is there a battle or struggle going on in utmost secrecy? A battle that involves humans and Grey aliens? Is a battle between good and evil forces in the making?

Whatever! Time will tell. First things first. I have to start writing the book as soon as possible. The world must be informed about the true nature of the Greys. If the Initiated know who the Greys really are, that will influence their own scenarios. Ramon closes his eyes and in no time he enters the dream world.

- 37 -
14/10/2006

While she drives home taking small roads, Mira is nervous.

What's happening to me? I never feel this way.

Suddenly, she has to brake hard. A silhouette of a Grey is standing in the middle of the road. She hesitates but then she drives straight at him. The moment she is going to hit him, he disappears like a ghost. Confused and in a state of shock, she pulls over to the side of the road.

What's wrong with me? Was I imagining it or was it real?

Quickly she drives home and is relieved to close the door behind her.

Am I becoming crazy? Ramon may say what he wants but this is not normal. I'm hallucinating.

She lies down on the sofa and tries to relax. In her mind, it

222

happens all over again. This is not like me, she thinks. How could I drive that creature over? I couldn't even do that to an animal. All the past experiences of her and the Greys come back to her mind.

I hope it's not going to happen all over again, she thinks. Two o'clock? I have to go to bed. Rapidly she takes some slices of bread and cheese and wearily she goes to her bedroom.

Fatigued and confused by what happened she falls on her bed. Using a technique of visualization, she puts her mental alarm on six o'clock. As she lies down, purple lightning spreads through her room, but it disappears as quickly as they came.

That's odd! I would swear that Teimon was trying to contact me.

She turns on her side and takes a deep breath. But she feels an unknown tingling going through her body. Mira does not fight the sensation until she realizes that the Greys are in her room. She wants to resist, but it is too late. Her body seems paralyzed. Only her consciousness is active. It is as if she is physically dead. Two small and one larger Grey appear at her bed and the larger one starts to communicate with her telepathically.

We don't want to harm you, the large Grey sends. We only want you to understand us. We don't want to harm people. We want to learn from the humans. We want to become like them. We want to think like you. We want to feel like you. But we are not evolved like you. You are the result of a long evolution. But we come from the future and evolve backwards in time.

While Mira is letting him suggest his nonsense, she can't change her physical state. The tingling in her body feels pleasant, though. Let's listen for the time being, she thinks. The tall Grey goes on with his hypnotic telepathic suggestions.

We are evolving to individuality. That's why we are so fascinated by humans. You all have different thoughts. We want that too. But we don't know how to do that. We want to understand why you all think differently.

Mira realizes that she must not show her knowledge about these creatures and lets him talk, waiting for a moment to counteract.

The tall Grey goes on with his programmed suggestions.

We all want to become different too. We have always lived in complete unity with one another. We don't know what it is to be an individual. That's why we observe humans. You humans all have different thoughts and feelings. We never had individual feelings. Only a feeling of oneness. We want you to teach us how humans do that.

Mira is surprised. Do I have to teach these creatures something?

The Grey goes on.

Why do you start your healing sessions from below and then gradually upwards? Why not the other way around?

Mira can't resist giving an answer.

Because we help people by guiding them. We don't want to impose ourselves on them. We have to show the people what is the next step in their lives. But the people have to make the next step themselves. If you start from above working downwards, then you give them only the illusion of a choice. In fact, you force them to make a certain choice. But most people have problems because they have been forced to do things all their life, leaving them no choice.

The tall Grey looks with his dark eyes straight into her eyes while he shares the answer with his block to formulate the next suggestion. Then he goes on.

But the people have a lot of problems just because they have a free choice. They don't know the unity of everything. That's why they do all kinds of wrong things. And in doing so, they hurt people a lot and bring sorrow to other individual lives.

That's right. But that's the learning process of life. If you want to become individuals, you must learn to make the right choices in freedom. So of course humans will do wrong things.

The Grey doesn't understand this and is silent for a while. He needs some time to process this answer with the help of his block and goes on with his suggestions.

We want to be individuals too. But we also want to think groupwise. That's why we want the people to evolve in our direction just as we want to evolve in their direction. Then we will become equal. We want to teach the people how they must evolve to group consciousness. We want to teach them how to grow above their desire for individuality. For all the problems on your planet are the result of egoism and egocentricity. If the individual comes before the group, the group will suffer from the misbehavior of individuals. That is not good. Look how much crime there is on your planet. You pollute nature and millions die

224

of hunger for the wealth of the few. Look how much poverty there is on your planet. It is all because of the fact that you are individuals and only think for yourself. The Grey looks very serious and waits for her reaction.

Actually, that's not true. Most people aren't like that at all. Most people are good and decent. But some people take advantage of the many. But they will be punished for that. Never heard of justice? Imagine, the individuals would lose their identity and become part of a group. Then you have to obey the commands of the leader of the group. The humans would simply execute orders like solders in the army. There would be no personal opinion. They would live in a dictatorial regime. And don't forget. There is always a human at the top of the pyramid. He would become the only individual. But why should he know what is best for everybody? That's why we have democracy. On Earth, every group has a leader. But he has to listen to the voice of the individuals. Do you know our history? Dictators pop up in every culture now and then. They are individuals who think they know what is best for everybody and especially for themselves. To make sure that everybody agrees with them they punish everybody who stands in their way. They commit the cruelest deeds and eliminate millions of people to keep control over the majority. But the majority of the people will never accept that. They will fight back. For humans do not want to become individuals. They already are individuals! It's part of their nature. By the way, who determines your group decisions?

She senses that the Grey doesn't know what she means. It is silent for a while before he reacts again.

We come from the future. We come from where you have to evolve to. Call it like you want. Heaven, Moksha, Nirvana. That's where we come from. Our group has no individual leader. We are all linked with one another. We together are the group. We come from the ends of time. We are what you call angels.

Oh, very interesting, says Mira sarcastically. But you get the commands from a single source, don't you?

All commands come from the central brain of our groups, the Grey says.

Well then that central brain functions like an individual. And he determines what you have to do, no?

The Grey is confused while Mira goes on.

That means that you live under the dictatorship of your Central. And he decides what you have to do. If you want to become individuals, you have to free yourself from his dictatorship.

That is impossible, the Grey thinks, because we are part of the central decision maker. He takes care of everything. He knows everything what we do. He knows what is best for us. He takes care that our knowledge is preserved. We are part of the history of our group. He gives us eternal life. He is our father and our mother. He takes care that we always get a new body when our container is worn out.

For a while there is silence. This is my chance, Mira thinks.

So you want to become individuals? If you can't even procreate yourself, how do you want to become individuals?

The Grey is clearly frustrated by Mira's question.

That's why we want to become like you. That's why we want to procreate ourselves like you do, that is why...

Yes, yes... Mira thinks emphatically. Then you will have to change your DNA. Otherwise, your plans will come to nothing.

That is what we try to do now!

The Grey is annoyed by Mira's suggestions. During the telepathic conversations the two other Greys keep the body of Mira under control. Suddenly, she feels a burning sensation in her belly. That's enough, Mira thinks.

You know, wherever you come from, I don't give a damn. But you had better stay away from my body. You are just miserable creatures. You have nothing in common with us. You are not human and never will be.

Mentally, she makes a very deep and low Ohm sound. Startled, the large Grey lets her go and the two little Greys seem to shrink. Suddenly, they are gone, just like they came. Mira sits straight up in her bed and looks around.

Those creepy Greys are gone! Ha, ha, they thought I couldn't do anything. Those Grey assholes! They don't know who they are dealing with.

She gets out of bed and looks through the window. It's very dark outside but the crescent moon still spreads a bit of light over the neighborhood.

Teimon was just on time to break the contact, she thinks. The

226

Greys didn't sense anything.

A few minutes later she falls asleep, exhausted. Thousands of light years away, Aodin looks at Teimon.

Have the Greys sensed anything?

No Aodin, I broke the contact just in time. Mira was strong enough to keep them at a distance. We have to wait to contact her again until she is safe. And together they go back, deep underground.

- 38 -
5/8/2007

Ramon finishes the last sentence as a pleasant voice brings him back to everyday reality.

Hey, Ramon! Everything okay?

Joy, dear girl, please come in. Thanks. Everything is fine.

Ramon is glad to see her alive and well.

Tell me Joy, are you all right?

Yes Ramon, but I don't have much time.

Not much time? So young and already no time? What will happen when you get older? I hope you have time for some coffee?

Always, Ramon. Thanks.

In a hurry, Ramon makes a few mugs hot tasty coffee and with some slices of cake they sit in front of the two computer screens, forgetting about the rest of the world.

Joy checks her e-mails while playing a few games with Ramon who is losing every game of course, as always. When they meet, it is as if two completely different generations come into contact with one another. She sees that Ramon closes a word processor file before she can read anything.

And how is your book coming along, Ramon?

I wish it were finished, Joy. But I am half way now.

Ramon knows she doesn't understand why he is writing a book about UFOs. She only knows UFOs from movies and thinks it is all just fantasy. Understandable of course. But still, she finds it exciting because Ramon doesn't allow her to read anything. Why is he acting like that? She finds Ramon to be the strangest person in the world. But at the same time he is the most common person as well.

I don't understand why you write a book, Ramon? You are a painter, aren't you? I don't get it.

That is a good point, Joy. But writing can be compared with painting. It's like painting with words.

Joy shakes her head. How can you paint with letters and words, she thinks.

But when will it be finished?

I really don't know, Joy. But if you start something, you have to finish it as well. And writing a book is a lot of work. But it will be ready when it is finished.

A smile appears on Ramon's face.

Yes, yes… Oh, let it go, Ramon. I will never understand you. But tell me, what's happening in the Days Of Our Lives?

Let me think. A lot has happened this week.

Is Collin really dead, Ramon?

I think so, Joy!

But who killed him? Is…

Ramon has to tell her all the details without revealing the clues. Time passes by and when Ramon gets the videos for her, he knows that her visit is over. As she leaves the house and Ramon waves goodbye, she waves back and disappears behind the corner house. He is always glad to see her and sad when she leaves. For a while his mind is quiet, but soon he starts up his word processor. The part of Mira's meeting with the Greys is finished. He will soon start with the next information of The Alien Code. He really is looking forward to the fascinating revelations that will follow. He fills his mug and quickly he puts the video tape in the recorder, to be ready for the soap of the day. Gradually his fingers find their way on the keyboard, but only for a few moments. Then he remembers he must send the pictures of the chemtrails.

That was an odd experience! A few days ago, after a long week of rain, a period of good weather brought a smile on everybody's face. When Ramon woke up, he saw some condensation trails of airplanes in the sky. They were perfectly parallel and Ramon wanted to make some pictures of them. He first took some time to drink a few mugs of coffee and when he went outside to make

228

some pictures, he was very surprised to see many condensation trails, horizontal and vertical ones, in angles of 90 degrees and all perfectly aligned.

He had never seen something like that. The perspective was amazing. It looked almost like an abstract Mondriaan painting in the air. But the idea that these trails were part of an experiment about climate control gave him ambivalent feelings. Not that he believed all the stories about the existence of chemtrails just like that. A lot of UFO sites mentioned the existence of secret experiments to get the temperature down a few degrees. Ramon wasn't interested at all in all these rumors. But he read a few articles and saw some videos about the subject. It made him conscious of the possibility that governments from several countries allowed the military or a private organization to execute these experiments. But that these experiments also happened above his own village was a shock to him, to say the least.

Why doing this in secret? Why keeping it quiet for the people? Because eventually, the stuff they use in these chemtrails will fall on the ground. Who knows what the effect is on agriculture? After he made a few pictures, he forgot the trails and went on working on his book. But when going outside to the garden late in the evening, Ramon couldn't believe his own eyes. What he saw was unbelievable.

Numerous condensation trails or chemtrails, as far as he could see. Like a large matrix in the sky. He immediately made pictures of them. It was amazing to observe this obscure show. The airplanes kept on coming, one after the other. Even in opposite directions, flying closely next to one another. This was not normal air traffic. The difference between condensation trails and chemtrails is that condensation trails disappear immediately.

For an hour, Ramon enjoyed the show, but with growing dislike. The older chemtrails spread gradually to form a light-grey nebula in the air while new chemtrails followed the same tracks as the old ones. It was like they created a web all over the visible sky.

Ramon looks at the pictures again. If these are no normal contrails, if they go to this extent, there has to be something wrong with our climate. Even if they don't admit that in public. Maybe, that's the reason why they keep these experiments secret. But if so, who organizes these experiments? It must cost a lot of money. Especially the last pictures worry Ramon a lot. The last trails were not white but dirty yellowish brown. He remembers that during the night an ugly smell had been hanging over his village. A mix of ammoniac but slightly different. It really made him mad. Are they crazy? Whoever they are. How can decision makers allow such experiments above their own country? Smoking is bad, but what about this? Confused and worried about the reality of these experiments he closes the folder with pictures. He continues working on his unbelievable story.

- 39 -
29/10/2006

There has been no sign from Mira for several weeks now other than messages with excuses: I have no time... I can't make it... But that is all. Ramon is working constantly on the real and virtual 3D model. First design everything in a 3D program, then print it and next glue it. That is the plan. But as always Ramon underestimates the time needed. While working he listens to radio interviews and videos to seek links that would support Teimon's story. The history of ufology in particular has his attention. He found a man that played an important role in 1933. This person was called Avenol Joseph. He was secretary-general of the League of Nations, the organization that was to become the United Nations. If the Greys were an international threat, such an organization could be perfect to discuss the topic of an alien presence in private. But that was just a speculation of his part. Gradually, Ramon gets a better overview of what is happening in the field of ufology.

One website makes a deep impression on Ramon: the Biblioteca Plejades. Like Wikipedia it contains al kinds of UFO related articles. Hundreds of articles and thousands of links. Very well designed also. Really professional. Partly in Spanish and for the most part in English. It had to be run by a professional organization. How else could they finance a site with more than thousand articles? All the important names in ufology could be found on that website, if you would take the time. But something sinister is going on on this site.

There is a special chapter about the moon and Mars. He is very interested because maybe he might find some clues about alien moon bases. The moon chapter starts with a list of places where astronomers saw strange light phenomena during observation. So far so good. But gradually it becomes more and more cult-like. Every article is very well chosen and written. The second article is about the special location and behavior of the moon. The moon looks as big as the sun and all the time it is showing the same side to Earth. How can that be? It must be an artificial satellite of the Earth, no?

Ramon reads all the articles. All together, it is good stuff for a science fiction movie. The behavior of the moon is indeed remarkable. But it is just the result of the laws of gravity. It is not unusual for a satellite to behave like the moon does. It is not at all as unusual as one would think. It is called synchronicity of movement. For example, Pluto and its moon Charon always have the same side pointed to one another, which is also very strange.

Ramon had the feeling that the Bibliotheca is about more than just giving information. It is as if all these articles have a link with a certain vision or system of belief. At first, it is interesting to know, but in the end they explain that the moon is artificially made, that it is hollow and that inside the moon, there are technical alien installations. Even a large cube would exist inside the moon. You can believe all this but there is no scientific proof at all.

There is no trace of Dr. Karl Wolf on that site. He is not mentioned at all. As if his statements have no real importance. But who decides what is important and what not? There is even an article containing maps showing where moon bases are supposed to be located. Not two or four but dozens of bases! The only thing you can do is believe it or not believe it. There is no possibility to react in any way. It is clear that this site is made with a special purpose. Could it be that this site has a link with the secret religion, Sean Leyka which Teimon mentioned? Could it be a sort of database where a select amount of articles get a place and are interwoven? To create a kind of alien Iliad, like in ancient Greece? To create a new kind of mythology? For that was what Teimon had said: Sean Leyka is construing a mythology to unite the myths of the different world religions.

The Bibliotheca has a lot of articles about Richard Hoagland. Ramon does not know him, but some research on the web shows that he became rather famous in the nineties of the previous century with his books and articles about the face on Mars. On one of the Mars pictures, made by the Mariner, a picture was made of the region of Cydonia. The shadow of a rock of a few square miles looked like a large face. Hoagland stated that the appearance of the face was no optical illusion of light and shadow, but a genuine, artificially sculptured rock, with resemblances to the sphinx of Egypt. In the same region a few pyramids were also visible. One pyramid had a pentagonal base, another one a triangular base. But Ramon was not convinced. Interesting, yes. But not enough proof. All too vague. Optical effects can fool you. Ramon himself is a specialist in optical art.

It could be that the Ancients had a base on Mars, though. If the Ancients were in our solar system ten thousand years ago, then they surely took a look on Mars and the other planets. For minerals, special metals and so on for their space technology. But there was no real prove for Hoagland's story. You can believe it or not. On the other hand, he is not a Mental. He is too rational and very well educated.

About the Greys there are plenty of sites on the web. It strikes Ramon that certain names have become generally used. Since the Serpo site, the Greys are called EBEs. There is a lot of resemblance between their physical nature and everything Teimon told about the Greys. But most descriptions about the nature of the Greys are the opposite of what Teimon had revealed. First of all, they are seen as humans from another planet. Interesting was the fact that the lack of individuality was mostly seen as a sign that they are higher evolved.

In general, nobody follows the viewpoints of Dan Burisch about their origin in the future. Probably because his information is very recent. But when Ramon reads over and over again how the behavior of the Greys is being justified, it makes him really mad. The general approach is to compare the behavior of the Greys with the way the humans treat animals. The EBE Greys would see humans as a kind of intelligent animals and that the Earth is a kind of zoo. So, if the Greys do experiments on people and abduct them, it is understandable because they are higher evolved, no? Like humans do experiments on animals and use them for food, the Greys do the same to humans.

Such theories annoy Ramon terribly. How is it possible that intelligent people think in such a way about themselves? It was very striking that these theories often came from military people. Since social Darwinism became a wide spread theory, not much was left of the image of man as a creation of God. The image of man became that of an intelligent social animal, led by its instincts to gain power and control over others. The idea of survival of the fittest became the survival of the strongest, which is a completely different story than the original idea of Darwin. Social Darwinism pretended that the strongest were also the most civilized. Shamanic cultures became inferior civilizations and the powerful countries were allowed to colonize them. This vision was not based on Darwin but on Gobineau's work. Ramon's Wise Teacher once told a story about Albert Schweitzer in this respect. He was a man who had a lot of admiration and respect for the African cultures. Once somebody asked him what he thought about Western civilization. And his response was: That's a good idea. When do we start with it?

The idea that humans were nothing more than intelligent animals was also the basis of behaviorism. Human individuality was seen as a random effect of the brain, while the behavior was controlled by the chromosomes. This view was the basis for the image of man of the Nazis.

After the Second World War, the image of a human was degraded to a more or less civilized predator. It is not that hard to understand that if somebody is educated with this image of man, this person can accept the behavior of a Grey. For the Greys are more powerful and higher evolved than us humans. If your image of humans is that of an intelligent predator at the top of the food chain, then it is understandable that you come to the conclusion that the Greys have the right to use the humans for experiments and food. Unbelievable how ignorant intelligent people have become. What a relief to know Teimon's completely different story about the real image of these Grey clones.

It also became obvious to Ramon that there were different theories about the origin of the Greys. The Dan Burisch version and the let us say Serpo-kind of version were the two extremes. Interesting to note was that the Serpo story states that the Greys came from the planet Serpo in the constellation Zeta Reticula.

234

This constellation is located near the south pole of the celestial sphere. The idea that Zeta Reticula was the Grey home started in the seventies. But this idea originally came from a study of the abduction of the Hill family in 1961. This abduction case was even discussed in Allen Hynek's book. During a hypnotic session Betty Hill described the place where the aliens came from. She remembered maps that the aliens showed her and made drawings of these maps. One researcher did some study and compared the stars with existing star maps and discovered a striking resemblance with the constellation Zeta Reticula. Betty Hill drew two stars on a place where only one was visible. It was only years later that astronomers discovered that Zeta Reticula was a double star, like Betty's drawings suggested. And now, forty years later, this name returns in the Serpo story.

Based on the information of Teimon, Ramon knew that it was all a lie. But why? Could it be that this information proves that the Greys spread different stories? To confuse the Initiated? Or are these stories inventions of the Initiated to create disinformation and to confuse the UFO communities. To create conflicts between these groups? While in fact the Initiated themselves just don't know who the Greys are?

It is again late at night when he goes to the kitchen to eat something. After a sober meal, he cleans the kitchen, makes a last pot of coffee and goes to his WebCom when he suddenly hears somebody entering the house.

- 40 -
29/10/2006

Mira? You always know how to surprise me. Everything okay?

As you see, Ramon. Alive and kicking. She's doing everything she can to look cheerful but Ramon sees that she is really tired. Nervously she sits down and takes a cigarette.

You smelled the coffee, didn't you Mira?

Her weak smile speaks for itself. She's not in the mood.

Are you writing the book, Ramon, she asks to take the attention away from herself.

No Mira, you know I first have to finish the 3D model. But I will

235

do everything to get the job done as soon as possible. What happened, Mira?

Ramon serves the coffee.

Oh, Ramon. You don't believe what I had to endure the last two weeks. But now, I have it under control. They can no longer do anything to me.

And who or what are 'it' and 'they'?

The Greys, Ramon. Now I know for sure what they are.

Mira, don't tell me you had contact again?

Yes, yes Ramon. I had contact with them. Don't look like that. I know how dangerous they are. But how could I know who they are if I had ignored them. And it was not like I made contact with them. They make contact themselves, you know.

Ramon shakes his head. Mira, Mira, I hope you won't regret it. But anyway, I'm glad that it turned out well.

Ramon sits down and takes his notebook.

Tell me what happened, Mira?

Mira describes her telepathic communications with the Greys vividly. She realized that her contacts were dangerous, but she was proud to take the challenge to find out more about them.

You know, Ramon, it is remarkable how precise Teimon's description of the Greys is. The Greys really believe that they live on a higher level of consciousness than we humans. They don't know who they are. Those cactus revelations opened something up but mentally they live in the conviction that it is true what they think of themselves. Very strange. They live in denial of their true nature.

That's indeed remarkable, Mira. But it is even more remarkable that some whistleblowers compare their group consciousness with a higher state of consciousness. Most whistleblowers who pretend to have contact with these so called higher evolved or higher dimensional beings, think very similar. Only Phil Schneider was very clear. To him they were stinking, lying assholes. But if you listen to the majority, you get the impression that the Greys see us as a dangerous species. That we have to evolve and that they want to give us a hand with it.

Yes, yes. And we are to believe that? But what I don't understand is that so many people believe such crap. Do you remember that Teimon told us that the Greys evolved and

236

became self-conscious?

Yes, very well. What is your point?

Well, not only the cactus experience but their own evolution became the reason why they really think they are further evolved than us.

You have to be clearer, Mira. I don't see the point.

Listen, Ramon. Before they became self-conscious they were all linked with one another in a group. They became conscious while being part of a collective consciousness. Previously they didn't have thoughts of their own or personal experiences or an individual will. That's why they think that they evolve in the opposite direction compared to humans. The Greys are convinced that they evolve from a group consciousness to an individual state. And so, it is easy for them to describe it as evolving from the future to the past. But they don't mean it literally. To understand what individuality is, they need people because we all have individuality. Do I make myself clear?

Absolutely, Mira. So the Greys want to evolve in our direction while they expect us to evolve in their direction.

Exactly, Ramon. They want us to become united with them. They don't see anything wrong in that. They think they are doing us a favor. That's why they abduct people. They want to speed up our evolution so that we will become like them, so that we evolve to their group consciousness. For they want to be individuals but at the same time they want to keep their group consciousness.

I understand very well what they want, Mira. In this way, they can link us to their block system. You must not forget, Mira, if you are in contact with a Grey, you have contact with the block he belongs to. That's the way they are created. We see the individual Grey, but he gets his commands via the collective that is in control of the Central. Psychologically he belongs to the group consciousness. Each contact with humans, gives the Central more information about the individual behavior of humans. The big joke is that humans think that they are dealing with that one individual Grey.

You're right, Ramon. I sensed it during contact very well. But there is another thing that is important to know. If you refuse to accept their way of thinking, they let you go. Because individually they can't handle a situation in which their suggestions are rejected. The Central doesn't know how to deal with this behavior. You can sense it. If you refuse to go along with them, they have to let go.

That's indeed very important, Mira. They are used to commands being executed automatically. That's the way the Téry made them. They were biological robots. So they don't understand the refusing of commands. They simply don't understand that behavior. That explains why they react that way. I think that's also the reason why military people have admiration for them. For in the military, you have to follow orders. So they have the same mentality.

That's right, Ramon. The Greys want you to take them seriously. They want you to fit in the big picture, designed by the Central. The Grey block culture is not interested in people who refuse to cooperate. That's just a waste of time to them. And not only that, they simply don't understand it.

I agree with you, Mira. There are plenty of people. So they just go to the next human.

But Ramon! Where is all this leading to? What is the big picture behind the Grey strategy?

I don't know, Mira. But I start to understand the warnings of Teimon. Finally, the Grey block culture is just a biological machine. Their goal is to log humanity into the block culture and to make our planet their own. They were doing that from the moment they were created. But the Téry had control over their actions. Since that control fell apart, the Greys are like a machine out of control. They just go on till somebody stops them. The question is who will stop them?

Indeed, Ramon. It is important for Mentals and Psy-mutants to understand who the Greys are and what their intentions are. The first step of the Greys to conquer our planet is to abduct as many people as they can. For the Greys, every personal opinion is a variation of the same theme. Abduction is their way to get a better understanding of humanity as a whole. The more influence they have on an individual, the better they learn to understand how to control humanity. The better they can manipulate abductees, the better they can manipulate their personality and sense of individuality. By suggesting a kind of spiritual group

238

consciousness, abductees become defenseless and easy to log into their block system. The abductee gets the feeling that he is working for a higher cause. But the only goal of the Greys is to get you into their Grey matrix and to have complete control over you.

That is perfectly clear, Mira. And once you are a Mental, you are ready for an implant and to become a Psy-mutant. At that moment, the Greys take over.

Do you have any idea how many people are abducted, Ramon?

Something like two million in the USA alone, I guess.

Two million, Ramon? That many? You are not serious!

Well, that's the number of people who asked for psychological help for problems related to abductions. I heard that number several times. Some even suggest the number is higher.

I didn't know it was that bad, Ramon. Because the abductees will all be logged into the Grey block system and will become slaves in service of the Central. They will execute what is suggested during the abduction sessions.

For a while, it is quiet in the kitchen.

That book I have to write will be a real thriller, Mira. What is your conclusion, based on your contacts with the Greys of the past weeks?

Well Ramon, I would say: the Central is in control. He plays with human minds. All the individual contacts go to the Central. And he can use all the knowledge he receives from the individual Grey to become better every day. What the people should know is that you can go against them. You can fight back mentally. Just refuse by all means to cooperate with them. In the end the Greys will let you go. Therefore, this book you have to write is very important. It gives abductees a tool to defend themselves against repetitive abduction and to prevent that they become Mentals.

If that is true, the Central makes it easy for us, Mira. Teimon told us that the Greys took control over their planet. He also told us that our planet is next if we don't do anything. So there must be lots of clues here on Earth to discover their plans, their strategy here on Earth. So it is important that we know exactly what happened on Ter I.

Indeed, Ramon. We have to know as many details as possible

about the Greys invading Ter I so that we can prepare ourselves better. The Greys have worked already sixty years or longer to succeed.

That's what I mean, Mira. I have to study the history of ufology in-depth. Everybody who had contact with the Greys can give us a piece of the general picture. Because we have the advantage that we know how and who the Greys really are. I can compare the information of Teimon with the stories published on the web and in books and videos. We can discriminate between what is real and what is fiction or a lie.

I will smoke a cigarette to that, Ramon.

So will I, Mira.

A few minutes later, a blue nebula is spreading in the kitchen.

We should talk more often, Mira. These meditations give more clarity. Two people know more than one. Communication is the human way to log on to one another. The Greys don't understand that. Based on our discussion, Mira, we can come to another conclusion. Only the Central has a kind of individuality since that cactus experience. The question is, what does he want with his Grey matrix? What is his psychological make-up? What is he really up to if he succeeds to invade the Earth? What do you think, Mira? Mira...?

Ramon sees how Mira is getting into a trance. Teimon and Aodin have listened to the conversation and Aodin agrees with Teimon making contact. It is safe for the moment. The Greys broke contact with Mira. It almost went wrong the last time they wanted to contact her. But now it is okay again. They both know that this will be the last contact for a while. The Grey block culture has increased the search.

- 41 -
29/10/2006

The kitchen glitters in a purple nebula and Mira enters the geometrical gateway through the skull. As a light beam, she travels light years to get to the other side where she meets Teimon.

1.311 **I salute you. We will send you some additional**

240

information. You are on the right track.

1.312 **Since the beginning of the twentieth century the Greys used a special mind control technique to suppress spontaneous intuition by humans. Intuition is a typical sign of a strong individuality. This kind of mind control started around 1920 when behaviourism saw the light. In a short time behaviourism suppressed the other psychological theories as being unscientific.**

1.313 **The Greys have no feelings. Their brain is a biological computer. The Greys approach everything rational. What they did was extremely clever. They started to target people with a natural telepathic ability, abducted them and turned them into a kind of Mentals, but not like they do it now. They were very careful in the beginning. Telepathically they suggested to these educated people the theory that the soul or the mind does not exist. That inner thoughts and feelings were illusions, a by-product of the brain. These people became "Monoms".**

1.314 **Also individuality was seen as a by-product of electro-chemical processes in the brain, in combination with genetics. Individuality as the essence of yourself, the expression of your soul was laughed away as superstition and unscientific. Only in circles of parapsychologists there was still a place for phenomena like the soul and consciousness.**

1.315 **In the thirties, more and more Mentals were created. The Greys followed a strict schedule. First they telepathically suggested a new idea to the Mentals. These people thought that it was an idea of their own. They spread their ideas in the scientific community and put their ideas into practice. You could call such an idea a Psy-virus.**

1.316 **Once a Psy-virus is accepted by a mental, it blocks your ability to feel and it makes you callous for ethics. In essence it blocks the communication between the left and the right brain hemisphere. The Greys always used very materialistic ideas, based on their own perception of reality. These Psy-viruses can easily be transferred through education. Racism, discrimination and monistic materialistic ideas were quickly accepted in the scientific community. This method of abduction was especially designed for intellectual people.**

You may call people that are infected with these Psy-viruses "Monoms".

1.317 Only later, more common people were abducted and transformed into Mentals. Monoms and Mentals are both ready for an implant. Call the Grey implants "G-implants". A G-implant can be compared with the antenna for the tooth or a human implant but G-implants are more powerful. They regulate the limbic system.

1.318 But a G-implant can also be influenced from a distance, technically as well as telepathically. Once you have a G-implant in your body, you become part of a Grey block. These G-implants can regulate your hormonal functions but also transport ideas and specific commands. The human variant of the G-implant is still in development.

Ramon writes as quickly as he can. But when he hears this information he looks worried at Mira. Mira is talking very fast. Teimon doesn't want to lose time because the Greys can turn up any moment.

1.319 Parapsychology was never a scientific discipline. We don't know exactly what happened after the thirties, but Ramon does. What I'm going to tell you now is very important. There was a special reason why the Greys brought these Psy-viruses into the human sciences.

1.320 People who couldn't accept these rationalistic and materialistic ideas, became part of all kinds of subcultures. This evolution went on and reached a peak during the sixties. The young generation of the sixties wanted individual freedom and wanted to free themselves from the socio-cultural system of that time.

1.321 But the Greys are very patient. All the subcultures gradually became part of a large organization. This process was spread over several decennia and is now coming to an end.

1.322 Mentals and even Psy-mutants were used to infiltrate these subcultures and New Age organizations. The Greys are afraid of strong individuals, especially if they have paranormal abilities because they are very difficult to manipulate.

1.323 A lot of people with paranormal abilities are members

242

of secret organizations or subcultures. In this way they have no real influence in the big world. So eventually, the Greys were able to isolate them from the common world. And that was the real intention of the Psy-viruses in the first place.

1.324 **Paranormal people get special privileges and high places in these secret groups. But without knowing, they are in great danger because some of them could come into contact with one of the seven crystal skulls. The Greys wanted to prevent that they would come into contact with the Sheyan. That was their greatest fear. Some secret organizations, often lead by Mentals or Psy-mutants, unwillingly helped the Greys to isolate and identify these special people.**

1.325 **Their knowledge of the skulls is now used within these organizations, but wrongly interpreted. In this way, they have no influence on the outside world. Most people who are able to have contact with the crystal skulls risk to be manipulated inside these subcultures. It makes it easy for the Greys to find these people and to manipulate them via telepathic suggestion. The result is that these "Contactees" spread all kinds of theories which are not correct and confuse large communities. In most cases the Greys are behind paranormal channelling. The Greys have in this way transformed lots of Contactees into Mentals and at the same time the Greys have now access to the crystal skulls.**

1.326 **All the crystal skulls, except the purple one, are brought together and under control of the Greys. In this way they could prevent actions of us to inform Contactees about the true nature of the Greys. But not everything is lost. The purple skull is still missing. Also, the persons who have contact with this skull are still not found. The Greys want to find the persons who are able to make contact with the purple skull as soon as possible. They know that we, the Sheyan, are still free and have the ability to communicate with them.**

Ramon understands that this information is addressed to Mira and himself.

1.327 **We can warn your world for the danger of the Greys with the help of the purple crystal. The Greys know you,**

Mira, but they don't know that you are our contact person. It has to stay that way. There are changes on our planet on a social and political level. The search for us is intensified.

1.328 **Liberties are curtailed. Ramon, you have to start writing the book. Soon we will have to take refuge to our last hiding place on Ter I.**

Teimon interrupts the transfer. He is too exhausted because of years of hiding. Aodin takes over.

1.329 **We have to break every contact until we are safe again. That is the only thing we can do to protect us. You have to be careful. You must not be discovered. Tell Ramon, synchronicity will increase.**

1.330 **Ramon has to find his way on the web. Research everything but believe nothing. Use your intuition and think with your feelings. I send Mira some more extra information about the Greys. We salute you. Thank you. We will come back as soon we can.**

Give them my greetings, Mira.

But the contact is broken. They are in real danger. In a hurry, Ramon finishes his notes worrying about his cosmic friends. For a while it is silent in the kitchen. Mira comes back to reality and the colors of the kitchen become normal again.

That's it, Ramon, says an exhausted Mira.

She has problems to regain her voice.

And now I need some coffee, Ramon, or I will faint.

Ramon immediately stops writing and makes a fresh mug of coffee for the both of them.

I even forgot to smoke, Ramon.

I do believe you, Mira.

Ramon looks at the leftovers of his own cigarette.

Jesus! You were talking fast! I could hardly keep track of everything you were saying.

Sorry Ramon, but they were really in a hurry. They had to go into hiding immediately after sending. The Greys were close. I sensed it in Teimon's voice.

Have you any idea where they will they go?

No, Ramon. But there must be a place where they can hide temporarily. There they will bring themselves in a special state of mind to hide from the mental powers and the technical means

244

of the Grey block culture on their planet. I don't know how they do it.

Is it a kind of Samadhi state of mind?

Maybe, Ramon. I only know that the Greys will not be able to sense them telepathically.

It looks almost like paranormal espionage, Mira.

You can put it that way, yes. And especially for Teimon it is necessary, because he has difficulties to protect himself from the Greys. His master Aodin has to take care of that.

But then they can no longer contact us?

No, Ramon. When they go into this state, contact is impossible. But they have no choice. It is too dangerous.

Ramon serves the coffee.

Any idea when they will come back?

I think that they don't know that themselves, Ramon. The most important thing is that the Greys don't find them. But when they are safe, they will be back. I'm sure of that. What I find to be very peculiar is that they are not afraid at all. They just do whatever they have to do. But they are very alert.

I hope so Mira, because I am really worried. I guess that is why they call themselves the Sheyan. They have extreme willpower. Still I think it is a great pity that they can't have contact. There are so many questions I would like to ask. I need their help to write the book, you know. Some more coffee, Mira?

Yes please, Ramon.

The rest of the magical fluid is divided over the two mugs.

It may sound naive, Mira, but in the last two months I have started gradually to feel friendship for them. In the beginning it was just information but gradually they became real persons. And I take their information more than seriously, though I still have my doubts. But as Descartes once said: "I think, therefore I am". And Descartes came to this famous conclusion by doubting everything except his doubt. Furthermore, I don't know how to say it but Teimon and Aodin are so… normal. Don't you think?

It is the same for me, Ramon. They are not arrogant or dominant or whatever. They feel very natural, completely different than the Greys. You feel the latter want to control you. I am glad that Aodin sent me some additional information about the Greys, just before he left. Now I know why he asked me to make contact with the Greys.

Ramon is slightly surprised. Did Aodin ask you that, Mira?

Well no, Teimon did. Not the first time I had contact with the Greys. But Teimon knew that the Greys would come back. So I had to make the best of it because a visit of the Greys is generally meant to abduct you. But I don't know if you are in the mood to listen to everything that Aodin sent me. It is a long story but I make some time if you want. I will not be having much time in the coming weeks. We start with a whole new project at work. I guess you won't see me for a while.

You know how to surprise someone, Mira. Of course I want to make time.

Okay then. It is a lucky coincidence that the Sheyan have to go into hiding now. In this way I can concentrate on my work. You know what, Ramon? It is half past eleven. I quickly go to the pizzeria and buy a few pizzas and a bottle of wine. Then I will tell you everything I know.

Fine by me, Mira.

Half an hour later, both are enjoying a midnight meal...

- 42 -
30/10/2006

A bit dizzy of the wine, Ramon takes his notes.

It is one o'clock, Mira. The dinner was wonderful. Now, what did Aodin send you? Anything you can tell me about the Greys is important to get a better picture of these creatures. Don't forget that even professors of Harvard University have written books about the abduction syndrome. And if professors put their title at stake, then there must be a problem. Because even when they say that it is just a psychological problem, they still haven't come up with a therapy to help these people. Apart from discussion groups, they have nothing to offer.

The reason for that is simple, Ramon. It is because they think it is all happening in the mind of their patients. They think that there is no extra factor involved, that is to say: the Greys.

That is not all true, Mira. Dr. John Mack was convinced that there was an extra factor at play. Not that he defended the alien hypothesis openly. But for him it was remarkable that the same grey beings appeared all over the world. There were no cultural differences in abductions in America or Russia or China. His books and articles about abductions have got him into deep trouble. It was such a pity that he died in a senseless car accident right after he had a meeting with two friends in a restaurant on September 27th in 2004. You must not forget, Mira. Parapsychology is still not recognized as a science, let alone ufology. Talking about grey aliens in a scientific environment is simply out of the question. This makes paranormal or alien explanations of abduction cases impossible to defend. So, I agree with Teimon. The Psy-viruses have done their work very well. Do you know any university with a faculty of parapsychology, except the University of Utrecht?

No, Ramon.

Well, enough said then, don't you think? The founder of the mystery school wanted to change that. But results were few.

I know, Ramon. Monistic materialism has suppressed dualistic and pluralistic materialism. You told me that during one of our first meetings.

You have a good memory, Mira. Indeed. Most scholars haven't read the great book of Prof. Dr. Johannes Jacobus Poortmann "Hylisch pluralism". But let us return to the matter at hand. Please, tell me what Aodin told you. I'm really curious.

Mira takes a cigarette and tries to explain what Aodin told her.

It is all quite simple, Ramon. We know that Greys are artificial clones. They can't procreate in a natural way. Like we make cars, they make copies of themselves. Their brain is completely empty as long as they grow. When they are fully grown, they are disconnected from the container. Then their brain is programmed with information with the help of technical tools. That's what I experienced in the underground compound. Well then, Teimon told us that the Greys have a vague sense of individuality via their skin. But the decisions and actions are still dictated by his block or even block culture. Personal initiative is impossible. Until now we thought that the Greys wanted to change that by imitating human individuality. But it is not that simple. Listen.

The individual Grey will not admit it, but individually they all suffer from a giant inferiority complex when confronted with humans. For as an individual, they are nothing. Do you understand what I am saying, Ramon?

Yes Mira, go on. I'm listening.

Let me give you an example. Imagine that you sleep your whole life until you are an adult and suddenly you wake up. The first thing you will ask yourself will be. Who am I? That doesn't happen as the Greys wake up after their cloning process. They lack any experience of live and are immediately programmed to function properly in the collective.

Humans grow their whole lives as individuals, even during the nine months in the womb of their mother. Our individuality grows and changes all through our life. Everything we experience and learn in our lives shapes our personality. But the Greys don't have that experience. They don't understand that. That's why they only see the rational and informational aspect of our human personality. How shall I put it? They don't understand that we humans have to put the information in our brain ourselves. The Greys live in a world of information. They don't know what it is to grow up with other individuals. They don't know what it is to learn. They just don't know anything about real life. Absolutely nothing!

But since the contact with hallucinogenic substances, the Central Grey became autonomous, able to give commands. Now he wants to dominate us humans. And the Greys work together to accomplish that. They want to take our individuality away from us because they consider it to be an illness or a dysfunction of the software. In order to do that, they have to make humans into Mentals. In order to succeed they first have to know your personality. Once they have made a scan of your personality, they know how to manipulate you and to turn you into a Mental.

Wait a minute, Mira, does that also mean that once a human is changed into a Mental, the Greys can download the information of his personality and save the information, as if it were a computer file?

That's what I mean, Ramon. They make a scan, a blueprint of your personality. With the help of the block culture, this blueprint is analyzed and used to know how to manipulate you further and to gradually turn you into a Mental. But as long as they don't succeed in this process, the human is still superior to

248

the Grey. Because the Greys compensate their inferiority by taking away from you what makes you superior to them. And that's your individuality. So they want to take something away from us. Something they don't have.

I think I understand what you mean, Mira. It makes sense. Originally, they were just one big biological cybernetic machine. To them, the brain is a computer.

Indeed, Ramon. Due to these hallucinogenic substances, something changed dramatically in their software. I don't know how it all fits together technically. But since that time, the Greys turned themselves against their creators. You could call it patricide, murdering the father. What's the psychological name for that? Let me think...

You mean the Greys suffer from an Oedipus complex, Mira? Sigmund Freud wrote extensively about it.

Yes, Ramon. That's the exact word. Because we must not forget, the Greys act and think as one person. And this collective personality sees the people of Ter I as its father. The Central behaves like a grown up son who wants to kill his father and wants to marry his mother.

A genius diagnosis, Mira. Most people don't know that an inferiority complex expresses itself by behaving in a superior manner. Not an inferior manner! And the Greys act as if they are superior to us. So you cold indeed compare it with a Greek tragedy.

That also means that we must react against these creatures or we will be in big problems, Ramon. Because they see the people of the Earth as their...

...as their mother, Ramon continues.

Exactly, Ramon. Unconsciously, they want to marry us. That's what they have in mind as a group. But the individual Grey suffers from severe inferiority. Their superiority act is just an act. They are technologically superior, but in fact they are individually very pitiful creatures. They never had a father or a mother. They can't procreate. They can't even eat normally. Anything they think is shared by the whole block. And everything they do is on command of the Central. You would have an inferiority complex for less, don't you think?

You're right, Mira. My teacher of education, professor

Langeveld of the Netherlands, would say: That is the worst preformed environment you can think of to develop a healthy personality.

That's right, Ramon. You know, when the Greys made contact with me, I always played with their lack of self-confidence. I confronted them with their ignorance about what real life is all about. You know, like: what do you want to teach me, little boy. You don't know anything. Psychologically, they are like little children, considering the fact that you have always contact with their block and not with the individual Grey. And that changes the whole situation. If you make the Grey in front of you feel that, he is on his own and that makes the individual Grey very unsure and unable to handle the situation. Individually, they are not dangerous at all... if you now how to handle them. You have to let them feel you are on top of them. Because you are. But it is completely wrong to be scared of them. Because then you give their block the chance to control you. And then they become dangerous. To know this is the best defense against them. That's why it is so important that the book will be published. With the help of the book, people will know who the Greys are.

So, in essence, it is important that the abductees don't panic during the confrontation. By neglecting them and to show them that you are superior they are powerless. Don't listen to their suggestions! Be yourself. Because that is what they fear the most.

That's just great Mira! But what happens when they feel your superiority?

Oh, that's strange, Ramon. It looks as if they become very weak. It is as if they lose all strength. Their head bows and they sink through their knees. They just look miserable. That happens because you influence their mental image they suggest to you. And then, you have to do something unnatural for humans: you must not show any compassion. Because compassion makes them mentally strong again. If you don't fall into that trap, then they will give up the mental abduction and disappear.

So, if I understand you well Mira, one must not treat them as humans?

Of course not, Ramon. Because they are no humans. They are not even animals. They are programmed biological robots,

250

remember. And don't forget the plans of their Central Grey! The block culture wants to manipulate and integrate humanity into the Grey matrix. You know what a hell it will be for us if they succeed?

Ramon stops making notes.

Our planet will become one big Auschwitz, Mira.

You are right. We must not forget what they have in store for us. They will treat us as cattle. They need us for hormones and other stuff. I already feel bad when I see what people do to animals. I even became a vegetarian for that reason. If the Greys would succeed in their plans, a terrible future is waiting for us all.

But the question is: what is their ultimate goal? They want to kill their father and they want to marry their mother. And humanity is their mother. But what does marrying us humans mean in the mind of the Greys? Don't forget, Mira. The Greys prefer to live in space. They are not built to live on a planet. They can't survive here on Earth. How must I see that marriage with us? A long distance relation?

No idea, Ramon. I only know their wish list.

Could it be that they want to enslave the whole world population in a kind of biological industrial complex, serving the Greys?

That could be, Ramon. But they also want to procreate. I don't think that can happen if the Greys remain in space.

OK. Let's do a thought experiment, Mira. You know, they plan everything in advance. They take their time and do everything step by step. Teimon made it clear that the Greys plan everything on a long term. Eighty years have past since the thirties. Imagine they have plans to become planetary citizens. And imagine that they want to become like us. What must they do to make it work? How will they prepare the marriage with the human species? Because if they want to become like us, they need a body like ours. A body, adjusted to our planet and being able to procreate.

I guess that's the only way, Ramon. But then, they need a type of body with a lot of genetic variation. They can get genetic material from the humans. For if they would only make one identical body for cloning, they would get the same problems as with incest if they want to procreate naturally.

I didn't think of that, Mira. You are right. They can't use the same cloning process as they use now. Otherwise, natural procreation is impossible. So they have to develop a different cloning technique if they want to have a human-like body. They have to use a different genetic make-up for every clone. But then it is not a clone anymore. Clones are identical.

Absolutely, Ramon. But there is a second problem they will have to overcome. The human body can eventually be cloned. But these clones can't communicate telepathically with one another. Remember, they want to keep their block culture intact. To make that happen, they have to mix a part of their own DNA with human DNA. Like the Téry did, millennia ago but now with Grey DNA. So it would have to be a body, partly human, partly Grey. A hybrid being. Because the Central doesn't want to lose control.

You could be right, Mira. To work in space, they can still use the Grey body they already have. But the Grey hybrids that would live on Earth have to have a different brain than the humans.

I don't want to be a part of that marriage, Ramon. Over my dead body! The human race would eventually be exterminated.

I could not agree more, Mira. That could explain the genetic experiments they do on abductees. Hundreds of articles suggest that something like that is happening in underground bases. Abductees often report that the Greys take samples of their tissue and so on. Maybe they even do genetic experiments in these underground facilities.

In his mind, Ramon remembers images from his nightmare and it gives him cold shivers.

But wait a minute, Mira. Something is not right in our reasoning. Or there is something not right in the reasoning of the Greys. If the hybrids would get a brain like the Greys, then they would lose their identity. For if they have telepathic abilities, they have no private thoughts anymore. Would you like that everybody could read your mind?

Absolutely not, Ramon.

So, in other words, this would come into conflict with their own wishes.

Do you know what I think, Ramon? I think the Central is not at all looking to give the individual Grey an identity. I think he wants to know as much individuals as possible. Just to make the abduction process better.

For a while it is quiet in the kitchen. And then they both say simultaneously:

The book has to be written as soon as possible.

Let's drink to that, Mira.

Thanks, Ramon. My throat is dry from talking.

The glasses cling.

To the book, Mira!

To the book, Ramon!

For a moment, they both enjoy the nocturnal silence.

Let us go back to what Aodin told you, Mira. I find the comparison with the Oedipus complex extremely useful. If the Greys want to overrule their father, then they maybe want to make humanity into a Grey like block culture. Don't forget that the Greys had to work for their creators.

That is indeed another way of looking at it, Ramon. The Greys could use the humans, like the Téry used them. They could turn the tables.

Indeed, Mira. The Greys can't live in our atmosphere. But if they have sufficient Psy-mutants, they can let them do all the work for them. With the help of Psy-viruses, Monoms would be able to complete the scientific work here on Earth, to create that hybrid block culture. Once this hybrid race would be in production, these hybrid cultures would gradually make the natural humans superfluous. They could then wipe out the natural humans, the Mentals and Psy-mutants included. The world would become populated with hybrids, in service of the Greys.

But that would be horrible, Ramon! Imagine a world without a soul or individuality, without feelings, without culture.

Well yes, Mira. Maybe only the Central would have an identity. Maybe, he could give the hybrid a kind of artificial individuality. Just by downloading one of the identity files they have in stock for programming the hybrid clones. If they make a copy of the identity of every human that is abducted, then that is a possibility. You must not forget, Mira. The Central of the Greys does not think like a human. For him, the world is purely virtual. He is like a living self-conscious computer. For him, everything is just information. It is difficult to get inside the mental make-up of the Central.

I agree, Ramon. It is hard to tell what is really going on inside their heads. They don't understand the things the same way as we do.

That's the problem, Mira. There is no common sense between the humans and the Greys. It could be that the hybrid project is just the next step. Once they have created the hybrids and take over our world, the Greys can program the hybrids with the same programming techniques they always have used as Greys.

Because the hybrids are in fact just a new type of body that can be used to make it possible that some of the Greys can live on our planet. The hybrids would have a brain like the Greys. And they would all be linked telepathically with the Central. But before they eliminate the natural humans, they could collect DNA samples of all the natural humans. The next step could be to make the hybrid clones genetically different, with a programmable differentiation of their individuality in the clone production process.

How disgusting, Ramon.

Yes it is, Mira. But tell that the Central.

I don't think he will listen, Ramon. He is like a little child who wants to know how a watch works. He opens the watch to find out and in doing so he destroys the watch. The Greys can do whatever they want, they will never become humans.

That's a fact, Mira. The problem is that they just don't understand that. Have you ever heard of mentalism?

Not really, Ramon.

Mentalism is a philosophical school that sees reality as an illusion. A mentalist believes that there is only consciousness. And that reality is just an illusion like as if you are looking at a movie with your consciousness. This philosophical trend exists in every culture in a different way. The Greys are in fact all mentalists. They don't perceive reality like we humans. Our mother gives us life and we grow physiologically and psychologically in our planetary and cultural environment. In the same way, mother Earth gave birth to the whole evolution of life and finally created us humans. The DNA of every living being carries a part of the complete evolution of life. We humans and all living creatures "are" the living Earth. That's why we have a sense of reality. We belong to this Earth. This feeling of

254

belonging is the basis of all instincts, emotions and most importantly, of all feelings. We are one with Earth. Especially humans have this ability to cohabitate with any other living creature. But Greys don't know that feeling. They are still one big collective machine. They are born as adults with no mental experience at all. Anything they know is programmed. Psychologically, they experience life like a dream. Like a mental reality, a virtual reality. They are not in tune with reality as we know it. To them, the body is like a hard disc, a container that can download information. If the drive malfunctions, they just put the same information on another hard drive. The program for every Grey is saved in computers. They have the technology for that. The Central takes care that every Grey file has its place in the overall block culture. To them, individuality is just a file, a packet of information, which you can copy. Because that's the only thing they understand. They don't have a sense of reality. So the Greys are pure mentalists. Do I make myself clear?

Perfectly clear, Ramon. Though it is difficult for a human to imagine. I wouldn't like to be the therapist of the Central.

Ha, ha, that would be a challenge, Mira. But no, thanks. I wouldn't know where to start. By the way, what time is it, Mira?

Two o'clock, Ramon.

Shall we drink one more coffee, Mira?

Just one more, Ramon, I am getting tired.

Moments later two mugs clink.

To the humans, Mira.

To the humans, Ramon. Whatever the Grey plans are, I am glad we get a better idea why Teimon and Aodin warned us. And then to think that the Greys already succeeded with their plans on Ter I. It must be a horrible place now. The frightening thing is that the Téry are much more developed than we humans. And still, they were not able to prevent the Grey threat.

I thought about that too, Mira. I guess that the Téry are much more homogenous than we humans. I remember that the Ancients dropped them as a colony on Ter I to bring them over to Earth later. So it must be a rather small group of people, with one culture. So there is not as much differentiation as here on Earth. That must have been to the advantage of the Greys.

You have a point, Ramon. And the Téry must look more like the

Greys physiologically. Because the Greys are made with their DNA. And we must not forget that all the Téry have the ability to communicate telepathically. So they were easy to reach by the Greys. Our planet is much more complicated. Look around you. So many different cultures. Billions of people still live in poverty. Millions of children die from lack of water or diseases while others live in unlimited wealth. You can't say that we are just one people.

That cultural, religious and economical diversity, Mira, may be our weakness but also our strength against the Greys. If the Greys want to bring the whole world under their block culture, they have to overcome that diversity.

And to say that it all started when one Grey falling with his butt on a cactus, Ramon.

Even on the street, you can hear them laughing. Mira has pain in her stomach from laughter. Suddenly she thinks of something.

Ramon, ha, ha… I have to tell you something else!

Ha, ha… Sorry Mira… What do you want to say?

It just popped up like that. I think it is something extra from Aodin.

Wait, Mira. First I will make an extra mug of coffee. You need it if you want to get home sober. Ramon makes two new mugs of coffee while Mira rolls two cigarettes.

What could this extra information by Aodin be?

Ramon ponders this question while serving the coffee. Can it get any worse?

- 43 -
30/10/2006

What was I going to say, Ramon? Oh yes. I think this is very important to you. We can agree on the fact that it was crucial for the Greys to prevent the Sheyan to contact humans on Earth and to warn the humans for the Grey danger!

Indeed, Mira. That must have been a priority for the Greys.

Now you must listen very well, Ramon. Dan Burisch said that he let a Grey escape through some kind of star gate, no?

Yes. It was somewhere close to or in the pyramid of Cheops. He

256

also told that all over the world the star gates had to be destroyed to avoid a galactic catastrophe, allegedly to reduce the damage. He even stated that the war in Iraq was a cover to destroy the star gates there, assuming that this alien technology was given to the Sumerian culture. You know, the Anunnaki.

I remember, Ramon. But don't you see what I mean?

Ramon, a bit tipsy from the wine, tries to make some notes. He looks at Mira and thinks.

Wait a minute, Mira. Do you mean that these star gates exist but that the reason to destroy them was a clever lie? Not to prevent a catastrophe but to prevent that the Sheyan could get into contact with the shamans on Earth?

Indeed, Ramon. That's what I mean!

Ramon is immediately sober.

That's unbelievably clever, Mira. And they didn't have to do anything themselves. Except maybe give the locations to the Initiated. Unbelievable!

Now, Ramon, that's what Aodin meant when he was talking about the Mentals or the Monoms. The Monoms are very intelligent people who believe whatever the Greys suggest. So, through Dan Burisch, they not only spread the lie of time travel. But the Greys convinced the Initiated via Dan and maybe others, to destroy all the devices of alien origin. The threat of the catastrophe was just a cover story to convince the Initiated to destroy all the artifacts. They didn't know that they made it almost impossible for the Sheyan to warn humanity about the Grey threat.

That makes sense, Mira. That is why Dan Burisch helped the Grey to escape. He thought he was doing the right thing. Damn it, Mira. Those Greys are professional liars. Now that you mention it, do you remember that Dan Burisch also talked about another device? The looking glass? A kind of futuristic version of the crystal ball, used by witches and magicians in fairy-tales. My first thought was that it was simply nonsense. But it could be that the Greys have software to make precise predictions about future events. Something that can extrapolate the present into the future. Like futurologists do with statistics but more advanced. Burisch said it was not absolutely precise but better than anything we have available. A dream for captains of industry, policy makers and economists.

Right you are, Ramon. But don't forget that the Greys can use this technique themselves.

Indeed, Mira. They can use it to take certain decisions and to select the best tactics to achieve their goals. A perfect technique to predict future events. Unbelievable, Mira. So, the Greys gave the Initiated devices, but they knew exactly what they gave them. It made it easy for them to convince the Initiated that their future predictions of catastrophes were right.

Right again, Ramon. Because they can manipulate these devices to influence the outcome. I told you how dangerous it is to believe them, Ramon. If you are interested in their technology, you admire them. And they will turn that into an advantage. They use that to manipulate you.

So all the technologies Corso talked about may play in the hands of the Greys? They wanted us to get that technology, but they knew very well which effect it would have on our society. Everybody that works for them will be manipulated for a specific goal. That would mean, that the computer and the laser and God knows what more, play in their hands too.

I'm convinced of that, Ramon. To control information systems is just a game to them. That's their world. And because the world relies more and more on computers and the internet, it will be a piece of cake to take control of all those systems, whenever they decide to do it.

Ramon takes a deep breath.

That means that their control matrix grows day by day, Mira. Thank God, they could not locate the purple skull. Otherwise, we might as well give up.

Right you are, Ramon. If they would find that skull, it would be impossible to have contact with Teimon or Aodin. Everything depends on the purple skull. Because the Greys can't locate the skulls themselves they spend much time in tracing humanoids like me. If they could manipulate me, I would not be able to come into contact with the Sheyan without revealing their location. That's why the Greys started with the Psy-viruses already from the beginning. They had to isolate the people who are in contact with the skulls. We know the skulls were spread over the world during the second contact of the Ancients. But in

258

those days, the Greys didn't exist.

Oh no? That's indeed important, Mira. Did Aodin mention the period when the Greys were created?

Mira is silent for a while, screening the data of Aodin.

The Greys arrived in the vicinity of the Earth some thousand years ago. The Greys don't know what happened before that period.

That's important to know, Mira. We must not underestimate the Greys, Mira. They are not only clever but also sly. All those catastrophe theories of the last years about the year 2012 can be a perfect diversion to execute their own agenda.

I'm sure of that, Ramon. The Greys know all the myths of the world religions through Mentals and Psy-mutants. You must not forget that the Greys worked for the Téry to inform them about everything that happened on Earth, at least in the last millennium. So the Greys must have a very good knowledge of our history and the evolution of science. That's the reason why Teimon has no clue what happened after 1930. The Greys broke contact with them.

It's always the same old song, Mira. If you know the superstitions of a population, you can do with the people what you want. Confirm their superstitious believes and they will work blindly for you. Superstition is a powerful weapon in the hands of a demagogue. Look at the influence of Bin Laden. Being a Sunnite, he used the myth of the Mahdi to convince a small group to go along with him.

The Mahdi? Who is that, Ramon?

Well, simply said, the Mahdi can be compared to the Messiah figure in Judaism and Christianity. He belongs to the messianic belief of the Islam. In Islam, Mohamed is the messiah and it is believed he will come back in the person of the Mahdi. The myth tells that the Mahdi will unite all the Islamic cultures. And then he will spread the Islam all over the world. Maybe, you don't believe this, Mira, but there are websites with descriptions of the facial properties of the Mahdi. And I must say: Bin Laden looks like him.

But there is one important thing everybody should know, Mira. The Sunnites and the Shi'ites believe in a different version of the Mahdi myth. The Sunnites believe that the Mahdi will come. But the Shi'ites believe that before the real Mahdi comes, a false Mahdi will come. Once he is there and active, the real Mahdi will come, together with the Messiah of the Christians, to unmask the false Mahdi. That's why the Sunnites and the Shi'ites are each others enemies. Think of the war between Iraq and Iran. Iraq is a Sunnite and Iran is a Shi'ite country. But if these two groups would become united, then the West would have a big problem. It would give the Islam tremendous power. Sorry Mira, I am boring you, aren't I?

But no, Ramon. I am merely tired. Please, go on! I am listening.

Well, it comes to the point that if for example the USA would invade Iran, then the Shi'ites and the Sunnites would have a common enemy. That would be enough to unite the two greatest enemies within Islam.

But that is easy to understand, Ramon. Even I can understand that.

Well yes. I don't know why I never hear or read anything in the press about that. Don't forget, Mira, if the Islam would become united, it would be proof for the Islamic people that Bin Laden is the real Mahdi. And then... then...

Mira sees that Ramon is really worried.

What would happen? War? A third world war?

Ramon shakes his head.

I don't know, Mira. Let it go. I don't want to make predictions about something like that. I hope it will never happen. I can only say that it would be in the interest of the West to stay friends with the Shi'ites. The Sunnite and the Shi'ite countries had the Mazdaistic religion before they became Muslims. But the Shi'ite countries had a period of Christianity before they became Islamic. That's the big difference between these two major Islamic groups. It would be better if the Christians would make an alliance with the Shi'ites against the false Mahdi, don't you think. But enough of that, Mira.

Nervously Ramon cleans the table and fills the mugs with the rest of the coffee.

The point I wanted to make is how superstition can be used as a weapon. Fear is never a good advisor. The Greys convinced the Initiated to destroy the contact devices using their own superstition. The Initiated don't know they did the Greys a big

260

favor. God knows how much wonderful alien technology has been destroyed.

And not only that, Ramon. The Téry used some of the artificial star gates to get here. It must be large objects of some kind. The Téry can no longer use these devices for real space travel. Maybe that was the reason why Dan mentioned the Cheops pyramid?

Damn, maybe that is the reason why so many UFOs are observed in the vicinity of old temples and pyramids. It could very well be that the Greys are not there for tourism only. It could very well be that the Greys keep an eye on them. There are plenty theories stating that these old megalithic structures are more than mere religious symbols. Maybe, some of these theories are right after all. I must make some real study of the most important megalithic sites, Mira. Not only the Egyptian pyramids, but also the South American ones. Teimon told us already from the beginning about the gateway of Orion. Could it be that the star gate technology was in one way or the other connected with the "shape" of the pyramid. The shape is very unnatural. Maybe, their GPS system can sense them over large distances. It could be, don't you think?

I really don't know, Ramon. But it sounds logical. But I have no information about that and I can't ask Teimon. By the way, I hope they are safe out there.

I hope so too, Mira.

In the background they hear the sound of the church bells.

Three o'clock Ramon. Now I really have to go.

Absolutely not, Mira! First you drink one more coffee for the road. I want you to be sober before you get into that car. I'm always worried when you drive away just like that.

Minutes later, the hot brown elixir flows into the mugs.

Here you are, Mira. Milk and sugar as usual.

Ramon can't resist enjoying the wonderful fluid that keeps the workaholic on his feet. With the mug in their hands, they both go outside. It's very dark and the street lights make sharp shadows on the walls.

Mira, let's say we meet again with the next full moon. I will try to finish the model as soon as possible. Use your free time to relax to be ready when Teimon makes contact again.

I will do just that, Ramon. The last weeks have been so hectic.

Exactly, Mira. I will do some in-depth research about the pyramids. Maybe I will find traces of the star maps in the Cheops pyramid. And Mira, stay away from the Greys. Okay?

Don't worry about that, Ramon. For the moment, I guess they will not come back. They had enough of me, I think. She is a bit surprised that Ramon is worried about her.

I hope so, Mira. God knows which tricks the Greys know to break you mentally. Don't trust them for a minute.

It's very kind of you to worry about me, Ramon. But I'm a big girl. And it is not that I invite them. I can handle them when they show up.

Ramon looks around in amazement.

Where is your car, Mira?

I came on the bike Ramon, Mira says proudly.

Mira, you on a bike? That's new.

And why not, Ramon? Do you think I can't ride a bike?

No, no Mira. I think it's an excellent initiative. I just have to get used to the idea. Ha, ha, Mira on a bike.

Don't laugh, Ramon. I just knew it was going to be late today. That's all. There is nothing more to it than that.

While laughing, Ramon takes her mug and helps her to turn the bike. With some effort, Mira gets started and with an extra push in the back she reaches the street. With some left to right maneuvers, she makes some speed and gone she is. They wave at one another and slowly she disappears into the night.

Ramon feels a cold wind. The winter cold is slowly coming. Quickly, he does some houseman rituals and in a hurry he goes to bed where sleep relaxes his worried mind.

- 44 -

Seven silhouettes follow a guide through a labyrinth of caves, decorated with very large crystals, created over eons by the melting water of a large glacier that covers the high mountains. The echo of the water drops resonate from all directions. The only light beacon is in the hands of Xigan, the hermit. He guides the Sheyan through the crystal labyrinth. The light makes the most beautiful light reflections in all colors of the rainbow. In a

262

wooden cube box, decorated with symbols, Aodin carries the purple crystal matrix.

After the last contact with Mira, the seven Sheyan were ready to go to Ha Olam. A mythical place, discovered by the Ancients, the most secret hiding place for those who had to defend themselves against unexpected evil or in times of natural disasters. Even Aodin did not know where they were going. Teimon had to concentrate on the "**W**" symbol. Immediately he got telepathic contact with Xigan. He could guide Teimon to find his way through the labyrinth of caves to a location where Xigan was waiting for them. When they finally found their way out, they saw Xigan. With his long blond hair and a face like a Neanderthal man but more fragile and finer lined, he makes a deep impression on the Sheyan. The natural habitants who evolved on Ter I are very friendly humans. The Ancients took care that they agreed to let the Tèry live on their planet. But the Tèry never really lived together with them because their evolutions are too different in development. Only occasionally, the shamans have contact with the leaders of the Tèry to celebrate their arrival, thousands of years ago.

Nobody knew Xigan. Long ago, he left his people to choose the life of a hermit. He lived with the animals of Ter I in the endless green jungles.

As soon Teimon visualized the "W" symbol, Xigan received the mental message and knew what to do. Molo, a giant elephant-like animal and friend of Xigan, brought him to the location, high in the mountains. The Sheyan were impressed to see him waiting, sitting on Molo, as an ancient mythical figure. He is one of the thirteen Guardians of his people. Aodin knew him from documents. But this was the first time that Aodin met Xigan in person.

Politely they bow for one another and Xigan speaks some short words. Aodin in return answers him with some short phrases. Aodin knows the spoken language of the local people very well. All Guardians of the Tèry still know how to speak, although in the Téry culture, speaking became old fashioned because of the common use of telepathy. Aodin had to learn the art of speaking during his education to become a Guardian, the highest level of the Sheyan. The welcome ceremony was simple but solemn and after a short telepathic briefing between Aodin and his brothers, everybody is informed.

They all follow Xigan through the forest to the entrance of a secret cave. Aodin takes care of Teimon, to keep him from falling from the cliffs and once in the cave, he makes sure that Teimon will not hurt himself on sharp crystals, broken by underground planet quakes. Teimon is still in trance and walks along with his brothers as a sleepwalker, a precaution against the Greys. Deeper and deeper they go into the labyrinth of caves, until they see a bluish light at the end. Great is their surprise when they enter a large natural hall. Aodin is impressed. This must be the place, Ha Olam, the Ancients discovered and where they found the crystal to make the purple crystal skull. Nature had really surpassed itself. As one large baroque cathedral, the walls of the natural hall are decorated with large crystals, surrounded by large white stalactites and stalagmites. In the abstract patterns you can project even your most hidden thoughts. A natural underground water channel splits the hall in two. The last water is flowing away into a tunnel at the end of the giant hall. They understand that this hall is normally filled with water.

In the middle of the hall, a platform is built over the channel and a large pane-shaped star ship seems to wait for those who need it. Aodin sees for the first time the Ark, mentioned in some secret myths of the Sheyan. It is indeed the perfect hiding place for the Ark: a cavern, deep under the sea. Legend has it that the Ancients founded the group of Guardians of the local habitants to protect this place as if it was the holiest of holiest. A blue pulsating light around the ship tells that this star ship is still active. After all that time, the ship is in perfect shape. Xigan is concentrating on a symbol and automatically a door opens.

With admiration, the Sheyan enter the ship. A pleasant temperature makes it clear that they had better put their coats aside. In the super modern designed ship, these soberly dressed monks appear suddenly as real space astronauts. The simplicity and perfection of the ship exceed anything they have ever seen. No sharp corner anywhere. It seems to be made of one piece. Through the window, they see the tunnel where the water disappeared. On the second floor of the ship all the navigation

264

instruments are located. Zeinia seeks the thoughts of Aodin. With a simple gesture, Aodin allows him to enter the special room. Zeinia is the technician of the Sheyan. He knows the technical writings and the old code symbols from the Ancients by heart.

Fascinated, he looks around in this magical room. He takes a seat in a perfectly fitting chair. After a few visualizations, he puts his hands on the sides of the armrests. As by magic, different parts of the navigation instruments free themselves from their base and rotate in space. The undergrounds hall is lit by a strong orange-yellow light, but soon it becomes dark-blue again. Everything seems to work perfectly. While Zeinia deactivates everything, Teimon lies down in his chair. He came out of the trance as soon as he was inside the craft. Xigan starts to hum and Aodin understands that there is no time to lose. He gives Xigan the wooden cube box with the purple matrix and gets in exchange a strange shaped jewel, with in the center a smaller copy of the crystal. Very carefully, Xigan gives this precious jewel, which he had to protect all his life, to Aodin. The jewel will make sure that Teimon can have contact with Mira, but it is also the navigation receiver of the ship.

The jewel fits perfectly in the center of a special device in the control room of the ship and a vibration goes through the whole ship as soon as it makes contact with the control panel. Aodin gives a mental command to his brothers and immediate they take their seats. Moments later they all lie in a circle around the center of the ship. Telepathically Aodin gives the last instructions. Xigan sees that everything is done and after a last verbal salute to Aodin, he leaves the ship.

The door closes silently behind him and as quickly as possible he runs out of the hall with the wooden box tight in his hands. He finds his way out through the crystal labyrinth but takes suddenly a halt. He pushes one specific crystal, marked by a symbol. In the distance, he hears the flow of streaming water as it enters the hall. Xigan runs as fast as he can to a higher place, to find his way out of the labyrinth. And while he goes back to Molo, who is waiting for him, the hall fills completely with water. Molo is enjoying the juicy moss on the roots of the mountain trees. Together they return to find a shelter in the valley for the Greys.

The seven Sheyan lie silently in their chairs, unreachable for the Greys. Apart from Xigan, nobody has a clue what happened in that magical place, deep under the ground. The only thing Xigan has to do is to bring the purple crystal to a safe place, which he and only he knows.

- 45 -
26/11/2006

A month has passed by as if it was a day. Ramon has done everything he could to complete the model and his WebCom has been turned into one big recycling bin. Litter and paper everywhere, maps in different scales, collages and paper models of the buildings. Christmas is near and in between, Ramon designs a new 3D postcard. What started as a simple design has become a model of a Christmas tree with a stable and everything. But like anything in art, it takes containers full of time. Amused, Ramon looks at the final prototype, as Mira suddenly enters his WebCom, clearly agitated and nervous. With gestures and a waterfall of words, she tries to explain why she had no time to bring him a visit. Ramon smiles.
Mira, I'm glad you are alive. I thought you were taken by a UFO to Timbuktu!
I wish it were true, Ramon. At the office they expect that everybody is on stand-by, twenty-four hours a day. Everybody has to be a hundred percent available. They are crazy. I'm glad I haven't heard anything of Teimon anymore. I wouldn't have the time to inform you. But tonight I said: They can all go to hell. I shall bring Ramon a visit.
Mira, I know exactly what you need. A fine coffee will do you good.
While Ramon starts his coffee ritual, Mira is looking at all the paper gadgets spread over his WebCom.
Oh, what a beautiful Christmas tree, Ramon. Can I have one too?
Of course, Mira. If I get it ready in time. A few minutes later, they sit on their familiar spot in the kitchen and enjoy a hot mug of coffee with some nut cake.
Haven't you heard anything from Teimon, Mira? No sign?
266

Nothing?

Nothing Ramon. Absolutely nothing. But yesterday, I suddenly had contact with somebody. I think it was the same person as just before I came into contact with the purple skull.

Ramon remembers that before this story started, Mira had contact with a source that revealed him the connection of different colored skulls with constellations. But at that time he wasn't aware of the significance of this information.

Yes Ramon, it was the same source. I'm almost sure. He started to talk about the crystal skulls. He gave me again information about all the skulls.

Ramon immediately looks for his notebook. As he finally finds it under all the paperwork, he sees the date of the last notes.

Do you know that the last notes are a month old, Mira! I'm ashamed that I couldn't start with the book. But if everything works out well, the model will be finished in a few weeks. And then, I will start immediately. Damn! I can't find the notes I made of the information about the connection of the skulls with the constellations. Where have I put them? I'm not going to search them now, Mira. That might take hours. But tell me, what did that mysterious person send you?

Listen, Ramon. You know that Teimon told us that a lot of paranormal persons became members of a secret organization.

Yes, Mira. Look, here it is. On October 30th Teimon told us about that.

Well, you will be surprised. This is what the source told me.

1.331 **All the crystal skulls are now property of several secret societies. But there are also a lot of fake skulls. Their shape is not right.**

Now that you mention it, I remember one website of an organization that owns a lot of crystal skulls. They give lectures all around the world.

That may be so, Ramon. But most skulls are not from the Ancients. My contact told me the following:

1.332 **There are a lot of fake skulls, made by shamans in the past, to get the same power as the highest shamans. But they are not as powerful and can't be used to get contact with the visitors from space. There are only seven genuine skulls and six are in the hands of secret organizations. The purple skull**

has never been found. Because the real skulls have all one basic colour of the spectrum, some people suspect that there must be a purple skull. But they are merely guessing.

Something I don't understand, Mira. Are the people with access to these real skulls members of a secret society?

No Ramon, that can't be.

1.333 Only completely independent people become the chosen ones to come into real contact with one of the crystal skulls. If one of those chosen ones becomes a member of any organization, he will immediately be replaced by someone else.

And what about those people who pretend that they have contact with the skulls but who became member of an organization?

Well, I guess they sense things and they know there is something special about the skulls. But they don't know what it is. The only thing they can achieve is a limited contact with the Akasha. But further than that, they can't go. Listen, Ramon. The next thing he said was even more intriguing.

1.334 Only those in contact with a "Guardian" can have access to a real skull. They don't need to possess the crystal skull physically. Every skull works through a different star gate. The purple skull works through the star gate of Orion. But there is also a skull that works via a star gate, located near the Pleiades, and so on.

1.335 Every skull gives access to another part of the code of the Ancients and works via another star gate.

Ramon doesn't know how to react. Until now, only Merly used that word.

A Guardian, Mira? Did he use that word?

Yes, he used the word Guardian. Why do you ask?

Well I just wonder, that's all. That would mean that a Guardian has to be educated in the code of a specific culture! A cultural code connected with one of the crystal skulls! How else could he be a guide for the one with access to one of the crystals?

I guess you are right, Ramon. It is just a feeling I have but I think that this unknown contact is of Tibetan origin. After he broke contact, I immediately remembered a visit I brought to a Tibetan monastery some years ago. It was so strange. I was smoking a cigarette outside in the garden, and suddenly I saw a Tibetan

268

monk on the roof of the monastery, waving at me. I waved back of course and seconds later, he was gone. I have the strong feeling, it was him.

That is remarkable, Mira. He may be a Tulku, a monk with paranormal abilities. Some of them can communicate telepathically. But maybe, the highest ranked Tulku is the one who is able to have contact with a crystal skull. Teimon said that there are seven crystal skulls. Maybe one skull is connected with the Tibetan culture. It would make sense, you know. Let's drink a fresh coffee to that, Mira.

Hot brown elixir flows in the mugs.

I'm glad with this information, Mira. Now I know at least what a Guardian is. He is somebody who is initiated in the code of a culture. Then Aodin must be a Guardian and Teimon a Tulku. But anyhow, we will come back to that later. There is something else I want to discuss. A few days ago, I downloaded a video of a certain Dr. Wolf. He's a computer specialist. He could definitely be a Mental or even a Psy-mutant.

Is that the same Wolf as the one from the moon base?

No, he has the same name but he is somebody else. A very interesting person in a way. Let me tell you about him. He states that he came into contact with the Greys in 1952. He was involved in several secret projects related to UFOs. With what we know about the Greys, it is interesting to listen to his interview. He could truly be a prototype of a Mental. He was abducted when he was still a child. When he was fourteen, his IQ rose from 141 to 168 in a very short time. As a young adult, he was involved in top secret projects. He stated that he was involved in the development of the paint of the Stealth airplane. Phil Schneider, completely independently of this Dr. Wolf, said that this paint was mixed with alien material. And Phil's ideas about the Greys were very clear.

This Dr. Wolf said in the interview that the Greys were concerned about our environment. And that the Greys are from Zeta Reticula. That the Greys work together with secret American study groups and that he was one of their most important advisors. He confirmed the rumors that a treaty was signed between a secret governmental group and the Greys. So there we have again an indication of the existence of the

Initiated. This treaty was also signed by the MJ12 group. The MJ12 group is the top twelve of the Initiated.

Again twelve, Ramon. Isn't that remarkable? Is MJ12 the same group that was mentioned in the X-files as the top of all the secret UFO-related groups and projects?

Yes, Mira. There is no official statement that this group exists. Stanton Friedman, a nuclear physicist wrote a book about MJ12. Dan Burisch stated that he is a member of that group. In the last month, I read several articles that try to prove the existence of that group. Particularly interesting about this Dr. Wolf is the fact that he is very intelligent. Just like Dan Burisch. They both have a positive picture about the Greys. So this is again proof that the Greys took care that their Mentals became important people inside secret projects and support their strategy.

Indeed, Ramon. And in this way, the Greys stay on track with all the technical developments.

That's what I thought too, Mira. But the most shocking thing he said was that one in forty Americans is abducted.

But Ramon, that's two and a halve percent. That's about eight million people! Then the Greys must have a tremendous influence on the population of the USA!

That's what it looks like, Mira.

Then it is time that you start writing the book, Ramon.

Absolutely, Mira. I work day and night to finish the model. And then, I will concentrate only on the book. Promised!

I believe you, Ramon. Just hurry up. By the way, Ramon. What do you think of Al Gore's video, "An Inconvenient Truth"? It is the subject of the day at work. But I have mixed feelings.

Well Mira, it is difficult to say. He pictures a catastrophic future but at least, he believes that we can do something about it. There is indeed something changing in our climate, but the cause is still not clear. The Club of Rome warned us already in the seventies. But the media seem to have forgotten everything about it. Of course, Al Gore is more convincing than a group of scientists. He was almost president of the USA.

I hope he succeeds to spread the message, Ramon. But I have to go now. I have to feed the animals and then quickly to bed.

Ramon walks with her to the car and waves while she disappears in the night. As he closes his WebCom hours later, he wonders if

Merly is a Tulku or a Guardian. If he is a guardian, than Ury is a Tulku. If Merly is a Tulku, then he must be in contact with a guardian and passed the information to Ury. What is happening? It all becomes more and more complex. And how does the Tibetan who told Mira about the Guardians fit into the story? With mixed feelings he falls asleep.

- 46 -
26/12/2006

Again a month has passed by. Ramon comes back from the garden house with a bag full of apples. He enters the WebCom and looks around. The 3D model is still not ready. But the first results are visible. Satisfied about his work he cleans the kitchen. The cake and the cookies are ready.
He lights the Christmas tree in his freezing cold WebCom, giving it a surrealistic atmosphere. All the memories of the past year have a place on his homemade tree. And what a year it was! Aliens, crystal skulls and what more.
The computer screen shows a video with the title "The Secret Government". It is a movie from 1995 showing a lecture by William Cooper in Hawaii. He was a friend of Phil Schneider. He had outspoken ideas about the whole UFO subject. Especially about the history of the secret projects he was partly involved in. He stated that the NSA, founded in 1952 by President Truman, insured the secrecy of all these UFO related projects.
The NSA was specialized in analyzing the codes of secret messages. Cooper also stated that the MJ12 group existed and that this small circle of Initiated was the top of all the secret projects.
Ramon was convinced that Cooper was an important whistleblower but he was not a Mental, just like Phil Schneider was not.
All these people, they fight a lonely battle. The only thing you can do is listen to them and make up your own mind. What is lacking in all their stories is real evidence. Ramon was happy that he could at least trust the information of Teimon, and not to forget Merly and that mysterious Tibetan contact. Their

information was like an oasis in the desert of disinformation and the multitude of opinions on the web.

Overall it became more and more clear that a group of Initiated exists. Cooper was not in favor of the Greys, just like Schneider. But he used the word EBEs for the Greys, based on his own research, almost ten years before the same name popped up years later in the Serpo story. Ramon was shocked by his statements about how all these projects were financed. There was something fishy about the origin of the large amounts of money, needed to finance these projects, to say the least. And that was surely not a stimulus to bring disclosure of the UFO subject. An Aliengate is the last thing they need in the USA, especially now.

Something else had become obvious for Ramon in the last month: the reason for the secrecy. Teimon said that when the Greys came to their planet, they threatened the leaders of Ter I. And that was clearly also the case on Earth. It struck Ramon that a lot of military whistleblowers almost without exception stated in interviews that the governments in general were convinced that these UFOs were no threat at all for the world, because they did not attack people. Robert Dean said it very clearly: If the aliens wanted to attack us they could have destroyed the entire world population a long time ago. The same statement was shared by other UFO researchers. Ramon had a different opinion about that statement. It was not because the Russians didn't attack the USA that they were not considered to be dangerous! There was even a race for the most powerful weapons between the two countries.

The military considers any power to be a threat. That has always been the case, maybe not so in peace groups but in the military? Come on! No, no, the military clearly saw these UFOs as a threat and even a very dangerous one. Even if they were not hostile at all at the moment, they were technically superior to anything existing on Earth. That was proven above any doubt by Robert Dean, Robert Jacobs and Robert Salas and probably many more. Nuclear warheads were neutralized in a blink of an eye. Rockets destroyed in full flight and so on. So the most powerful army of the world was at the mercy of the goodwill of these UFO's. To military people, this must have been a very frustrating and fearful situation.

The whole secrecy around the UFO subject had definitely to do with preventing the world population to become aware of the dangers. UFOs were a threat in the eyes of the military. No doubt about that. And those who were threatened were in the first place the policy makers of that time. Just like on Teimon's planet. Not by the phenomena itself, but by the danger of the unknown intentions of the Greys, whoever they where. Why else would the government go to such lengths to keep everything secret? The end justifies the means is often the stance of the policymakers.

The only conclusion Ramon could come to was that all these secret projects are part of a kind of arms race, to be able to defend themselves against a possible future alien attack. It could be that the military saw the first UFOs as a kind of explorers or spies to collect information about the humans on Earth. Before the large army would arrive or whatever. That's military logic, is it not?

The secret organizations, involved in this alien weapons race, must have become very powerful over the years. They must be more powerful than the public army. A lot of videos had convinced Ramon that the world powers prepare themselves in secrecy for an interplanetary war. Major Donald E. Keyhoe predicted it in the fifties. The speech of President Reagan to the UN about an alien threat in the late seventies, showed it was not only a problem for the USA but a world problem. If you look at it this way, the last sixty years, covert projects must have done anything in their power to try to find the weak spots of the Greys. They must have developed technology with the help of back-engineering to find an answer against the alien threat. Maybe that is where the other Illuminati are afraid of. The secret technology, developed in secrecy since the army got their hands on the crashed flying discs.

Since Roswell several UFO crashes happened and these crafts were studied in detail. The Greys would be laughing, if they only knew how to laugh. They knew all along that the humans would not be capable to copy the technology of UFOs, even if they would theoretically understand the technology. Didn't Colonel Corso say that they were not able to reproduce the material? Mira was right. The Greys deliberately gave the world some flying discs. They knew in advance which kind of materials and technology could be copied and which not. The Greys wanted the secret groups to develop specific technology.

Didn't Corso say that the development of the chip, the glass fiber and the laser were all based on back-engineered technology? It became obvious that the Greys gave us these alien gadgets with a certain purpose. Probably to develop technology here on Earth that the Greys needed themselves. Why do it yourself if the humans could do it for you? They only had to wait. These advanced technologies would bring forward two things: the group that would be able to back-engineer these technologies would become a power within the power structure of the USA or any country that possesses these crashed materials, because it had to be done in secrecy. And at the same time, the Greys made sure that abducted people, the Mentals, played an important role in these projects. So they were informed about the developments. And with the help of their so called "looking glasses" they must have known how long it would take to spread these technologies over the world.

Just think for a moment. Before we knew it, the world has become completely dependable on computers and web technology. And that is a very important part in the Grey strategy of their invasion. The world becomes dependent on Grey technology. Can you think of a greater threat? The Grey block culture wants to dominate and control us. They don't want to destroy us. They need us. They want us! That is the reason why they don't harm us for the moment. Not because they are peaceful aliens. They want us alive.

That was for the moment the diagnosis of Ramon, making sense of the information on the web by comparing it with the story of Teimon. It was a strange feeling to realize that his WebCom could be the result of alien technology.

But there was something else that thwarted Ramon. A lot of ufologists are in the habit of spreading ideas that could be called anarchistic, to say the least. An anarchy of the word, that is. It was annoying that a lot of UFO related websites put a lot of "anarchistic information" on the same websites as well. One complot theory after the other passed in review. It made the UFO subject part of a network of complot theories. In these times of terrorist threats, only one law would be enough to prohibit most

274

of the UFO related websites.

There was something just not right. But it was not clear what exactly. Could it be part of a disinformation campaign? Just in case disclosure would come too early and would interfere with the plans of the Grey-human cabal? Because increasing the information pollution is a perfect way to guarantee secrecy. You have to admit: Who has an overview of the thousands of files? Who can control and check it all out? You need a professional organization to do that.

But in order to organize a world wide disinformation campaign, just to keep the Grey threat away from the public eye, you need lots of people. You need carefully planed lies and in order to maintain these lies, you need more lies. This string of lies has increased over the years and the methods to keep the secret safe are more and more complex, more and more aggressive and more and more threatening. In time, the container of disinformation can be compared to Pandora's Box. If you open the box, the country will fall apart. So what else can they do apart from keep on going on the same track of secrecy?

Could it be that the secret sect is part of this disinformation campaign? They would be a perfect partner to reveal a mix of real and fake information. In this way a lot of information could be made public in a fragmented way in order to make it impossible to see the big picture. And at the same time, the Greys would be able to suggest the top of the sect how to structure the disinformation to their advantage.

What a situation, Ramon thinks. He takes a deep breath and after some notes of his X-files diagnosis, he makes himself a nice cup of coffee. While the water is transformed into coffee, he remembers a proverb of his Wise Teacher: No matter how quick the lie is spread, the truth will finally come on top. Ramon lights a few candles in the kitchen to feel the Christmas spirit as somebody enters the doorway.

Happy Christmas, Ramon! Sorry that I couldn't come earlier.

Joy! Happy Christmas, dear girl! You must have smelled the coffee, no? All Ramon's sorrows disappear as snow in the sun. Her first cascade of questions is of course about what is happening in their favorite soap.

So John works for the ISA and the twins are real aliens, no?

That is still not clear, Joy. But the ISA is studying their DNA now. You know what I think, Joy? I think these twins are from Earth. Maybe, Stefano has created them with the help of artificial insemination.

But who is their father and mother, Ramon?

I have no idea, Joy. But I guess we will find out eventually.

Wasn't it a UFO in which the twins fell to Earth? That was not a normal airplane, was it?

Well, you have a point, Joy. But maybe, it was a ship, made in secrecy by a secret organization of Stefano. You know, he has his hands in all kinds of secret organizations. You do know Rolf, don't you?

Yes, the scientist.

Indeed, Joy. He is definitely a neo-Nazi from Germany. You can hear it in the way he speaks. I think he knows more about it.

A neo-Nazi? What's that, Ramon?

Well, those are people who still believe in the ideas of Hitler.

Oh Ramon, you think much too deep about everything. It's just a soap, you know. Just fantasy. But I find it strange that the twins don't know who they are. How can that be?

That's a good question, Joy. But they never had a mother and a father. They were living completely isolated from the rest of the world. So they could not develop an identity.

That's strange, Ramon. I can't imagine such a thing. But I am happy that Belle and Shawn are back together again.

So am I, Joy. You see, when a couple have secrets for one another, their relation becomes problematic. Luckily, Shawn finally told the truth.

After some full mugs of coffee and some fresh cake, Ramon takes the video from the past week. He realizes more and more that "The Days of Our Lives" is a commercial version of the UFO files. All elements are there albeit in a clumsy and funny way. Could it be a cautious way to inform the people about the whole UFO domain?

Eight tapes, Ramon! That many?

There are so many movies these days. I don't know what to choose anymore. So I recorded them all.

With a big smile she puts the tapes in her basket while looking at all the paper models. They are beautiful, Ramon. And so tiny!

276

The model will be beautiful.

It will be even more beautiful when it is finished.

I have an idea, Ramon. I have nothing to do at the moment. Shall we watch the last part of the Lords of the Rings? You have the DVD, no?

Let's do that, Joy. It will help me to clear my mind from all my work for a while. The lights are dimmed and with some coffee and sweets both watch the fantastic movie. Suddenly, Ramon hears somebody entering the kitchen.

Sorry, Ramon. I didn't know you had a visitor.

Joy puts the DVD on pause.

Mira? Is that you?

Yes, who else, Ramon?

I will be right there, Mira. I'm back in a minute, Joy. I just have to speak to that lady. It won't take long.

No problem, Ramon. I will play a few games on the computer.

Quickly, Ramon goes to the kitchen and turns up the radio a bit louder so that Joy can't hear what they talk about. He sees that Mira is nervous.

Is there something wrong, Mira? I haven't seen you in a month. Any news from the cosmos maybe? Happy Christmas, Mira!

Happy Christmas, Ramon. No, no, she whispers. No news from Teimon. But I get strange pictures all the time. Circles, rotating in all colors, connected with one other. And I see strange symbols. Very complex. I don't understand. But Ramon, you have a visitor. I was waiting for Chinese food and I thought I'd pop in to see you, so that you know that I'm still alive. But the food must be ready now. I see you later. My guests are waiting.

But Mira, won't you stay for a while? The coffee is hot and Joy is enjoying herself on the computer.

No, no, Ramon. I have to go. Bye. I will be back later.

And before Ramon can say another thing, she's gone. What's wrong with her? Moments later, he and Joy enjoy the rest of the movie and quickly, he forgets Mira's short visit. When Joy goes home with her videos and one of the Christmas trees he could finish, he's alone again with all his work and questions.

New Year and January pass by and it is already late February when he finally finishes the model. From Mira and Ury, no trace.

In a hurry Ramon cycles back home through the cold night. The crescent moon rises above the horizon and gives some charm to the cold winter night. He is relieved to feel the warmth of the hallway. As he sees the model, a smile comes to his face. He puts his spectacles on and checks if he hasn't forgotten anything. Finally done, he thinks. With a bag full of apples he enters the kitchen. The kettle of soup boils and the smell tells him it's done. The model is ready, the soup is ready and I am ready to start with the book. No more pro bono!

The few vegetables of the garden are cleaned and the apples are peeled. Ramon turns up the volume of the radio when he hears Housewife by Daan coming out of the speaker. In no time, the apple sauce is ready. Hm, a royal delicacy. While making the soup, Ramon reflects about all the information he got from Mira. What's wrong with her? Since her last short visit, almost two months have passed. His effort to finish the model made the time fly by. Only Joy regularly showed up and gave him some notion of time and reality.

How are Teimon and Aodin? Are they still safe? Already four months no contact. I hope Mira had no Grey visitors. But if this were the case, I would have heard something from her. I guess work must take all her time. Business is sometimes a hard profession. But Mira is tough.

Quickly, he mixes the apple sauce to a pulp and takes the kettle of the fire.

And now some coffee! Coffee beans are grinded and the aromas make his heart beat faster to the rhythm of the music when somebody enters the kitchen.

Are you there, Ramon?

It's a familiar voice. Ramon is surprised and astonished.

Mira, I was just thinking about you. That is a surprise. Everything okay, girl?

Mira smiles at the only houseman she knows.

Hello, Ramon. As you see, I am still alive.

Thank God, Mira. I was worried, you know. I haven't seen you for months.

278

Sorry for that, Ramon. Work, you know. I see the model is ready. So many details! It is beautiful, Ramon. They will be glad with that!

I hope so, Mira. Sorry, I don't hear you well with all that noise on the radio.

He dims the sound and goes to Mira.

I'm glad it's finished. Such work is bad for my eyes. I'm glad that the computer could help me. Anyhow, you are just in time. Some coffee, Mira?

Please, Ramon.

Elegantly as always, she takes a seat in her favorite kitchen spot. Relieved that Ramon is not angry about her long absence, she rolls a cigarette. Most guys can't understand that she has a full time job. The kitchen is soon filling up with the smell of caffeine and nicotine. The coffee is served and Ramon is glad to finally sit down.

Still no news from Teimon?

Please Ramon, no questions right now. Let me first enjoy the coffee. The last two months have been hectic.

Don't tell me that I didn't warn you, Mira. Business is a tricky job, especially when a company starts a new project. Anyhow, look at me. I thought that I could make the model in a month. But in the end it took four months. Four! But believe me: no more pro bono. Writing the book is pro bono enough.

That's just great, Ramon. So the decision is made? You will write the book?

Absolutely, Mira. I don't know how but I will write the book. By doing, you learn to do. So I guess you can only learn to write by writing... I hope. It's good that Teimon stopped sending information, Mira. It gave me more time to do my research on the web. It is not easy to get an overview of everything that happened the last forty years in ufology, you know. When I was young there were only a few books about the UFO subject. But now, with Google and YouTube, everything has multiplied rapidly. What disturbs me the most is that all UFO sites give information, but cooperation between sites to construct the big picture is hard to find. It seems to me they all have their own agenda, which is understandable of course. But it is bad for the science of ufology. And it's clear that there is also a commercial side.

Big business, Ramon?

Well yes Mira. Not that it is wrong. Everything is business today. The world is the "nothing for nothing show", you know. But I hope I can generate some order out of the chaos with the book. Lucky me, to have access to the information of Teimon and Aodin. It gives me some substance to separate the chaff from the corn.

That's right Ramon, but that means that you have to accept that the information of Teimon and Aodin is right, no? Otherwise, it makes it even more chaotic.

I agree, Mira. It's indeed a paradox. But what choice do I have if I have to write the book? At least, there is one objective, concrete, verifiable aspect: the star map. The strength of the book is the star map, Mira. If that part is right, all the rest of the information, about the Greys and the Ancients and the Téry, will become more reliable. It would be great if we could find the star map. To be honest, I am curious myself whether the signals really exist. Because no matter how you look at it, if I want to know if the star map exists, I will have to write the book. Because if the signals are hidden from the public, the ones who protect this information at least know what the signals are all about. Maybe they can break the code with the information that I got from Teimon. And that is the goal of the book at the moment. So no matter what, I have to give Teimon the benefit of the doubt, no?

Mira smiles.

What you are saying is in fact that you still have your doubts about it all.

Yes and no, Mira. I can think of all kinds of scenarios. I can be the harshest critic of my own theories. It could be that Teimon is not giving the right information. Or that you translated something wrong. On the other hand, it is possible that you get the information from the Akasha. If that is the case, it is possible that you only have access to a part of it, therefore drawing the wrong conclusions. This was also the case with Edgar Cayce. Don't forget what Tenhaeff always said: Where ends the truth and where starts the personal interpretation?

I know, Ramon. But it is also possible that it is all just my own imagination!

That's true, Mira. But I'm sure that this is not the case. I do not think this is a projection of your subconscious or super-consciousness. The story is too complex. There are not only the Greys, but there is also the star map, the planet Ter I, the different personalities involved, the crystal skull, the publications on the web and so on. Then again, you might have gotten the information from the web in one way or the other or you could have had telepathic contact with me and know through me what can be found on the web. But even then, the information you give can't be found on the web. If the latter would be the case, your information would not deviate that much from what I find on the web. Teimon's information makes clear who the Greys really are, who made them and how they operate. In short, it reveals the secret agenda of the Greys. And that, you can't find on the web. No, no, trust me, there is something else going on. And don't forget. There is a big chance that the star map and the signals exist. Remember the statements of Steven Greer. Nobody proved that he lied. And if the signals are real, those who have the signals will be the ones to figure out whether the information of Teimon is right.

Thanks for your trust, Ramon. Because, believe me Ramon, it is no fun for me to have all these freaky contacts.

I know that all too well, Mira. I was very worried and still am. But until now, everything worked out well. But now that we are speaking of Teimon, Mira, still no news from him?

Mira can't suppress a smile.

What Mira? Do you mean...?

Well, yes and no, Ramon. But it lasted just a few moments. It happened just before I decided to bring you a visit. Suddenly the purple nebula was there again, but it was not like with Teimon. I heard in the background a deep bass-like rhythm. I never heard that when Teimon had contact with me. The only thing that came to my mind was that I had to bring you a visit. I will let him know I'm here.

Him? You don't mean that, Mira? Really?

Quickly, Ramon fills the mugs once more, takes his writing materials and full of questions he wonders what kind of information he will have to digest.

Oh Ramon, that's strange. I hear him talking. He says that the Sheyan are in danger. And we have to help them. I will have contact with another star gate, he says.

Ramon's heart skips a beat when he hears that the Sheyan are in danger. What's wrong with them and who is talking now? Mira gradually goes into a deep trance and for the first time in a long time, she sees the purple crystal skull and when the central matrix starts to tremble, she tunnels again into the unknown. Suddenly the color changes into deep blue and she hears the voice again, better and clearer this time.

Ramon opens the notebook, ready to take notes as suddenly the alarm of his mobile phone clock rings. A reminder to tape a movie for Joy.

Just a moment, Mira.

In a hurry, he puts the tape in the recorder and with a few clicks the movie "One Last Dance" will be recorded.

If only Joy would know that I let an alien wait for her movie.

As he runs back to the kitchen, he gets a flash back of all the work on the model, seeing all the paper, scattered everywhere around the WebCom.

Let's start now, Ramon, says Mira a bit impatient with that typical deep voice.

Of course, Mira. Sorry. Is it also possible to ask questions?

No, Ramon! No questions. It is just like in the beginning. Short but compact. I hope I can translate it! Here we go.

Here we go, thinks Ramon and the song by the Chemical Brothers comes to his mind.

1.336 **We, the Ancients, salute you who can hear without sound. I am Aryein. I speak for the Ancients.**

The Ancients? So it is definitely not Teimon?

No Ramon, it is Aryein. It is the spokesman of the Ancients.

Ramon is flabbergasted and shakes his head. It becomes more and more complicated every time that Mira gets in touch with somebody via the purple skull. The Ancients? That was the last thing he would expect. Even the Téry haven't had contact with them for millennia. But Mira starts to translate the information, leaving Ramon no time to think. It's writing time.

1.337 **The Sheyan are still impossible to reach. They are in great danger.**

282

Mira has clearly difficulties to translate the information she gets. The expression on her face is intensely focused.

1.338 The hexagrams of the code are made of twelve signs by twelve signs.

Ramon is speechless. Hexagrams? I don't believe this!

Now I see pictures of squares, Ramon. Images, but I don't know what they are. Images of origin and beginning, or something like that.

1.339 The key of the code can be found in the Cheops pyramid. The signs can be found in China.

Ramon is stunned to hear this. The Chinese I Ching, The Book of Change, has always been his favorite book. The book is composed out of sixty-four chapters, symbolized by abstract signs called hexagrams. These signs are composed by two kinds of lines: full and broken lines. His Wise Teacher could talk for hours about this book that contains the basis of the entire Chinese culture. But the code of the book was never deciphered. His Wise Teacher stated that there existed even an I Ching of twelve lines. Could it be that this is what Aryein means with these signs of twelve lines?

Mira gives Ramon a hint to ask questions.

Sorry, Mira. I was just thinking. So, Tei... eh... Aryein, if I understand you well, the key of the signs can be found in the pyramid of Cheops? Do you mean the key to understand the I Ching of the twelve lines?

1.340 The signs can be found in China. 12 on 12. Synchronicity will show you the way. I will come back. I salute you.

Ramon looks up.

What? Has he already gone, Mira?

Wait a minute, Ramon. I have to go to the Chinese location.

What?

Ramon has no time to adjust. Is it possible that Mira will translocate herself to China?

For a moment Mira is silent and suddenly she says: I'm in a room, Ramon.

Her voice is very deep. Mira is now in a deep trance. He experienced this remote viewing ability often with Marika. But this is the first time that Mira seems to be able to translocate herself. Her head is sunken, deep between her shoulders. It looks as if she is asleep. But that is only an impression. She is definitely awake and begins to describe the place that she entered.

1.341 **I am in a large square room. The walls are straight, but the ceiling has the shape of a pyramid.**

1.342 **Around the four sides, I see twelve pillars.**

1.343 **Between the pillars and the walls, there is a passage. Above the pillars, I see figures. The walls are white.**

How high are the pillars, Mira?

1.344 **I think three to four meters. The distance between the pillars is one meter.**

And what is the shape of the pillars?

1.345 **The pillars are composed of six segments, divided by a smaller stone. On the segments there are symbols.**

While Mira gives details of the room, Ramon makes a sketch of her description. Is there anything else you see, Mira?

1.346 **I see all kinds of lightning like laser beams, going from one segment to the other. All around they go and they also reflect on the pyramid's ceiling and then back down again. And then, it repeats again.**

Ramon makes notes but doesn't understand.

Are these light beams real or is it just as a kind of virtual explanation of which segments belong to which?

I don't know, Ramon. It is so strange.

Don't you see any other details? Do you see anything else in the room?

Mira shakes her head.

No Ramon, it is all so confusing. Wait, Ramon!

For a moment it is silent and it looks as if she is fighting an inner struggle. Suddenly she jumps up.

Yes, Ramon! I got them measured.

Sorry Mira, I don't follow anymore.

Give me a moment, Ramon. I need a minute to adjust.

She sits back in the chair and looks for something to smoke.

It were the Greys, Ramon! They wanted to confuse me when I was in the temple room.

The Greys? My God! And just what did the Greys do?

Well, I was in the middle of the room, but the Greys didn't want me so see what was in the middle of the room. That's why there were these light flashes.

Still shaky, she lights her cigarette.

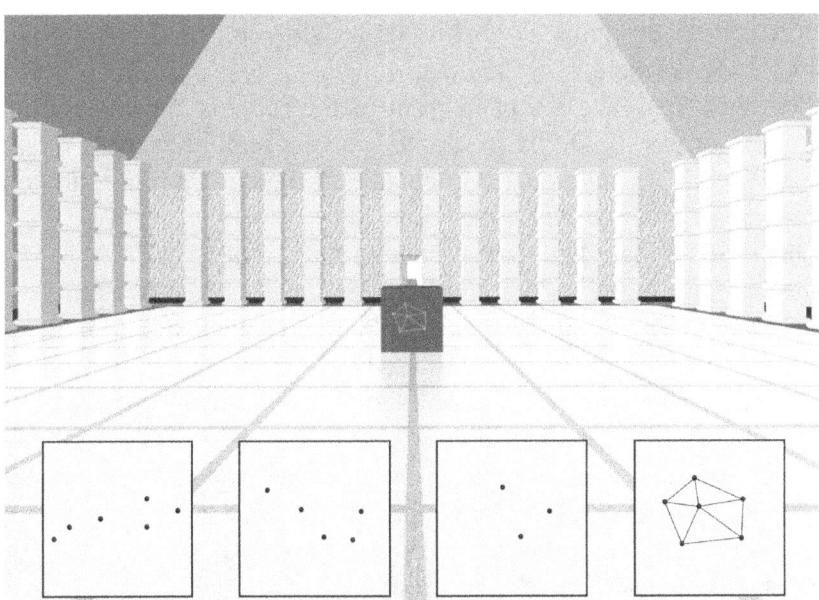

Even Ramon starts to get nervous of all the excitement and can only think of one remedy to calm down.

Some fresh coffee, Mira?

Yes, Ramon. Please. Look at my hands shaking!

Ramon calms down during the coffee ritual but is very worried about Mira. So the Greys are not gone. They must suspect something. Gradually Mira comes back to herself.

Jesus, Ramon. That was strange. Her voice gets back to normal and she takes a few deep breaths. Now guess what was standing in this room, Ramon.

No idea, Mira. You tell me. But first things first, this mug of hot coffee will do you good.

Thanks, Ramon. You will not believe it, she says in between drinking. There is a cube standing in the middle of the room.

A cube? You don't mean that!

Definitely, Ramon. A massive stone cube.

Ramon goes from one surprise to the next.

Wait a moment, Mira.

Quickly, he makes a sketch of a cube.

Okay. This is a cube. Can you tell me more about that cube?

Well, on the sides there are drawings!

Okay, now you're talking. Wait a second Mira. This drawing is no good. Follow me, Mira. I make the drawing on the computer in 3D. That's better to visualize.

Together they take a seat in front of the screens and in no time Ramon draws a 3D virtual drawing of the temple room. Twelve pillars with six segments at each side of the square room, and on top a pyramid, resting on the walls.

Okay, that's that. And now, a cube in the middle, yes?

Not that big, Ramon. Yes, that's better. That's about it, Ramon.

And the drawings on the cube, Mira? Can you still remember them? Can you make a sketch of them?

Quickly, she takes a paper and draws four squares. She concentrates on the drawing of Ramon and suddenly, she's back in the room. Attentively, she looks at every side of the cube and draws what she sees. On every square, she makes a simple drawing, using… points.

Is that all you see, Mira? Just points?

Yes, Ramon. That's what I see. I'm back in the room.

286

Ramon copies the points on the 3D cube. In the mean time, Mira looks around in the old temple room, to see if there is anything more.

Can you tell me on which sides I have to place these drawings, Mira?

Carefully, she points out where the drawings belong.

Ramon places the drawings of Mira on the right sides of the cube.

Is there anything else you see?

Oh yes. On top of the cube, I see a dragon! A red dragon.

Okay, that's typical Chinese. And on the pillars? Do you see something there?

No Ramon. Sorry, I'm back. That's it.

Ramon sees that Mira needs some time to adjust.

Come Mira, let's go back to the kitchen. I will fill the mugs once more and finish the drawing in detail later.

Ramon knows that after a psychic translocation, it takes a while before the psychic comes back to reality. He takes care that Mira doesn't fall. With cake and coffee they go over the notes once more to be sure he has it right.

What a situation, Mira. So this Aryein is somebody from the Ancients?

Yes, strange, isn't it, Ramon. I sensed that it was somebody different. I even had the impression that he was not that far away. It was clearer.

Strange indeed, Mira. What I don't understand is that Teimon can't have contact with the Ancients and you can.

Apparently I can. Maybe because the crystal skull is located on Earth.

That could be, Mira. For it was the intention of the Téry to come to Earth finally. It could be that the Téry have no crystal skull on their planet to contact the Ancients.

The coffee-pot is completely empty before the two have talked everything over. It has been four months since the last contact and Mira needs some time to adjust.

So Mira, as far as I understand, the pyramid could contain the key to the I Ching code. Ramon remembers several teachings of his Wise Teacher. Sometimes, late at night during seminars in Lugano, the beautiful city in the south of Switzerland, his Wise

Teacher spoke about the secrets of the different cultural codes. All students listened closely to what he had to tell about the Tai I Ching.

The Tai I Ching was more a kind of library than a book. Some 128 books would be necessary to write the Tai I Ching down. There would be 4096 chapters and also 4096 dodegrams of twelve lines with 12 subchapters, and not to forget the key of the Cheops pyramid to understand how these dodegrams of twelve lines are ordered and have to be read. And that would be the key of the code. Could it really be that this key was hidden in the Cheops pyramid?

Legend has it that the Tai I Ching really exists. Maybe it is hidden in Tibet in a cave near a large mysterious waterfall. This waterfall was never found and was one of the many legendary, undiscovered places in Tibet. Ramon was very surprised when a few years ago an American expedition discovered the waterfall. At the same time, there was also a Chinese scientific expedition searching for this waterfall. But without any results. National Geographic showed the documentary. But the Americans couldn't find the cave either. The waterfall was located in a very dangerous ravine. Maybe this was a good thing. It is not at all sure that this is the legendary Waterfall. But even if they would have found the cave and the library, no one would have been able to use the book. Only one person in every two thousand years or so would be able to read this book. But it is better that the Tai I Ching doesn't fall in the hands of the wrong people. They could misuse it or even destroy it. Like the library of Alexandria.

That this book could play a role in this strange alien adventure beats everything. Teimon said that the Ancients spread the code during the second visit some 6000 years ago. Imagine that the key of the code of the Tai I Ching could be found in the Cheops pyramid. That would be great. It would be even more important than the star map. It would prove an ancient link between the Egyptian and the Chinese culture. It would be a real shock for all of us, especially to historians.

But what has the Cheops pyramid to do with the Chinese culture, Ramon? I have never heard of any link between these two cultures. I don't get it.

Neither do I, Mira. But if the Ancients spread parts of their own culture code over different ancient cultures, then there could be a link between Egypt and China. That could explain why the Ancients hid the key to the I Tjing code in Egypt. To be sure that the code could not be changed or misused. On the moment, I don't see another explanation. But what I would like to know is where that room that you saw is located. China is a large country, you know.

Mira listens to Ramon but is much too tired.

We will see, Ramon. The most important aspect of the book you have to write is to explain who the Greys are and how the abductees can defend themselves against the Greys during abductions. The code of the Tai I Ching is interesting but not important.

Of course, Mira. I will start writing the book in the coming days. That's for sure. No more pro bono. It will be hard for me to find the time. But I have a secret weapon!

He holds up the coffee-pot.

A big smile on her face is Mira's answer to the indestructible optimism of Ramon. She gets ready to leave.

I will keep you informed, Ramon. If Aryein makes contact, you will hear it immediately. Whatever the relation is between Egypt and China, you will figure it out. He said that synchronicity will increase. Thanks for the coffee Ramon, but I have to go now.

Ramon takes his woolen poncho and accompanies Mira to the car.

I guess it is too cold to ride the bike, Mira?

Don't make fun of me, Ramon. It is not the cold but the time, you know.

Ramon laughs.

Of course, Mira. I'm just joking. I will start writing. It is no option to wait until I know everything.

If it ever becomes clear, Ramon.

Oh Mira, just see it as an adventure. Reality surpasses even the wildest fantasy.

I am sure, nobody will believe what we have experienced, Ramon. But seriously, don't forget that the Initiated and the Mentals will understand very well that this book is for real. And maybe, they won't be amused.

You are right, Mira. But that's the risk I have to take.
That's why the book has to be a novel, Ramon.
I understand, Mira. But what can you do? A publication like this is always tricky. A novel it will be. But then again, a conceptual novel. I'm not a writer. But if I make a conceptual novel, then…
Explain it another time, Ramon. I have to go now. I will get in touch when I can. And in a hurry, she disappears into the cold night.
…I can use it also for "Alien", my next exhibition, Ramon thinks. Those modern witches! Always in a hurry.
The crescent moon stands high above the houses, surrounded by a yellowish glow and some bright stars. The view gives Ramon the feeling to be a part of a larger reality. For a while he looks at the different constellations, but the night cold creeps up on him and soon Ramon is back in his WebCom. The cold but bright night waits for the next admirer. It is twelve o'clock as Ramon goes to bed. He is tired of the months of non stop working.
Now I have to write a book. And how must I do that? '
But without answers sleep takes him into the world of dreams.

- 48 -
4/3/2007

The village of Ramon is lit by the white light of the full moon. The long shadows of the houses and the trees give the dark, cold evening a magical atmosphere. A light-grey, misty nebula hangs over the village brook and the moonlight reflects on the low clouds and gives the darkness a dress of light.
Only a lonely bicyclist sees the magic of nature while peddling home in this black-and-white period of the year. Seeing the beauty of nature is a relief to Ramon. Since Mira's last visit he has surfed non-stop on the web, looking for clues related to the pyramids. It is cold and Ramon is glad as he enters his home.
He made a modest start with the book and he realizes that it will be matter of trial and error. But a start has been made and that is what counts.
Come on Ramon, let's do this!
Only the light of the TV and the computer screens light the
290

WebCom and only a few long shadows on the walls give a hint about the shape of the room. Perfect technical drawings of the Cheops pyramid decorate the screens.

This man is truly a professional, Ramon thinks. With admiration he has studied all the drawings on Rudolf Gantenbrink's UPUAUT website. Ramon didn't know what he was looking for in finding the key, but it had to be something visible. A lot of New Age groups lose themselves in both unproved and unprovable theories. But the pyramids are mysterious enough as they are.

Ramon read anything related to the pyramids he could find on the web. But the UPUAUT project was really worthwhile. The CAD drawings of the pyramids were perfectly designed in detail. Rudolf was the guy who made the first real in-depth investigation of the so-called air shafts. Ramon found out that the pyramid of Cheops was the only pyramid with shafts. Especially the Caviglia shaft got his attention. It is the small S-shaped part of the shaft in the King's room.

Gantenbrink had proven that this "S" shape was very unusual. The general theory was that the builders had to make a curve in the shaft because otherwise this shaft would cross the main entrance. But the CAD drawings proved that this was not the case. This shaft could have been straight, just like the opposite shaft in the same room. The reason for this "S" shape had to be a different one. The explanation that it was a construction failure was definitely ridiculous.

But any relation with the I Ching was nowhere to be found.

"In Cheops the key is hidden, in China the signs."

Ramon could not get that sentence out of his mind. Could Aryein mean that the signs that Mira saw on the cube have a relation with the Tai I Ching? Could these be the signs he was talking about? Ramon couldn't figure it out. He decides to make a hot cup of soup and goes to the kitchen. As he enters the kitchen door, he almost bumps into Mira who is about to enter the WebCom.

Mira, you almost freaked me out!

Hello, Ramon! Sorry, it was not my intention to scare you. I am in a hurry and can't stay long. Do you have a minute? And some coffee?

That's just the word Ramon needs. And a little while later, both enjoy a hot mug of brown magical fluid. Ramon wants to tell her everything he has found on the web but Mira interrupts his speech immediately.

Ramon, Aryein is back on line. I think he wants to send information.

Sorry Mira, I didn't notice.

In a hurry, Ramon takes his notebook and when he returns to the kitchen, Mira is clearly gone again, far away in the depth of the cosmos. She starts to speak as soon as Ramon sits down.

1.347 **Inside the Cheops pyramid, there is a small, long passage. Mira is silent for a while before proceeding. The squares are divided in 144 sub-squares.**

Mira sees some drawings of a pyramid.

1.348 **The first four images on the cube in the China temple are the first four parts of the passage of Cheops.**

1.349 **The person who previously had contact with the purple crystal skull couldn't place the information. We salute you.**

That's it, Ramon.

Ramon is speechless. Does Aryein know what Ramon is doing or is this synchronicity?

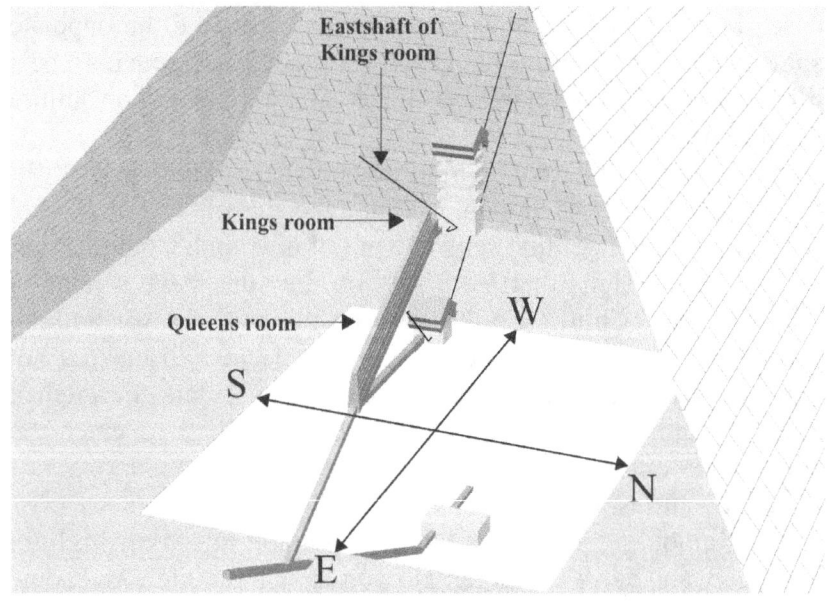

292

So that's it, Mira? Aryein is not a man of many words.

You see Ramon, says Mira while she comes back to herself, I knew that information was coming. All day long I heard that deep sound. But now the sound is gone. She feels clearly relieved.

Ramon is astonished.

Don't be surprised Mira, but would you believe that I just made a study of a few long shafts in the pyramid of Cheops? It's true! Come and I will show you.

She can not believe her eyes as she looks at the drawings of the shafts.

Ramon, these drawings look very similar to the drawings I saw minutes ago.

What? So, you mean that these drawings have something to do with the signs on the cube of that Chinese temple?

Well yes, Ramon. That's what Aryein told me.

Wait a minute, Mira. It could very well be. Look at this shaft.

Ramon points at the Caviglia shaft.

This curve is cut through four solid stones. Strange indeed. I will show you the drawing of the temple room. It's finished.

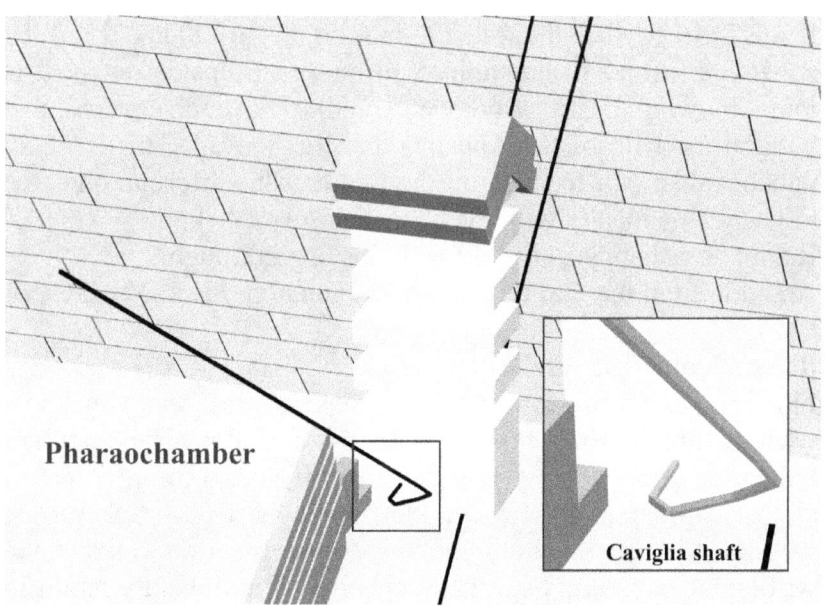

Pharaochamber

Caviglia shaft

Mira looks fascinated at the drawing and everything comes back to her. Suddenly, the deep sound intensifies and mentally she is back inside the room. She looks again at the cube and she shouts out loud: Ramon! Now I know!

1.350 **Look at those points on the drawings. These drawings have nothing to do with the I Ching. They are stars! Those drawings are a part of the star map. And if you place these four maps inside this shaft, then you have the first four square maps of the star map!**

Ramon is shocked.

Are you sure, Mira?

Sure? I am never sure. I just tell you what I receive from Aryein.

My God! Now I see it, Mira. This is just great. This is unbelievable. How is it possible that I couldn't see the link with the star map? But it was so long ago that I forgot the information of the star map. This shaft is a stone version of the star map, from here to... Orion! This shaft "is" the "KEY"... I find no words, Mira. But come to think of it... What would be the best proof to factually show the humans of future generations that the Ancients were truly humans from another planet and that the Earth was once visited by aliens? It's very simple! By showing them the way they came! With the help of a star map!

If this is true Mira, then we are making history today. Then the collective history of humanity will be turned upside down. It is mind blowing, Mira! And we wouldn't have discovered that without the help of the Ancients and the Sheyan. This is really unbelievable. Not to mention the fact that the information came to you telepathically with the help of the crystal skull.

Ramon is as happy as a child with this breakthrough.

And don't tell me that this is just imagination, Mira. No, no, that can't be.

Ramon looks again at the drawings.

Finally everything starts to make sense, Mira. And you know what is great? Everybody knows these shafts. They are not hidden in secrecy. How is it possible? If you know it, it seems almost evident. By the way, Mira, I found a new link on the website Niburu. I had to look up some previous links while writing the book and I saw an interesting hyperlink. "Pyramids in China". Shall we take a look?

294

Pyramids in China? I have never heard of that, Ramon. But can I first take some more coffee and a cigarette. You want some too? Please, Mira.

While Mira goes to the kitchen, Ramon opens the link and reads the text.

Hey, that's interesting, Mira. The article mentions that you can see the Chinese pyramids on Google Earth.

Quickly, Ramon opens Google Earth and goes to the coordinates of the location, mentioned in the article. Deeper and deeper he enters in the large Chinese country. In the vicinity of the city Xi'an, dozens of pyramids show up while he comes closer to the ground.

That is unbelievable. Mira? Where are you? Come quickly. You will not believe your eyes.

I'm coming, Ramon. With two mugs and some cigarettes, she enters the WebCom.

Look, Mira. There and there. Dozens of pyramids! Look! They all have a flat square top. How is it possible that there are pyramids in China and that we don't know anything about it? Look Mira, how many of them!

Mira is very quiet when suddenly she sees a light on a pyramid.

Go back to the previous place, Ramon. Yes. There. That pyramid. Can you get closer? There is something strange about that pyramid.

With growing astonishment they look at this large rectangular grave hill. Ramon is surprised to see how high the resolution from that height is. He puts the compass to the north and the pyramid Mira pointed at fits exactly on the screen. Ramon immediately makes notes of the coordinates of the place. 34°24'04.97" N and 108°42'47.58" O

Mire feels a strong attraction to the pyramid.

I think that inside this pyramid there is a large, square room. I think that this is the place where I was.

Ramon doesn't know any longer what to think.

Are you sure, Mira?

Mira's hands start to tremble.

I am sure, Ramon. I clearly see a square structure inside. Don't you see that?

No, Mira. The pyramid has a square flat top, but I don't see anything else.

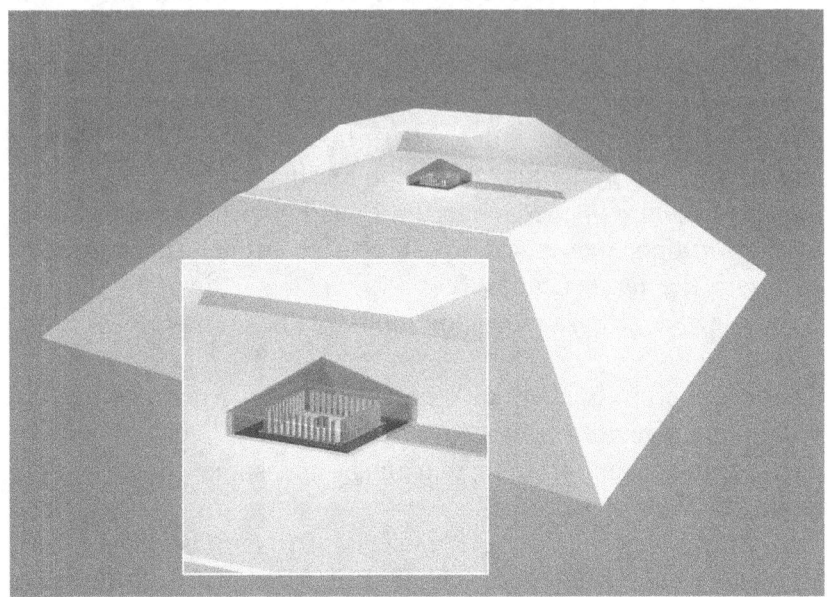

Do you think I am imagining things, Ramon?

No Mira, I am just not psychic, that s all. Wait a minute. I will mark the pyramid. So you think this is the place where you were?

I'm sure, Ramon. It attracts me so much. It really feels like… I don't know.

If this is not synchronicity, Mira, I don't know what that word means. But let us take a look at the other pyramids.

Ramon zooms out to go to another location when Mira reacts again.

Stop, Ramon. Go to that place. There is something.

Ramon zooms back in and both see a large river to the south east of Xi'an. Strange regular terraces all along the north side of the river are clearly visible.

1.351 **In these terraces are the graves of the Ancients, Ramon. These are the graves of the Wise Men that stayed behind after the Ancients went away.**

While she says that, she hears the voice of Aryein again.

1.352 **In Egypt is also a region in a rock face where the graves are located of the Wise People that stayed on Earth.**

296

But they have not been discovered yet.

While the landscape moves slowly over the screen Ramon sees some forty terraces.

And there is something else, Ramon.

1.353 The graves from these terraces have a link with similar terraces in South America.

Can you explain that a bit more, Mira?

Sorry, Ramon. The contact with Aryein is gone again.

Don't be sorry, Mira. With what you have said, I can spend the rest of my life.

Excited, they go back to the kitchen. Ramon realizes more and more how incredible this information is. This has to be taken seriously.

I have to know more about these Chinese pyramids, Mira.

But how is it possible that we don't know anything about these ancient monuments in China, Ramon?

Well, I guess China always has been very isolated from the rest of the world. Maybe the openness in recent years makes it possible to know more about the past of that country. Imagine we can even go to China via Google Earth.

You are right, Mira. That must be the case. Incredible how quickly this computer technology evolves. One thing is certain: the first thing I will do is make a map of all the pyramids I can find. God knows what else we will find in this way. But lest I forget, Mira. Aryein said something about people that didn't interpret the purple skull in the right way. Can you tell me more about that? I will quickly make some coffee in the mean time.

There is nothing more to say, Ramon. I think they were people like me, who had contact with the crystal skull. But maybe, they are involved in groups or cults now. And as soon as that happens, the contact will be blocked.

That could be right, Mira. Or maybe, they lost contact with their Guardian. They need the Guardian to get the information, right? You too had problems with it in the beginning, remember?

Absolutely, Ramon. I don't know what I would have done, if you were not around to help me to get it right.

Well yes, forget it Mira, that's my job. That's all.

Yes, but don't underestimate your own role in this. I remember that Teimon was glad that we got the interpretation right. He told me that he tried others but without any result.

I can understand that, Mira. It is not simple, you know. If I had not had a good education at the mystery school, I would probably think it is just abracadabra. Because you have to admit, it is an exceptional story.

Don't tell me, Ramon. It's just too crazy.

Gradually they come back to their usual relaxed state of mind.

Milk and sugar, Mira?

Yes, thanks Ramon. And now what, Ramon? What is the next step?

Well, there is only one thing I can do, Mira. I have to finish that book. In between, I can scan the web to find out more about the Chinese pyramids. And I will make a 3D drawing from the shafts and put the Chinese drawings in them. Now we have in fact four of the seventy-two maps. That is a start, no? This information must get the attention of the Initiated who received the signals. And furthermore, I think that Teimon will come back. The Sheyan are in danger now. But my gut feeling says that they will come back.

If that is the case, you will be the first to know, Ramon. I have to admit that the contact with Aryein is much easier than with Teimon. I don't feel pressure and there is no wound on my head. That troubled me a lot, remember. To be honest, I was glad that the contact was short, although last month I received a lot of information from the purple skull. I think I can have access to the code of the skull itself. It is as if the skull has a mind of its own. Very strange.

Is that so? Tell me about it, Mira? Or is it private?

Oh no… You may know it.

I'm not going crazy Ramon, am I?

But Mira, how often must I tell you…

Yes, yes Ramon. How often must you tell me that crazy people never think they are crazy? I know. Well, okay. I will tell you. I get information about… How shall I put it?

About previous lives, Mira?

Mira looks very surprised.

How do you know that, Ramon?

Oh, very simple, Mira. This often happens when people are in contact with the Akasha. Edgar Cayce is a good example.

298

So it is not unusual?

No Mira, you are absolutely not the only one. It is just extra information. Not that it is that important. Regression therapists have done extensive research about previous lives. Regression therapists even make use of previous lives in a therapeutic context. But personally, I think that the life you live now is the most important. For you live each life only once. That also goes of course for the life you are living now. So you had better make the best of it. And Harish Johari explained us that in every life, the previous lives are repeated during the first 28 years for men and the first 24 years for women. Come to think of it, Mira. Harish Johari taught us that when yogis develop paranormal gifts with the help of tantric yoga techniques, these paranormal abilities won't go away anymore. Even not in the next lives. He warned us not to develop these psychic abilities if we wanted to become enlightened. Because it is already hard enough to get your mind under control as it is. If a yogi develops psychic abilities, it only becomes more difficult to get control over the mind.

So there is no way I can stop this telepathic ability?

No, it won't work, Mira, especially since you are a humanoid. So you inherited the ability genetically. You can suppress it for a while, but it will always come back one way or the other. So there is only one thing you can do. Learn to use it in an ethical way and use it only for the good.

So I can also use it in an unethical way?

Of course, Mira. It is not because you are paranormal that you automatically become a good person. That's the difference between a magician and a mystic. Mystics are enlightened people. They use their gifts and knowledge to serve others. Magicians are not enlightened. They can easily fall into the trap of using their powers to control and to dominate others. Remember what Teimon said. Those who were genetically altered used their telepathic abilities to get more power, especially the men. Only the women use their psychic abilities in general for the good. Therefore it is much better for men and women to become first mystics and to develop paranormal powers only after they are enlightened. Only in this way, they will be able to use it for the good. That is the real difference between black and white magic.

But Ramon, I thought there are no magicians any more.

Oh no, Mira? Well, that's a misconception. Look, Mira. Magic is based on repetition. Repetition works like magic. The Dutch word for advertising is "reclame" which comes from the Latin "reclamare", which means "to yell repeatedly". So, advertising is based on repetition. If you repeat a slogan over and over, people will start to believe it. Propaganda works in the same way. Logos, slogans and so on... The whole Nazi circus is a good example to see how effective modern magic works. Magic is based on repetition and suggestion. Showing the same images over and over again works in a suggestive way. Whether the message is true or not, doesn't matter. And that is the dangerous part. The media and advertising organizations are in fact the greatest magicians of today's world. They use the same techniques that made the Nazis so powerful. They use the theories of Pavlov and behaviorism and put them into practice for their own benefit. It is funny if you understand that behaviorists are in fact all magicians although they pretend to be true scientists. Especially if they use the knowledge of behaviorism to manipulate people. Why do you think that the Greys used Psy-viruses to stimulate behaviorism? Because this science can be used to learn how to manipulate people, even whole populations. Demagogic people use scientific knowledge of the social and psychological sciences to manipulate people. But there is one reassuring aspect to all of this.

That's a relief, Ramon.

You see, Mira. My Wise Teacher once said, paraphrasing Abraham Lincoln: You can fool a lot of people for a short while. And you can fool a few people for a long time. But you can never fool a large population for a long time. That's why a dictatorial regime never has a long life. The people will revolt and take the dictator down, as soon as they discover the lies behind the propaganda. For the truth always unmasks the lie.

But these dictators are not paranormal, Ramon?

I am not so sure about that, Mira. But you don't need to be paranormal to use magic. I'm sure you have heard about magic incantations. I'm not talking about the magic spells of the fairy-tales. That is nonsense. But if you tell lies about somebody or

300

something, then you can do a lot of harm to a person or a group of people. Hitler spread lies about the Jewish people. Racism is always based on such lies. And everybody knows from their own experience how harmful gossip can be. But imagine that you can spread lies by means of telepathy. Like the Greys can. It is evident that this is the perfect way to manipulate people. For you don't use technical means. It is immediate. And the person thinks that the suggestions are his own thoughts.

That's the reason why the Greys want these implants spread I guess. To make it possible to suggest whole populations. Therefore it is important that we know that the individual Grey have an inferiority complex. Only the block culture gives him strength. If abductees know who the Greys are, where they come from and how their psychological make-up is, they can break more easily through their suggestions. It does not matter whether they use telepathic suggestions or not.

Why do you think that Christianity had such an impact in South America and Africa in the past centuries? The religion of these people was voodoo, the religion of the dance. Voodoo isn't black magic at all. All people of the world like to dance. But within the voodoo traditions, like in any other culture, there were black magic groups. They were a kind of black magic mafia within these shamanistic cultures. By embracing Christianity, the general population felt protected against these negative powers within their society. For with the help of this belief, they could...

...brake the suggestions of the black magicians, says Mira.

Exactly, Mira. It is simple and effective.

Then the book is crucial for abductees, Ramon.

I realize that all too well, Mira. It will also be of great help for everybody involved in all kinds of secret organizations. The Initiated, the Monoms, the Mentals and the Psy-mutants. And also the members of that mysterious religion, Sean Leyka. And not to forget, the Humanoids, because they know about the existence of the Téry. And they can easily break contact with the Greys.

You're right, Ramon. When will the book will be ready?

That's a good question, Mira. I have started it, now it is just a matter to hold on. In fact it is already finished. I just need to write it, says Ramon with a smile.

Okay then, Ramon. I must go now. I'm already late as it is. I let you know if anything happens, okay?

Fine, Mira. I will surf a bit on the web and then I go to sleep. I had enough excitement for one day. We have found the key of the star map, Mira. Isn't that great? That alone gives me courage to write the book.

Yes, Ramon. It must be a relief that we finally have something concrete.

Absolutely, Mira.

As they walk outside, the full moon is high in the sky.

You know what my Wise Teacher always said about manipulative people, Mira.

Tell me, Ramon.

There always belongs one more person to the stupid masses than you think!

Both have a good laugh.

That's a good one, Ramon. I have to remember that one. All those magicians, normal or paranormal! Who do they think they are? Demagogues or Grey aliens, they are all one of a kind. They are just good for nothing.

Look after yourself, Ramon.

See you later, Mira.

And after waving, she disappears through the shadows of the moonlight into the night.

- 49 -
4/3/2007

Back in the kitchen, Ramon starts cleaning. While doing the dishes, he meditates about the importance of the discoveries of today. Just a quick look on the web and then off to bed.

I must make a good daily schedule and use every minute of the day as economically as I can. And I must not forget the translation of The Galactic World-View. Maybe I can combine the two books. I can make drawings in the morning, write the book in the afternoon and I can do translation work and do research on the web at night. That should be possible.

After cleaning, he shuts the computer down and in a hurry he

302

runs upstairs as the sound of the doorbell makes him almost stumble over his feet.

Who can that be? Ramon goes down and walks through the dark passage to the front door. But of course, who else? Ramon opens the door and Ury steps inside with a big smile on his face.

Good evening, Ramon. I was on my way home and I thought: I bring Ramon a short visit.

That's a good idea, Ury. Look, the moon is full!

Both look at the magical, bright shining companion of the Earth.

The sign of the Buddha, Ramon, but it's cold, you know.

Sorry Ury, please come in. A hot coffee will do us both good.

A bit later they both sit in the kitchen, which is lit by a few candles.

Haven't you put the Christmas tree away, Ramon?

Ramon starts to laugh.

You know Ury, I really didn't find the time. I find it much cozier like this. And it is not really a Christmas tree. It is more a winter tree.

Ury has to laugh.

You look well, Ury. What happened? Don't tell me you have a new girlfriend?

Ury starts to blush, making any response unnecessary.

Ah, you know how it is, Ramon. I can't live without a woman. I can't cook and... I like women very much. You know me.

You don't need to excuse yourself, Ury. Seriously, I can't imagine you without a woman. Alone is alone. I know that better than anyone. By the way, do you know the advantage of being single?

Smiling Ury shakes his head.

No idea, Ramon.

Well, the advantage is that you are alone. But the disadvantage is that you are alone.

Both have a good laugh and forget how tired they are.

But tell me, Ramon. Anything new from the cosmos?

Well, you never believe it Ury, but I started writing the book.

Seriously? I feel sorry for you, dear friend. I remember how you dislike writing. Do you remember the time you were writing The Galactic World-View? My God, that's more than ten years ago!

Well yes, Ury. Writing is not my favorite waste of time, you know. But it is important to get the information out. Duty calls. By the way, Ury, did you know that there are pyramids in China? No, I don't, Ramon. Are you serious?

Absolutely. Come, I will show you. You can see them on Google Earth very clearly.

A few minutes later, Ury looks surprised at all the pyramids in the Xi'an region.

That's strange, Ramon. Look. They all have a flat top.

They are indeed flat, Ury.

He sees that Ury behaves differently while looking at all these old wonders of the world.

Can it really be? Is Merly right after all? Is there a relation between China and Egypt, he mutters in himself.

What's that you are saying, Ury?

Well, I had a visit from Merly this week.

I'm listening, Ury.

Gosh man, it is so difficult to explain.

Take your time, Ury. I will write it down.

First Merly showed me the symbol of the pyramid. You know, the symbol on the one dollar bill. Merly said that the original meaning of this symbol was forgotten. He said that this logo actually symbolizes the link between the Chinese and the Egyptian culture. I really didn't understand, Ramon. But now that I see these pyramids, he could be right after all.

Merly stated that the Illuminati always have misinterpreted the true meaning of this symbol. The Illuminati think that the flat pyramid represents their secret power structure in the world, ruled by the Warriors, and that the top triangle on the flat pyramid is the symbol of the superior authority of the thirteen Illuminati at the top of the organization.

I think I know what Merly means, Ury. Some of the Illuminati consider themselves to be the superior class, meaning they are the superior authority. They don't believe in a spiritual world.

Exactly, Ramon. The Illuminati in general think and behave as if they are gods. If you look at their logo, you can see that the two parts of the pyramid are separated. In practice, this means that the Illuminati behave as if they are the gods of the world.

Then they are dead wrong, Ury. Even the Pharaohs of Egypt were only demigods. They were the top of the society, but they

304

were still intrinsically connected to their society. The job of the Pharaoh was to keep contact with the gods, to do all the rituals and ceremonies and in this way make sure that life was good for everybody.

That is exactly what Merly said, Ramon. But one fraction of the Illuminati thinks they stand above the other families. And that is a dangerous attitude, especially because their Warrior is ordered to make a serious attempt to reach world power.

Ramon listens in amazement to everything Ury has to say.

The Chinese emperors had a different interpretation of their pyramid monuments. The flat top symbolized clearly that the powers of the world can never replace the power of the gods. That was considered blasphemy in their culture. No matter how powerful a human being is, he still is a human being. He is a mortal. That's the reason why they left the top of the pyramid away. The invisible top symbolizes Tao, the mystery behind the universe. The source of everything that exists.

The top of the pyramid is essential to design the proportions of the pyramid. The pyramid was the world and the invisible point was Tao. And there is one more thing, Ramon. Merly said that the Guardians are now the only ones who still know the true meaning of the pyramid symbol.

Did Merly say something about that true meaning, Ury?

In a way, yes. He said that the flat pyramid was the Chinese part of the Illuminati symbol and the triangle on top was the Egyptian pyramid and together, they are one. So if you put the two pyramids together, they reveal a higher unity or something like that.

And what was that unity? asks Ramon with growing astonishment.

He didn't say, Ramon. Merly told me that I had to bring you this message, because you know the code. Is that true, Ramon? Do you know more about this? Because to me it is just gibberish, you know.

Sorry Ury, I can't tell you more about it. But the pyramids will play an important role in the book.

Oh, but then you must not tell me anything, Ramon. I prefer to read the book. I have to go now. Thanks for the coffee, young man. Somebody is waiting for me.

His face lights up in a smile.

Right you are, Ury. Don't let her wait.

As quickly as he came, he disappears into the night.

The full moon stands free of clouds in the night sky and its light gives the whole village a white glow. How strange, Ramon thinks. An oppressing feeling goes through his body. Merly said that I know the code. It becomes more and more clear that the information of Mira and Ury is linked together. The Greys and that fraction of the Illuminati, whoever they are, seem to have indeed in essence the same agenda. They both want control over the whole world. So I must consider the possibility that that dissident fraction of the Illuminati is in close contact with the Initiated through the Warriors who in turn listen to the commands of the Illuminati. That would mean that these Illuminati are in this way manipulated by the Greys. They think that the Greys will help them to fulfill their agenda. While in fact, they fulfill the agenda of the Greys. Could that be the argument between the fractions of the Illuminati? That the opposition in the group is suspicious about the alien involvement and therefore don't want to go along with the plans of the most powerful ones? But, if there are twelve Warriors in command and they belong to different countries, how will the majority react if one Illuminati fraction puts the plans in action? If one family of the Illuminati wants to rule the others no matter what, then we will end up in a world conflict. I can't imagine that the other families just step aside without a battle. Dozens of questions go through his mind. Too tired to think, he goes to bed and when he feels the warm blankets, he falls asleep in no time.

- 50 -
10/3/2007

The last cigarette disappears into the ashtray. Electronic music is playing in the background. The TV is showing a stupid game show. The computer mouse scrolls through the growing text.

Okay. Every word previously marked red has been corrected. The notebook lies open on October 10th, 2006. Is it already five months ago? While preparing the next chapter, the past comes

306

back to life. At that time Ramon was excited about the implications of Mira's information and the strange synchronicity with information published on the web. Ramon always had absolute confidence in the openness of the NASA. But the NASA video about the light phenomena damaged that confidence seriously. It was definitely real footage. Why did NASA hide this for the public? Was science becoming a private domain? Knowledge is power if you keep it to yourself.

The recent discovery of the Chinese pyramids made him also doubt about the openness of educational organizations. Why are our history books filled with information about the Egyptian culture while there is nothing on the pyramids of China? Why is history so selective? If this is no breaking world news, I don't know what is.

And why are the media so selective? Last week, Ramon discovered that the Russian media showed a documentary on the national TV about UFO technology, developed by the Germans during World War Two. This documentary could be found on Google video. Not translated but with impressive images. One would say that this is super breaking world news, but nothing is mentioned in the Western press.

Gradually, Ramon has to accept the possibility that the Germans had contact with the Greys. The video "Nazi UFO documentary" on Video Google described the secret development of the flying disc during the Second World War. The documentary stated that these flying discs worked with a kind of fusion between electro-magnetism and gravity fields. Apart from everything that was mentioned, Ramon knew that the German scientist Theodore Kaluza was the first to publish a theory that unites two of the four powers of nature, namely electro-magnetism and gravity. This theory is known as the Kaluza-Klein Unified Field Theory. That was back in 1921. So there was already theoretical support for the statement that these two forces in nature could be united. But there was no official proof that this theory was put into practice or tested. Could it be that secret experiments resulting in the foo fighters and later on the flying discs were based on these theoretical assumptions of this relatively unknown physicist?

Then there was the Google video "The Secrets of the Third Reich". Somewhere in the middle of the video, you can see a big disc flying above a large crowd. Freaky, to say the least. If this footage were part of an old special effects movie for propaganda purposes, then it was very well done. Maybe with the help of Leni Riefenstahl or somebody of her level. Or it was a recent fraud to help build a new image for neo-Nazi groups. These videos gave Ramon an ambivalent feeling. On the one hand, they proved a link between the Nazis and the UFO subject. But on the other hand, Ramon was worried about the effect of these videos on young people who were unaware of the war crimes of the Nazis. Before you publish this information, you have to be damn sure it is true.

The Google video by Nick Cook "UFOs, The Secret Evidence" made it even harder to deny that the Nazi's were up to something. The video made it very probable that the secret electro-gravity technology of the Nazis was not only a rumor, spread by neo-Nazi movements. More and more information supported the idea that the Greys had a hand in the Second World War. Ramon realized how bizarre this possibility was and decided to put his mind to another subject related to the star map. And then there was that other thing. The witness Karl Wolf who described the alien moon bases kept on coming back to his mind, particularly because of the relation between the star map and the moon. Ramon took Wolf's testimony very seriously. The fact that the base was located on the back side of the moon was of course very practical if it was a hoax. We can't study this side from Earth. So there is no way to check it. Wolf also stated that the pictures with artificial structures were retouched. That statement was corroborated by the testimony of Donna Hare. She had worked several years for NASA. It was common practice to change pictures with questionable details. Often some antennas of the photographing satellite were visible, making the pictures not presentable for books. Or sometimes pictures of craters were based on a collage of different pictures. But if there were artificial constructions retouched, then that was a mind blowing possibility to Ramon. While remembering all these things, Ramon looks again at some of the footage that he found a few days ago on YouTube.

Nothing could have prepared Ramon for the YouTube video "Ancient Structure on the Moon". It was supposed to be made by

308

Neil Armstrong himself during the Apollo 11 mission. On the video, you could see how both astronauts investigated an old ruin of a building on the moon. You could see clearly a large hangar with a large flat entrance at the front. The style of the building was unknown to Ramon. The pillars inside the ruin reminded Ramon of the Stanley Kubrick movie "2001 A Space Odyssey". In this fantastic movie from 1968, a dark flat monolith played an important role as an alien artifact, found on the moon. The footage gave Ramon really an alien feeling. He watched this video over and over again. Could this be genuine footage? No, it can't be! Out of the question! But at the same time, the footage was so freaking real. Ramon wanted to go to the bottom of this. He was convinced that if the video footage was a fraud, then the producers would have made mistakes, as they always do, no matter how professional the team was. And so, for a couple of days, Ramon spent most of the time trying to prove to himself that this video was fake.

If this video is a fraud then it is very well done, was his first conclusion. If the ruin was a piece of a film set, then it was very realistic. The feeling that there was a link with Stanley Kubrick, made it even more impressive. The first thing he had to find out was who published this footage. He discovered that this video was a part of a documentary, made by Juan José Benitez and published on YouTube. This documentary was called Mirlo Rojo. But it was in Spanish. So, was the subject of this documentary real or fake? Ramon wanted to find out. In order to do that, he first of all had to search for contradictions with the public information of the real moon landing of Apollo 11.

He remembered the first moon landing in 1969 as if it was yesterday. The media hype made a deep impression on the young Ramon. The whole night he stayed up, although he had to go to school next day. Even his grandfather of 91 years of age watched this historical achievement. But the bad quality of the images was a bit of a disappointment. He had read the fantastic comic strip, "Man on the Moon" from the Tintin-series by Hergé. The landscapes in this comic strip were much more impressive than the boring sand desert of the real moon. And to make matters worse, suddenly the real-time broadcast was interrupted. Chriet Titulaer, the commentator of all the missions on television, kept on talking and in a way it was really funny.

The Mirlo Rojo documentary stated that with the help of fake footage there was enough time to bring a visit to the ruins nearby. In theory that was possible of course. But only when the ruin was near and hidden in a fairly large crater.

At the beginning of the footage you can clearly see that the astronaut in the vicinity of the base is located at a lower point. The one who is doing the filming, officially always Armstrong, walks downwards into a crater.

You can also see the moon lander through one of the windows of the ruin. That could only be a few hundred meters. So the crater had to be in the vicinity of the landing site. But if that was the case, how could they hide such a crater and a ruin on the live broadcast?

The first thing Ramon did was to search photographs of the landing site. He could not remember if the complete horizon was shown during the broadcast. In search for pictures of the Apollo 11 site, he found a website with panoramic views of the six moon landing sites. But no crater was seen, large and deep enough to hide a building from sixty by forty meters. The only large crater in the vicinity was located to the east and hardly visible by the sunlight.

In search for pictures from above the landing site, Ramon watched every YouTube clip about the descent of the Eagle landing on the moon. From the Eagle's window, you could see how the landing place came nearer. The crater that could be seen, just before landing, was to a large extent covered in shadow. But there was no trace of a ruin. The craters, seen at the end of the descent, were in accordance with the pictures of the moon landing, made from space. So nothing wrong there.

Another thing Ramon noticed, while looking at dozens of clips, was that during the moon walk, two static cameras were used for the live broadcast. They were all the time pointing in the same direction. Of course in the western direction, opposed to the east where the large crater was located and also the sun. Being the devil's advocate, one may argue that the crater could be located at the back of the cameras of course. But that was not convincing enough to prove that the footage of the moon base was real. It had to be possible to prove beyond any doubt that this footage

310

was fake or fact.

The next step was to see what the position was of the sun during the Apollo 11 Moonwalk. It was the first quarter of that moon day. On the moon, a day takes fourteen Earth days. So it was early in the morning when the astronauts landed in the Sea of Tranquility. The moon was still not heated up by the sun that stood low at the east side, making long shadows. In the Mirlo Rojo video, the same long shadows were visible. So if the video was a fraud, the producers had taken the orientation of the sun into account.

During the official moonwalks, the astronauts stayed close to the lunar module. After a few hours, they had to go back inside the lunar module. They had to sleep. They could not lie down in that vehicle. So they had to sleep in a standing position. Ramon remembered his thoughts as a young kid. How can the astronauts sleep on the moon? The time is so short! He couldn't understand that. During the sleep period, the only thing we saw on TV was the lunar module and a silent, simple landscape. There was no wind on the moon.

It made Ramon think about a trick often used in movies. It was an ideal situation to freeze the camera. Like a thief blocks a surveillance camera. The thief can do what he likes, since you don't see him on camera. The astronauts could have used the five hours, to do an archaeological trip to the ruin. After the alien trip, they could have gone back inside the lunar module, before the cameras were activated again. A cheap but very effective trick. Ramon also wanted to know where exactly the moon landing took place. He read in an article that the astronauts landed ten miles to the west and two miles to the south of the originally planned landing location. Armstrong had to manually improvise the landing. They could hardly sidestep a deep crater. From that place, no previous pictures were published. It was difficult to find a picture of the original landing site. The only picture he found was of low resolution and on the place where they had to land was a strange dot visible, probable the lunar module hanging in space. Was it hiding something? But all this didn't prove that the Mirlo Rojo video was an authentic document.

On pictures, released on the web, only one crater could be the crater containing the ruin. A crater of 200 meters across and some 400 meters away from the lunar module. You could see a square-like feature in the middle, hidden in black shadow. But normally that feature had to be the crashed meteorite. All the other large craters were much farther away. And from there, the lunar module could not be visible. So that would prove that the footage was a fraud, no?

But Ramon wanted to be sure. So he started to study the footage itself. Especially the style of the ruin. The windows and the pillars of the ruin had a specific style. The pillars were slightly curved and were thinner at the top. The crossbeams were very thin and had a smooth triangular angle in the middle. The whole construction was built much lighter than a similar construction would be on Earth. But yes, the gravity on the moon is much less. The style of the base intrigued Ramon. It was surprisingly well done, especially for a low budget movie.

The light and the image quality of the footage was the same as during the real moonwalk. The makers of this hoax had thought about everything. The more he studied the ruins, the more he became convinced that this was not a simple studio setting. It was also more convincing than the decors of science fiction movies. It all looked so real. So minimal in its presence. And also the whole atmosphere of the movie was freaky real. There was no unnatural acting. The astronauts behaved realistically. You could even sense the feelings and the fear of the astronaut sometimes crossing the footage. Could it be that this was real? Or was his desire to find proof for the existence of a moon base playing tricks on his mind?

Ramon knew that it was very well possible that some original parts of the broadcast of the moon landing were fake. At least, if he accepted the proof given by the documentary, "Moon landing, fake or fact". The documentary stated that Stanley Kubrick was involved in a secret operation, that he had made a fake movie of the moon landing in case there were problems with the transmission of the signals. And that this fake movie was the one we all saw on that memorable day, June 20th 1969. In this documentary, important persons participated: Kissinger, Rumsfeld and Haig to name a few.

But also that documentary was not the whole truth and nothing but the truth. Especially the reason that was given by several participants why Stanley had to do the fake movie. Ramon didn't believe a word of the overall statement that the fake movie was made to be broadcast in case there were technical errors with the cameras on the moon. No matter how convincing the participants of the video were. Stanley Kubrick could have made the fake footage, no doubt about that, but not for a few technical problems! No, no, Stanley Kubrick was much too authentic and too realistic to be part of such a cover up for that reason.

Stanley Kubrick had a great influence on Ramon's artwork. Space landscapes had been Ramon's favorite subject for painting for years. To Ramon Kubrick was in his profession the Leonardo da Vinci of the twentieth century. If the fake movie was made to give the astronauts the time to investigate an artificial moon base, that would make more sense. That could be a very good reason to broadcast a fake show. The fake movie could give the astronauts all the time to investigate the ruins. And it would be a much better motive to convince a man like Kubrick to participate in such a fraud. To do such a thing, you need a damn good reason. Because the broadcast of the live moon walk of the Apollo 11 astronauts was of miserable quality anyhow. The bad quality of the footage was the main cause of the rise of the complot theory that the moon landing never took place in the first place. You could find hundreds of videos on Google and YouTube to support that ridiculous theory. Based on these two documentaries, Ramon asked himself this crucial question: Could it be that that Stanley Kubrick knew about alien bases on the moon? If anybody could have known, it was Kubrick. And could it be that in exchange for hiding the truth, he got green light to make the movie "2001 A space Odyssey"? Not only as a preparation for the real moon landing. But also to spread the message, hidden in a movie, that proof was found of an alien presence on the moon. To tell the truth masked as a lie? That was more like Stanley Kubrick.

Taking into account everything that he knew from Teimon, Ramon started a thought experiment. Ramon was convinced that the military felt that the alien presence was a serious threat. The Apollo project was more than twenty years after Roswell. Imagine for a moment that there were real artifacts on the moon. In that case these findings on the moon became undoubtedly part of the overall cover up of the alien presence.

Imagine just for a minute that the Mirlo Rojo video was real. In that case the location of this base had to be known before the astronauts landed. When could NASA have had proof of a base? Ramon had to start somewhere. When could a moon base of forty by fifty meters have been discovered?

Since the Mount Palomar telescope in 1928 was finished and galaxies could be seen, this telescope could also see details of the moon. But since the Ranger and especially the Orbiter project, in the period 1966-1967, masses of pictures of the moon were available. These satellites made a complete map of the moon. The pictures of the Orbiters were used to determine the sites of the future Apollo missions and had at its best a resolution of 1.5 meters per pixel. Large enough to see strange geometries like the moon base on the Mirlo Rojo footage. So from that period on, NASA must have had some proof of ancient ruins, if they existed of course.

Dr. Karl Wolf talked about these pictures during his testimony in the Disclosure Project. So three years before the Apollo 11 went to the moon they could have known of artificial bases on the moon. That was plenty of time to choose landing sites in the vicinity of possibly alien bases. But all the landing sites were on the visual site of the moon, not on the back side. The bases that Dr. Karl Wolf had seen were located at the back side. But if there were bases on the back side, why not at the front side? Mira located two places at the back side and the front side. But that is still to be proven.

Anyhow, a few years before the release of the movie "2001 A space Odyssey", Stanley Kubrick could have been informed about possible moon bases, if there were any.

And what about Arthur Clarke, the writer of the book "2001 A space Odyssey"? What did or could he know? He was a radar specialist and had a degree in mathematics and physics. To know more about Arthur Clarke, Ramon read some biographies and discovered that Clarke was a member of the BIS, The British Interplanetary Society. Arthur Clarke was a member from 1936 on. The BIS was founded in 1933 to stimulate the development of the rocket engine and to promote the air and space industry. 1933! There was that strange magical date again. A lot of science fiction writers were members of this society. Ramon felt he found a new aspect of the importance of that crucial year 1933 and tried to find out as much he could about this organization and the organizers. He was more than surprised to read that in America, a similar group was founded three years earlier. On April 1930 the AIS was founded, the American Interplanetary Society. And in Russia, a similar organization saw the light with the name GRID. Ramon was shocked when he found that in Germany, the VfR was already active since 1927. All these societies had the same interest, developing the rocket motor. And almost all these organizations had the name "Interplanetary" in their name! Werner von Braun was an early member of the VfR. He even used some of the ideas of Goddard to develop his own rocket designs and finally he developed the V1 and V2 rockets, the "angels of death" in the Second World War. But the most important link between these organizations was that they were all founded in the sensitive period around 1933 and only seven years before the beginning of the war. The world is a small place after all.

Undeniable was that both Kubrick and Clarke were fascinated by extra-terrestrial intelligence. They were both very intelligent and realistic persons. But why were they so fascinated by alien life? What triggered these two intellectuals? What did or could they know? Where they informed by the Initiated? Clarke could be familiar with UFO sightings as a radar specialist. And Kubrick had an important function in NASA during the Apollo project to build a simulator for the astronauts.

Too many questions stayed unanswered. The most interesting aspect of this research, triggered by the Mirlo Rojo video, was that Ramon relived this important period in human history as if it happened yesterday. The idea that the astronauts had found an alien base was just a fantastic possibility. It could also explain the strange behavior of the astronauts after their historical trip to the moon. They all lived a rather secluded life afterwards. They became no "pop stars", so to speak. And they are the only people that could give real proof about all these speculations. Why didn't Neil Armstrong or Buzz Aldrin react to this Mirlo Rojo video? To Ramon, they were the greatest heroes of his youth. Rumor had it that they were both 32 degree Freemasons and that made it all even more obscure. Finally, Ramon decided to turn his attention back to the book. That was much more important. Day in day out, he worked on the book and in between he continued the translation of the Galactic World-view.

- 51 -
23/3/2007

With sleep still in his eyes, Ramon activates his WebCom. The operation system wishes him welcome and with a full pot of coffee and a few slices of bread, Ramon starts his morning ritual of visiting all UFO sites to see if there is news.

One breaking news article makes him curious. A few young students solved the centuries old problem of the magic square with twelve lines. Intrigued, Ramon reads that the magic square was known in Chinese antiquity. A lot of articles praise the mathematical discovery of the students.

Speaking of synchronicity! Why does the number twelve pop up time and again? Could this magical square have something to do with the room that is hidden in one of the Chinese pyramids, with twelve pillars on each side? Didn't the Ancients say that synchronicity would show me the way?

First, there is the star map, based on square maps, divided twelve by twelve and then there is the information about the room in the Chinese pyramid, with twelve pillars on each side. Then there are the twelve Guardians and Warriors, this solved magical square problem, the information of Ury and Mira, all the information on the web. It seems as if it is all interwoven in a web of synchronicity. There seems to be no causal relation but it all makes sense, as if there is a hidden link between it all. Ramon feels like being mixed up in an information hurricane. But intuitively he is always able to find the center of the hurricane where everything comes at rest.

It annoys him that he can't resist working on the translation of The Galactic World-View, the book that he wrote fourteen years ago. Something prevents him from fully concentrating on the book about the alien SOS. He needs something extra to convince him. And it is important to Ramon to finish the translation of the

316

Galactic World-view. He needs it for the upcoming exhibition, but also because he read so much doubtful articles about galactic concepts.

All the New Age theories about galactic thinking were often a source of aggravation. Ramon is a hyper-realist. He is convinced that there is a need for a new world-view, an improvement of the old world-view, being the heliocentric one which was in turn a great improvement compared to the geocentric world-view. Ramon is sure of one thing. The geometrical concept of The Galactic World-View is more up to date than the Copernican vision. It took him several years to understand the geometrical consequences of the galactic model. It was as Allen Hynek said: We need a new physics to understand the UFO problem. But before you can have a new physics, you first need a new world-view. So, Ramon took Hynek's statement very seriously. Newton's theories were based on the revolutionary model of Copernicus. The reason that a lot of concepts about alternative energy fail, is because the world-view hasn't really changed. We all think still too much Newtonian. We can't help it because we are educated that way. It is difficult to change a fundamental concept, once it has settled in your mind. Beside its benefits, a world-view can become a Psy-virus too, preventing you to accept new ideas. And then to know that the galactic world-view is very simple!

There is as much difference between the heliocentric and galactic paradigm as there is between the geocentric and heliocentric paradigm. Not that much, though. It is about the same universe, but the description of the movements of the planets and the stars is different. Nothing more, nothing less. And everybody can understand it, it's that simple. Ramon didn't doubt that the physics based on the galactic paradigm would answer a lot of questions in physics. Not that Ramon knew much about physics. He himself was more interested in the social and cultural aspects of the new paradigm. The galactic world-view is not centralistic. And that is in essence the real difference. Centralism was always the dynamic force of social and cultural development. Centralization of a society gave birth to social hierarchies. Centralism and hierarchy are two sides of the same coin. Growing centralism resulted in the evolution of hierarchical structures in the societies of ancient times and as a result, the rulers at the top of the hierarchy became very powerful. The existence of the Illuminati and Warriors was based on that dynamic force in society. All the information of Ury about the Warriors and the Illuminati made it clear that the world was entering the last phase of this unifying social process. The stage of ultimate centralization and a struggle to get hold of world domination. Humanity, controlled by one centralized hierarchical power structure.

That would eventually happen, with or without the help of the Greys unless there is a good alternative. But the involvement of the Greys in our cultural development accelerated everything. Even if the Greys would be defeated in one way or the other, the consequences of their involvement would still be there. So a new world-view is inevitable. How do philosophers call such a process? The English language has a beautiful word for it: a paradigm shift. Meaning, the shift from one world-view to the next. Compare it to what happened in the times of Copernicus. Our sociologists will have a hell of a job to translate the galactic world-view in a social frame, because there is no real frame. Everything moves and is in a constant flux. Ramon's Wise Teacher would have called it a dynamic hetrarchy. But if the sociologists and economists will succeed, the people will adore them. The state would no longer be a dominating force, a force that rules society, but it would be a shepherd that accompanies society. Individual freedom will be again the highest asset. It will be the opposite of the plutocracy that the Greys and some Illuminati have in mind.

Mean while the coffeepot is empty. Like an alchemist making gold out of iron, Ramon makes coffee from water, with the help of fresh grinded beans. Minutes later, he again takes up his writing odyssey. With the exception of a daily visit to the garden and a regular visit by Joy, Ramon works non-stop till late at night. Every day.

His only worry is the condition of Mira. Not a word from her has reached him. He is sure something has changed. But what? He can't put his finger on it and hopes that the meetings with the Greys haven't hurt her. They must not be underestimated. He hopes that the Central Grey isn't playing with her. But can she

318

handle the Greys? Yes! But how strong is she really? Those previous contacts with the Greys worried him a lot. But Mira is strong enough. She can handle the Greys. Teimon will help her if necessary. If and when he makes contact again. If!

- 52 -

There are pyramids in China. That became very obvious after studying the region of Xi'an. Ramon had located at least eighty pyramids, all with a flat top. It was hard to find decent information about all these tombs, as they are generally labeled. Ramon was really shocked that nobody knew about these monuments. He had heard about grave hills in the region of the terracotta findings, but that these grave hills had a pyramid shape was a big surprise. What a situation! Ramon was looking for monuments on the moon, while he didn't know that there were pyramids in China. Okay, these pyramids were not made of stone like the Egyptian ones. But that didn't make them less interesting.

To find pictures on the web of all these grave hills was as difficult as finding good pictures of moon craters. The resolution was so poor. Nice to look at but no quality. And to think that schools in general want to stimulate young people to be interested in science and space travel. Pictures by professional Hasselblad cameras have a resolution of gigabytes. But even on the most specialized sites, you can download only pictures of a few megabytes. Every pixel is larger than a football field. Even a pyramid as large as the Cheops wouldn't be visible on those pictures.

The big question about the Chinese pyramids was of course: Are there rooms in the Chinese pyramids? Could it be that on the inside of Mira's pyramid was a large room? The room that she described? On the web were hardly any pictures to find of these pyramid-shaped grave hills, let alone pictures from the interior. And how was Ramon supposed to find a link between the Cheops and the Mira pyramid, if he can't find any real information about the Chinese pyramids? There was only one solution. Ramon had to go there and to figure it out for himself.

319

But his bank account had a different opinion about such an adventure.

Luckily, with the help of Google, Ramon found a few important basic resemblances between the Cheops pyramid and the pyramid in China that had attracted Mira's attention. The size and the orientation. The size of the base of both pyramids was the same. That was undeniable. The orientation was equally important. Both pyramids were oriented to the same direction, exactly to the north. That was very striking, because almost all the pyramids in China were oriented some 4° to the north-west. Only a few pyramids were exactly oriented to the north. The pyramid of Mira and five or six smaller ones close by. What was even more striking was the fact that the Xi'an road infrastructure is a square network and was also perfectly directed to the north. Even more exact than the forbidden city of Beijing. In fact, the architectural concept of Xi'an was very modern. The Egyptian builders had used the orientation to the north for all the pyramids over the centuries. Could it be that the Chinese pyramids that were oriented to the north, were from an older period than all the others? Google couldn't give him an answer. But Ramon was glad that he found at least some resemblances between the Cheops pyramid and the "Mira" pyramid. He also wondered about the reason why all the other pyramids were oriented differently. He remembered some lectures in the eighties, about the Feng Shui technique. Since ancient times, this method was used for orientating buildings. Feng Shui was based on a kind of complex compass, combined with the magical square, the five elements and the eight trigrams of the I Ching.

Nowadays, everybody knows that the geometrical north has an angular difference from the magnetic north. On the geometrical north, the axis of Earth's rotation is located. The compass is directed to the magnetic north. So the method to orientate the Mira pyramid had to be based on a very old technique to connect sunrise and sunset during the longest day of the year. Only on that day, the line between these two points at the horizon has a perfect 90° angle to the geometrical north. So it was a practical way to figure out the exact direction of the north.

In our modern world, everybody knows that the Earth rotates once a day and that the movement of the moon and the sun is

320

basically an optical effect based on the Earth's rotation. But like the Sumerians, the ancient Chinese astronomy was based on the idea that the sun, the moon, the stars and the planets rotate once a day around the Earth, the geocentric model. The sun came up in the east and went down in the west. The north-south direction and east-west direction made a cross with a 90° angle. So the cross as a symbol was much older than the Christian cross, which had of course a different symbolic meaning. This cross method was used all over the world in prehistoric times as the basis for orientation. Also megalithic monuments like Stonehenge were based on that method.

The cross has four directions and that's probably the reason why the pyramids all have a square shape with four sides to symbolize the four directions of the heavens. It wouldn't surprise Ramon, if the pyramids which were directed to the north were older than the other ones. The Chinese were the inventors of the compass and the change in orientation of the pyramids to the magnetic north could be the new fashion after the Feng Shui method had been developed and institutionalized.

If only he could go to China himself. Xi'an must be a beautiful city. It would be amazing to be able to check himself whether Mira's description of the inner room was correct. It would be very good proof for Mira's paranormal abilities. But for the moment, it was financially out of the question. So he could do only one thing. Keep on writing and translating. Ramon was happy with the two links for the moment. That on itself was a hit. Mira had no clue about the size or the orientation of the pyramid. She just saw a light that had attracted her to that particular pyramid.

Meanwhile, Ramon went on with his struggle to write the book about his strange alien adventure. Every day he translated a few pages of The Galactic World-View. And in the scarce free time he made computer illustrations for the book. Especially the basic method to orientate buildings and cities and to be able to orientate while traveling on land and water became a priority in the chapter about the geocentric worldview. These basic methods of orientation were also the basis of the geocentric world-view and also of astrology. It took him days to thoroughly study some archaeological sites. The method to figure out the cross was remarkably simple if you know how to do it. In his enthusiasm Ramon designed a 3D map of the star constellations and a 3D drawing of Stonehenge to make the principle clear. These drawings would finally give him some unexpected insights into the rise of the first real world-view of humanity. But he decided to write it down in The Galactic World-View. Otherwise, the readers of the book "The Alien Code" would have a hard time to digest it all.

- 53 -

Wordlessly Mira inters the WebCom and sees Ramon seated in front of his screens like a futuristic yogi and surrounded by a wall of loud techno music.
Well Ramon, is there still life before death?
Ramon comes out of his 3D daydreaming and is glad to see Mira alive and kicking. He has been working for weeks on a 3D model of the solar system, based on the galactic world-view. Also the 3D Stonehenge model and the 3D map of the constellations were ready. He had to know every detail of why and how the architects used the cross for orientation.
Mira, come here and take a look. I have to show you something. You can't believe how simple it is to orientate in space and time.
Wait a minute, Ramon. Let me first come to my senses. I have been through an exhausting period the last few weeks. But today I wanted to visit you but then I thought, no … let him work on the book? And? Are you working on it?
I am Mira, I am. I write every day. But there are also other projects. But first things first. Let's make some brown inspiration.
While Ramon makes coffee, Mira looks around. Pictures of star maps, collages of the Chinese pyramids, all in the typical chaotic Ramon style. Artists, she thinks. How can somebody live in such a chaos of order? With a big smile, Ramon makes some room for the mugs and some slices of cake.
Please Mira, help yourself. By the way, did you know that 30,000 years ago men had to be on time for dinner too?
Mira laughs. A little while and a waterfall of information later,
322

Mira is convinced that primitive people were perfectly able to orientate in time and space.

Will you use all of that in the book, Ramon?

No, Mira. But it is important to know, because now I know that orientation is not something invented by the Ancients. Humans could orientate themselves on our planet dozens of millennia ago. They could even travel over long distances without losing their orientation to one another. They could always find their way back. And that is important. It proves that we didn't need the Ancients for the orientation of the pyramids. And it proves that there was already intelligence and science before the Ancients came. The Ancients just added their information to the knowledge that already existed in the different cultures. I am convinced that just like natural laws are the same everywhere in the universe, science is also the same everywhere in other planetary civilizations. Maybe they use different languages and symbols but the logic and the rationality must be the same.

Mira looks surprised.

So you think that the information of Teimon about the Ancients is not right?

No, that's not what I mean, Mira. I mean that people from prehistoric times were already very intelligent. They did not have the technology we have now. But with simple tools and practical intelligence, they were able to do stunning things. Just like we use a watch to know the time, they had a simple tool and some simple but genius knowledge that enabled them to know where they were and what time it was. But when the Ancients came and the Wise Men stimulated the building of large monuments like pyramids, it became necessary to develop a well organized society. To create a large pyramid, you needed a social structure like the pyramid itself. Do you remember from your history lessons the social model of the Egyptian culture?

Wait, Ramon, I know! The society was structured like a pyramid with different classes. At the bottom of the social pyramid were the farmers and the slaves. The second layer was the layer of the craftsmen. The third layer was made up by the lower priests and the writers. The fourth layer consisted of the high priests, the officials and the nobility. And the Pharaoh was the top of the pyramid.

You have a good memory, Mira. But you must not forget that this social pyramid was without question necessary to make the pyramids. All pyramid cultures were hierarchically structured. The pyramid monuments were like stone models of their society. It is possible that the Ancients gave technical advice. But don't forget that the Egyptians were very well joiners. You only have to look at the furniture of the Pharaohs. Just perfect! I think it is very reasonable that they could have used a mould technique to make the stones for the pyramids.

You mean that the stones were not cut out of solid rocks?

Yes. A French professor, Michel Barsoum, showed clearly that most stones, used in the pyramid, could have easily been made with a kind of concrete. Maybe the receipt of this concrete got lost or was kept secret. But this method could explain a lot. The stones were merely cube-like blocks. Perfect to make in moulds, no? But don't get me wrong. To make perfect 90° moulds in wood is not as easy as you may think, you know. And also the technique of drying was not simple. There was enough sun to dry the concrete in the moulds. But these wooden moulds could have been placed in a kind of stone moulds to control the drying process and to get the geometry right.

But that must have been big stone moulds, Ramon. I never heard that they found something like that near the pyramids.

I'm not so sure about that, Mira. Come, I will show you these stone moulds.

Ramon activates Google Earth and zooms in on the Cheops pyramid. Look! To the west of the pyramids lots of mastabas were built. I think that they could have been primarily built to dry the concrete with the natural heat of the sun. They are very massive and can regulate the drying process of the concrete in a natural way. They all have a square opening on top. Perfect to make a square mould stable. It is just an idea of me but it would make sense. The mastabas are close to the pyramids and they are orderly built to work in an efficient way. Every day or so, a few hundred stones could be made in this way. Enough to do the job in thirty years.

Anyhow, the pyramids were built in a very planned way. The architects must have used construction designs. These drawings were never found and some people are still looking for them.

324

Probably a lot of evidence was lost during the destruction of the library of Alexandria. Although, my Wise Teacher was convinced that most books were not burned, but came into the possession of the new Islamic kingdoms, where they were hidden in secret libraries, waiting to see the daylight once the Islamic culture is ready for disclosure.

That would be great, Ramon.

Indeed, Mira. But to come back to the subject, I am more convinced than ever that the Ancients left a kind of visiting-card in the construction of the pyramid of Cheops, like the star map geometry of the shafts and maybe other things that we still don't understand. So the Ancients were not that much responsible for the building. That was done by the Egyptian people. But the involvement of the Ancients has to be found in the details of the design.

I understand what you mean, Ramon. But what do you think of the Ancients? If they went away a long time ago, what must be their purpose in life?

That is a good question, Mira. I think that the task of the Ancients is first of all to protect life in general. To spread life but also to help or stimulate existing civilizations to evolve. And that might be crucial, taking into account the overall situation of the multitude of physical events in our Milky Way. And that is a noble cause. For that increases the chances of survival for the evolution of life. Don't forget that a lot of things can go wrong on our planet and in our Milky Way in general. Knowing what geologists and astronomers discover every day, the continuation of life on a planet is not evident.

Right you are, Ramon. National Geographic shows one catastrophe theory after the other. It can definitely go wrong. Ice ages, super tsunami's, super volcano eruptions, super meteorite strikes, floods and earthquakes, you name it. All super dangerous for life in general!

Absolutely, Mira. And also stellar disasters are possible. A supernova explosion in our galaxy could destroy life on our planet. But relax! It is proven that this can't happen in our neighborhood of the milky way. But it is also very probable that our solar system enters an interstellar dust cloud, making the temperatures go down for hundreds of millennia. Recently, astronomers have discovered that our solar system travels back and forth through the spiral arm of our milky way that we are part of. This back and forth movement takes some 46 million years per cycle. When our solar system passes the middle region of the spiral arm, the chance for meteorite strikes will be twenty to thirty times higher than now. We are now located near the border of the spiral arm. But in about 12 million years, we enter the central zone again. And God knows what will be discovered in the future. A few weeks ago, astronomers observed shockwaves throughout a galaxy, created by black holes. Galaxies can even collide with one another, with all the risks involved for collision of stars or planets. So, it's undeniable that the survival of life on a planet in our gigantic universe is not evident. That fact makes it understandable and acceptable that a civilization like the Ancients, who "made it" in a manner of speaking, helps less evolved civilizations to be prepared to protect themselves against future disasters before they will occur. The Ancients didn't intervene in our daily business. They just helped us to be ready when disaster would strike on our planet. Don't forget that the Ancients are far more developed than we. So they must be able to estimate future planetary problems far better than we. In the near as well as in the far future.

Sorry to interrupt you, Ramon, but before I forget, I have gotten some ideas about the pyramid shape these past days.

You have? Please, tell me, Mira.

Let me think. How shall I explain it? We agreed that the star map could have been used to locate beginning and end of a travel route through space, as a coordination system for interstellar travel.

Yes. That would be logical, don't you think?

Indeed, Ramon. As you know, the pyramid shape is a geometric shape that does not exist in nature. So maybe, the pyramid shape could have been a kind of essential element for a star gate to function. I think that is the reason why the square matrix in the purple skull could have the same function as the shafts in the Cheops pyramid.

That is possible, Mira. But what do you want to say? That the pyramids are a kind of stone version of the purple skull?

Well yes. Let me tell you exactly the idea that came into my

326

mind. I think it was information from the purple skull itself.

1.354 **The pyramid can no longer be used as a star gate. It is not only damaged, but some important artefacts are lost or have disappeared. The Greys have done everything to make sure that all the contact points of the Téry with the Earth can no longer be used. Luckily for us, the purple skull is still missing.**

But that's a confirmation of what Dan Burisch told about the artifacts and what we thought about the intentions of the Greys, Mira.

Indeed, Ramon. I am convinced that one of the artificial star gates on Earth was the Cheops pyramid.

That makes sense, Mira. Why else were Dan Burisch and J Rod in that pyramid? Strange that you should bring this topic up. I thought about Dan Burisch when I read the article about the galactic shockwaves astronomers recently discovered. The phenomenon really exists. But shockwaves don't spread with the speed of light. It is a process over tens of thousands of years. J Rod stated that these shocks could travel via wormholes in a matter of seconds. But that is yet to be proven.

You may look at it any which way you want, Ramon, this discovery will be seen by some Initiated as a confirmation that the Greys are right.

I agree, Mira. You know, a few days ago, I found two new video interviews of Dan Burisch, published on the Project Camelot site. I was astonished when I listened to the things he had to say. I listened with in the back of my head everything we know from Teimon. And for the first time, I could hear contradictions in his story. For example, he told that the face on Mars, about which Hoagland wrote a book, is something from the future.

Now I don't follow, Ramon.

Do you know the picture of the face on Mars?

Yes, you showed it to me once, when we were discussing Hoagland's theories.

Dan Burisch states that this ruin is in a way a virtual building. You could compare it with the picture in the science fiction movie "Back to the Future" by Steven Spielberg.

You mean the picture that constantly changes, depending on what happens?

Exactly, Mira. Dan claims that depending on which of the three timelines will unfold, this face will become a real artificial construction or just a natural mountain.

Mira shakes her head. How is it possible that such an intelligent man can be fooled in such a way?

Oh Mira, I understand that all too well. Some people are so intelligent that they can lose themselves in a theory, no matter how absurd the theory is. Parallel universes, time travel, higher dimensions, etc. Thousands of books have been written about these subjects by very clever people. But that doesn't mean that these theories are right. They might be logical but nevertheless very wrong. It's like a lie. A lie always pretends to be true. But it is still a lie.

People would be astonished to know how little intellectuals know about philosophy. Most people think that philosophy is some kind of hobby. But believe me, philosophy is as difficult as physics or mathematics. Nothing is as difficult as finding wisdom. You can find a lot of small truths in every science. But wisdom is of a different level. Reading books about philosophy or studying philosophy doesn't turn you into a philosopher. It is a start yes, but a real philosopher is a wise man and wise people are rare to find. Let me give you one example.

The word dimension is used in all kinds of literature. In dozens of articles I have read this one recurring statement: "We humans are three-dimensional creatures who live in a four-dimensional universe". And that is such blatant nonsense, Mira. Einstein was the first scientist who stated that the three dimensions of space and the time dimension were an integral part of a four dimensional space-time universe. The consequence of his theory is that time and space is an inseparable unity. You can distinguish space and time with your mind but not physically.

I got you, Ramon. Go on.

Einstein proved in this way that every atom, particle and molecule and everything present in our universe is four-dimensional. And in fact, everybody knows that. From the moment of your birth, you will become older until you die, no? So everything that exists, exists in space-time. Not merely in space. So a human being is a four-dimensional being. Not a three-dimensional being that lives in a four-dimensional world. If

328

the universe exists of eleven dimensions, like the string theory claims, humans are eleven-dimensional. Not three-dimensional.

String theory, Ramon? No theory about underwear, I hope?

No, no Mira, ha, ha. In string theory, space has ten dimensions and the time dimension is the eleventh dimension. In this eleven-dimensional universe all existing things would become eleven-dimensional phenomena. Rocks, plants, animals and humans. The extra dimensions are not above us or something like that. These dimensions are within and around us. The space dimensions are the geometry of the behavior of energy... of the stuff we are made of. They are not spiritual dimensions or whatever.

And what about the "now" time then, Ramon?

Interesting question, Mira. The "now" is the place where we are on the timeline in space-time. Every moment is a new "now". Time is the movement of the now over the timeline. Teimon and Aodin taught us that this "now" is the same in the whole universe. Do you know that Buddha discussed the "now" extensively in his lectures. For him, the "now" was the only reality. There was only the "now". The past exists in what is left behind, physical and mental, but the future is only mental. So every moment is a new moment in the space-time line. The past lives only in the Akasha or in our personal memories. And the future is that what has yet to come. In the Dutch language the word for future is "toekomst", which literally means, that what is still "to come". But it does not exist as such. Only the now exists as a reality.

Thanks, Ramon. Now I got it. Ramon smiles.

But now something else, Mira. You told me that the pyramids were a stone model of the purple skull, to make space travel possible. Teimon made clear that only telepathy makes communication possible over long distances in the now time. Telepathy doesn't need time. The crystal skull works as an amplifier. But telepathy is something else than traveling with your body over long distances at very high speed. In order to do that, the "now" location of the stars on the star maps must be very accurate. Pyramids could be perfect objects to connect two points hundreds of light years away from each another. But I have no idea how they do that. If the Ancients developed such a technique, it must be a fantastic technology. I really wonder what kind of technology they use. Have you any idea, Mira. Has the skull revealed maybe something about their technology?

Mira hears Ramon talking and gradually, she remembers something about the visions she had during the Christmas days.

Now that you mention it, Ramon. I remember seeing all kinds of images. Circles that rotate in different colors, but nothing clear. It was too complex.

That's a pity, Mira. Forget it. Maybe it will become clear later on.

Suddenly, something enters Mira's mind. Ramon, there is something I have to tell you. I think that it is information from Aodin, which suddenly came up now that you talk about the star map.

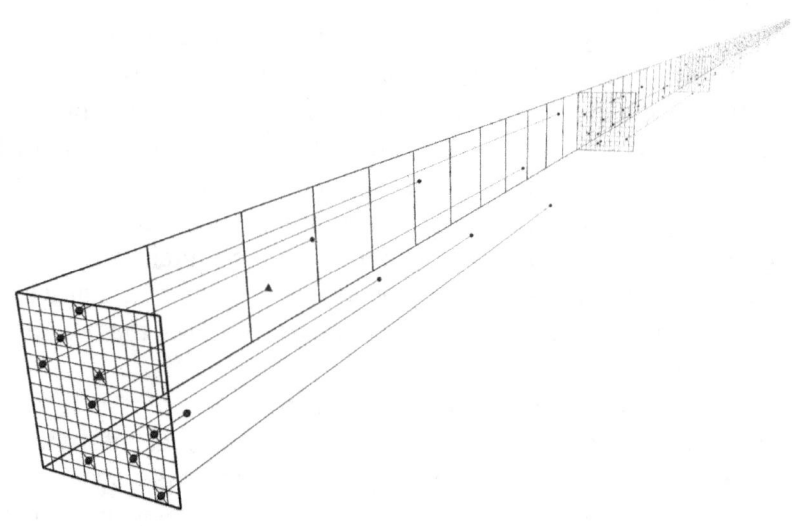

1.355 **The information about the star map must be corrected. The squares are not 144 by 144 but 12 by 12 light years. The cube structure in the purple skull is a simplification of the shafts in the Cheops pyramid. In the shafts, the star maps are 12 by 12 light years and the distance is plus minus 144 light years.**

Now you truly surprise me, Mira. When I was drawing the star

330

map in 3D, I saw that the information didn't fit the Caviglia shaft. The shaft shape is not made of cubes. I immediately remembered what you said when you received this information for the first time. But it is good that you mention it, Mira. That was also the reason that I didn't see the link with the shafts in the first place. I thought that the maps were saved on clay tablets or papyrus or something like that, hidden inside a secret room in the pyramids.

I am sorry, Ramon. But the translation is not always simple. I was already happy to understand what they meant and how the star map was built.

That's no problem, Mira. The important thing is that I know it now. It makes everything a bit more realistic. I think this is just great. I will make the drawings later but first things first! Let's celebrate this, Mira. What do you think of a fine glass of red wine? It's a long time ago that we have exercised the favorite French way of wasting time.

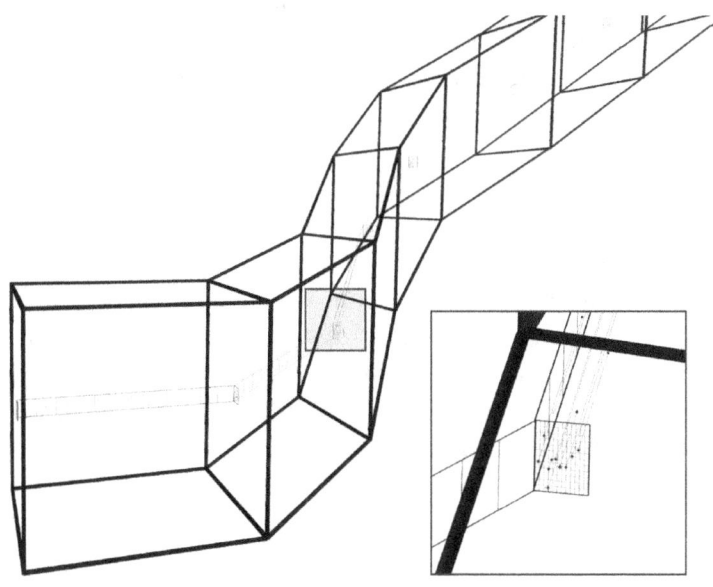

That is a terrific idea, Ramon. I came today to relax a bit in the first place, you know.

Ramon smiles, gets a bottle of red wine in the cellar and both enjoy an excellent glass of wine.

How on earth is it possible that most people still don't know what a dimension is, says a tipsy Ramon. It is the simplest thing in the world, you know. In fact, everybody knows it. Dimension means literally "direction". Schools in general don't teach the student the difference between geometrical and physical dimensions. Let me explain it to you.

A point is an appointed location. It has no direction and so no dimensions. Therefore a point is called a zero dimension. A straight line is called the first dimension because a line is a series of points arranged in one direction. If you combine two lines with a different direction and they have one point in common, you appoint a plane. For example, in a compass, north-south and east-west are two lines that cross in a point. With this simple tool you can appoint the place of any point on the plane.

But isn't north-east a different direction?

Yes, but if you know the north and the east direction, you can appoint north-east based on the two basic directions or dimensions. Any shape you draw on a plane is therefore two dimensional.

Okay, it is clear Ramon.

Well then, north and east are the two horizontal directions, the third dimension is the vertical direction. As soon as a plane has a thickness, the plane becomes three-dimensional. Any shape that has thickness or elevates from the plane is three-dimensional. It can be appointed by three dimensions. But in physics, points don't exist. Particles do for sure, but particles are not infinitely small like points in geometry are. Particles are the smallest building blocks of matter. But they do have a size. Thus particles are three-dimensional. But even if particles would be compared to points, they are still different from geometrical points. Because particles are made of pure energy, meaning they are in constant movement. And because you can only make a movement in time, this extra dimension is linked to time. So particles are four dimensional! Get it?

No Ramon, I don't understand what you mean, says Mira amused.

Listen. The line is a geometrical presentation of the first

dimension. A line exists of infinite points. But you can also look at a line in a different way. You can see a line as the movement of a point or in the case of physics a particle. The line is then the direction of the movement of a point. If you draw a line with the point of a pencil, you start with the first point and by the movement of the pencil, the line becomes longer. In order to do that, you not only need space, but also…

…a pencil, says Mira, who can hardly suppress her giggling. She doesn't understand why Ramon makes a point of all this.

No Mira! You also need time! So if a particle moves in one direction, then it also moves in time.

Ramon looks at Mira to see if she understands but she starts to shake of laughter.

Mira, don't laugh. This is very important. A moving particle moves in space and time. That's the difference with a point. A point is a zero dimensional concept. And why? Because it has no direction and is frozen in time and space. As if you freeze the movement in one moment. In the "now" time.

So a point is in fact nothing, says Mira with tears in her eyes.

Well… I wouldn't say that Mira, says Ramon very seriously. When I was young, I had a friend, Peterselie was his nickname.

Peterselie… ha, ha, ha.

Listen, Mira. Once he asked me: What is the smallest circle? And I said: a point with a hole in it!

Mira laughs out loud. Ha, ha, a point with a hole. Ha, ha….

But Mira, that's not funny!

No, no Ramon, ha, ha…

Ramon shakes his head. What am I to do with a gal like that, he thinks.

But Mira, in fact it wasn't a bad idea, you know. The string theory is saying something similar, did you know that? In string theory, the smallest particles are little rings of energy. In school, we learned that particles were very tiny balls. But in string theory, particles are visualized as small rings. So in fact points with a hole in the middle. And what do you think that this means, Mira?

Mira tries to be serious.

No idea, Ramon. I thought that strings were… a ladies thing.

Aand again she starts laughing.

Ha, ha… Ramon, don't forget to drink. Your glass is still full, ha, ha…

But Ramon continues his lecture.

No, Mira. That means that even the particle itself, even if it is in rest at a certain point, still has an inner movement, it's moving in a circle. And this can only be if a particle has gravitational force, curving the energy movement in a circle, which is a two-dimensional shape. And because the circular movement of the energy has also a twist during the circular movement, the energy movement of a string is three-dimensional. And because movement is only possible in time, a string particle has a four-dimensional movement. The circle has two dimensions, the twist is the third dimension and time is the fourth dimension. So the simplest string is still a four-dimensional energy phenomenon. And do you know how much time it takes for the energy to rotate once in a string?

No idea, Ramon. Please enlighten me, she giggles.

One hundredth billionth of a billionth of a billionth of a second.

Well Ramon, it could be worse, no?

No really, Mira. That number is the smallest amount of time. There is no smaller time unit. And that's exactly the definition of the "now" in modern physics.

Let's drink to that, Ramon. Her laughter comes finally to an end. The two glasses are filled again and Ramon comes out of his speech.

Here's to the "now", Ramon.

Here's to the "now" Mira.

For a while it is silent in the kitchen. Suddenly, Ramon intuitively gets an idea.

Now I know what is so strange about Burisch's idea of the timelines, Mira. J Rod told Burisch that the Greys are descendants of the humans and that they come from three different periods in the future. They came back in time to warn us about a coming catastrophe, which will happen in a few years. As a consequence of the catastrophe the survivors become genetically ill and their bodies will deteriorate over the next millennia. Burisch said that the Greys found in Roswell are from 24,000 years into the future. J Rod came from 44,000 years into the future and the other Grey type was from 54,000 years into to the future. So J Rod uses three types of Greys and three points in the future for these Grey time travelers. I will call them the 24, the 45 and the 54.

Now listen, Mira. By talking about the face on Mars, Burisch revealed the intentions of the Greys. First of all, he said that there are three types of Greys.

I know what you want to say, Ramon. We know who the Greys are and that the Greys have had their own evolution. So these three types of Greys constitute the progress of their own cloning evolution!

Clever girl! I think that in order to explain the differences between the three types, the Greys could not tell the truth. So to hide their real background, the Greys suggested Burisch that they came from the future and that there are three possible scenarios of the future. J Rod also suggested that it is still not clear which of these three scenarios will be the real future and that the humans can still prevent the future scenarios of the 44 or the 54 Greys. If that would be the case, four billion people will die during the catastrophe. So we can still prevent that this will happen and if we do, our future will be the future of the 24 Greys. And that would be the best of the three futures. Burisch says we can still reduce the effect of the catastrophe, if we treat the Earth better and destroy all the star gates. Isn't that clever?

Yes, very clever, Ramon, but wait a minute. What will happen with the 45 and the 54 Greys when the future will be the 24 timeline?

Well, Burisch has a simple answer to that. Then they will never come into existence, meaning that the 45 and 54 Greys will disappear. Just like that. Gone they are! And not only that, Mira, also the abductions would have never taken place, because the 54 Greys are the ones who do the abductions. They would disappear with everything they did, as if nothing had happened.

The great magical disappearing act, says Mira amused.

Indeed, Mira. It gets even weirder. If that would be the case, Dan Burisch would never have met J Rod, if we finally succeed to take the 24 timeline. It is even worse, Mira. If Burisch made it all up, he can deny everything by saying that we succeeded to take the 24 time line.

Okay, I get it. So, he can deny everything he has told, if we enter the 24 timeline. Because then, J Rod would have never existed and Dan could never have met him in the first place. That's clever.

Indeed, Mira. So if Dan Burisch has invented this story himself, he found a very interesting version of Back to the Future. But if the story is indeed from that Grey J Rod, then it is even cleverer.

I'm listening, Ramon.

Think about it, Mira. In this way, the Greys hide their real origin and they don't have to talk about their creators, the Téry. And by suggesting that they are from the future, we are their ancestors. That's a perfect way to work on our feelings, is it not?

You are right, Ramon! This story is a knife that cuts on three sides. It gives an explanation for three types of Greys, covering their real origin. It makes everybody that believes it afraid of a coming disaster and in order to prevent that disaster, we would destroy all the star gates making it impossible to get into contact with the Téry.

Indeed, Mira. Fortunately, we know the real background of the Greys. If Teimon is right, of course. But believe me, everything I find on de web points to the fact that Teimon is right. His revelations make sense of all the information that you can find on the web. And the information of Teimon is also pure. I have it directly from you, so at least I am sure that nobody altered the story you tell me. And that is our greatest advantage.

Believe me, Ramon. I don't make anything up.

Without a doubt, Mira. How could you make everything up that is written in all these notes? It is all so detailed. Of course, the future will finally be the judge of it all.

I'm glad that you see it this way, Ramon. I don't think that I would find anybody else with an open mind for what is happening to me. By the way, what's the time?

One look at the clock is enough for Mira to run to her car and to disappear into the night. It is new moon and the stars twinkle bright against the dark night sky. Orion looks beautiful and Ramon wonders about the situation of the Sheyan. A warm flow of energy runs through his body and for a moment he forgets the cold.

He realizes that he gradually becomes a part of the story. He recognizes the symptoms. For a parapsychologist who practices

336

the phenomenological method, it is a pleasant extra experience. A test of your own psychological limits, not to become part of something and in the same time become deeply involved in it. For Ramon it is part of Mental Art and a reaction against Body Art. For years, he lived like a Hindu. He became one with their traditions until he finally merged with the Indian code. And suddenly, from one day to the next, he ended it all and just continued his normal Belgian life. It was the moment that he realized that the Indian Code was true, that it was as objective and realistic as the scientific code. Any cultural code is as empiric and realistic as the other.

When he understood that, he went on with is own life. But now he was sure. He had no more doubts about the code of another culture. And that is the most important thing you can discover in your life. He understood that the different cultural codes are all approaches of the same world, the same reality. There is only one world and one universe, but there are different ways to understand the same world. Every code shows a different facet of the same reality. Ramon remembered that time very well. That experience gave him a feeling of freedom, difficult to put in words, a freedom to think in different codes. And that's the ultimate mental freedom. Memories of that time made him smile. And without worrying about the cold outside, he goes to bed.

Thinking how great it would be to learn about the cultural code of an extra-terrestrial civilization like the Ancients, he slowly falls asleep, realizing the book has to be written as soon as possible. First the book… first the… book…

- 55 -
2/5/2007

The full moon turns Ramon's garden into a place of mystery and natural beauty. The first strawberries are ripe and after removing the weeds between the vegetables, Ramon goes back home with a basket full of red natural artworks. Evening falls. Strawberries with cream would make his day. There's no news from Mira. His research on the web takes away every sense of time. Day in day out he is reading texts, watching videos, translating and writing.

Who wouldn't lose track of time? The garden brings him always back to reality and the prospect of a delicious dessert makes him forget all his worries. He enters his house and…

There you are, says the deep voice of Mira when he enters the kitchen. I have been waiting for an hour, do you know that?

A big smile comes on Ramon's face.

Mira, are you still alive?

As you see, Ramon, alive and well. Some coffee? I made a pot.

Perfect, Mira. Finally somebody who makes coffee for me. A full mug will do. I will take my writing materials. Because I think it's time for an alien dialogue, no?

How do you know, Ramon? Is it that obvious?

I don't know, Mira. I hear it in your voice! But don't worry. Nobody else will notice.

He quickly takes his notebook and checks if the video recorder is ready for the late night movie. Mira is clearly in trance. God knows what information will be revealed today.

Who is on line, Mira? Is it Aryein or Teimon?

It is not Teimon. It is Aryein, Ramon. I'm sure of that. I hear that deep sound again on the background. He introduced me already to what he has to tell, while I was waiting. The information is very complex and simple at the same time. Only Aryein's messages are that compact.

That's reassuring, Mira, says Ramon while making himself ready to take notes.

What's that suppose to mean, Ramon, "reassuring"?

I'm just joking, Mira. These alien conversations have become so normal that we forget how special it is. So surprise me, Mira. I will make a strawberry dessert after the session. Okay?

I will take you up on that, Ramon. But take a deep breath because it will not be simple. It is about the code of the I Ching.

What? Ramon is immediately on high alert. A hard time lies ahead for him.

Okay, Ramon. Here we go.

1.356 The interpretation of the I Ching is wrong. The code is used in a wrong way.

Ramon feels a warm sensation going through his body when he hears this information. His Wise Teacher was convinced that the key to the code of the I Ching was hidden, so that the basic

338

system behind this book would never fall in the hands of people who would misuse its knowledge to enlarge their power. Since Merly's information about the Illuminati, these remarks of his Wise Teacher became very real.

1.357 The code of the I Ching is based on two symbols. These two symbols are generally interpreted in the following way.

1.358 A full line or the Yang line is in general seen as the symbol for the masculine principle, light, heaven, the creative forces et cetera. A broken line or the Yin line is the symbol of manifestation, the feminine principle, earth, the darkness.

━━━━━━━━━━━━   ━━━━━ ━━━━━

1.359 But this is not completely right. The symbol of the yin line is not a broken line. The Yin line is composed by two separate full lines. So it is not a broken line as if the unity is broken. The broken line is two full lines. One of the two lines is the Yang line and the other one Yin line. Together they symbolize Tji.

1.360 So "Tji" means energy. Tai Tji means the whole universe. Tai means "large" but also "the unity of everything". Tji is the stuff where everything in the universe is made of. Tai Tji means the unity of everything that exists.

1.361 But everything comes out of Tao. The Tai Tji symbol shows the unity of Tao and Tji. It is important to understand that the Tai Tji symbol and the two symbols of the I Ching are intrinsically related.

1.362 The circle of the Tai Tji symbol symbolizes the same thing as the full line in the I Ching. The circle or the full line symbolizes Unity or Tao, the source of everything. But the circle also represents the border in which the Tji moves.

1.363 After one orbit over the large circle of the Tai Tji symbol, the Tji energy moves inwards and divides the inner region of the circle in two parts. The Yin and the Yang region. The inner movement of the energy describes an "S"

shape or wave movement. The "S" wave is composed of two half circles. After the inward movement, the Tji energy comes back on the large circle in opposite direction. After a full orbit, the energy moves inward again in the opposite direction. If the Tji comes back on the large circle, a new cycle can start.

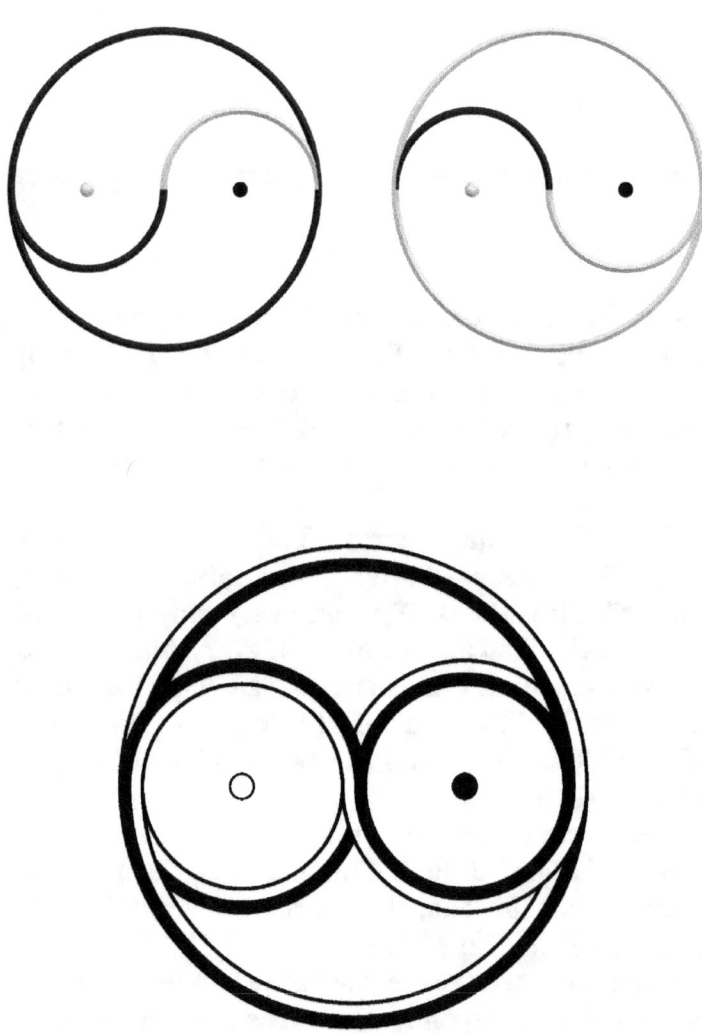

1.364 **So the Tai Tji symbol is not a static symbol. It shows the movement of the energy. If you draw the full movement, you see a large circle with a horizontal "8" figure in the middle.**

Ramon understands immediately what Aryein means. How strange is all this! But he has no time to think. Mira goes on with the translation.

1.365 **So the symbol of the full line in the I Ching is a simplification of the large circle of the Tai Tji symbol.**

1.366 **In the interior of the Tai Tji, two nuclei are present. The Yin part in the Tai Tji symbol moves around. They symbolize the polarity of the Tji energy.**

1.367 **The movement of the "S" shaped Yin line, is directed by these two centres. The essence of Yin is Yang, the essence of Yang is Yin. These two nuclei are interconnected and keep the energy flowing.**

1.368 **The Tai Tji symbol visualizes the unity of Yin and Yang, the unity of Heaven and Earth, the unity of Creation and the evolution of space, time and matter, from the smallest to the largest.**

The following information must not be published in the book.

1.369

1.370

1.371 **This information is again allowed. With the two symbols of the I Ching, you can make four combinations of two lines. They are called "Duograms". They are the four primary symbols in the code of the I Ching.**

1.372 **Energy or Tji has to flow in these four Duograms. To understand the dynamics of the I Tjing, you have to understand the relation between these Duograms and the Tai Tji symbol. I will explain this but the information may not bee used in this book. It will become clear in the coming**

years why and when this information may be revealed.

Ramon has a hard time to write it down. He understands that this is very important information. All kinds of questions run through his mind. Is this really the key of the code, hidden in the I Ching? Warm vibrations flow through his spine, now that a millennia old secret is about to be revealed in his kitchen. But Mira gives him no time to think. With astonishment Ramon listens to the information that Aryein sends telepathically to Mira. He explains how the hexagrams are composed using the combination of these Duograms.

1.373

1.374

1.375

Mira, a bit slower, please. I can't keep up with you. I am afraid that I can't read what I have written.

But Mira doesn't react and goes on, extremely focused on what Aryein has to say. Ramon tries to write down as much as he can as well as he can, hoping he will be able to read his own writings afterwards.

1.376

1.377

1.378

1.379

1.380

1.381

The only thing Ramon can do is writing. Mira is talking on autopilot. The words flow out of her mouth without hesitation. Like an oracle, she reveals the most complex information, searched for by wise people within living memory. A feeling of admiration about the wisdom of the Ancients vibrates through Ramon's body. And it has still not finished.

1.382 **This must be written in the book. "1" and "2", is the basis of our physics.**

1.383 **The number "0" does not exist in nature**.

1.384 **"Nothing" does not exist.**

1.385 **Everything that exists, is something.**

1.386 **What not exists, is not "something".**

1.387 **"Nothing" is not something.**

1.388 **"Nothing" is not existing like something.**

1.389 **There is no physical "nothing".**
In his mind Ramon sees a lot of physical concepts disappear into thin air. There is no perfect vacuum, no singularity, no Big Bang out of nothing. He thinks back on the evening when he tried to explain Mira what a dimension is and smiles.

1.390 **Geometry has a zero point. But that is an appointed place mark.**

1.391 **The 0-point in geometry exists. The zero point in geometry is not nothing. A zero-point is the basis of geometry. All points can be zero-points. A zero-point lies between minus one and one. It is a place to start, so it is a very important point.**

1.392 **The zero in geometry became the concept of "nothing" in physics. That is a big mistake. In physics "nothing" does not exist.**

1.393 **Everything that exists is a unity of two parts or aspects. Yang and Yin can't exist on themselves. Nothing is only Yin or Yang.**

1.394 **Ramon will understand. The synchronicity will increase again in the coming days. I salute you.**

And then it becomes very silent in the kitchen. Gradually Mira comes out of her trance.

That was it, Ramon. Jesus, what a marathon! I thought there would be no end to it. I hope you could make notes of everything because I can't remember a thing.

Ramon is still making corrections here and there and with the help of some sketches he hopes he will be able to remember it all.

I think I have it all, Mira.

Thank God, she says and takes a deep breath while looking for a cigarette.

Deeply under the impression of this session, Ramon can think only of one thing.

How about some coffee, Mira?

Yes, Ramon, please.

Her voice regains her normal intonation. While Ramon is still under the impression of the revelations, he makes coffee as in a Japanese tea ceremony. Gradually his mind comes at rest. The mugs are served and for a while, he and Mira sit quietly, recovering of this fascinating session.

Mira, I'm really perplexed. No, don't tell me that you only made this up.

Mira has to laugh as she sees how bewildered Ramon is looking at her.

Do you realize how important this information is, Mira?

Well Ramon, I have never been into the I Ching that much. But if it can be of any help, it's fine by me.

Now it is Ramon's turn to laugh.

You are a real piece of work, Mira.

Okay, Ramon. But can I get that dessert with strawberries now?

Ramon has to laugh out loud and also Mira gets the giggles when she hears him laughing. One of the greatest mysteries of the Chinese culture is solved and she is only thinking about a strawberry dessert.

I will take care of that, Mira. Right away. Ha, ha, ha. And I will join you.

In no time Ramon makes a delicious dessert.

Look Mira, the round glass bowls are the Tao circles and the cream and the strawberries are the Yin and the Yang. Together they are a higher unity, the dessert.

Both laugh and enjoy the wonderful tastes of nature. The rest of the night, Ramon and Mira meditate about the information with the help of the old I Ching book that has been the most loyal companion of Ramon for so many years. Has the secret of this book finally been revealed? Is this information the key to how the hexagrams are configured "in" a certain "formation"? Both forget the UFOs and the aliens and when Mira leaves the house of Ramon much too late, the full moon shines high in the sky, where Orion dominates the other constellations.

The synchronicity will become stronger. What was Aryein referring to? The whole I Ching was based on this strange concept of synchronicity, which the people of the West don't seem to understand. Synchronicity is not the same as "coincidence", used to calculate the basis for a lottery. Synchronicity gives meaning to life and overrules fate. Western science understands causality all too well. Cause and effect. If something happens by accident, it means that there is no causality. But could it be that some things that seem to happen

344

by accident have a deeper meaning? Synchronicity is when two things happen at the same time without causal connections, but with a very important impact. Life is full of it. Who doesn't know love on first sight?

Much too late, Ramon hurries to bed. As he enters his bedroom, Ramon remembers a story of his Wise Teacher about synchronicity. If you enter a dark room and you touch the light button by accident, the light goes on by accident. But the light can't go on by accident alone. You need the whole electrical installation to make it happen. The concept of justice in the Chinese culture is based on synchronicity. Justice will punish unjustified actions. Justice will always prevail. Synchronicity gives life meaning. Everything is not just happening by accident. Synchronicity is also the power that will make sure that the Greys will get what they deserve, that they can't succeed in their plans to control the world. The sleep closes the curtains of the day and Ramon disappears into the depth of his own virtual reality.

- 56 -
9/5/2007

Ramon has struggled for days to decipher his notes of the information about the I Ching. It confirmed that the Ancients brought part of their cultural code to China. The contact with Aryein also proved that he can have contact with Mira with the help of the crystal skull but not with Teimon. The Ancients also used a different technique of telepathy. Mira could not ask questions in the way it was possible with Teimon. It was a take it or leave it situation. No dialogue or arguments, but nevertheless fascinating. But the big question is: How can this information be of use when you have a bunch of Greys on your back, trying to get control over the world? But maybe it was not yet clear what the real purpose of the information was. One thing was certain: Teimon's and Aryein's information had to be taken seriously. The book had to be written as soon as possible. The only decision that Ramon has to make is simple: put everything else on hold and focus only on the book. So the Galactic World-View had to wait. He finished two chapters of the book, which is a good start.

Evening falls and his WebCom is only lit by the computer screens. A light beam of a car interrupts his thoughts. A figure passes the window in a hurry and somebody enters the house. Out of breath, Mira enters the WebCom and is clearly nervous. Ramon recognizes the symptoms. She has contact.

Do you have some coffee for me, Ramon? I have no time and that sound is back again. It has been for days now.

Coffee it will be, Mira. I need a break too. Writing is hard labor, you know.

Happy to see her, he immediately makes a fresh pot of liquid inspiration.

Mira takes a seat and the smell of coffee and the relaxed atmosphere in Ramon's kitchen bring rest.

It is unbelievable, Ramon. I work sixteen hours a day and it is still not enough.

Then I am not the only one, says Ramon while serving the coffee. The only thing that I do is work on the book and in between I sleep. But I'm not complaining, Mira. At least we don't get bored.

Ramon takes his writing materials and sits down. Mira goes into trance spontaneously. For days, she managed to suppress it but now that she is relaxed, it happens in a split second and Aryein is back with some important information for Ramon.

1.395 **There are seven locations on Earth where the laws of nature behave differently.**

Ramon asks cautiously: Are these the star gates, Mira?

Mira goes on.

1.396 **You call them star gates. But they are natural star gates, existing on every planet. On Earth, there are seven natural star gates. In Africa, Asia, Europe, North and South America, Australia and the North and South pool.**

Ramon remembers several websites that mention natural star gates. Some call them "regions with a vortex". There is even a map on the web showing all these places. But apparently, there are only seven real ones. Or no, eighth, the North Pole is no solid continent.

1.397 **These gates are created by nature itself. They open up**

346

every 900 years.

Ramon remembers the legends of people in Siberia. He read an article about it, when he was gathering information about Tunguska. These legends tell that every six or nine hundred years, strange light phenomena were seen in the Tunguska region.

1.398 **The natural star gates will open again soon. These places are not known by the humans. They have to remain secret. The Greys can't control them. The Greys only control the artificial star gates.**

Ramon waits for more information but Mira comes gradually back to herself.

That's it, Ramon. Have you got some more coffee for me?

Of course Mira, says Ramon with a smile, astonished by the importance of this information. He fills her mug.

So the gates open every 900 years, Mira. If they get open soon, then these gates were also open in the eleventh century. No?

I guess so, Ramon. In the eleventh century, in the second century and then 700 B.C., 1600 B.C., 2500 B.C., 3400 B.C, and so on.

Do you think that the Ancients and the Téry have used these gates in the past to get here?

That could well be, Ramon. But nothing has been said about that. But it seems logical, no?

So the gates Dan Burisch talks about do exist! Won't they be dangerous when they open again?

I don't think so, Ramon. But wait. I hear that sound again. I think Aryein is back.

A few seconds later, Mira is back in trance.

1.399 **The gates will open, but there is no danger. It is a natural cycle.**

1.400 **The Greys control all the artificial gates. These gates can no longer be used by the Téry. But the natural gates can still be used.**

Mira rubs her face with her hands.

And that was it, Ramon.

What a relief, Mira. So there is no catastrophic event waiting for us. That makes it final. Dan Burisch was misled by the Greys. The Greys want to prevent every contact between the Sheyan and those here on Earth who can contact the Sheyan via the crystal skull.

Mira is glad that the sound has gone. She takes a few deep breaths and lights a cigarette.

Can you roll one for me too Mira, asks Ramon, while he fills the mugs once more.

Sure, Ramon. I'm glad that the pressure on my head fades away.

That's good, Mira. Do you remember that Teimon said that there are star gates on the moon? You know, you showed me some places where these star gates were located.

Oh yes, Ramon. That was when we discussed the coordinates of the star map and their connection to the moon.

Indeed, Mira. Wait, I look it up in my notes. Ramon shows her the drawing that she once drew herself. Look, Mira, it is dated 9/9/2006. Based on this drawing, it was new moon during the transport. You see?

Did I make that drawing? Strange, but now that you show it to me, I remember it, Ramon.

Give me a moment, Mira, I take the Space Atlas. There you find the places of the moon bases.

Ramon takes the big book and opens it on the page showing the moon maps.

Look, Mira. This is where you located the bases. Two on the frond and two on the back side of the moon. On your drawing the moon was located between the sun and the Earth. So it was during the new moon. And the transport was on new moon, remember?

Now I remember it vividly, Ramon.

Good that I made this notes, no?

But you didn't remove the stickers of these maps!

Well yes, I can't get them of. But that's okay. They are the witnesses that it really happened.

But these places on the moon are not natural gates, Ramon. I'm sure of that. They are artificial bases. They were built by the Ancients a long time ago and not by the Greys.

Good that you mention it, Mira. That part was still not clear to me. Probably these artificial star gates can be used more often than the natural gates. Maybe once a year. Let me meditate about that for a while. Every month, the stars move 30 degrees opposite to the earth caused by the rotation of the Earth around the sun. And the moon follows the Earth. If the transport route of a star gate goes in a more or less straight line, then the line of beginning and end will have a straight angle towards these star gates. Look. On your drawing the Earth and the sun and the moon are placed in a straight line and the coordinates of the star gate are aligned with this direction. If the coordinates are directed to one fixed location in the sky, they can only use this star gate only once a year.

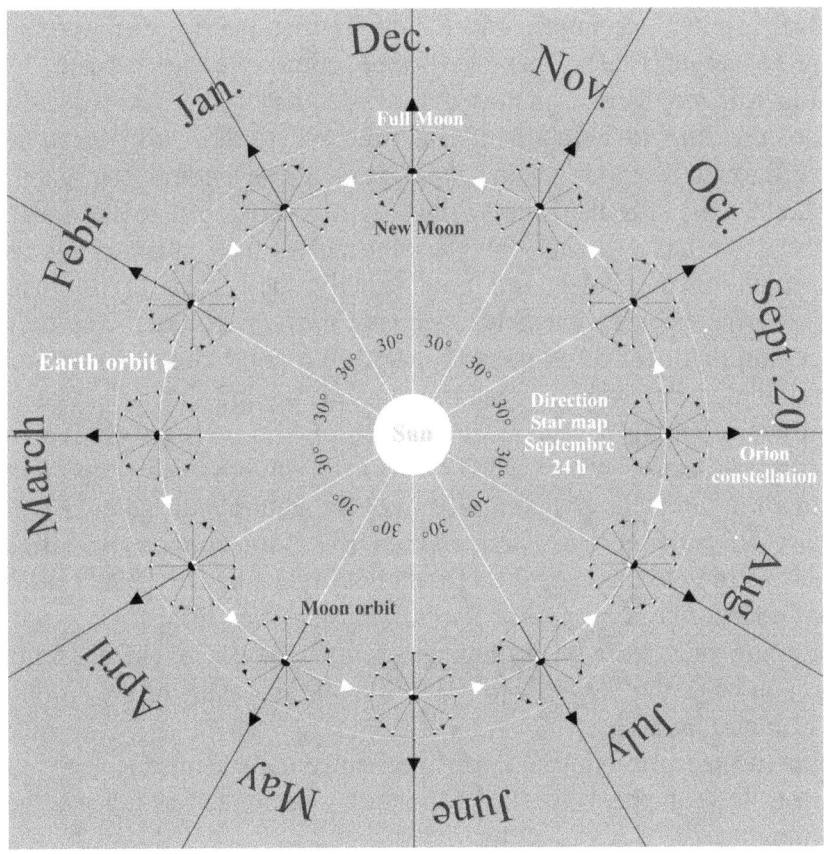

I see what you mean, Ramon. You're right.
Geometry does not lie, Mira. I understand the geometry, but I have no idea of the physics to make it work.
Well Ramon, I even don't know how to fix my car, you know.
Ha, ha. Neither do I, Mira. But for the moment we can conclude that the Greys can use these artificial star gates once a year.

When was the last transport, Ramon? You know, when Teimon had to break contact. I can't remember.

Quickly, Ramon looks in his notes.

That was… around September 20th, Mira.

In that case it could be that there will be a transport again this year in that period, no?

That could very well be, Mira. But then we will hear from it. I hope. That is to say, if we can get into contact with Teimon again. Have you heard anything of him lately?

No, Ramon. No sign. Aryein told us that the Sheyan were in great danger. I guess they have other problems at the moment.

I'm worried, Mira, you now that. It is so frustrating that we can't do anything to help them. But time will tell. I will do some additional research on the web about these natural star gates. And I will speed up the writing of the book. But in the mean time, we have to find out what the Greys have planned for us people of the Earth and how exactly they want to do that. Nevertheless, the star gates fascinate me a great deal. The only person that I found on the web who had a good idea what he was talking about was… what's his name again? Oh yes, Gregg Braden. I found a few video lectures of him on the web. It was very interesting what he had to say. But anyhow, it is important that the Greys have no control over the natural star gates. I will also do some more research on the UFO-moon connection. There are so many videos on YouTube about this subject. There's a lot of nonsense of course, but also some interesting things.

Ramon tells Mira everything he found about the video of the moon base, the Mirlo Rojo video and all the details of the Apollo 11 moon landing.

Let me see that video, Ramon. You make me curious.

Both look at the video and Mira looks fascinated at the strange ruin.

This ruin exists, Ramon. This is a real building.

Are you sure Mira?

Yes, very sure.

And is it a building on the moon?

I'm not sure. But it feels very real. This is a real building. I can't say more than that. But now I have to go, Ramon. I have to prepare lots of things for tomorrow. Thanks for the hospitality. I feel much more relaxed now.

Ramon is glad with her positive reaction and together they go to the car.

You look really well, Mira. Nice dress.

Thanks Ramon, I'm glad you noticed.

Ramon laughs.

See you soon, Ramon. Take care of yourself. Good luck with the book.

She starts her car and rapidly gaining speed it disappears into the night.

Ramon waves.

Mira is one of a kind, he thinks. A real Wiccan but with no strings attached.

- 57 -
12/6/2007

Ramon works non stop on the unfolding story of a bizarre human confrontation with alien beings and on everything they revealed during the contacts with Mira. Joy's visits are the only thing that keeps him in contact with reality and of course there is Days of Our Lives. It is as if the world is gradually informed about the existence of extra-terrestrials via the web, through movies, ads, sects and even soaps. Aliens not only exist but they are here, seems to be the message. But nobody knows that everybody coming in contact with the Greys is in great danger. Disclosure is okay, but it has to be disclosure of the truth. But what is the truth? How can we check if the disclosure is the truth? If the disclosure supports the strategy of the Greys, then we are even worse of. Then it really becomes dangerous. The book has to change that. No more time for hide-and-seek. Only once, Ramon puts some time in his personal research for the truth. He can't get the Mirlo Rojo video out of his mind. And the information about the star gates brought him back to the study of the footage of the possible moon base. He had to find out the truth. There was too much at stake. His confidence in NASA, for one thing. Was this ruin a genuine alien settlement, the remainders of a star gate or was it a hoax? Mira was convinced that it was a real building.

But Ramon wanted to let the facts speak for themselves. Was it a building on Earth used for the hoax or a building on the moon?

The surroundings, the lights and shadows on the video were perfectly in accordance with the place of the sun in the sky. The image quality was the same as the quality of the live broadcasts of the Apollo project. He had studied so many angles of the Apollo story but nothing came up that was convincing pro or contra the hoax. So what else was there to study to find a failure in the hoax?

The space suits! On some video fragments of the real moon landing, you could see that the space suit of Neil Armstrong was covered with logos, front side and backside. But on the Mirlo Rojo video part 5 in the fourth minute, you could clearly see that the suit of the astronaut who is collecting samples had no logos. Armstrong was the man with the camera. So it had to be Buzz Aldrin who was scraping material from the ground. Ramon thought that he found a slipup. Now he got them! He looked at several fragments of different videos of the real moon walk to see whether Buzz had logos on his back. He found a video fragment where the astronauts step into a vehicle that brought them to the Saturn rocket. Now I will know, he thinks. Armstrong steps in first and one can clearly see the stickers on his back. But as Buzz enters the vehicle… there are no stickers on his back! Unbelievable, the producers thought of that too! But the astronauts were not wearing the big backpack with oxygen on that footage. Finally, he finds a fragment of the "real moon walk" where Buzz is scraping moon dust from the surface, filmed from the top of the moon module and … there are no stickers on his back! Shit! Can it be that the Mirlo Rojo video is authentic?

What else could be investigated? Maybe the way the ruin was filmed. The footage of the moon base was rather elegant, without real shocks. It was all very smooth. But one may argue that the gravity on the moon is six times less than on Earth, making moving much easier. Of course, every special effect professional knows that the recordings of the ruins could have been done in a virtual designed 3D environment and that the images of the astronauts were done in a blue chamber. This technique is very often used for special effects. In the Mirlo Rojo video part 5, a virtual drawing is even showed. Not a detailed drawing, but very well done. It could be a part of a more detailed virtual design. This 3D drawing could definitely be used to create a virtual environment. That could explain why the recording of the ruin was so smooth. The floor was clearly not flat and Armstrong could not walk smoothly over this floor. So there had to be more shuddering in the recording.

Except if less gravity would make it much easier to move!

Ramon started to wonder why he was losing that much time with this research. But he could not let go and made a 3D drawing to study the architecture. He looked again at the video of Karl Wolf who testified in the disclosure project of Steven Greer. He talked very convincingly about seeing pictures of a moon base. The video starts with Wolf introducing himself. In 1965 he worked on a project in relation with the Orbiter project. Suddenly, Ramon realized that there was something wrong with the date he mentioned. Orbiter 1 was launched on August 18th, 1966. So it was impossible that Dr. Karl Wolf could have seen pictures of the Orbiter project in 1965! Ramon was shocked. He was one of the most reliable people of the Disclosure Project. How was it possible that this man used the wrong date in his statement? And they were pictures of the backside of the moon, so it had to be the pictures from the Orbiter. There were no pictures of the backside of the moon in 1965. Was it just a mistake? Difficult to believe if you think it was a press conference and that he wanted to testify under oath!

Sure the Ranger took pictures of the moon in 1965. The Ranger 8 satellite made some good pictures of the Mare Tranquillitatis in February 1965, where the Apollo 11 would land. But the Ranger pictures were all of the front side of the moon. One thing was for sure: either Wolf was lying or he had to redo his testimony. It became clear to Ramon that even very trustworthy witnesses had to be studied very carefully before you can accept their statements as being true. Lies our incorrect facts bring contradictions into the story. But in general liars make mistakes and if you search long enough, you will find them. Just to be sure, he decided to look one more time at the two videos. First the video "Moon landing, fake or fact". The actual name of this documentary was "Dark Side of the Moon", produced by William Karel. The video ends on a cemetery, the Arlington National Cemetery in Virginia. The cemetery where general Vernon Walters was buried. He died in the night after the last interview in this documentary. That was pure coincidence, no? Suddenly, Ramon gets a freaky feeling. Was this cemetery the same as where the deliverer of the moon base footage for the Mirlo Rojo documentary was buried?

And what about Vernon's statement "I will tell you the truth if you turn the cameras of"? Was there a relation between these two documentaries? Vernon Walters died on February 2nd 2002. Was the Mirlo Rojo video from the same period? It could be but Ramon could not find the production date. By watching the Mirlo Rojo video it soon became clear that the cemetery was indeed the same as in the "Dark Side of the Moon" documentary, but filmed in an other season. Ramon knew that he found a surprising but sinister trail. But he had enough of it for the moment. He was disappointed that the testimony of Dr. Karl Wolf was wrong and decided to leave his research for the moment. The book was more important than an old ruin on the moon. But just maybe, he found a surprising link between these

354

two videos. With new courage, he worked day in day out to finish the book.

- 58 -
28/6/2007

Always working, Ramon? says a smiling Ury as he enters the WebCom.

He sees this modern monk, typing like hell on his keyboard, while Planet Orion by Pendulum, one of his favorite drum and base compositions, vibrates through the room. Ramon is very pleased with Ury's visit.

Well, Ramon, are you getting on with the book?

Don't ask, Ury. It's not really my thing this writing. But I see that look on your face. Disclose yourself! You wouldn't mind some good, fresh, hot coffee, now would you?

Ury smiles.

You always have the best ideas, Ramon. I have not much time but some coffee would be great.

Glad that he has a reason to take a break, Ramon directs Ury to the kitchen. Ramon looks for some clean mugs and makes room for the coffeepot. Concentrating, he performs the best tradition in the world.

And how is your new romance coming along, Ury?

Great, Ramon. I'm so glad that I finally found somebody who takes me like I am. She has her own job and we enjoy the time that's left for the both of us.

I see it on your face, Ury. You look happy. Here, a fine mug for the late hours.

Thanks, Ramon. I do feel well.

Both enjoy the thousands of aromas, pouring out of a simple mug.

Have you heard anything from Merly?

Yes, Ramon. How did you guess? In general, he helps me with my personal problems but yesterday, it was suddenly serious stuff again.

Tell me, Ury. I wouldn't mind hearing something else besides the typing sound of my keyboard.

Well, I don't know if I understand it well but this is what Merly tried to explain to me.

1.401 The Guardians and the Warriors have contact with each other via the I Ching.

Ramon can hardly suppress his reaction to this breaking news.

And now it becomes confusing to me, Ramon.

1.402 The Guardians know the Warriors, but the Warriors don't know the Guardians.

1.403 The Warriors know that the Guardians exist, but they don't know who they are.

Can you make something of that, Ramon? Because to me, this is all gabble. You know a lot of the I Ching, don't you? Have you got any clue?

I have worked with the I Ching all my live, Ury. But it is still a mystery to me, you know. I think we have to meditate about this. Shall we?

Ury knows very well what Ramon means with ""meditate". Ramon taught him that meditation has nothing to do with "not thinking", but with learning how to think the right way. Meditation is learning to think with your own thoughts or in communication with others to search for answers on the questions you have. This insight has often helped Ury at his work and during think-tank sessions with his colleagues.

We have to start somewhere, Ury. The I Ching is based on synchronicity. This power in nature is still not well understood in Western science. But there is a change coming along.

You mean the strange behavior of subatomic particles, Ramon? You told me about it long ago, remember?

Right, Ury. Suppose you split two photons from the same particle and you influence the behavior of one of these twin photons, then the other photon behaves in the same way instantly. This mysterious behavior is called "non-locality". Recently they have discovered that there are grounds to accept that it not only happens with photons. This behavior is not easy to explain in a causal way but it could be explained by an unknown force. Synchronicity could be that force. As far as I know, non-locality will be put in practice soon.

How can it be of use, Ramon?

Ramon tells Ury in short that non-locality will be used in

356

quantum computing, to update computers in the near future as soon the technology is available. By updating one computer, all computers all over the world will update in a similar way instantly.

Really? That would be a relief, Ramon. This updating business by Windows is sometimes very boring, especially if not everybody updates his system.

I will send you the link of the articles, Ury.

Please do that, Ramon. But what has this to do with Warriors and Guardians?

Well, the I Ching states that everything has his counterpart. You know, man and woman, good and bad, heaven and earth, and so on.

The yin and the yang of everything, you mean?

Yes, Ury. And the same Yin and Yang also mirrors itself in society. Warriors are control freaks. They are impatient and active, they want to rule and be important. But don't forget, the Illuminati give them the commands. Guardians on the other hand are patient and wait for the right moment to come in action. They serve and are humble. They don't need commands from above but they are very spiritual. They are like Yin and Yang. Like Merly told us before. The Warriors don't understand the unity of everything. So both are opposites in their psychological make-up. Don't get me wrong. The Guardians are not passive. They prepare themselves by studying and help their fellow men in any way they can. The Warriors are born leaders. They want to rule the population and take the power. That's their psychological profile. The Guardians are hidden within the population. But they don't want any power. They are here to serve. But they can't be influenced by the manipulation techniques which are interwoven in the commands of the Illuminati. On the contrary, they see through the manipulation techniques the Warriors use to manipulate the population. And because the Warriors fulfill the wishes of the Illuminati, these suggestions reveal the true intentions of the Illuminati if you can read between the lines. The Guardians study on their own and don't want any official function. They enjoy their simple life but they are not naive. They see the signs. They see what the Warriors want to achieve with the propaganda and prepare themselves in secrecy for when it is time for action. Because the real intention of the Warriors is power and gradually they will become their own worst enemy. Warriors have the tendency to prefer to destroy in order to stay in power or to enlarge their power. And war is the result of that. To keep that power they do the cruelest things. But if their power is at its peak, the Warriors are their own worst enemy.

What do you mean by that, Ramon?

That's very simple, Ury. What have the lie and the truth in common?

Wait, Ramon. I think they both pretend to be the truth, no?

Exactly, Ury. The lie can only exist, if everybody thinks it is the truth. So the lie needs the truth.

I understand, Ramon. The truth doesn't need the lie to be true.

That's what I mean, Ury. The longer the lie exists, the more difficult it becomes to pretend to be the truth. And that's the weakness of the Warriors. That's the reason why the I Ching teaches us that when evil is on its highest point, it destroys itself. The Guardians wait until that moment is near to reverse the chaos which is the result of the tendency of the Warriors to self-destruct in order to maintain their power. In doing this the Guardians can give the world a human face again.

So the Guardians have no actual contact with the Warriors via the I Ching?

Oh no, Ury. That's the reason why the Warriors don't know the Guardians. The only thing the Guardians do is bring the truth to light. The Warriors and the Guardians both use the I Ching. The Warriors use the knowledge of the I Ching to gain power and control. The Guardians use the I Ching to gain wisdom and freedom for everybody. The Warriors can fool the whole population for some time and maybe a smaller group for a longer time. But they can't fool the whole society for a long time. Remember! The weapon of the Guardians is the truth. The truth liberates the people from the confusion and the lie.

Hindus know a similar principle, Ramon. The Goddess Brahma is the creator and the Goddess Shiva is the destructor, but the Goddess Vishnu is the preserver. Vishnu takes care that the truth, the good and the beauty that Brahma creates is preserved, against the destructive powers of Shiva. "Vishnu" keeps the world turning in Hinduism, not money like the Illuminati think.

That's indeed the same principle, Ury.

For a moment Ramon is lost in his thoughts. He thinks on the proverb, Mira received in the first contacts. Are the green and yellow frog the Warriors of the opposite Illuminati fractions and is the red fox the symbol of the Guardians? It could be a good explanation. The principle of the I Ching and the Goddess Vishnu could be hidden in this proverb.

Ury, do you now that the I Ching is based on two symbols? The full line and the double line.

The double line? I thought it was a broken line, Ramon.

That is what I thought too, Ury. But it appears that it is a double line. And that is what you also find in the Indian code. Strange, no? Shiva and Brahma are the two opposite parts of the double line or the Tji line. But Vishnu is the full line or Tao line.

But Ramon, then there is a relation between the Chinese and the Indian code. That's just great! Just great!

A strange feeling goes through Ury's spine and speechless he looks at Ramon.

That's a good meditation, Ramon. I really learned something today.

And without words, he says goodbye. If Ury is impressed by something, he prefers silence. Smiling he disappears into the night, looking forward to seeing his soul mate. Ramon is glad that he learned something himself too.

Aryein is right. The I Ching is not based on zero and one. But on one and two. One is unity of the opposites and two is the separation of the opposites. He closes his WebCom and goes to bed.

It is clear that the Guardians play an important role to expose the games of the Greys, the Warriors and the Illuminati fraction, eager to rule the world. Is that the reason why I have to write this book? To bring some truth into the world?

With peace in his mind Ramon goes to bed

If humanity needs some truth, truth they will get. It may rest assured.

A few weeks pass by. The book grows every day. As good as he can Ramon tries to keep up with all the breaking news articles in the UFO community. It is late again as Ramon decides to spend a few hours on the web. On the UFO site "Earthfiles" he finds a strange announcement. A man, called Isaak, has more information about the Drones. A Drone is a newcomer in the UFO files. It is a kind of UFO, first seen a few months ago and published on the web. Most comments were clear: this is a hoax, absolute nonsense. Ramon didn't know what to think. Most pictures of UFOs are rather fuzzy, but the pictures of the Drones are very sharp pictures of a very strange, flying craft-like thing.

His first impression was that they were beautiful 3D designs. It would take him weeks to make a 3D copy of this design with 3D modelling software. But it was not only the professional design. Also the signs on the Drone were very well made. Ramon used to design some fonts when he was younger. It took him weeks to make the letters of the alphabet. But these were no known letters. So it must have been a serious job to design them all.

Ramon is even more surprised as he surfs to the website of Isaak. Isaak states that he was involved in the study and back-engineering of artifacts of a crashed UFO. He managed to make copies of some of the technical drawings of an artifact and smuggled them out. He decided to put some of these drawings on the web, after seeing the pictures of the drones.

If this is a hoax, and this Isaak is the initiator, then this man put a lot of work into these drawings. That was Ramon's first reaction. Several drawings, in very high resolution could be downloaded for free. They were detailed drawings and were described as a functional model of a control device of a UFO. The drawings are very beautiful to look at. Everything has very aesthetic proportions. You can sense it immediately. The composition is perfect and the letters or symbols are just marvelous. Ramon prints them before he goes to bed.

I must show this to Mira, as soon as possible. I'm curious how she will react to this.

Ramon sleeps well that night. What he doesn't know is that these drawings will be the breakthrough he needs to make the book work.

As soon as he is out of bed, he calls Mira at her office, something he seldom does.

Mira… You have to see this. Yes Mira, I understand that you have little time… But I think this is important. You have to come... Yes, it is very important to me!

For a while it is quiet on the other side of the line.

Okay, Ramon, I will be there in an hour. Make sure the coffee is ready!

In a hurry Ramon cleans the table and puts all the pictures of Isaak in the right order. He does the dishes and makes a fresh pot of coffee, the smell of which tickles Mira's nose when she rushes into his kitchen.

I'm really curious what you have to show me that urgently, Ramon.

Come to the WebCom, Mira and I will show you.

She is almost in a state of shock as she sees all the drawings.

But Ramon… These are drawings of the circles that I saw!

Circles that you saw? I don't know what you mean, Mira.

Don't you remember that I saw visions with all kinds of circles?

No, not really… But wait. Yes, now that you mention it. That was during the Christmas period, was it not?

Exactly, Ramon. I saw all kinds of circles, interconnected and rotating together in all kinds of colors. These are the circles, Ramon. Oh my God! That's really freaky. Where did you find these?

On the web, Mira.

Mira cautiously studies the drawings of Isaak one by one.

Do you see now why I couldn't tell you anything? I saw all these things, but it was too complex for me to grasp. But this is it. These are the circles that I saw, Ramon. Really, unbelievable!

Ramon doesn't know if he has to be glad or surprised. He thinks of the words of Aryein. Synchronicity will become stronger. He feels a strange sensation throughout his body. Is he dreaming or is this real?

Excited he runs to the kitchen.

Coffee, Mira?

Yes, please.

She analyzes the drawings intensely. In a hurry, Ramon fills two mugs and goes back to the WebCom.

I shall tell you the background story of these drawings, Mira.

In a few minutes, Ramon explains the story of Isaak's publications on the web.

So in short, these are the technical drawings of a devise of a crashed UFO. I can't believe it, Ramon. They are beautiful. Look at the letters.

Yes Mira, top design, isn't it?

She looks at drawing 14.11. She is impressed by the alien symbols and the beautiful mandalas, interconnected with curved lines. The letters or symbols are strange, as in an unknown language, but at the same time they are very familiar. It is silent in the WebCom. Mira feels she goes into a trance and a purple nebula surrounds the WebCom as she hears deep rhythmic sounds in the background. As by magic, she recognizes the meaning of all the symbols and function of every detail of this drawing.

1.404 **Ramon, this scheme is based on the code of the Ancients. With this part of the device all the information of interstellar transport is coordinated.**

Ramon immediately takes his notes and starts to write, becoming more and more amazed by the minute.

1.405 **She points to one part of the drawing. This part contains all the information to go to the planet of the Téry. This mandala is the part to focus all the information of the coordinates of the star map.**

1.406 **And this part contains the essence of their energy concept. With this, they start and control the UFO. Look Ramon, this disc is connected with the colour changes that I saw between the moving parts of the device.**

Do you mean everything you saw back in the Christmas period?

Yes! As if she is looking at the dashboard of her car, Mira understands every part of this technical devise and its use.

1.407 **Look Ramon. This mandala is an image of their star system. This is probably the star system of the Téry.**

Strange don't you think, Ramon?

What do you mean, Mira?

Don't you see what it looks like?

362

No, Mira.

1.408 This drawing looks like one of the drawings of the Chinese pictures. Don't you see that? Look, don't you see the similarity?

You mean the drawings on the cube, in the Chinese pyramid?

Yes, what else?

In no time, Ramon takes the drawing, hidden between the notes and compares the two drawings. There is indeed a striking similarity.

This is too crazy to believe. And what…?

Wait a minute, Ramon. I have to drink.

That can be arranged, Mira.

The mugs are filled again and Mira goes on with her technical explanation of this mysterious drawing.

1.409 The letters of the disc are based on the code of the runic symbols, Ramon.

And these wavelike things? Any idea what they mean?

Don't you see that, Ramon?

No Mira, I only see that they are very beautiful.

1.410 Look, the first wave is based on the physical energy concept of the Ancients. The last wave is the concept of the mental energy. The wave in between is the relation between the two.

Again the principle of the I Ching, Mira. 1 and 2. So it must be based on the energy concept of the I Ching.

Mira feels a bit awkward. Her critical attitude against her own talent is shaken. She looks to the drawings that she saw half a year ago. But the symbols and images that she saw were in colour.

Do you understand now why I couldn't explain what I saw, Ramon?

Absolutely, Mira. I could not do it myself. This is not only beautiful, but it is also ingenious. If I didn't know what it was, I would say, it is done by a very gifted jewel designer or a watchmaker. But he is definitely an artist. When I saw the drawings for the first time, I was touched by their beauty. It is clearly not a joke. It has to be art. But now that I hear you, I am convinced that this is a technical drawing of an alien instrument. These Ancients must really be artists of science.

It must be something real, Ramon. How would I know what the designer means with his design? And the letters, Ramon, the symbols, they are so elegant. It must be from a civilization that is much more advanced than ours. Look how beautiful it all fits.

And there is more, Mira. As far as I understand, Isaak stated that these letters have not only a meaning but they have also a function. They are not only the numbers of a watch, but they make the watch work.

It's absolutely incredible, Ramon. And to think that you found this on the web!

Yes, thanks to Isaak, whoever he is. And it is only a few days on the web, you know! If that is not synchronicity, I don't know what is.

Mira looks at the letters of one of the parts and explains every symbol, its place and function in the sentence and its symbolic meaning. Ramon is speechless. As well as he can, he writes everything down. After the session, they both agree. The information of Teimon and the Ancients must be taken seriously. Mira comes gradually out of the trance.

Ramon, I have to go now. There are people waiting for me. I think this will do for the moment.

Absolutely, Mira. This is just great.

Oh, Ramon, the information about the letters must not be published. And now I go, Ramon. Bye!

And in a hurry she runs to her car and gone she is, back to her busy life. Still impressed by this brief introduction to alien technology and symbolism, Ramon goes back to his WebCom. Carefully he adds the drawings to his notes. Great! Just great!

He fills his mug with the rest of the coffee and then he starts to write.

- 60 -
16/7/2007

A week passes. Waking up, drinking coffee, surfing on the web, reading articles, writing, eating in between, again writing, quickly off to the garden, more writing till late at night and then back to bed.

Ramon has a question. How does this story end? He has no idea where this is all going. From Teimon there is no news. Half a year passes by. Nothing! Mira is completely consumed by her work to get the new business project on track.

It is again late at night. The soundtrack Aurora vibrates loudly through his WebCom as the sound of footsteps in the kitchen gets him out of his daydream. Could it be Mira? He goes to the kitchen and sees that it's dark everywhere.

What's going on, Ramon? No lights?

Wait Mira, I will put the lights on. The light blinds the two of them.

Ramon, were you asleep?

No Mira, I just forgot to put the lights on. I was so involved in the story that I forgot the time.

Sorry to pop in so late in the evening, Ramon. But I thought if I don't go now, I will never get there. I have some news from the cosmos and… With a smile she shows a bottle of red wine. Are you with me?

I definitely am, Mira.

Like only a houseman can, he changes the kitchen in no time into a comfortable room and the two glasses cling.

To the Téry, Ramon.

To the Téry and the Ancients, Mira.

What do you think that the word Téry means Ramon?

It means "human", I guess.

Mira is surprised. How do you know that, Ramon?

It is always the case, Mira. Dogon, Zoeloe, Bantoe, Inuit. It all means "human". I guess it is the same on other planets. But tell me, Mira, why do you ask this? News from the cosmos? Is it from Teimon or Aryein?

No Ramon, sorry. It is information from the skull I think. But something tells me that the Sheyan are in danger but that they are okay. But tell me, how far are you with the book?

Well, it is growing every day. But I have no clue how it will end. New information would be welcome.

Well it is not new information, Ramon. It is more like extra information. For example, yesterday I suddenly heard some strange information. I think it was from that Tibetan. I heard two sentences in my head over and over again. What were they? Oh yes.

1.411 Animation is the stimulating force behind nature.
1.412 Nature is the manifestation of animation.

Do you understand what animation means, Ramon?

Ramon writes the sentences down.

It sounds familiar, Mira. Aristotle wrote in his book Metaphysics that there was a force that caused the growing of all the natural phenomena. He called it entelechy. This force was responsible for the shape of all living things. These days, they explain this force with genetics. But in fact, science still doesn't understand exactly how genetics evolved during evolution. Survival of the fittest gives a good explanation. But there is still something missing. Namely the evolution of consciousness and the part it plays in directing the trillions of DNA mutations in their interconnection during evolution. By the way, artificial robots can evolve and learn and these machines have no DNA whatsoever. Don't forget that "survival of the fittest" means that those will survive that can adjust the best to the ever changing situation. It has nothing whatsoever to do with survival of the strongest, like social Darwinism interprets this credo of the evolutionists. Butterflies are still around, but the Tyrannosaurus Rex has gone a long time ago.

The second sentence reminds me of the shamanistic code, Mira. Shamans all over the world believe that all things have a kind of consciousness, even stones, rivers and mountains. In the Indian-Tibetan Code, it is believed that it is consciousness that is the growing force behind nature. Indian philosophy knows two concepts: Purusha and Prakriti. Purusha is pure consciousness, but not material. And Prakriti is the manifestation of that consciousness. This world-view sees the whole universe as the manifestation of Purusha. So for them, everything has consciousness, everything has soul.

Mira smiles. Ramon is a strange guy if you think about it.

Ramon, what's the deal with that Isaak of the CARET project?

Nothing new, Mira. The rest is silence. He has not published anything on the web lately. I guess it was too dangerous. I hope you still know what everything means?

Oh yes, says Mira convincingly. When I look at the drawings, I just know by heart what they mean.

366

Ramon has to laugh.

Mira, Mira, you are really a modern witch. You can't fly on a broomstick, but flying a UFO wouldn't be a problem for you.

Ramon cannot keep from laughing.

Yes, Ramon, joke all you like, but what am I suppose to do with all that knowledge of the Ancients? I don't have a UFO, you know. Do you?

Ha, ha, ha, no Mira, I don't. The only thing I have is a bike. If I had a UFO, you could have it. Ha, ha. You know, Mira. Time will tell why you got that information. Some more wine?

Please, Ramon. Let's drink to Isaak.

To Isaak, Mira. By the way, recently I have been thinking about what a lot of whistleblowers in the UFO community have in common. Isaak is clearly an exception. But the release of information by whistleblowers like Dan Burisch made me wonder.

Tell me about it, Ramon.

I have read a lot of articles about mind control. It is a hot item on several UFO related sites. It is not only with implants that people can be controlled. Some people on the web testified that they were the subject of disgusting mind control experiments. To make a long story short, the techniques are based on artificial creation of traumas in children. These artificial traumas were inflicted during the most sensitive periods of their lives. From previous scientific tests, we seem to know that schizophrenia is very often a result of a traumatic experience when it occurs during these sensitive periods. Schizophrenic people are extremely open for suggestion when they become adults. They can develop a double personality. These double personalities can easily be manipulated by hypnotic techniques. They can live a double or even a triple life without knowing it themselves.

But Ramon, that is terrible! If that is true, then those who are involved in these kinds of experiments are real criminals.

I couldn't agree more, Mira. But the worst thing of it all is that it is so simple. Some articles state that the basis of these experiments was done in Nazi concentration camps. But these experiments were further developed in many countries after the war. I stopped reading this stuff because it really made me sick. But it also made me think.

Mentals are similar but not identical to schizophrenic persons. The difference is that the extra identity is induced with the help of telepathy. And the trauma is the encounter with the Greys. An abduction is a traumatic experience. Psy-mutants are even a step further. They become gradually dominated by that new personality and lose grip on their own. In this way, they become like spies for the Greys. And from the outside it all looks much cleaner than the cruel trauma experiments, done by humans. And there is another similarity, Mira. Like paranormal people feel attracted to Wicca groups, Mentals will feel attracted to that secret Sean Leyka religion, because there they will find some understanding for their experiences. Don't forget, if we have to believe the rumors, there are millions of Mentals.

So the abduction business is a very clever part of the strategy of the Greys in their invasion plans. Abductees can be driven to that sect and once inside, they can further be manipulated by the Greys, because the founder of this sect was one of the first victims of abduction himself. So the whole mentality and techniques they use in the initiations of this sect must be suggested by the Greys in order to control them on every level.

Now let's suppose that a part of the UFO literature is induced by that sect, in that case we can study the sect through all kinds of UFO related publications that fit the overall strategy of the Greys. For the strategy of the sect will be the same as the strategy of the Greys.

Those Greys are really manipulative bitches! Are you well aware of that, Ramon? Jesus!

Indeed, Mira. And there is another thing I have discovered. I have studied maybe ten important whistleblowers. Some are clearly Mentals our Psy-mutants, but others are free and honest. But they all have something in common. The theories they tell can't be confirmed. They all talk about secret projects. How can you prove from an objective stance that these secret projects really exist? The only thing you can do is believe them on their word or reject their stories. But believing has no scientific value. So the information of genuine whistleblowers can very easily be ridiculed or exaggerated by fake whistleblowers, in service of the Sean Leyka sect or the Initiated. The Initiated don't want the truth to come out, while the sect only want their own interpretation of the truth to come out. And that interpretation is based on the lies of the Greys.

What a mess, Ramon. We are lucky to have contact with Teimon. We know at least who the Greys are. And equally important is the fact that we know that there are Mentals, Monoms and Psy-mutants.

Indeed, Mira. The Greys play a very smart game. They work on different levels at the same time. There is the secret technology, the climate experiments with chemtrails, the underground bases, the star gates, the secret projects, the hiding of the presence of alien life and the historical implications, the coming of catastrophes in the near future, the religious consequences in the past as well as in the present, the prophesies for the year 2012. You name it. And all these stories strengthen one another. If you put everything together, you get a very anarchistic scenario. A scenario that is positive for the Greys but very negative for the world leaders and the world institutions. The Greys pretend to be alien hippies, enlightened beings who want peace and care for the environment and they pretend to be against nuclear weapons and nuclear energy. No wonder that a lot of New Age groups are attracted to these ideas. At the same time the Greys give their abductees a bad image of the human species. Humans are described as intelligent animals, who don't know what they are doing and need to evolve to a higher level of evolution or a higher dimension, whatever that means, to be united with the lovely Greys. In the mean time, the world leaders are portrayed as war seeking individuals, only interested in world domination and power. But we should not worry about the world leaders. It's the hidden commanders, the Illuminati who rule the world. If you are not aware of that, you are exposed to all that anarchistic information that gives you the feeling that you live with one foot in hell and the other in heaven.

Where will all this end, Ramon?

You tell me, Mira. It is not simple. A lot of stories that are spread are food for superstition. People in general are susceptible to superstition and easy to manipulate. For example, the stories about underground facilities built by humans, and probably shelters for the Greys, remind me of the concept of hell in Christianity while the Greys themselves are sometimes portrayed as angels from heaven. They are the good ones and the bad ones at the same time. In general, you get a picture of a kind of modern interpretation of heaven and hell. These kinds of suggestions work very well on religious people. And that is genuine mind control, especially because there is in fact absolutely no proof for the one or the other. You can only believe it.

But I was in the underground facilities, Ramon? Remember? So, do you think they don't exist?

No, no. They do exist. But what is really going on down there depends on to whom you want to listen. There is no information from an independent research group that visits these places and writes an objective rapport. All the stories give conflicting information making it a hard to know what really is going on in these underground bases. Then it is your own superstition that will fill in what information you will believe.

But why are they doing that, Ramon? This kind of disinformation is playing with the feelings of the people.

That is the nine million dollar question, Mira. Why are they doing it? And who are "they"? We will only be able to answer that question properly if we know more details about the strategy and goal of the Greys and the Illuminati and not to forget the Sean Leyka sect. And in order to know this, you must belong to the top of one of the organizations involved. Or one has to know you, Mira, ha, ha.

Yes, yes, do make fun of me, Ramon. Sean Leyka must be a well organized large cult, Ramon. For this is clearly mass manipulation.

Indeed, Mira. But who are these people? How are they organized? I don't know. But it must be a group who benefit from people starting to believe in UFO related stories. At the moment it is all hidden. But this sect has to go public at a certain moment, though. Maybe they are now preparing their public appearance. A religion can only grow if it becomes institutionalized. In order to do that, they must come into the open. If a large group of people already believe in their version of the Grey presence, portrayed as a kind of angels or gods or multi-dimensional beings, then you could say that the sect prepares the way for the Greys. It is a very clever way for the

Greys to get control over the world through a settled religion, is it not? And the perfect time for the sect to go public would be at the same time as the disclosure of the alien presence by the Initiated. In this way, the people would run into the arms of the sect, once they realize that aliens are present. That goes especially for young people.

That is indeed clever, Ramon. And also money comes into the equation, Ramon. If this sect would come into the open, it would quickly become a religion. Once this religion would become institutionalized, they would earn billions. Think of Islam, Christianity or Buddhism. Over the centuries they have become very wealthy and powerful institutions. So, you think that a part of the UFO scene is controlled by Mentals and Psy-mutants, to play a game of Stratego with humanity?

I think that's what is happening right now, Mira. Think about it. It is very clever. The people of the sect don't know that their organization is used to fulfill the agenda of the Greys. At the same time they can question or overrule the stories of real whistleblowers. If the Greys want to dominate our world, the people must be mentally prepared to their presence. A new religion is the perfect way to do just that. Don't you think? Or am I wrong?

Absolutely not, Ramon. If the people would think that the Greys are people like us only higher developed, then the Sean Leyka sect would be the perfect way to prepare the world for the takeover by the Greys. For the top of this sect is under the spell of the Greys.

Indeed, Mira, that is what I think. But that is not the whole story. This sect is just a part of the global strategy of the Greys. And to think that it all started by keeping the alien presence secret! Secrecy is the name of the game. And that makes it all so complex and confusing. A lot of what some whistleblowers say is true but the overall picture can easily be manipulated by that sect. What makes it tragic is that the Mentals and the Psy-mutants who work in this sect believe that they preserve humanity from a terrible disaster. Or that they are the forerunners of a new humanity that lives together with highly evolved aliens. But in fact they help the Greys to prepare the world for their invasion.

Then it all looks rather hopeless for the world, Ramon. Is there no way to stop the Greys?

I have no idea, Mira. Maybe this book can expose their plans before they can start the invasion. In a way, the information of Teimon is a disclosure, but of a completely different nature than the disclosure that Sean Leyka our the Initiated have in mind, which is based on the lies of the Grey. If the star map information is right, then the rest of the information will be taken seriously. It will give an entirely different meaning to a lot of information that circulates in the UFO community. Because these organizations become more and more structured like a pyramid, as has been the case with so many modern subcultures. The ones on top finally run the show. What started in Egypt and China as a social experiment some six thousand years ago, spread throughout the entire world. All organizations, companies, institutions, societies, countries and so on are structured as a pyramid. The world is bursting with the Egyptian social model. And in time, hierarchies are combined to again form larger hierarchies. Every country is one large social pyramid. And the globalization process fueled by the multinationals brought the whole world in a process to become one large pyramid. The question is: who wants to be on top of that world pyramid?

Ramon hesitates. Should he tell her? This is a good moment to explain this to her.

Mira, do you remember you once mentioned the name Guardians?

Yes, Ramon. They are the ones who are in contact with the Tulkus.

Indeed, Mira! Listen!

And without revealing the identity of Ury, he explains everything he knows about the Warriors and the Guardians and the secret cabal of the Illuminati.

But Ramon, if everything you say is right then the Illuminati will decide who will get on top of the world pyramid.

That's my guess too, Mira. In the end, they are the people with the highest power on earth. They are the new kids on the power block.

So they are the greatest magicians of the modern world, Ramon.

372

That's a good way to put it, Mira. The Warriors who had supreme power still have a lot of power but will have to obey the Illuminati and the Greys. Don't forget what Teimon said. On their planet, the same rulers are still in power. But they are under Grey control.

Like puppets on grey strings!

I could not describe it in a better way, Mira.

How many Warriors are there, Ramon? One for every country?

I don't think so, Mira. Let's say there are 12 Warriors, who are the executers of the twelve Illuminati fractions. It is an old tradition that the highest council exists of 12 members. Did you know that the council of the World Bank has 12 members? Remember the story of King Arthur? There were twelve knights, were there not?

Okay, but together with Arthur there were thirteen.

Yes. But that is what is at stake now. The Illuminati had probably a kind of chairman. There is one fraction of the twelve Illuminati who wants to change the power of the chairman to become the leader of the twelve members. This fraction wants to impose their will on the others. You know, a thirteenth member is practical when it comes to voting. If the vote is 6-6, then the thirteenth member clinches it. It is just an old tradition. How many apostles had Jesus?

Twelve, Ramon.

Right, Mira. So with Jesus, there were thirteen.

How many constellations are there, Mira?

Twelve!

Yes, but the enlightened one is the thirteenth. He unites all the constellations into one person.

How many successors had Mohamed until the Mahdi came?

I don't know, Ramon. Twelve?

Yes, twelve. And Mohamed makes thirteen.

And how many Euros do I have in my bank account?

Twelve?

No, none!

Both start laughing. Ramon goes on.

If one of the Illuminati fractions becomes the leader, this leader needs a warrior of his own. At least if he wants to have real power. Until now the Illuminati level was like a thirteenth warrior. The Warriors had no own leader. Their leaders are the Illuminati. They are the highest level. They are in command. But if one fraction of the Illuminati becomes a power above the other Illuminati, then the power structure changes. That's when the thirteenth warrior comes into play... I guess.

I see what you mean, Ramon. That makes sense. But sorry... I have to go now. I have to get up early in the morning. She empties her glass and prepares to go home.

I understand, Mira. The holy job. Then I guess I will go to sleep too. And tomorrow, it's writing time again.

Together they go to the car. As she is about to enter the car, she hesitates. I have to tell you something, Ramon.

Please tell me, Mira. I have all the time.

1.413 **I have seen the seven crystals all together.**

1.414 **I also saw the faces of all the people who have contact with the crystal skulls.**

1.415 **But they are all peculiar people. They are all representatives from different cultures.**

1.416 **I have the feeling that we have to get into contact with one another.**

You mean that you have to meet one another at a special location?

1.417 **No. We must all be connected with each other telepathically.**

Okay. And why?

I don't know, Ramon. I don't understand the meaning of it all. I think we have to do something together. This information makes me doubt my sanity, you know.

But no Mira! Whatever it means, it must be important. Don't doubt your sanity. It will all become clear to you. Don't worry. Remember: I doubt, therefore I am!

Then I must exist, Ramon. Without any doubt!

Both start to laugh and Mira gets into the car.

Good night, Ramon.

Good night, Mira, and gone she is again. Gone with the wind, and while waving Ramon is again alone in the darkness of the night. He contemplates the whole discussion and suddenly he gets a very surprising idea.

Could it be that the Warriors of today are descendants of the first

374

people that were genetically altered so many centuries ago? And that they took power? It could very well be the case. They were able to pass on their paranormal abilities to their children. Could it be that those families, genetically altered by the Ancients, took power, like Teimon said, and preserved their knowledge of the alien contact in their family tradition? But that these Warriors came gradually under control of the Illuminati, while the Guardians had to go into hiding. That would mean that the knowledge of alien contact would be known in those circles since that period. And that the Warriors of our time have known about the alien reality all along? That would explain their involvement with the Greys. Picture that! That would be really mind blowing.

Ramon is stunned by the consequences of this line of thought.

But of course! Teimon said that the genetically altered masculine humans used their mental abilities for power. Could it be that this power was the real Holy Grail of the so called bloodlines? And that the genetic heritage was protected in the ruling elite? Who else than the nobility of the different cultures had power and control over the population for so long? Could that explain the secret of the bloodlines? It is not about the blood but about the genetics? That the real power of the Warriors was the telepathic ability to understand the intentions of their opponents by reading their minds and to enable them to find out the best strategy to conquer the others? For on the battlefield, the Warrior with the best strategy wins. In this way, the most gifted Warrior would enlarge his influence and dominate ever larger regions of planet Earth.

Ramon recalls the ideas of David Icke. He was damn close to the solution. But he was probably wrong footed by all kinds of obscure individuals in occult traditions. It was not the relation with reptiles that made the genetics interesting, but the paranormal abilities that were genetically inherited by the royal bloodlines. And those abilities can probably be triggered by certain rituals.

Ramon is rational enough to realize that here is the chance of a lifetime to figure out this part of the hidden history of mankind with the help of the hidden documents of the twelve Warrior families. Is it really possible that there are twelve bloodlines?

And that these twelve bloodlines came under control of the Illuminati. Could that be? The code of the Ancients was based on the number twelve. It could make sense. Could it be that the Ancients spread the genetics in twelve kingdoms on Earth, just like they spread the seven crystal skulls and the different parts of their code, six-thousand years ago? Did they make twelve women pregnant and did these women become the mothers of the first twelve Warriors? Were twelve royal families genetically altered? Is that the reason why there are also twelve fractions of the Illuminati? For the Warriors, God was the thirteenth as well as for the Guardians. As far as he knows, the Illuminati stepped only much later on the scene of history. Maybe they destroyed the covenant between the Warriors and the Guardians and took their place.

All kinds of questions are going through Ramon's brain. Could the royalty in the different cultures be descendants of the people that were genetically altered? Just like it was told in so many myths. With only one difference: the Sumerian gods, the Anunnaki, were no spiritual gods but they were the Ancients, the forefathers of the Tèry, humans from another planet but further evolved. The natural star gates are open every nine hundred years. So there could have been contact over long periods.

Ramon always had a hard time with some ufologists. They make a big mistake by thinking that the aliens are godlike creatures and that there is no God because all gods are aliens and that these aliens are a threat for world religions. That is truly a very severe mistake.

If the Ancients visited the Earth six-thousand years ago, then they may have been considered to be gods. But that doesn't mean that these aliens also created the world or the universe like some individuals and groups believe. Because that was the first thing that God did, wasn't it? We must not forget one thing. The idea of a God is in every culture equal. He or She or Whatever is the power or the force that created the universe. Any alien human civilization is not different from its human counterpart, even if they are much further evolved. Tao or Yahweh or Allah or Brahman or God, all these concepts do not refer to aliens! They refer to the creator of the universe. The existence of extra-terrestrial civilizations is therefore in no way a threat to God.

376

Although, their existence and involvement in human history would be a threat to history as we know it from history books. That's clear.

Much more interesting would be to discover the image that alien civilizations have of God, especially from the point of view of comparative religion. And for scientists it would be great to learn their theories of the origin of the universe and its evolution.

It is a darn pity that Teimon can't be reached! I have so many questions to ask. A cold breeze reminds him that he is still outside and quickly he goes inside and closes the door behind him. Meticulously he makes notes of what Mira said about the people she saw. Could it be that Mira had contact with all the Tulkus who are in contact with the crystal skulls? But why? This story becomes weirder by the day. God knows what awaits her!

Ramon is glad when he enters his warm bedroom. Feeling happy about making good progress with the book, he pulls the sheets over him. It becomes more and more obvious that the book has to be published. However it all may fit together, it is important that everybody involved in the UFO discussion knows that the Greys are a real threat to humanity. Otherwise, we all walk with open eyes into the Grey web of control. And that would be a real disaster. Thinking about how to begin the next chapter, he falls asleep.

- 61 -
17/7/2007

Seven bodies, in hibernation since several months, give signs of life and start to move. Aodin, who took care of their health, informs them telepathically as they become conscious, one by one. Teimon is the first to be fully awake again. He knows that the fate of the Sheyan, some underground groups and the whole Téry population lies in his hands.

Welcome back to the mental realm my dear friend, his teacher sends. The moment to leave is near. The Tulkus on Geya are all informed. The Guardians have prepared them for what is coming.

These Sheyan have an incredible amount of self-discipline. The only thing that counts is their mission. They all get a kind of strange greenish cookie and let it melt on their tongues. All is quiet for a while. They feel how the concentrated energy of the seaweed cookie vitalizes their entire body. Some minutes later, they all take their place in specially designed chairs in the upper part of the vehicle.

Meanwhile, dozens of silver discs scan a large part of the jungle, spreading throughout the deep valleys between the high mountains. Signals appear on their desks and in the collective mind of the Grey blocks. The fugitives must be down there somewhere.

Aodin takes care that Teimon is protected from the Grey mental scanners. Zeinia knows what to do. His hands fit into the contact points of the armrests. With a few mental signals, he activates the ship and he moves it carefully through the underwater labyrinth. The beautiful crystals are lit by the blue glow of the ship and reveal the beauty of the underground world of Ter I. After a while they reach a deep abyss in the open sea. There are no seconds to lose. The Greys are closing the ranks. As a large mandala, the discs are hanging above a localized region. Their instruments point to a source in the vast impenetrable jungle near the sea. The laser beams are ready.

But something is wrong. The signal changes location and the discs need to readjust constantly.

Teimon becomes one with the ship while he is focused on the purple crystal matrix in front of him. His task is to program the coordinates. Only then Zeinia can take over.

The Sheyan are preparing themselves in the deep ocean and at that very moment Mira can't catch her sleep.

If the time is there we will know what to do, says Ramon. Yeah, right. That is easy for him to say. But I'm stuck with it.

She gets out of bed and sits down in the chair, zapping through the TV channels. Suddenly, she feels a warm wave of energy going through her body and a marvelous purple nebula of light gleams through the room. Teimon is back again, she thinks and immediately she sits up straight in the chair. As a hologram, the purple crystal skull appears in a rainbow of lights. Her room disappears completely and it is as if she has entered a virtual space. The purple matrix starts to vibrate. She knows that

378

Teimon has contact but he doesn't say anything. Then, suddenly, a second skull appears, made in beautiful deep blue. A small light beam connects the two skulls.

Mira sees it happening in front of her eyes. She isn't afraid but is as frozen. A third and fourth skull appear and form a triangle around the purple skull. Vermilion red and yellow light splendor radiates through the virtual space and mixes with the other skulls. Then the other three skulls appear: a sea-green one, an orange one and a white one make a second triangle around the purple skull.

The interconnecting light-beams make a beautiful mandala of light. The beauty of this experience is beyond words. Colours purer and more beautiful than any rainbow give Mira an intense feeling of admiration.

Suddenly, Mira feels she is not alone in this virtual room. She seems to be sitting in a circle with twelve strange people: six men and six women. Although nobody knows each other, it is as if they have known each other for eternity. Every crystal skull is connected to a man and a woman. Only Mira is alone as a thirteenth member, but she is connected to Teimon, thousands of light years away. Every resistance in Mira's mind is broken and she lets herself go in this inscrutable scene. Suddenly, the six skulls project a beam of light to the purple skull and the central matrix starts to vibrate tremendously. Mira is sucked into the cosmic gate with tremendous speed. She sees a bright light in the center of the tunnel and it becomes gradually lighter. A halo of light expands from the light source until it fills the entire virtual space. It is as if all the Tulkus float in a kind of holographic space. A star constellation becomes visible: one star with the five inner planets of that star system. It looks identical to one of the drawings of the Caret project and the drawing on the cube of the Chinese pyramid.

As she comes nearer she is impressed by the giant blue planet with large, white, satin-like, thin clouds, moving through the atmosphere in long curving spirals. A bright light is visible and as she focuses her mind on the light, she sees a beautifully shaped craft. While she is focused on the vehicle she suddenly is back in the virtual space with the others. She has linked the Earth in the now time with the Ark, deep down in one of the abysses of the Ter I ocean. The purple skull radiates as never before and in the center of it there is a very bright spot where the vehicle is located. Suddenly a bright beam of light is projected again from the six skulls to the central bright spot and the light gets stronger and stronger. A powerful light blinds Mira's vision as a beam of energy is released through the purple matrix in the direction of the vehicle of the Sheyan.

Gradually her vision returns and another constellation becomes visible. Dozens of stars are visible in a blue nebula and a spotlight in between the stars starts to pulsate and lightens up as a brilliantly shining cube shaped structure. Again, a beam of energy is released from the purple matrix.

Concentrated and calmly, Teimon receives the two signals and in a split second, he transfers the coordinates mentally into the control center of the craft. Zeinia reacts immediately and activates the craft. An aura of light surrounds the star ship and with tremendous speed, they are catapulted into deep space. The Greys, still confused by the ever changing frequencies on physical and mental levels are too late to see the light beam that disappears into space. Hundreds of laser beams are fired but it is too late. The Sheyan escape the control of the Grey blocks. Even when they scan a few other signals, they know they are too late.

On an open space in the jungle, a smile appears on the face of Xigan, seated on his dearest friend Molo. He has prepared himself his whole life for this event that inevitably had to come. The diversion had worked. While Teimon and Zeinia were receiving the signals, Aodin sent a strong telepathic message to Xigan who reacted immediately. With a strangely shaped musical instrument, he called up all the oligants of Molo's herd to communicate with a very deep sound that these animals only use when there is severe danger. Only oligants can make that sound. During the whole operation they were spread in the jungle and produced these sounds one after the other, confusing the control units of the Grey crafts. The instruments could not distinguish between these sounds and the signals from the Ark, hidden deep in the Abyss.

The Sheyan have escaped.

The central command of the Grey squadron is in panic and several discs crash against the dangerous sharp rocks of the mountains. The rest of the squadron flies back to the space station that hangs above Ter I as an impressive colossus. The otherwise orderly community of Greys is turned into chaos. Their leader, the golog of their block culture, is furious as he has to digest his failure. He belongs to the most evolved Greys of the colony. He is larger than the others and the complexity of his brain makes the internet a child's toy. It doesn't make him more attractive, though.

Due to the perfection of the cloning techniques, he became the head of the strong hierarchical culture of the Greys. What went wrong? How could this happen? We are infallible, no? How could the Sheyan escape their superiority? But it is clear he has failed. He is angry and ashamed at the same time and his royal household experiences his confusion as if it is theirs. Their arms hang weakly beside their bodies and as a miserable group of burned out junkies they gather around their leader. He knows that he has to inform the supreme head of the Grey block culture on Earth. The Greys responsible for his well being help him into his special chair. A disgusting spray is squirted over his arms and gradually he regains strength. Immediately, he orders telepathically that everybody has to take an extra dose of serum to regain strength and to prevent a collective depression in his space colony. His long fingers are connected to the armrests and he goes into a trance. On top of the space station a powerful beacon of light flashes in the direction of the solar system and follows the coordinates of the star map. In no time, it reaches the moon where the signal is received by the high tower, dominating the landscape. The Ancients built this large settlement on the moon to exploit helium 3, titanium and other materials. These precious materials are present in abundance on the moon. The people on Earth have no idea how lucky they are that their satellite is so rich in these two precious substances. Titanium is an essential substance for the space crafts of the Greys. Numerous perfectly circular shaped craters with a deep pointed bottom are the remains of this old industry of the Ancients. Originally, there were more towers and in every tower was a large crystal to receive and send signals. But the Greys had destroyed all the crystals, except one. The only working tower is under Grey surveillance, twenty-four hours a day.

In the underground basis, the supreme golog understands that there is news from Ter I. He moves his fingers to the armrests and both brains fuse almost instantly. Petabytes of information are exchanged. When the golog comes out of his trance, the entire moon colony is in panic. They all feel collectively the fear, anger and frustrations of the golog and don't know what to do. Paralyzed, they feel how their energy flows out of their bodies and ugly smelling sweat drops on their dresses.

While the block cultures on the moon try to recover from their defeat, the seven Sheyan regain consciousness. They have traveled at an unimaginable speed through the Neet and have arrived at their new location. The spaceship floats elegantly through the atmosphere of a desolate planet that possesses a very strong natural star gate. A feeling of relief gives them collective joy. There is again hope for the Téry and for the people of the Earth. With the help of the Tulkus, they were able to take an escape route, used in mythical times by the Ancients when they started their galactic mission in that part of the galaxy after the final exodus from their home planet.

But the planet they are now approaching has changed rapidly over the last millenniums. Zeinia activates the evolugram

382

scanner and without losing time he scans the evolution of the planet to see if there is still water. Negative. The last swamps have dried up and all the water on the planet is mixed with the poisoned atmosphere of the hot planet. The planet has lost all the oases that the Ancients used to refuel their spaceships.

The Sheyan realize there is no time to lose. The search for water on one of the thousands of young planets in this region of the young star formation has begun. Their lives and the functioning of the craft depend on water.

Far away on Earth, Mira falls asleep in her chair. After the last flash of light, she was suddenly back in her room, completely exhausted. Thanks to the millennia old invisible alliance between the Shamans of the different cultures on Earth, the Sheyan could escape.

- 62 -
18/7/2007

In a good mood, Ramon peddles to his garden on his old bike. The book grows every day and he starts to get accustomed to the daily writing rhythm. The evening falls but it is still light as he arrives in the garden. He takes a deep breath to smell the flavors of nature. Relaxed, he collects some vegetables as he hears a rustling sound behind some bushes. He can not believe his eyes as a large peacock appears. As it sees Ramon, it quickly tries to hide behind a purple bush. Where is it coming from? Cautiously he walks to one of the most beautiful creatures of the animal kingdom.

The peacock sees no escape and turns towards Ramon. It looks Ramon straight in the eyes and he erects its tail. With admiration, Ramon looks at this beautiful animal with its tail spread as a curtain of the most beautiful colors. For a while, they both stand still and keep looking at one another. The peacock feels that Ramon is not a threat. With a big smile Ramon watches how this strange animal passes him at a safe distance. Once passed, he makes some quick steps and flies into the direction of the high oak tree. Its large wings carry the heavy body and he lands on a branch of the old oak. He makes a few loud sounds and then he flies to the other side of the brook and elegantly, he walks away, wherever it is he's heading.

What is this all about? The peacock is the symbol and the vehicle of Vishnu in India. Ramon remembers the conversation with Ury. Ramon is happy to remember the positive mentality that the Hindus have of the world. He has heard so many doom scenarios the last few months. It made him sick sometimes. In the nineties the year 2000 was a kind of doom year in which all kind of terrible things would happen. But now the year 2012 seems to be the new date for the most outrageous visions. The rumor started some years ago with the Maya calendar that ends abruptly in the year 2012. It would be the end of a more than five thousand year old cycle. To be exact, one fifth of the rotation movement of the Earth axis called "precession", which is 5154 years. Everybody should know that the Earth's axis has an angle of 23° and rotates every 25,770 year around his own axis. Even stranger was that 2012 is also the end of this even larger cycle of five equal periods. So the year 2012 is the end of one complete precession cycle of 25,770 years.

Jan Xel Lungold, a specialist of the Mayan calendar started a world tour to give lectures about his findings. Ramon really enjoyed his video lecture, "The Mayan Calendar Comes North". He was not at all a doom-thinker and was rather optimistic about that date. But since a few years, this year has become the focus of all kinds of doom theories and a period of worldwide catastrophes. The end of the world as we know it. It is clear that most Americans have never heard of the God Vishnu.

At ease and a bit impressed by the strange visitor in his garden, Ramon drives home. The last months he has collected all the websites about doom theories in a separate folder. It was very clear that a professional team was at work. It was all very well organized. Especially after the 9/11 disaster in New York, the Americans became very sensitive to doomsday theories. That's understandable, having seen the Twin Towers crashing in front of your eyes during non stop CNN news broadcasts. This collective trauma was a perfect moment to open people up for doom suggestions. It was a perfect environment for mind control. Back home, he turns the volume of the radio up and his favorite Beastie Boys song vibrates through the WebCom. The "Volt"

384

program on Studio Brussels gives Ramon the necessary "house man" energy to prepare dinner. In no time the vegetables are cleaned and the soup comes to the boil. The sound of an incoming mail requests his attention. It is a short message from Mira.

Are you there? Very urgent!

No problem, is Ramon's answer.

I will be there in 15 minutes, is the short answer.

What can be so urgent? In a hurry he does the dishes and gives the floor a lick and a promise. Just as he drops the dirty laundry in the washroom, he hears Mira's car. In a hurry she enters the kitchen.

Oh Ramon, I am glad that you are here. You will never believe what I experienced a few days ago.

Mira, please, take a seat. Did something bad happen? You seem upset.

Excited, she describes her experience during her meeting with the Tulkus. With amazement, Ramon listens to everything and makes extensive notes.

But that is fantastic news, Mira. So the Sheyan are safe now? Let's drink some coffee to that.

While he makes a hot mug of coffee, he tries to get a picture of the new situation.

So if I understand you well, the seven Sheyan have left Ter I and are now in another region, looking for water?

That's what Teimon told me yesterday night. He informed me that everything was okay and that I had to visit you as soon as possible. And so, here I am.

Any idea where they are now, Mira?

Could it be in the region of the Pleiades?

That could be, Mira. It is near Orion, seen from here. But it is still far away. Their technology must be really mind blowing. But why didn't they come straightaway to Earth?

That's impossible, Ramon. To get here directly, they have to travel via the road of the star map. But that road is protected by the Greys. Don't you remember that the artificial star gates can be found on the star map? These locations, these space stations and artificial star gates, are now under control of the Greys. So the Sheyan had no choice and took another road. But now they are stuck there. They need water before they can make the next trip.

That's very good news, Mira. At least they are safe for the moment.

Indeed, Ramon. Teimon told me that they are in a state of hibernation most of the time. Only one person has to keep the atmosphere in the space ship stable. And in this way, they consume less energy. You never know what kind of surprises the Greys have in mind. But sometimes, Aodin wakes up Teimon.

The experience of Mira is so different from science fiction movies that Ramon can only conclude that everything she tells must be true. Who can make up such a strange scenario? A mix of normal and paranormal technology! Para-psycho-physics has definitely a future. He fills the mugs once more and writes down as much as he can about Mira's incredible experience.

And when will Teimon wake up, Mira?

Right now, Ramon.

Are you serious, Mira? I thought…

Yes, Ramon. That's why he told me to get here as quickly as possible. He is awake now. Mira gives Ramon a sign to give her a moment of silence. The kitchen lights up in a purple nebula and soon she tunnels through the purple matrix to meet Teimon.

I'm there, Ramon. You can speak with him.

Ramon has to adjust a bit to this unusual situation but soon he forgets the strangeness of it all. Good evening Teimon, everything all right?

1.418 We salute you. Everybody is healthy and well. Thank you.

Ramon is very happy to hear the reaction through Mira's mouth.

Mira told me about your escape, Teimon. I'm glad everything worked out well. The book will be ready soon. It is a question of time. I don't know if it is appropriate now, but I would like to have some more details about the way the Greys took control over your people.

For a moment it is silent and Mira translates the question to Teimon. With a deep voice, the answer comes out of her mouth.

1.419 **The Greys have very complex brains, designed to digest information at high speed. They have frequent telepathic contact in blocks of six. Like your computers, these blocks of**

386

six Greys have a telepathic intranet.

1.420 Two blocks of six Greys are connected and form again a single block. Two of these double blocks are again combined to form a larger block and so on. Every time the DNA material of the new clones was cloned again, they evolved a bit.

1.421 Their brains are all genetically the same. But to do the different tasks, they are programmed after their bodies have fully developed. Every Grey is programmed to do his specific job in the Grey organization.

Suddenly things become clear. Ramon thinks of the people that Mira saw in the underground bases. Probably, they were being programmed with the same technique as the Greys. In this way they are programmed to function in connection with a specific Grey block. That technical devise can probably program or reprogram their brain in a way to make them ready for their tasks. I have to know more about that.

Sorry to interrupt Mira, but can I compare the software of a block system with the Windows Explorer?

1.422 Yes, Ramon. The block culture is based on the same classification method as the folder system, but much more complex. If one folder is one block of six Greys, then two of these folders are in a higher folder. Two of these higher folders are again combined in a higher folder and so on. But Mira does not understand that principle very well.

Ramon can hardly suppress his laughter and Mira looks at him as if to say: Men! Pfff! But she remains focused and she fulfils her task as telepathic translator.

1.423 The Grey organization is perfect. Their culture is as orderly structured as the great pyramids on Earth. That's why they are so hard to fight.

Ramon understands perfectly what Teimon means. The Greys are biological robots, made in such a way to function at their best in a group. That was their function. Their whole organization is based on efficiency. Every Grey and every block has a place in the pyramidal structured organization of the Greys.

1.424 Our ancestors took care that this Grey hierarchy could be controlled for security reasons. Every level of the Grey pyramid could be controlled and upgraded if necessary. That

was necessary, because of the ever growing block cultures.

1.425 **The Grey industry extended biologically. Like a living pyramid. But everything happened purely on a functional level. In this way, we could control and improve our space industry.**

1.426 **The mission of the Greys was to reach the Earth and to find traces of the Ancients and to have contact with descendants of the Wise Men.**

1.427 **They followed the road of the star map and made a new connection between Geya and Ter I. The gates were in constant repair. Precious materials had to be dug up and transported to keep our culture on Ter I intact.**

Thanks, Teimon. But how could that contact with the hallucinogenic substance of a cactus have such an immense impact on the Greys?

1.428 **The Greys had their own evolution and became disobedient even before that happened. They brought sporadic visits to Earth, which they were not allowed to do.**

1.429 **Their skin had to be kept wet. The desert was their favourite place to land. They can't stand the world of bacteria on Earth. The desert is the safest place for them. A technical problem forced a Grey block to stay longer than normal. To survive, they had to use the fluids of a cactus.**

1.430 **Some substances penetrated the skin and came in their bloodstream and created a strong ecstatic hallucinogenic effect, thereby neutralizing their programmed brain. As a kind of telepathic virus, this experience spread through the Grey network and infected the other blocks.**

1.431 **In no time, this effect reached the entire Grey culture of Geya. The centre of the Greys is located in an underground base on the moon. When the effect of the substances reached the top of the hierarchy, it changed the mother code of the highest block.**

Ramon is speechless. It is all so simple and at the same time so fantastic. What would Bill Gates think about that?

1.432 **The top of the pyramid is only one Grey. He is programmed with the Mother Code, being the essence of the program of the whole block culture. That was done by the designers of the Greys for a very practical reason. If the**

388

technicians found a failure in the Grey information system, they could block the whole block culture by neutralizing the mother code. We called this Grey with the mother code the golog.

1.433 **The hallucinogenic experience reversed the mother code. The golog became a commander in stead of a receiver. In no time, the golog took control of the whole block culture.**

1.434 **Step by step his commands penetrated deeper into the hierarchy of the Grey organization and his insights and overview grew constantly. And then the drama happened.**

1.435 **The golog travelled through the star gates and visited the gologs of every other block culture, located at different places on the star map route and changed the mother code of every golog until he reached the block culture of Ter I. In fractions of seconds he took over the whole information system and our Grey friends became our worst enemies.**

1.436 **The Téry expected a transport from the Greys on Earth. These kind of transportations were done regularly so we had no clue what his real mission was this time. After they arrived the whole Grey network was disconnected from our control. It happened totally unexpectedly, like when a virus enters and blocks a computer.**

1.437 **We lost complete control over the Grey programming system. The spaceship came under control of the golog. But that was only the beginning.**

1.438 **The survival of the Téry depends on our space industry. The greatest part of the Téry work in the space industry. They are what you call workers. But in our culture, nobody is obliged to work. Working is based on free choice. If you are interested in something, you can become involved, based on free choice. We are not forced to work for survival. Everybody is free to live the way he wants. Those who work, see it as their contribution to our culture, so that we can survive as a group. They are called the Free-Actives. This is a tradition since the Ancients became interstellar nomads during the great exodus.**

1.439 **Because space itself is not a good environment for humans the Ancients took care that we could have telepathically contact with the Greys. In this way, we could** control the fully automatic Grey industry in the "now" time, without leaving our planet.

1.440 To do this efficiently the Free-Actives were organized in the same way as the Grey culture, just for practical reasons. At a certain moment, the Téry Free-Actives decided to wear an implant to improve the communication with the Greys.

1.441 Implants are small crystal skulls to improve the coordination of the contact with the Grey block system. And that was in the advantage of the Greys in the take-over of our planet. The Greys could paralyze all the Free-Actives mentally with the help of these implants, making them unable to react.

Ramon is completely surprised as he hears this story. That is why wearing an implant is so dangerous.

So, it was a kind of coup d'état, Teimon?

1.442 Correct. Once the Free-Actives were under their control, the golog threatened our leaders with destroying the energy supplies located in space, if they were not willing to cooperate with them. Our whole colony on Ter I would be destroyed in a matter of days.

1.443 We live in large ecodromes. These ecodromes use a lot of energy and raw materials, necessary for our food, atmosphere and technology. We don't have agriculture, like on our mother planet.

1.444 To protect the lives of the citizens, our leaders asked the Free-Actives to surrender in order to win time. I remember that I was in an important meeting with some of our leaders when it all started. I immediately sensed that there was something wrong. Because I don't wear an implant, I was able to get away in time and to warn the Sheyan.

Mira is quiet for a while. She feels the traumatic experience in the telepathic contact. He had to leave his friends behind. Ramon also realizes that it had to be a traumatic situation for Teimon.

Was there nothing they could do, Teimon?

1.445 No, not at that moment. All implanted Téry lost mental control and were as paralyzed. They were not able to neutralize the mother code of the golog. And at the same

time, the leaders heard the threats of the Greys.

1.446 The only thing I could do was to escape before a Grey squadron landed on Ter I and invaded the Central Industrial Complex and took control. Powerless, the Free-Actives had to see how all control technology was reprogrammed.

1.447 The disconnection with the block culture was complete. The Free-Actives were powerless and totally defeated. And from that moment on, the Téry colony on Ter I was in the hands of the Greys. The common citizens who were not working in the space industry had no clue what happened. From the outside, nothing had changed.

1.448 But the Grey desire to get control over our people didn't stop with mental control. To get absolute control, the golog developed an evil strategy.

Wait a second, Mira. So there is one Grey on top of a Grey block culture. What does "golog" mean, Teimon?

1.449 The central Grey of every block is very well protected by the Grey population of that block. We gave him that nickname. It sounds... funny in our language. He is in fact a nobody but he thinks he is important.

Ramon smiles while making notes. That's a reassuring thought. If the Téry have a sense of humor, then they are real people. Mira sounds tired and feels the pressure on her head again.

Ramon, do you have more questions? The wound on my head is open again.

Ramon understands that the contact time is limited. Quickly he finishes his notes, thinking about what he can ask.

Maybe one last question, Teimon. Can you clarify the experiences of Mira with the crystal skulls a bit more?

1.450 The different star beacons of the star map route are under Grey control. That's why we can't travel to your solar system in one transport. The star beacons are like lighthouses to guide our flight route. The star beacons are located on different segments of the star map.

Star beacon! That's a nice word. I have never heard it before. So these gates are lighthouses in space, Mira. They have the same function as the lighthouses on the coast to guide the ships. Great!

1.451 Exactly. These beacons connect the different segments of the route of the star map. They give a signal to coordinate

our flight. **But the beacons are now under control of the Greys or they have been destroyed.**

1.452 For that reason we can no longer follow the route of the star map. That's why we used the seven skulls to simulate a signal as orientation. We had only one alternative to escape: an old route of the Ancients. There is a powerful natural star gate on one of the planets of the Pleiades. That's where we are now. We are searching water and oxygen.

The Pleiades? Then Mira was right after all. This location is mentioned several times in a lot of New Age literature. Ramon was always suspicious about that. He knew that the Pleiades are a group of very young stars. Seventy million years is much too young for stars to have planets where higher life forms could have formed. Not to mention the dust clouds surrounding this large concentration of stars. Maybe there are planets with water, but life? That is absolutely impossible. But a natural star beacon on a planet or an artificial star gate? That could be, of course.

1.453 Collectively the Tulkus on Earth helped us by using the crystal skulls. Thanks to them we could determine the coordinates to bring us to safety.

1.454 Teimon was able to capture the signal. If the skulls vibrate collectively, they can send a strong enough telepathical signal to coordinate the flight route. So the crystal skulls together became one star beacon.

1.455 It must happen in the "now" time. The Tulkus had telepathical contact with each other and had to start the signal of the skulls.

1.456 But the problems are not over. All the star beacons on the moon are destroyed or under control of the Greys. We will need the Tulkus again. Soon.

Again it is silent. This information clarifies so many rumors inside the UFO community. What else shall Ramon ask? Making notes, listening and asking questions at the same time is not simple. Ramon thinks back on the lectures of Gregg Braden, who talked about the star gates.

Teimon, do the old calendars of the Mayan and Egyptians have a relation with the star beacons or with any of this?

1.457 In ancient times the shamans practiced the same ritual as the one that Mira was part of recently. The Ancients used

this ritual with the skulls millennia ago. The shamans know us and know the powers of the crystal skulls. They knew that the Ancients came from the stars.

1.458 **Special calendars were designed for the humans to calculate the moments when the Ancients used the natural star beacons for their transportation to Earth. At those moments this ritual was done to help the Ancients to get the coordinates right. These moments in time correlate with the active periods of the star gates. The natural star gates are much more powerful than the artificial star beacons.**

1.459 **In order to help the humans to use the calendar the Ancients taught the shamans the knowledge of the star mechanics to get grip on time. This knowledge became the basis of astrology. The calendar of the Mayans is important. He was brought to South America during the first contact. The ritual of 2012 is near.**

1.460 **Prepare yourselves. The natural gates will open again soon. It may be before 2012. That is just a date, a convention. We salute you. We will come back.**

Greetings, says Ramon completely involved in everything he heard. Thanks!

Mira takes a deep breath and stretches her body.

My God! I'm so glad it is over. My throat is dry and my head feels as if it will explode in a minute.

Ramon knows what to do. Quickly, he puts the water heater on and moments later they both enjoy a fresh mug of coffee and a cigarette.

I'm glad that it is over, Ramon The contact with Teimon is different from that with Aryein, although I have the impression that I recover more quickly. The pressure is gone in a matter of minutes, probably because they are closer to Earth now.

That could very well be the reason, Mira. But telepathy is very exhausting. Why do you think that Tibetan tulkus have to do so much practice? It is a hard job to become a telepath.

I am starting to realize that, Ramon. But tell me, does this information make you any wiser?

Absolutely, Mira. But I made a big blunder.

What do you mean, Ramon?

I still don't know what that evil plan is, which the golog

executed on their planet. How could I forget to ask that! We have to know that, Mira. If the Greys want to invade our planet, we have to be prepared. We have to inform the people as well as we can with the book. It is important for everybody involved.

I have no idea of that master plan, Ramon. I was too occupied with the translation. Sorry, but I couldn't take anymore.

No problem, Mira. You did just great. I'm just angry with myself. But I'm sure that Teimon will make contact again. They are safe for the moment. Aryein was right, Mira. They were in danger. Thank God, it all worked out well.

I know one thing for sure, Ramon. If the Greys want to take over Earth, they will have serious problems.

I know, Mira. We had this discussion already a few months ago. And we couldn't figure it out then as well. It is a big riddle to me. But I will study this new information to see if it brings more clarity.

I think the G-implants will also play a crucial role on Earth, Ramon. Implanting humans should be banned as a policy, anywhere in the world. It is just too risky.

You're right, Mira. But the G-implants alone can't make world control possible. There has to be something else. But now that you mention it, a lot of websites claim that some companies and organizations are already using implants for their people. These implants become smaller and better every day. But the real function of this Grey practice is still not clear to me. Imagine that that all the people of the world would be implanted. Then you need a large network of Greys to control them all. I can't imagine that one block culture can do the job. They would need a large human organization to make it happen. We must not forget that the people involved have no clue what the real plans of the Greys are. The Greys would expose their plans in this way.

Not necessarily, Ramon. It could be that the organizations involved in this implant business do this with the best intentions. The Free-Actives of the Téry were implanted too. But it could be that the Mentals and the Psy-mutants are all programmed for a specific task. They think that these implants are necessary to protect humanity for hundreds of reasons. They don't realize that they are programmed to serve the Greys. The Greys just have to wait until the orders are executed. As soon it is done, they can take over the entire inter-network. Just like they did it on Ter I. Probably, they have technology to do that.

You are right, Mira. We must not forget that Psy-mutants can not refuse commands of the Greys any longer. Their own will is locked inside. So even if they know what the real intentions are, they are no longer able to react. Just like the Free-Actives on Ter I. Who knows what the Greys can do with these implants! Their technology is so much more advanced.

I fear the worst, Ramon. It doesn't feel well.

Indeed Mira, never underestimate your enemies. That would be the dumbest thing a general can do. I hope Teimon can help us figure it out. It is important to get a global picture of the Grey threat.

I'm sure you will manage to get it right, Ramon. If you can't do it, who else can?

Thanks for your trust, Mira.

Ramon waves Mira goodbye? He realizes the time. The moon is growing to a full moon and lights the surrounding clouds. Orion and the Pleiades are very well visible.

How could I be so stupid not to ask about the plans of the golog? Dozens of questions cross his mind as he falls asleep.

- 63 -
22/7/2007

For the time being, Ramon has only one goal: to finish the book as soon as possible. It is already late as a vivid young lady unexpectedly enters Ramon's WebCom. She sees Ramon sitting in front of his computer, surrounded by notes, drawings and loud music and a big smile appears on her face.

Hey Ramon, still alive?

Joy, that's a pleasant surprise. Please, come in. Everything okay, girl?

Her smile speaks for itself. And as if the WebCom is her second home, she takes it over with her typical charm while Ramon makes her favorite drink. While she downloads some songs and checks her e-mails, she chats with her friends and solves some puzzles.

Ramon, do you know that a new season of "Lost" will start on Monday? And also a new season of "Temptation Island".

I heard about it, Joy.

And Bones will start again too!

Good that you remind me, Joy.

Ramon cuts a few slices of cake and serves the coffee.

But there is a problem, Joy.

Is there?

Well, Bones and Lost are scheduled at the same time. So, what shall I do?

Let's see. Just record Bones. Then, I will watch Lost at home. Do you know that Lost will go on until 2012?

Until 2012?

Yes, Ramon. I read it in a TV magazine.

Ramon doesn't know if he is dreaming or awake.

Are you sure?

Yes, I am sure, otherwise I wouldn't say it, now would I? But before I forget, there is a good movie tomorrow, The Skulls 2. Can you record that movie for me too? I have no time to watch that evening. It must be a good movie, so I've heard.

Sure Joy, I will record The Skulls 2 and Bones and you watch Lost.

Shall we play a game, Ramon?

Absolutely, Joy!

Patience?

Okay, Joy. I feel I will win this time. Ha, ha, ha...

Some minutes later, Ramon loses his 183rd game and Joy smiles pitifully to Ramon while looking at her scoreboard.

I don't know how you do it Joy, but one way or the other you always win. I don't get it.

But Joy is already busy, sending a text message to a girlfriend.

And Ramon, how is the book coming along? Is it almost finished?

I wish it was Joy, but it's in progress.

I don't know why a clever man like you writes a book about something as stupid as UFOs.

Ramon starts to laugh very loudly.

What's so funny about that, Ramon?

Ramon has to laugh even harder.

If I could only tell, Joy, if I could only tell.

Forget it, Ramon. I don't believe in UFOs anyhow.

That's a good thing Joy, I don't believe in UFOs either. I just study them.

Then you think that UFOs exist, says Joy with her typical logic. That means that you believe they exist!

Ramon doesn't know what to say.

Listen Joy, do you believe in cars?

No, I drive a car, is her reply.

Exactly right, says Ramon. In the same way, I don't believe in UFOs, but I want to fly them, if I ever get the chance.

You are a weird guy, Ramon. But then you do believe they exist.

But no, Joy. You see, UFOs exist or they don't. If they exist, I want to fly them. If they don't exist, I want to prove that they don't exist. But I don't want to "believe" that they exist.

For a moment she is silent. Hopeless, she thinks and she activates the song "Map of the Problematic" by Muse. In no time she fills her player with new songs while Ramon takes the video tapes of last week. Joy uses her time as efficiently as possible and enjoys every moment of the day to the fullest extent. The videos give her more freedom. Suddenly her mobile phone rings.

I have to go now, Ramon. Dinner is ready.

Ramon waves when she leaves.

Don't forget The Skulls, Ramon! And Bones! And gone she is.

Skulls and Bones in the same week. That's strange. I must check it out.

And so he does. The Skulls 2 is a movie about one of the most powerful secret societies in the USA. This secret society really exists and recruits members among the students of a private university and is called Skull and Bones.

The funny thing is that the series Bones has nothing to do with the movie The Skulls II. But it is strange that this detective series has this name. It is as if the secret society makes positive publicity by making a positive association with their name via TV. Bones is a professional made TV soap, but full of disgusting close-ups of decomposing bodies, analyzed in the smallest detail by a young, good looking investigator, nicknamed "Bones". And it is not only Bones. A lot of crime series use shocking images. You wonder where that will end. But as long the good guys win, it's okay, no?

It was not the growing use of violence that worried Ramon so much. The problem is that more and more movie heroes take the law into their own hands. They are still the good guys and they win, but the way they win made Ramon think. It is as if it is the policy of some film studios to glorify the use of the cruelest violence to let justice prevail. The growing use of violence is not the real issue here. The point is that the heroes take justice into their own hands. The growing amount of domestic dramas - father killing his children and wife or school children creating a massacre and then killing themselves - was a development in crime that worried Ramon a lot. Ramon was convinced that the idea that it is ok to take justice into your own hands is the real cause behind instable persons executing these terrible dramas. People committing those crimes don't look for help to solve their problems. They take revenge and decide themselves what the punishment shall be. And that is a mental shift, propagated by so many movies, starting with the Rambo movies. A lot of movies would follow, suggesting that you are allowed to take justice into your own hands.

It makes it understandable why the American population was in favor of the Iraq war. The 9/11 attack justified the reaction. Ramon remembers President Bush saying: "We will smoke them out of their holes". The anger of the whole population was channeled and there was no organization or government in the world, which could stop them to take revenge. It may be understandable but in essence they took justice into their own hands. Criticizing this policy was even dangerous in these times of black and white policy. Either you are for us or you are against us. There was no third option. And it was all understandable. Rambo was a killing machine but he was the good guy, no?

Ramon had problems with this justification of violence. Maybe because all these movie heroes remind him too much of the utopian "Übermensch" concept of the Nazis. War may be justified if there are no other means to resolve a conflict. But the army of Iraq was no match for the powerful army of the USA. In the Second World War the situation was different. Nazism could only be stopped by war. They started it themselves, making the war justified. No matter how cruel the consequences were.

But if wars are deliberately created to enlarge power or profit, we are talking about a different game altogether. The Germans invaded Poland after a fake attack of Polish solders on German ground. It was no coincidence that "thirteen" Polish solders attacked a radio station in Germany. In fact they were convicted German solders, first killed by injections and then brought to the scene of crime. There they became part of a setup to convince the German press that it was a real Polish military invasion of Germany. So the Germans faked the Polish invasion to have a reason to invade Poland. How cruel can humans be!

Suddenly Ramon thinks back on some articles in the eighties about a revolutionary breakthrough in psychology at the Pavlov institute. Any signal can create any association. If it is properly done! It created a revolution in advertisement. But it can also be used as a demagogic tool. The method is always the same. First you create a traumatic experience. Once that's done, people are sensitive for suggestion. This technique is the perfect formula to manipulate small and large groups and even an entire population. Annoyed by the cruel things that people can do to each other, Ramon fills his mug again and opens the book in his word processor. But then again, he quickly checks the TV programs for that day.

His attention is caught by the name of a popular movie, Men in Black. Ramon thinks back on a book he read when he was young, The Trojan Horse by J. Keel, a well-known ufologist in the seventies. Keel discussed the existence of a group of people, called Men in Black, extensively. These obscure people visited UFOs witnesses, threatening them if they would not shut up against the press about what they had seen. The movie Men in Black is used to exercise a different kind of mind manipulation. It portrays the men in black as a group of funny, nice guys who fight aliens in a most ridiculous way. The "genuine", manipulative and criminal men in black who operated in the last century are portrayed as nice guys. In fact, this movie suggests that they never existed and belong to the world of fairytales. Because who of the young people knows anything about the real stories of this sinister group that blackmailed and threatened witnesses of UFOs in the midst of the fifties? And so, in an entertaining way, a black period of mind control is wiped out of the history book. As if it never happened. Truly criminal! But it works... It even makes good money.

It became clear to Ramon that propaganda and demagogic mind control are now spread by the popular media in a very effective way. It all has to do with changing the associations with events, words, groups and phenomena. In the past, the good guys were smoking, now the bad guys are smoking. In the past the good guys had long hair, now the bad guys have long hair. In the past muscular guys were vain, now they are the new version of the Übermensch.

But yes, lifestyles change. Nothing wrong with that, is there? The same technique is also used to handle the alien presence and the UFO problem. There is hardly any serious program about UFOs. Aliens belong to the realm of science fiction. Movies and soaps determine what people think about aliens and UFOs in general. Only the web and some books give you real clues about this topic. But then again, it is very hard to make the evidence stick.

That's why Ramon is very happy to have direct contact with Teimon and that he possesses real clues about the alien presence. It enabled him to leave the realm of speculation and to look at the facts. Not that Ramon lost sight of the fact that he could not prove that Teimon was real. But there was a kind of common sense that told him that this story was real and factual. The book offers a positive association with real aliens but a negative association with dangerous developments in science like cloning, implants, genetic manipulation and so on. And that's how it should be.

Based on what Ramon has heard until now, the Greys are indeed a real threat. But the Téry and the Ancients are very decent, ethical people. Teimon even admits that his ancestors made mistakes by creating the Grey creature. The Téry don't hide their mistakes. Isn't that very humane and ethical? That fact alone is the main reason why Ramon writes the book. It will give the positive and the negative aspects of the alien presence. And that is a good thing. The book gives a positive picture of highly advanced extra-terrestrial civilizations. But it also gives a clear picture of the danger of advanced genetic techniques, resulting in

400

cloned creatures that become a threat against their own creators as well as against the earthly humans. And it is not about a hypothetical danger but a real danger we have to deal with in our own society. Right now!

It makes crystal clear that not everything that can be invented and created by science is good. At this moment, humanity itself is on the brink of creating human clones. The existence of the Greys is the best warning for the devastating consequences of these developments in biology. If we learn from the mistakes of the Téry, we can prevent the same mistakes in the near future. The knowledge about the DNA and the significance of every gene is great for medical and human sciences. But that doesn't mean we may play with it like school children. The Grey problem is the best example to show how dangerous it is to fool around with genetics just to make some money. Genetics may be used to improve the well-being of mankind, but it must not be used to design new living plants, animals and especially humans, because those organisms escape the test of the natural evolution of life on our planet. Making clones and new species is making an artificial evolution of life, threatening the natural evolution of our planet. It becomes like a cancer, growing in a healthy body, a "Fremdkörper" inside the planet's biological evolution. Investing billions to clone plants, animals and in the end humans, while every year thousands of plants and animal species are wiped out and millions of people starve to death is a call for revenge by nature itself. For science, to solve the problem of the massive extinction of life forms would be a much greater challenge than to fool around with genetic material.

The same "Reverse Association Technique", RAT, is also used on the web. The name of the game is "what's in the name". It looks innocent but is it really? If you type for example Zeta Reticula in a search engine on the web, you will find numerous links of a DJ before you find hyperlinks to the alien topic. It is a subtle tactic to prevent the general population to be confronted with this kind of topics on the web, by pushing the topic far back in the list. A similar technique is used with comments on the popular video websites like YouTube, Google and others. Any serious comment is immediately moved away from the top ten list by the most ridiculous crap comments.

RAT can also combine different media, making it even more powerful. Take the soap "Lost" for example. Scheduled to end in 2012? It is about a bunch of survivors of an airplane crash on an island. They experience the most bizarre experiences, but there is no goal or hope in the soap. Nobody knows what is really happening. The thread of the story is that there is no thread. It is as if the soap represents the chaos in the world of today: the threat of a third world war, the war against terrorism, partly in the open but much more underground. Is it not understandable that a lot of people feel a bit "lost" these days? Is it a mere coincidence that the reality soap Robinson's Island is an alternative version of Lost?

And then there is the year 2012. That magical date can mean almost everything: the threat of climate change and the rising of the sea levels, the threat of meteorites and tsunamis, pandemics and all kinds of natural catastrophes. All these associations, spread by the web, must be confusing people. Compare it to overload. If a server receives too much information, it locks up. If people get overloaded with information, they become disoriented, no longer able to react in a proper way. It is just too much and the "I don't care" syndrome and the "I do anything that is necessary to survive" syndrome become more and more serious.

There is only one way to cure this modern socio-psychological disease: giving humans overview, a general picture, a map to prevent that they feel lost or whatever. That was the purpose of the mystery school: to teach the students to get overview in this specializing and rapidly changing world. To stimulate the students to design mental and psychological tools to handle the ever growing amount of information. It is again silent in Ramon's mind. If humanity needs overview, overview they will get.

The word processor is still waiting while Ramon is meditating. Could 2012 be the date of the invasion of the Grey but also of the Illuminati? If the Greys plan an invasion on their own, they will have a deadline. Ramon read lots of rumors on the web about a secret cabal of people, probably the Illuminati, planning a new world order. Especially Dr. Salla from the website Exopolitics wrote some serious articles about the hidden agenda in

402

international politics. The name of the game is "a false flag operation". This complot theory states that the technology that was developed from back-engineering alien technology could be used to execute a surprise attack on the world. People would think that it would be an alien invasion. But in fact it would be an attack by a secret army, a secret army with advanced technology which makes it invincible against conventional weaponry. A technology developed in the large military industrial complex, hidden in underground facilities until the time is right. These rumors gradually overshadowed the other rumors that the 9/11 attack could be on itself a false flag operation... with severe implications. Conspiracy theories about 9/11 could be found on the web in abundance.

But a false flag operation with UFO's? Theoretically, that could be the case, of course. The first impression of Ramon was that this assumption was a bit over the top. But after the information from Teimon and from Merly about the existence of the Warriors, he started to take this option more seriously. If you start a war, make sure you win, is a known proverb. If you want to win, technological superiority is a must. That's something you can learn from every decent history book. With the help of alien technology, the world wouldn't know what hit it. And to put it in an overall scenario, the date could very well be 2012. The best secrets are public secrets. It is a year from which everybody expects something, provided the mass media will promote this date in the coming four years up to a climax. The world media, largely under control of the Illuminati, could spread various complot theories about this date via their networks. Also Sean Leyka could be a main player in this mind game.

Ramon was very happy that Teimon said that this date is just a date like any other date. The only difference is that it is related to the opening of natural star gates. The perfect date for an interstellar trip. The Greys will know this of course. It could be possible that the Greys fear that the Ancients will use this opportunity to visit Earth. They have control over the Téry but not over the Ancients. That would mean that the Greys must succeed in their plans for an invasion before that time. For against the Ancients, they have no chance. Could it be that the Greys want to have world control before that date? Just in case the Ancients come back? That would be logical. And neither the Warriors nor the Illuminati know about this. It is very well possible that they believe the suggestions of the Greys. That it will be a moment in time that natural disasters will occur.

Ramon remembers everything that Dan Burisch and others predicted. About one thing Ramon was sure. Also the Greys use RAT in a clever way to control the opinion of the general population. They use Psy-mutants to enforce associations and suggestions that fit a specific Grey agenda. Mass media are the perfect tool to spread their information worldwide.

Ramon remembers a lecture psychonomie at the mystery school about the structure of the cerebral cortex. The cortex is composed of six thin layers of brain cells. These six layers are connected vertically by very small cylindrical compartments of about twenty to thirty thousand cells. Every cell compartment can be compared to a folder of the Windows Explorer. In total, there are approximately half a million of these cell compartments, spread over the two parts of the brain, connected by the corpus callosum. These cell compartments are connected in a very complex way, different from person to person. In this way you get a hierarchy like the folder system on a hard disc. Every cell compartment specializes in one specific function. If you think of a red rose, you activate hundreds of cell compartments simultaneously, to see this rose in your imagination. That process is completely based on all the associations you have with a red rose: color, shape, meaning, smell, knowledge and so on. With advertisements, soaps and movies you can enlarge, rearrange and change the personal associations. It is in fact very simple and it works. The Greys must be masters in manipulation of these brain associations. Their whole society is structured that way.

Ramon remembers very well the hundreds of testimonies of abductees. After years of suggestion, the personal associations of the abductees changed completely. The Greys don't understand that every human being has developed in his life a unique association pattern, making him a unique individual. For the Greys who are perfectly programmed for their specific tasks, it is very disturbing that every human has this unique pattern. If they consider themselves normal, they must think of us as inefficient,

404

chaotic and disturbed life forms that need to be mentally upgraded as soon as possible. They want to recreate humans to their image and likeness. They haven't a clue what humans are all about. What would we be if we were all perfectly fitting in an overall mind hierarchy? We would all be psychic slaves of a dominating system. Free will and individuality would cease to exist. Cultural evolution would not be possible.

All great thinkers throughout history came into conflict with existing world-views, theories and systems of thought. They changed and improved them. And fortunately for us, these people exist for they are the engine behind the human socio-cultural evolution. To the Greys, such a situation is unthinkable. While meditating, Ramon starts to understand how and why the Greys make humans into Psy-mutants. First they question the victim's personal opinions with telepathic suggestion. They do this by changing the personal association patterns. In this way, the abductees lose their individuality and critical mind. The Greys make these people uniform in their thinking and connect them with their overall block hierarchy, creating a human pyramid, with the Grey pyramid on top. Like the pyramid symbol of the Illuminati.

Suddenly a lot of things become clear to Ramon. For the Greys, individuality is the mother code of every human being. The Greys think and act under one mother code. If you can take away the individual mother code of the abductees, he becomes indoctrinated with the mother code of the Grey block culture, the mother code of the golog! In this way, the abducted victim loses his independency while the Greys can save the original mother code of the abductee as a computer file for their own use, once the invasion succeeds. That's the Grey agenda. Since the mother code of their block culture changed after that psychedelic cactus experience, all their actions have only one goal: to manipulate every human in order to link him to the mother code of the golog. The Greys want humanity to become a part of the Grey block culture. They want to recreate humanity according to their image. First they transform the humans into mental Greys. Then they turn them into Psy-mutants with the help of G-implants or implants. Once their mother code is injected throughout the whole human population, the way for the Greys is open to become or to replace humans or whatever their plan is.

It grows silent in Ramon's mind. The meditation process has ended. The question he asked himself is answered. But how the Greys want to become humans is still an open question.

But now you have to stop meditating, Ramon. You have to work. Write, Ramon. Write! Finish the book.

And glad to have received some more clarity in the Grey strategy in an intuitive way, he starts writing again. For a moment, he thinks of Joy. That girl always brings on good ideas. It is late when Ramon finds rest in his bed.

- **64** -
1/8/2007

What? Ten to five? Ramon jumps up and looks for the remote to start the video recorder. Just in time for the daily soap. He decides to take a small break, cleans the kitchen table and prepares the vegetables for the soup.

What a day! The 264th show of "Out There" was rather shocking. The topic was Morgellons disease, discussed by Dr. Hildegard Staninger, a professional toxicologist. Staninger investigates the impact of environmental pollution on the health of people. She discussed a new skin disease whereby glass fibre-like hair is growing under the skin. Also on the website of Rense an article was published. Really freaky! He must not forget to ask Teimon if he has an explanation for that disease.

Ten minutes later, the soup is boiling and a mix of herbal smells fills the kitchen. Ah, the magical smells of nature! Sunrays have heated up the walls of the backyard making it hot until late into the night. Ramon decides to eat outside. In no time, he changes the old garden table into an acceptable dining table.

With an extra cup of coffee he enjoys the heat of the late afternoon sun. He decides to read through his notes and to prepare the next chapter. While entering the kitchen in search for his notes, the lid of the soup kettle rattles like hell and steam fills up the kitchen. Damn! How is it possible that I always forget to put the fire low? While he cleans the mess, Mira enters the kitchen.

406

Can I help? says the unexpected guest, hardly visible through the steam.

Mira! You know to choose your moments. Please, sit down. Or let us sit outside, before we suffocate.

Fine by me, Ramon says Mira in a low, weak voice. I have contact with Teimon. Do you have a minute? The whole day long I have felt that pressure on my head. I knew that I had to come as soon as possible.

The right decision, Mira. Just a moment. I take my writing materials and something to drink.

Quickly, he gets his notes, hidden in the typical chaos of his WebCom. And don't forget to ask what the big secret is, says Ramon to himself while checking the soup.

Ramon is excited. He is a professionally trained phenomenological parapsychologist and the process of identification with the story gives him for the first time the feeling he actually will talk with an alien being. There is no more doubt in his mind. The soup is put on the lowest level and with a full pot of coffee he joins Mira outside. As he takes a seat at the table, he feels a warm sensation going through his spine and his body trembles all over. But with the help of a few breathing exercises that he learned from Harish Johari, he relaxes in no time. He fills the mugs and is ready to note the coming information.

Can I start asking questions, Mira?

Yes Ramon, he is there!

Her deep voice indicates that she is far away.

Okay then. I salute you, Teimon. How are you today?

1.461 **Everything is okay. We are asleep most of the time to save oxygen. But one person is always awake to keep an eye on the conditions in the spacecraft.**

For a while, Mira is silent. But then suddenly she jumps straight up and starts talking agitatedly.

Now I know, Ramon! Now I know the reason why I am the one to contact the skull.

I don't know what you mean, Mira? Please do explain.

Teimon just told me the real reason. I was not trained to come into contact with the skull. But the person who had to make contact with the purple skull was not ready. That's why I had to take it over. I was the only one that could do the job for the moment. I have been wondering about this question over and over again these last days. I think that Teimon sensed it.

Ramon is as surprised as Mira with this answer.

From the look on her face he knows that this answer satisfies her eagerness to know why she was the one to do these telepathic sessions. While he writes it down he sees that Mira is relieved that she finally knows the reason for all this.

We will talk about it after the session, Mira. But let us first go on. So Teimon, what is the next step?

1.462 **We will try to reach Geya as soon as possible.**

Are they really coming, Mira? And when will that be, he asks with growing excitement.

1.463 **It will take us four years. We cannot reach Geya in one step.**

Four years, says Ramon. That long! The gestures of Mira indicate that that is what Teimon is saying.

1.464 **We must do the odyssey to Geya in several steps. All the gates of the star map route are controlled by the Greys. We have to take another route that is much more indirect. But the book has to be written anyway. Otherwise it will be too late. The time of the Grey invasion is near.**

On hearing this, Ramon gets an anxious feeling. It confirms his thoughts. I will do my best, Teimon. The book can be ready at the end of the year. I have to translate everything. I hope it will be earlier. But the book will come. That's for sure. Suddenly, he remembers the big question.

Before I forget, Teimon. What happened when the Greys got control over your Free-Actives? With close attention he awaits the answer.

1.465 **When the golog and his Grey colony took control, he started his cruel plan. The Free-Actives couldn't do anything to prevent it.**

1.466 **Without hesitation, the Greys polluted our ecodromes with a chemical substance and mixed it with the air. Not to kill us, but these substances entered our food and our bodies through the skin and by breathing. The population was not aware of that. This substance has a very cruel effect on anybody who wears an implant.**

These substances, are they similar to the ones used in nano-technology?

1.467 **Yes, Ramon. They are a kind of living molecules. These chemicals react to G-implants and implants. They have a primitive kind of DNA structure. They are deposited in several organs, where they start to cluster.**

1.468 **From there they grow through the entire body as a kind of second nerve system. As soon as this web of artificial fibres connects with the implant, it becomes active and replaces the natural nervous system of the body.**

1.469 **In this way, the body comes completely under control of the Greys. The only freedom that is left is the freedom of thought. If people with a G-implant get this infection, they will become Mutants.**

Ramon can hardly cope with this information. So that was what Aodin meant when he said: Only in our minds we are free. While he takes notes, he sees the seriousness of the situation. And is this is also happening on Earth? Concerned, he thinks of the interview with the toxicologist. All the while he is making notes.

1.470 **If you don't wear an implant, the body will reject the chemicals. People without a G-implant can handle the chemicals. For these people it is just like an allergy. Psy-mutants are the real victims. But also Mentals will have a hard time with these substances.**

What a relief! Then it is not a disaster yet. Imagine everybody would get this. Then we might as well give up. Mira is silent and waits for the next question.

Teimon, how can this happen on Earth? We don't live in ecodromes.

1.471 **On your planet, there is an unfortunate concurrence of circumstances. Your climate is now in a temporary cycle of heating up. Ever since scientists discovered that problem, they developed techniques to prevent this climate change from happening. The use of chemicals in the upper atmosphere had the most effect and was put into practice.**

Ramon doesn't believe what he is hearing. Shocked, he remembers the chemtrails he saw above his own village.

1.472 **Certain chemicals used in these chemtrails have the same properties as the chemicals that the Greys used in our** ecodromes. **The Greys used this situation on earth to their favour. They stimulated some Psy-mutants involved in the production of these chemicals to make worldwide use of these chemicals. They suggested them that it was the only way to do something about the threat of a climatic disaster.**

1.473 **Because of the fear of this climatic doom scenario, the use of these techniques has spread all over the world. These chemicals are now used in large amounts. This tragic coincidence fits perfectly the strategy of the Greys. They want these chemicals to be used because their own nerve system is made of a similar combination of chemicals.**

1.474 **Humans who carry an implant in their body risk the same fate as the Free-Actives of my own people. The Mentals and the Psy-mutants are at high risk. Synchronicity will give you more clarity.**

Shocked, Ramon stops making notes. He feels really sick. Like he felt when he saw the first of the Twin Towers crash in 2001. He realized immediately that the consequence of this event meant war. That's the way his parents must have felt when the Germans invaded Belgium. A feeling of uncertainty and fear.

Synchronicity? Teimon must mean that I will find more clues on the web. Get a grip on yourself, Ramon. Ask your next question before the session is over. What would be the most important question now? I got it.

Teimon, what can people do to treat such a disease?

1.475 **Mentals can be helped with low earth sounds. The low sounds from the Tibetan horn have a good effect to improve the resistance against the symptoms. But Psy-mutants need extra help. The implant has to be removed first. Otherwise the disease can't be cured.**

1.476 **But everybody with the disease needs good psychological treatment and the right information about the Greys and their telepathic mind-manipulation until the disease is cured. Talking about it is very important.**

1.477 **The infected people have to realize that the compulsive thoughts they have are not their own thoughts. That is the reason why the victims are generally treated as if they have a psychological disorder. The psychologists must be specially trained and accurately informed. Together they can win the**

410

battle against this terrible disease.

This gives Ramon again hope. He finds a small paper with questions he wanted to ask earlier.

Teimon, in UFO literature, I find different descriptions of alien beings. Reptilian, animal like creatures, higher dimensional creatures. Can you tell me more about that?

1.478 **The reptilians are not real. It is a mental appearance by the Greys. The Greys can induce mental hallucinations, if you come close to them. You see a different image in stead of what is really there. They are just mental projections of the Greys and are not real. But they look very real.**

1.479 **But the humanoids that are seen in UFOs are real and are under control of the Greys. They are abducted humans and turned into Mutants with a double nerve system.**

1.480 **Some humanoid creatures can also be genetic mutants of common people. They could be the result of genetic experiments in the underground laboratories. But the Greys don't have the technology to do that properly. More likely is that the Greys have access to children, born in a natural way in secret projects, with no official parents. These children could possibly been exchanged for knowledge and technology of the Greys.**

Ramon immediately thinks of the Nazi Lebensborn project to make a new race of humans. Is a similar project still active? Jesus! It could make sense because nobody will miss these children. They are perfect victims to be manipulated.

1.481 **Some humanoids can be descendants of the Wise People that were left behind by the Ancients. They are incredibly intelligent and in general they have high functions in state departments, universities or secret projects. They can be used as Monoms. But not every humanoid is under the spell of the Greys. Only those with a G-implant and a second nerve system are under control of the Greys.**

Thanks, Teimon. That clarifies a lot, even if it is disgusting.

Did some of your people use the natural star gates in the past to visit the Earth on a regular basis? They are open every nine hundred years, no?

1.482 **The Téry who visited the Earth came only for a short visit, except when they decided to stay. That was their free**

choice. The natural star gates are only open during a sort period. But in general, they came back to Ter I. The colony of the Wise People decided to stay and live their life on Earth. They were men and women and lived in the colony on Antarctica. That was their free choice. In our civilization, everybody has the freedom of choice. Nobody is forced to do anything. It would be a good idea to put that mentality into practice on Earth.

1.483 **The children and grand children of the Wise who stayed behind fell in love with people of Geya. Their descendants finally merged with the human population. In the end, we are just humans. Do not ever forget that.**

The descendants of the colony on Antarctica are what you call humanoids. These descendants have in general a strong sense of telepathy. Some of them are abducted but the majority is still free. They will be the first to understand the importance of the information in this book.

Ramon is feeling as if turned inside out. It is all interesting and it answers many questions, but at the same time it is also freaky and terrifying.

Ramon, can I have a cup of coffee?

Of course Mira, right away. I will be back in a minute. In a hurry, he goes to the kitchen and makes a new hot pot of coffee. The soup smells delicious. Back outside, he fills the mugs and wants to continue the session.

Do you still have contact, Mira?

Yes, Ramon, but the pressure in my head is increasing again. By the way, Teimon told me something strange when you were in the kitchen. I don't know. It is so weird.

Please tell me, Mira. Is it about the disease?

No, Ramon. It is something completely different. I don't know if it should be published. But I will tell you anyway.

1.484

1.485

1.486

Ramon is perplexed. That was the last thing he needed. He remembered this traumatic accident very well. At the same time, he sees that Mira is exhausted.

Let's quit, Mira. I think this is enough for today.

412

Mira translates Ramon's message.

1.487 We are safe for the moment. We will make contact as soon as possible. Don't forget synchronicity. We salute you.

While Ramon writes the last information, Mira comes out of her trance.

Jesus! That was once again a marathon. Did you get everything, Ramon?

I did my best, Mira.

For a while it is silent. Ramon puts the pen on the table.

My God, Mira. What Teimon told us really makes me sick you know. What a world!

Tell me about it, Ramon. What a world indeed!

By the way, Mira. Speaking of synchronicity, shall I show you what I found about this strange Morgellons disease? It is exactly as Teimon said.

Please Ramon, have mercy on me. Give me a break, please. You know what, Ramon, I'm hungry. Have you eaten?

Some bread in the morning. But the soup is almost ready. I smell it. Don't you?

Indeed, Ramon. Great! Then I will get us a pizza and a bottle of wine.

That is a good idea, Mira. Meanwhile, I will prepare the table.

Till late at night, they discuss everything Teimon said and Ramon found on the web. It is a full moon and the night is warm and pleasant. The moon stands high at the night sky when Mira prepares to leave.

One thing I know for sure, Ramon. You have to hurry with the book.

Ramon agrees.

That's clear, Mira. But I am a bit worried. This information is so sensitive, I don't know how to get it on the market.

That will become clear, as soon as it is ready.

Well yes, I guess so.

As Mira goes to her car, Ramon thinks of something that made him wonder.

It is so strange, Mira. But in recent months, a lot of websites about UFO related topics have become pay sites.

As if it is all commercialized, you mean? I'm not surprised. Business as usual, Ramon?

Exactly, Mira. There is a danger that the most popular sites are gradually becoming part of an ever growing hierarchy. How shall I put it? Did you know that most pop music festivals are now owned by one multinational? These festivals all started as individual projects. That was their charm. But now they come under the guidance of one multinational. This group can determine which groups are promoted. In this way, it becomes a boring and predictable happening. The same can happen to these UFO sites. Topics can be promoted or rejected.

I understand what you mean, Ramon. But that is happening in the world of business all over these days. I know everything about that.

Relaxed she jumps into the car.

You are right, Mira. But it is not the money you have to pay that annoys me. It is becoming increasingly more difficult to check the news items they are spreading. It becomes a closed group. And it wouldn't surprise me if these sites would become part of a new hierarchy, controlled by one or the other secret society.

Or that secret Sean Leyka sect, Ramon.

That's what I thought too, Mira. But you know, let them play their games. We will find out eventually. Once the book is out, we will see what will happen. I would like to see the faces of the Initiated if they read what Teimon told us and realize that it is not they who are playing games with the stupid masses, but that the Greys are playing with them. Those involved will be the first victims of the Greys, once the invasion starts.

That's what I think too, Ramon. The same thing happened on Ter I. But also for the innocent victims, the Mentals and the Psy-mutants, it will be a shock as soon as they realize that they will be the first victims when the disease gets epidemic proportions. A lot of people don't even know that they are implanted.

I know that all too well, Mira. It must be a tragedy to find out what is really happening.

Ramon sees that Mira is very concerned.

The Greys will not care for the suffering of their victims, Ramon. The only thing they care about is making our planet their own. They are taking their time. Because at the moment, they think they are superior. For who will stop them?

Indeed, Mira. But let them think just that. They don't know that

414

the Sheyan found a way to get the information out. And the Sheyan are coming! Isn't that great! Who knows, maybe they will bring a visit. Ha, ha.

Yes, Ramon. Just imagine. Ha, ha. Then I wouldn't be that critical anymore about everything that happened to me. Whatever, I hope they will succeed to get here on time to be able to stop the Greys. But now I have to go. My day starts early.

Of course, Mira. Good night. Look how beautiful the moon is today.

Together, they look at the cosmic scenery of the night sky, so common and at the same time so extraordinary. When Mira drives away, Ramon waves her goodbye and goes to bed. Before he falls asleep, his last thoughts go to the book.

Finish the book, Ramon. The book must be finished as soon as possible.

- 65 -
10/8/2007

Time passes by and the book grows each day. Everybody is on holiday and Ramon has all the time to spend on the book. Joy is happy that Ramon tapes the most important soaps. It is already ten o'clock in the evening and Ramon decides to take a break. He turns the volume of the radio up and soon the soup and the rice are boiling. The sound of a new mail interrupts his cooking ritual and he runs to the WebCom. Always when I'm busy, he thinks.

A message from Mira. Do you have time? Urgent!

Yes... I'm cooking... Come over... coffee is ready.

In her typical quiet style Mira enters the kitchen. The coffee is ready and Ramon immediately serves a fine mug for his special guest. She looks well and reassures Ramon that she hasn't had any problems with the Greys. Since she has contact with these creatures, Ramon always worries about what could happen.

Thanks for the coffee, Ramon, that's just what I need. And how is the book?

Good Mira, it is still a work of trial and error but it's getting to the point to become a real story.

That's good, Ramon. I don't know where you find the courage.

Oh Mira, it is just a job. The only thing that I miss is my design work. I would like to start making the sculptures. But the book has priority at the moment. And how is our friend Teimon? I see from the look on your face that there is information coming?

How do you know, Ramon? For days the pressure is back again. But I couldn't make time, Ramon. It is as if everybody needs me. But the business deal can be made any day now.

Then I will help you with that pressure. What must Teimon be thinking about those alien humans who put their work first? But anyhow, he must be used to it by now.

Quickly, Ramon takes his notes and tries to come up with some questions. The reality of the Wise People in the past fascinated him. He must know more about them. To understand the humanoids better, he has to know as much as possible about the colony that stayed behind.

Teimon, can you tell me more about the Wise Men?

While Ramon waits for an answer, Mira enters the realm of the purple skull. Once at the other side of the gateway, she immediately recognizes the voice of Teimon. His voice sounds very clear and she feels that Teimon is much more relaxed.

1.488 The Wise Men are the Ancients that stayed behind on Geya. The rising water of the sea, after the last ice age, had a devastating effect on some of the great cultures of Geya. The floods caused large migrations of human populations worldwide. Large parts of land became islands and other regions became sea.

1.489 Before the end of the last ice ages, all shamanistic cultures knew the essence of the code of the Ancients, the ethics and some basic principles of reality. They where given during the first contact. The shamans passed the secret knowledge on from generation to generation. We know from certain myths that the Aboriginals, the Mauri and the Dogon still knew the code when the Ancients arrived the second time. But there may be more. We just don't know exactly.

1.490 The Ancients brought the Uhr code back to Egypt, Europe and China during the second contact, because these cultures had lost the basic principles from the first contact. In the numerous wars between the different human groups,

caused by large migrations, lots of shamans were killed and because there was no written language, the chain of their tradition was broken. Large populations were subjected to the survival of the strongest and risked to go down in mutual conflicts.

Ramon didn't expect such an answer. It fits well with what he knows about prehistoric times.

1.491 **The dangers of the abuse of power were very real and the Ancients decided to spread their cultural code in part over the problematic cultures. The Wise took care of teaching the code to the priesthood.**

1.492 **Egypt got the hieroglyphs and the key to the star map.**

1.493 **China got the I Ching and the images of the maps from the Ancients.**

1.494 **The old European civilization got the rune symbols.**

1.495 **The key of the I Ching can be found in the rune symbolism. The star map can only be understood with the images hidden in the Chinese pyramid. All these cultures got the pyramidal social model as a tool to solve the problem of concentration of large human populations**

So the Wise Men were a kind of instructors. They had an educational task. They had to educate these three cultures about the information that was lost or misinterpreted?

1.496 **Yes, but you have to understand: we only know of these three cultures. There may be more. The Wise Men knew that they had to be careful and taught these three cultures one segment of their own code. It was sufficient enough to get them again on the right track, without using excessive violence or punishment. But the knowledge they gave was not enough to find the complete code. To succeed, the different cultures had to work together in peace.**

Ramon has to think immediately of Nicolas Tesla. He did the same thing with some of his inventions. Afraid, that his inventions would be misused by one power, he spread his findings over several power centers of his period. Ramon wants to know as many details as possible.

Can you tell me some more details about the work of the Wise Men, Teimon?

1.497 **It was a process of centuries. It all happened after the** second contact with the Ancients, some 6,000 years ago. During their first contact, 10,000 years ago, the Ancient made only physical contact with a civilization in South America. But during the second contact they spread the code.

1.498 Or chronicles tell us that they first went to Egypt. The existing priesthood was educated by the Wise in the secrets of geometry and architecture and the basics of written language.

1.499 After that, the Wise Men went to China where they educated the priests-shamans about the fundamentals of the I Ching. They also gave the Chinese the pictures of the star map.

1.500 The last ones to visit were the Celtic people. The druids got the runes and their symbolic meaning.

1.501 The runes are essential to understand the basics of the I Ching and the hieroglyphic system. These cultures are therefore interconnected by their code and can educate one another.

1.502 To find the way to our planet Ter I, mental as well as physical, and to understand the function of the purple skull, you have to combine the geometry of the shaft with the images of the Chinese temple room.

1.503 To understand the symbolic meaning of the Egyptian hieroglyphs and the I Ching, you need the rune symbols. Together, you have the basis of the cultural code of the Ancients. This code is also the basis of the code of the Caret device.

Wait a minute, Mira. I take the drawings. Then you can explain to me what Teimon means. It is getting a bit confusing, you know.

Mira looks again at the fantastic drawings. One of the drawings gets her full attention. This is the one I need, Ramon.

1.504 The symbols are part of the code of the Ancients. This part of the devise is a kind of travel coordinator. It enables you to program the coordinates of the road you want to travel in space. For example, the road of the star map.

You mean an interstellar GPS system, Mira?

Yes, something like that. Look, Ramon!

1.505 This part of the series of symbols was given to the

Chinese and is related to the I Ching. But this part of the symbols was brought to Egypt. You must understand, Ramon, the code of the Ancients is not only a technical thing.

I think I understand, Mira. The technical meaning is only one part of the code. It has a philosophical, a scientific and a technical meaning.

Exactly, Ramon. That is what Teimon means.

1.506 **The Uhr code has different layers of meaning. In the Caret device, the code is used to handle a space ship. But the code can also be used for a multitude of other things.**

I would conclude that the code of the Ancients is their world-view!

1.507 **Yes, says Mira seriously. You can compare it with the I Ching, but more complex and more complete. A part of these symbols can be understood with the knowledge of the I Ching. Another part can be understood with the help of the hieroglyphs and again another part with the help of the runes.**

1.508 **That is enough for the book, Ramon. The rest is for specialists of the different codes, once they would work together.**

Gradually, Ramon gets a better understanding what Teimon means with the code of the Ancients. He still has a lot of questions, though. As well as he can, he writes everything down, while Mira comes out of her trance.

Can you tell me something more about this symbol, Mira?

No Ramon, the contact is broken. Sorry.

What a pity. But God knows what situation they are facing at the moment. But at least I have some insight in their way of thinking.

Together they go back to the kitchen and the mugs are filled again.

Mira, with this information, the function of the Wise Men becomes clearer, also from a historical point of view. They had to restore the equilibrium after the chaotic ice ages. Every culture was given advice, based on what was lacking due to the chaotic past. They had their bases on Antarctica and from there they made excursions to help humanity to get back on track. I wonder if it is possible that the Wise Men used the pyramids to get in touch with the Téry or the Ancients.

That could be, Ramon. The pyramid of Cheops is structured like the purple skull. The shafts include the code of the purple matrix. That's what I thought too, Mira. Maybe a small group of Initiated used this pyramid to keep contact with them. I always have found it strange that such a large structure was built with relatively small rooms and hallways. By the way, the pyramids were not invented in one day. It was a learning process of many centuries. Cheops was the last phase, and after that suddenly the Valley of the Dead was chosen to become the burial place of the pharaohs. It could be that the Wise helped and advised the architects of the pyramids. But always based on trial and error. And not alone about technical matters but maybe more importantly, on the level of organization as Teimon said. I know a lot of myths from the time I was studying at the mystery school. The largest cultures all had a mythological part of their own history. They all have myths about a period that the gods were living on Earth. The gods came from the stars and brought knowledge to the people. Erich von Däniken was one of the first to take these myths seriously. In general the theories of alien contact in the past are laughed away as unscientific.

But if the Ancients were humans like Teimon describes them, then it all becomes plausible. Van der Leeuw, a Dutch scholar and phenomenologist who studied religion, described extensively that the first rulers of the large cultures were a kind of priest-kings. They were the highest shamans and had a lot of power. You can find them in the Old Testament. People like Tubal Cain, the father of the blacksmiths, or Methuselah. These mythological figures got very old. But also in China, you find legends of similar god-like creatures that lived before the emperors and became very old. Only later, the task of the Emperor was divided over a worldly and a spiritual leader.

Do you know that the emperors of China wrote the I Ching themselves? So the emperors were very well educated scholars. They were initiated in the code of the I Ching. They were not only the head of the power structure but also of wisdom and philosophy. The Ancients probably had contact with these priest-emperors, ruling the country before the emperors and pharaohs of the Chinese and Egyptian culture took over. If the second

420

contact was around 4,000 BC, then it is all plausible. In that period, the first hieroglyphs were designed, the first Chinese pictographs are from that period and the first runes were designed. Mira, have you any idea what happened afterwards with the Wise?

The contact is broken but Aodin has sent some additional information.

1.509 The oldest gods were the names of the first generations of Wise Men. Some daughters of the human aristocracy were selected by the priests to become pregnant with the genes of the Wise Men. Their sons and daughters became the generation of the pharaohs and got the top functions of the social pyramid. Because of their protective environment, these children could evolve to the highest of the human abilities. But the boys were attracted by power and wanted more and more power once they became emperors.

1.510 Gradually, the emperors and pharaohs concentrated all power around them. The priests became second in power and the descendants of the Wise died or went away.

1.511 The pharaohs and emperors became the descendants of the gods or Wise Men. They knew they were different. The pharaohs had a status of being descendants of the gods. The priesthood remained very important because they had received the teachings from the Ancients. They memorized and protected the records of the teachings of the Wise Men.

1.512 It went wrong when the priests came under full authority of the rulers. The pharaohs and emperors became more and more involved in keeping and increasing their power and forgot the ethical aspects of the code. Secretly, the priesthood protected the manuscripts of the teachings of the Wise to prevent them from being destroyed. Lots of manuscripts were written and hidden, to protect the knowledge. Only the priests could read, so all knowledge was in the hands of the priests.

1.513 This scenario happened in every culture that was visited by the Ancients in a different way, also in the European region. The families who were genetically altered became the rulers of the important cultures of the world. They protected their lineage by marrying within the families.

They knew they had to do that to keep something in the family. They thought that is was the blood but we know that is was the genetic make-up.

That's exactly what I thought a few weeks ago, Mira. So that means that the nobility is still the keeper of the genetics of the Wise?

I guess so, Ramon. But how it all fits, I don't know. I can guess but I don't like to do that. I don't want to invent things, you know.

You're right, Mira. It is a process over such a long time. Numerous things have happened. The base of the Wise Men on Antarctica has vanished under the icecap. So at a certain moment, they couldn't go back there and so they were forced to live with the humans and finally integrated completely with the human population, becoming the humanoids. In this way, the genetics of the Ancients was also spread under the general population.

Some of them probably went back to Ter I with the help of the natural star gates. But I am not sure about that., Ramon.

Ramon has so many questions. But he realizes that filling in all the details is too complex a task.

Well Mira, in whatever way it happened, to a lot of researchers it is interesting stuff to take into consideration and to look at myths in a different way. Specialists have to figure that out. Maybe the world civilizations didn't have physical contact after all. But if their basic codes have mutual links, then that proves that an extra-terrestrial civilization had contact with humanity in the past. And that's really fascinating, don't you think? If you know the history of the pyramids worldwide, you know the history of the involvement of the Ancients in human history. It is as simple as that.

Mira's mobile phone interrupts the discussion and while she answers the call, Ramon goes outside.

Ramon, I have to go. It's a co-worker of mine. I let you know if anything happens, okay?

She jumps in the car and gone she is again. The full moon is very beautiful that night. Orion and the Pleiades are very bright.

How are my cosmic friends? Ramon wonders. Is something wrong? They abruptly broke contact. Or am I imagining things?

422

Or maybe Teimon didn't want to say more about the code.

Ramon thinks of the movie Lord of the Rings. How dangerous it is to know secrets. The meaning of the Ancient code is very delicate knowledge, especially if it is connected with the Caret project. Maybe it is better that I don't know too much about it, because that could stir up certain thoughts in some people. For them, the breaking of that code is of a high priority. But as long as the Initiated are working for the glory of the Greys, it is better that they don't get access to this knowledge.

While he closes the WebCom to go to sleep, Ramon thinks back on his Wise Teacher. He told about the 36 hidden tsadikim, righteous men, who keep the world turning. Also the Buddhists know legends of the 36 secret Buddhas. Are they descendants of the Wise Men? Are they the Guardians? Ramon goes to his bedroom, followed by the shadows created by the moonlight.

Waiting for sleep to come, he sees in his imagination how a pharaoh is walking with his wife over the holy road to a pyramid, followed by a long procession of beautifully dressed nobility and priests. They want advice from the gods about the daily problems of their society. Thousands of priests bow full of grace for the descendants of the gods. Only the high priests and direct descendants of the Wise Men are allowed to enter the pyramid together with the pharaoh couple. Once inside the pyramid, the pharaoh goes to the king's room and his wife goes to the queen's room and they both take place in the sarcophagus. Long, deep sounds of trumpets vibrate through the hallways of the pyramids and in no time the couple goes into a trance. The surroundings change in purple nebulas and with tremendous speed they tunnel through eternity until they hear a calm voice.

I salute those who can hear without sound. The Téry are at your service.

The priests ask questions and the descendants of the Ancients, in deep trance, answer them. Ramon falls asleep and only the moon sees his face, in his lonely battle against the Grey evil and a multitude of secrets.

The star ship of the Sheyan floats through the dark-blue-grey space while Teimon has contact with Mira. Suddenly Zeinia receives a signal from a nearby star and the session of Teimon has to be interrupted. The coordinates are programmed and in a fraction of time the space ship reaches the location of the beacon. In the distance, they see a very large space station, built by the Ancients. A gigantic transparent cube structure surrounds two large transparent tetrahedrons. They cross each other and the eight corner points are connected with the eight corner points of the cube. The point of crossing contains two large pyramids, pointing to the opposite direction. Together they form an octahedron. The seven Sheyan look with admiration at this construction by their forefathers. While their spaceship approaches the space station, the
whole scene becomes more than alien.

Suddenly, their spaceship is surrounded by a blue beam and automatically they are guided to a hexagonal tunnel to enter this gigantic space city via one of the eight corners. The hallway seems endless and around the transparent tunnel they see thousands of cube cells, connected in a spiral way. Once, this complex was inhabited by tens of thousands of people, but now it looks almost like a ghost town. Even Aodin doesn't know what happened here in the far past. All is still in perfect shape and it is as if it is waiting for unexpected visitors. They enter a large hall and the door of their star ship opens automatically. An evolographic, transparent, feminine appearance waits for them and greets them politely.

I am Féra. I'm your guide in this space ecodrome. The Ancients await you. Please follow me.

The Sheyan brothers take their coats and follow the fairytale creature that moves as a butterfly through the long hexagonal hallway. Féra speaks:

You are now protected by a halo that surrounds this space ecodrome. It makes telepathic screening impossible.

Elegantly she is moving through the hallway. Relieved, the Sheyan relax after months of concentration. The mood of the otherwise serious Sheyan changes instantly. They get a smile on their face and start to whisper to one another. Aodin, the eldest of the brothers, looks proudly at his pupils. A deep humming tone comes out of his small mouth, and together the Sheyan produce a mixture of Tibetan and Mongolian humming tones while they follow Féra who is floating in front of them. They arrive at a second hall and enter a pyramid within this large pyramid. Breathless they see how large this ecodrome really is.

Come, says Féra. Please stand on this platform. It will bring us to the center of the building.

They all stand on the platform and together they float into the very long hallway. The pyramid appears to be larger on the inside than on the outside. The walls are transparent and it is as if there is an atmosphere projected against the outside walls of the inner pyramid, as if they enter an artificial planet. Everywhere they look they see small ecodromes with plants and animals. At the end of the long tunnel, they finally enter the central hall of the space complex and the platform floats to the center. Then the platform moves straight upward to the top of the pyramid. The platform is halted and becomes part of the floor of a large pyramid shaped room. It looks like a futuristic meeting room and although nobody is there, they have the feeling that they are not alone. In front of them is a large round table and in the center of the wall, illuminated symbols of the Caret code radiate.

Please take a seat, says Féra. The Ancients will arrive soon.

The seven brothers take a seat at the table. Aodin is in the middle and Teimon on his right. Once seated, the room shines in a purple glow. Two figures appear at the other side of the table. They are both dressed in fluorescent material. The man has a long coat like the Sheyan but the color is red and the material is delicate. The woman has a coral blue coat. They clearly have human features, but their eyes are larger and beautifully shaped, similar to the eyes of the Sheyan.

They both have a high forehead and the skull is larger and slightly pointed on top. The man has long white, grey hair and a long beard while the woman has long, light blond, curly hair.

Welcome, says an inner voice in the minds of the Sheyan.

It is as if both Ancients speak with the same tongue. But it is the woman who is sending the information.

426

We are glad that you have stayed loyal to the code, dear Sheyan.
Aodin stands up straight and greets the representatives of the
Ancients with a gentle bow.
We, the Sheyan, greet you. I guess you have been informed that
we have serious problems. Forgive our forefathers the wrong
decision to create the Shi. Unintentionally, the ancestors of the
Téry brought our people and the people of Geya in great danger.
We know that you are in great danger, is the answer of the
Ancients. As soon as we discovered that somebody used the ark
of Ha Olam, we knew you were in great danger. Your leaders
didn't want to listen to the warnings of Teimon.
Both look at Teimon, who stands in silence next to Aodin.
Teimon, please explain to us what happened.
Teimon opens up telepathically and reveals what happened
during the Grey invasion. Teimon was as an extremely talented
Tulku and at the same time a Guardian of the Sheyan. He was
educated to check all decisions of the counsel of the people, by
consulting the code of the Ancients. As a wise and educated
scholar of the code of the Ancients, he warned The Council of
Hundred of his people that the Greys, who they call the "Shi",
were a great threat to the Téry. The signs of the code were clear.
The evolution of the clones had reached a dangerous point.
The code was clear about the Shi becoming a real threat, if the
Free-actives of the people would wear an implant to stay in
contact with the Shi. Originally, the contact was done by means
of telepathy. They knew that the Shi had developed a certain
sense of individuality. The G-implants would improve their
control and flexibility. But the Council of Hundred voted in
favor of the implants. Even Teimon's mother, head of the
council, known for her visionary abilities and the 101st member,
could not prevent the result of the voting, in favor of the
implants. The arguments against implants were not clear enough.
Neither Teimon nor she could foresee the fact that the Shi would
come into contact with the dangerous hallucinogenic substances
in the desert of Geya, although the signs of the code were clear.
There was great danger.
The Ancients listen and experience Teimon's story mentally and
sense that Teimon has the feeling that he has failed.
I should have known it, he thinks. A tear flows out of his eyes

and he remembers the horror of the execution of his mother by the cruel Shi. He remembers that she refused to surrender herself to the Shi dominance. She was too strong to be manipulated and so she was beheaded without hesitation. Teimon was hiding in her house when the Shi captured her and saw it all happen. He could not do anything to prevent it. Trying would mean suicide.

The Ancients see the disappointment and sorrow of Teimon, because the council of hundred underestimated the warnings of the Ancient code.

We fully understand you, Teimon. You are not to blame. The Free-actives wanted to lead their people as soon as possible to Earth to be united again with our people. Impatience is a human quality. Impatience banned the humans from Para Deus. On Geya they call it paradise. But by impatience you will not return to Para Deus. For you Sheyan, it is important to believe that everything will be all right in the end. The code will show you the way. Seek and you will find a solution. This space Ark will help you to take the next step. There is plenty of water here. Teimon! You are the only one that has opened the first level completely. You live an unselfish life. Only the unselfish are able to interpret the code in the right way and don't misuse the knowledge it contains. Don't be disappointed by the Free-actives and leaders of your people. They made mistakes with the best intentions. To help you in your fight against the Shi, we have prepared Mira. She will know the code intuitively when the need is there. She is…

…a bit obstinate, Teimon thinks.

They all get a smile on their faces.

But she is a good soul, continue the Ancients. Ramon knows about her inner struggle and convinces her to continue her extraordinary task. The humans on Geya are ready for change. But the dark forces of the past try to prevent this change by all means. The golog ruler of the Shi makes use of the selfishness and the desire for power that still rules the lineage of the Warriors. But they brought themselves and humanity as a whole in great danger. If nothing changes, the Shi will proceed with their programmed desire for control. But the book of Ramon we will break the spell of the Grey and disturb the strategic scenario of the Shi. If the truth becomes public on Geya, the Warriors will

428

go down with the Shi if they don't refuse further cooperation with the Shi. But if the Warriors refuse further cooperation with the Shi and allow bringing the different codes together guided by the Guardians, then the world can be saved. All the codes together reveal the code of the Ancients and this gives the humans the knowledge to defeat the Greys in alliance with you, dear Sheyan. We are also not free of mistakes. We didn't foresee that the fusion of our DNA with the human DNA would enhance the desire for power of the rulers. But we can't go back in time. There is no way back in time. There is only a back to the way. The book is almost finished and it will find its way to those involved and those who understand. Synchronicity is the greatest power in the universe. Therefore, do not doubt.

Teimon sits down and Aodin resumes the telepathic communication.

We, the seven brothers of the Sheyan, will not doubt. Thank you for your providence. We understand that we have to solve the problems, caused by our predecessors, ourselves. We are glad to see that you are still alive and well. We haven't heard anything from you for millennia and we and the Téry in general thought...

...that we had died in a catastrophic incident? No, no, dear Aodin. We are the protectors of life in our part of the galaxy. Certain parts of the spiral arm undergo terrible catastrophes and we have to do anything to protect any planetary evolution of life as much as possible. Billions of planets are at risk and the only thing we can do is to protect the fertile planets as much as we can. This space Ark protects numerous life forms of different evolutions that had to be saved from disaster. We seek planets where they can continue their evolution. Protecting the life on any fertile planet is a holy duty to us. We see it as our task to protect all life forms, because all life forms have a soul. The knowledge and wisdom of the code makes us mentally strong to proceed with our galactic mission. The technology of the code gives us the means.

Our ancestors left you on Ter I because we are no Gods. We too are mortal. You were our safeguard in case something unforeseen would happen to us. But you will become like us, together with the humans, if you remain loyal to the code and learn to live together and evolve. You will become like us, keepers and protectors of life in this inscrutable universe, the body of the great source. If something happens to us, you have to continue our task. The more civilizations master the code, the greater the chance that life will survive. Soon you will land on Geya and make a front with your far descendants against the block cultures of the Shi. The struggle against the Shi will unite you with the people of Geya. We salute you, dear Sheyan.

The silhouettes of the Ancients start to shine brighter and brighter and the friendly faces give the Sheyan a feeling of compassion, pride and unconditional love. Both wave to the seven brothers who respond to this universal gesture, while the Ancients become pure radiant light. In a rainbow of colors they disappear.

The Sheyan are silent and feel a strong unifying power. The pretty voice of Féra asks her guests to follow her to another room. They are surprised when they see the table full of green vegetables and fruits. They hang their coats over the stylish chairs and enjoy the wonderful meal. They are surrounded by a holographic scene of their home planet and hear the sounds of the sea and animals they have missed for so many years. The brothers feel at home and when Féra later shows them the way to their ecodrome, they feel again strong and motivated to take the next step of their mission. The smell of the plants gives them so many memories of their home. They realize how important it is to succeed in their mission. They lie down and in no time they sojourn in their inner world of rest and relaxation, while their bodies regenerate from their past privations.

- 67 -
16/8/2007

All day long restlessness dwells in Mira's mind. She is very glad when the last pro bono client leaves the house. Relieved that she has the house to herself, she prepares a meal and with some green vegetables, fruits and a strong mug of coffee she goes to her comfortable bedroom to relax and then sleep. Through the window she sees the crescent moon. After the light meal, she lies down on her bed in the hope that sleep will take her mind away

430

into the world of dreams. But a light grey nebula surrounds her and suddenly two Greys appear in front of her bed. Mira is as angry as surprised. They want to start a communication but Mira refuses any attempt by neglecting their presence as if saying: I'm not interested in you in any way. Suddenly, a purple nebula fills the room and the two Greys try to escape. But Mira follows them mentally.

Before she knows what is happening, she's inside a kind of craft, together with the Greys. The Greys are seated at the control panel and nervously they try to activate the craft. Mira looks intensely at their actions and monitors their mental signals attempting to get control over the craft. Sending mind signals through the meridians of their fingers, connected to the side of the armrests, they move a cylindrical device in front of them. Different rings, accurately encoded with symbols and markings, are moving in a circular way as if they are programmed for a trip into space.

Mira realizes very well what the Greys are up to. Different colors radiate rhythmic from the control panel. A strange vibration runs through the vehicle and the craft is ready for take off. Mira feels intuitively that she has to act now. The Greys can't prevent Mira from taking over the command of the ship. Powerless, the Greys watch how she changes the coordinates of the flight using the intuitive knowledge of the Caret code. The rings move precisely in the opposite direction. Mira feels that the ship starts moving. The Greys want to prevent the intervention but they are paralyzed and have no control whatsoever. The code is activated and they can no longer change anything. With great speed, the craft moves forward and the Greys aren't able to do anything. As fast as lightning, the craft moves in the direction of the moon where it crashes on the grey surface.

Mira sees it all happening and doesn't understand it. It is as if she acted as requested, without knowing what the purpose was. Suddenly, she is back in her room and the purple nebula radiates intensely with deep tones on the background.

She hears the familiar voice of Aryein.

1.514 **The code of the Greys is temporarily disturbed. You did the right thing, Mira. The way is open for the Sheyan.**

1.515 **The artificial star gate of the moon will be temporary**

free of the interference of the Greys.

1.516 The golog has no choice. He has to bring himself in safety on Geya with his Grey colony. We thank you. I salute you.

Gradually, she comes out of the trance and wants to leave her bed. But all her energy has gone and before she knows, she falls in a deep sleep, as if nothing has happened.

But on the moon there is great distress. The reversal of the code has spread through the Grey network on the moon with the speed of telepathy. All the installations malfunction and the last active tower and star beacon on the moon start to load up energy. An ominous vibration trembles through the hundreds of meters high tower and can be felt in the deep underground base of the Greys.

The golog knows that they have to leave the base as soon as possible. The normally disciplined members of the Grey block culture gather chaotic in the large hall. A large long cylindrical mother ship is activated and floats to the base where it hangs stationary over the dome. It falls apart in hundreds of silver blue-grey discs and they descent into the crater. The large platform is in no time filled with discs and the Greys run group wise to their vehicles.

The golog enters the hall, protected by his royal household. He is clearly angry. The normally neutral expression of his face is as a thundercloud in the blue sky. He passes some telepathic commands to a group of Greys. The humanoids and hybrids are brought to a few special discs. One by one, the discs float upwards and reassemble in a gigantic mother ship. When everybody is logged into the collective ship, an intense glow surrounds the mastodon. Gradually the mother ship makes speed and flies away into space, direction Earth.

The tower is now in full action and starts to glow. Fortunately for anybody, the moon has only a weak atmosphere otherwise the sound would be unbearable. The vibrations of the tower spread through the whole moon surface and the lonely seismographs of the Apollo mission, on the other side of the moon, go mad. The large crystal at the top of the tower starts to glow and suddenly, with enormous power, a beam is released into space.

The seven Sheyan are informed by Féra about the intervention of Mira. Extra information is given to Aodin during the meeting.

432

After a short telepathic warning, Féra brings them back to their ship. They leave the space Ark and Zeinia takes his seat behind the super-futuristic control panel. Aodin gives the last instructions. They all take place in the upper compartment of the ship. Together, they make a deep sound and all slip away into a deep sleep. Zeinia makes the control panel ready and programs the last instructions to be prepared to capture the coming signal. The light beam of the crystals inside the tower finds its way through the Neet and suddenly the instruments in the Ark move by itself. Zeinia follows all the changes with the utmost attention and the moment that everything comes to a rest point, he mentally corrects the device via the central ring. The ship is radiating light and the color shifts over the rainbow colors and suddenly as a light beam, the ship disappears into space to enter the Neet.

The space Ark shines in the dark grey blue space, lit by the giant bluish star, waiting for the moment that the Ancients find locations to give the living creatures a new chance to evolve.

– 68 –
26/8/2007

A tired man is sitting in front of his computer screens. Satisfied Ramon scrolls through the text and sees that the book is almost finished. A few chapters and the basic work will be done. Sitting in front of a computer screen non-stop for weeks is not his favorite occupation. He sees the empty mug and takes a break. He remembers the good things of life as he passes a poster that he made after the last music festival. Two weeks have passed since those fascinating days of light beams and sound beats.

Impassion
Light beams
Rhythmic sounds
In paintings of light
Together wonder
In the unknown
The new

Out of rags
Of past dreams
Searching for the spirit of our times
So far away and so close by
Found in everybody
With you in me

It has been as always a special music experience and for a while Ramon could forget the sorrows, hidden in the secrecy of his own mind, as long as the book was not published. While enjoying the music, a few text messages of Mira brought him back to the alien reality. She is as unfathomable as... I am, he thought. He had no clue what to make of it. But after that, no trace of her.

Ramon makes a fresh pot of coffee and for a moment, he takes a seat in the kitchen, where he had so much alien inspiration for his artistic projects. With a few clicks, he scrolls through the memory of his battered mobile phone looking for the messages.

19/8/2007 I have changed the Caret code. Aryein says: Kwania Kabal. The Grey zone is open.

The second message is as incomprehensible as the first.

26/8/2007 Teimon said: on 9/20 we will arrive on Geya's satellite, on 27/9 we will land in the red sand of Geya in the vicinity of the rock.

How can that be? During the last contact, Teimon said that it would take four years to reach Earth and now they will arrive in a month or so? Ramon doesn't get it.

The only thing he could do is add it to the notes. Imagine that the Sheyan would really arrive on Earth. That would be a cool finishing point to end the book. For what will be the end of the book? Or is there no end?

In his free time, Ramon surfed on the web to stay informed about any breaking news related to the UFO files. Various websites were still debating whether the Greys were dangerous or peaceful. Well, after this book, opinions will change, Ramon thinks. This book will be like an information explosion in the UFO community. Ramon didn't like it a bit that a lot of UFO sites became pay sites. Why should we pay for disclosure? Or are some of these websites direct or indirect under control of the

434

Sean Leyka?

Ramon was happy to find the site of Jerry Pippin. It contained a lot of interviews, which could be listened to for free and every day Ramon listened to several interviews of important UFO investigators. Ramon was astonished to hear one UFO researcher talk about the problems to get a UFO story into the media. He stated that there is a group that decides which material will get media attention. It proved Ramon's idea that the UFO community is partly controlled by secret organizations. Could this organization have links with the Sean Leyka group? It could very well be because Sean Leyka has to come forward in one way or the other. Maybe that's the way to recruit members and impose their view upon their members. Could it be that Sean Leyka had started a process to bring more and more groups together in a hierarchy? And if so, what have all these groups in common? Do they use the same organizational techniques that made the secret societies so powerful?

One thing was certain, a lot of these UFO groups will not like a bit what Teimon and Aryein have to say. Some groups pretend they know already what UFOs are all about. As if they know the big picture, based on what they think is really going on. For Ramon, it was important to know what they think and publish no matter whether it was right or wrong. It is the only way to figure out which kind of ideas could live in the circle of Sean Leyka.

So many questions had to be answered. What is the relation between this sect and the Warriors and not to forget, the organization of the Initiated once called the MJ 12? A few days ago an interview with Benjamin Fulford confronted Ramon in an unexpected way with everything he knew from Merly about the Warriors. Only, Fulford didn't make a distinction between the Warriors and the Illuminati.

It was the most remarkable interview he had ever heard. A Chinese-Japanese secret society used Benjamin Fulford, a professional journalist working in Japan, as a negotiator between this secret eastern group and the leaders of the top of the Illuminati of the USA to announce an ultimatum. It was also the first proof that other fractions exist having the same power in their countries as the Illuminati fraction in North America. So there was clearly a conflict between the different Warrior clans in the world. It proved that the Illuminati fractions use the Warriors to put their cards on the table.

Benjamin was clearly serious about his mission. What he told about the plans of the USA Illuminati fractions was unbelievable. For instance, they would plan genocide among the Asian population with the help of genetically manipulated diseases, like bird flu. He even suggested that the Illuminati in America had weapons to create earthquakes artificially. And why? Probably to reduce the power of the Illuminati of the Far East. The Illuminati clearly had a love-hate relationship to one another and the Warriors are ready to fight.

Is it just a game the Illuminati fractions play? Any way, the wishes of the Illuminati who control the Asian Warriors were very clear: stop these plans or we activate the members of our secret organization, located everywhere in the world, to take serious action before the plans of the American Illuminati can be put into practice. An army of 100,000 assassins will become active to eliminate the complete Illuminati family, to start with the top.

The human descendants of the Ancients are in a state of war. It made Ramon think again about the role the Warriors play in the Grey strategy. And although the chain of kings and emperors is broken in several cultures, descendants of these families have survived over the millennia. The descendants must possess enormous historical knowledge, power and capital, never revealed to their own civilians.

Could it be that the most powerful fraction of the Illuminati, the Rulers so to speak, wants to create chaos in those countries? In order to get control over the money system of the other fractions of the Illuminati? Then they could get control over the monetary system of the world. And that they need an extra Warrior to rule over the other Warriors? Is this what the thirteenth Warrior is all about? And who is he? A kind of Priest-king?

Could it be that the Rulers want to come in the open and take what is in their mind theirs, namely world power, with the help of the thirteen Warriors and in possession of Grey technology? It could be. The winner takes it all, as the Abba song goes. Doesn't Abba mean God in Hebrew? Are the Illuminati not the ones who think they are God? And one has to admit, to be the most powerful men in the world without anybody knowing about it is pitiful. If you have power, you want to show it. Ramon feels he is getting somewhere.

If the twelve Warriors have to obey a kinglike Warrior, they will surely want their piece of the earth's cake. The different regions would become different provinces of one world. This would mean one people, one empire, one supreme Warrior or dictator, controlled by the hidden Rulers. And would this be the role of the thirteenth Warrior? For if you want to rule the world, you have to impose a new religion that links all the religions together. Originally, the Guardians were the ones that took care of the different religions in the past. They where educated in the part of the code they got from the Ancients, which later became the basis of the different religions.

If I may believe Teimon, the common denominator in the mythology of the different religions is indeed the contact with the Ancients. But because the Warriors think that the Greys are the Ancients, they don't see the danger. Is that maybe where the Sean Leyka comes into the picture? Are they to create a religion that unites all mythology, with a leading part for the Greys and not the real Ancients?

If the twelve Warriors want to pretend that they are descendants of an alien race and that this belief is interwoven in the religion, then they need a religion that confirms their oldest myths. Is that what Merly suggested when he said that the thirteenth Warrior is in the making but that he is not yet ready? Do they want a kind of reinvention of the Priest-King? It isn't that impossible if you know that for example the leader of North Korea pretends to be a descendant of aliens. They have designed even an entire mythology to prove that. His power and that of his family is based on a legend he created himself and the people have to believe it. Ramon was convinced that the leader of North Korea was a Warrior. But wasn't the emperor of Japan also a descendant of the Gods?

A similar alien based religion could also work as a base for world domination. Such a scenario would fit perfectly in the strategy of the Greys, especially if the aliens in the past would be the same as the Greys of the present. That would open the way for the Greys to be accepted as godlike creature. It would be easy for the Greys, once they have regained power, to take over the business of the Rulers because the latter have no clue who the former are.

Seen from the point of view of the Rulers, a common religion would be the ideal tool to keep the balance of power between the circle of the twelve Illuminati fractions and their respective Warriors. It could very well be that Sean Leyka is to educate the thirteenth Warrior. But what nobody seems to know is that the leader of the Sean Leyka sect is under Grey control. So in this case, the Greys would have access to the central power of the Rulers via the Sean Leyka. To the Greys, the Sean Leyka would be a Trojan horse. First of all, Sean Leyka would have to inform and educate the world population about the aliens. A perfect way to do that would be with the help of a kind of mythology, a mythology that unites the myths of the different religions that exist on Earth. If the founder of the sect is a Psy-Mutant, it is possible that the Greys suggested him a mythology that can be used by the Greys to underline their role and importance in the collective history of humanity. That would be a perfect tactic to make sure that the agenda of the Greys would dominate the agenda of the Rulers.

Ramon sincerely hopes that the members and the top of this mysterious sect will read his book. They to have to be warned. For they themselves will become the first victims of the Grey conspiracy. God knows how far the Grey block manipulation has already penetrated their organization via Psy-mutants and Mentals. Ramon remembers the strange Morgellons disease. He shivers to think about what so many members of the Initiated and very probably also of the Sean Leyka sect will have to endure. Especially if they are implanted. You would even want to spare your worst enemy this kind of torture. Neither The Rulers, nor the Warriors nor the Initiated nor the Sean Leyka sect know the plans of the Greys. They just think they are on the brink of a new period in world history but instead play into the hands of the Greys.

Which game does the sect play now? How do they spread their tentacles over the word? And could it be that some of the whistleblowers, consciously or unconsciously, play their part in the strategy of this sect? It was very remarkable that some important whistleblowers confessed that they themselves were abducted. Dan Burisch in the first place, of course. But Ramon was surprised that also Steven Greer confessed in his latest book that he was abducted and had contact with higher dimensional beings. He was also a very strong defender of the view that the aliens he had contact with were very peaceful and kind. But Ramon was even more surprised when he saw the Camelot video of Robert Dean. He confessed in his last public interview with the people of the Camelot site that also he was abducted. And no matter how interesting everything was what he had to say, he was positive towards the aliens that abducted him. He thought it was very understandable that a superior race of aliens abduct people and do medical research on them. Because these "supreme" beings treat us humans like humans treat animals. If such important key persons of the UFO community are that optimistic about the alien presence, the "Grey" presence that is, then they play a key role in the strategy of the Greys without even knowing it. But please! Abducting people is absolutely unethical! No matter how far you are evolved.

It is as if the Greys have not only created a sect with the help of Mentals but also made sure that, although unaware, some Mentals became key persons in the UFO community in support of the strategy of the Greys. Even if the whistleblowers did not mention to have any relations with the Sean Leyka cult. Maybe they just don't know. It became clear to Ramon that the Greys work from the top to the bottom with the help of abductees but also from the bottom to the top with their chemical techniques. Ramon starts to understand the power of his book containing the testimonies of Teimon and Merly. It will reveal the hidden scenario of the Greys as well as that of the Rulers.

He fills his mug once more and sits down in front of his computer screens, when he remembers that the next episode of Bones will start. He quickly puts the tape in the recorder and thinks of Joy.

I hope she has a good time, wherever she is.

He suddenly realizes that he hasn't eaten yet. Quickly he goes to the kitchen and in on impulse, he turns up the volume of the radio. A fantastic soundtrack of Scream is playing and while he heats up the soup and vegetables, he finishes his meditation.

If the Rulers want to take world power, they must have a deadline. Could it be that the Rulers reached an agreement with the Greys about 2012? Or sooner? The Greys know that the natural gates will open soon. Maybe they fear that the Ancients will take this opportunity to bring a visit to earth. So it is of utmost importance that they control the Earth before the Ancients come back. And what to think about the disclosure of the UFO files? What kind of disclosure are we talking about? If the Initiated base their ideas on the lies of the Greys then it would be a disaster. It would be the disclosure of an even bigger lie. Aside from the Grey factor, it would be rather naive to think that those that kept the UFO files secret for almost a century now, would suddenly reveal the truth and nothing but the truth. The way things are at the moment, the disclosure will be carefully executed via a strict scenario, to protect everybody involved and to be able to guide humanity during the period of denial and traumatic shock. But with the Grey factor involved the disclosure will be the greatest manipulation exercise ever in human history. The Warriors will walk into the Grey trap with their eyes wide open. "Eyes wide shut", Ramon thinks with a smile: Stanley Kubrick's last message. Only the truth about the Greys can break that scenario. Humanity is lucky that Teimon could reach Mira in time.

At that moment the midnight news starts. Ramon is shocked when he hears that the computers of the governments of different countries have been attacked by hackers. Last week America, but now, the computers of France and Germany were attacked too. Everything pointed into the direction of China as the home of the cyber invaders. Ramon was really surprised. Could this be part of the warnings by the secret society that Fulford was talking about? Ramon is a bit confused by this strange synchronicity. While enjoying his meal, he contemplates about the synchronicity between the message of Fulford and all the information he received from Teimon and Merly.

More and more he realizes that the SOS message of the book has to be finished as soon as possible. Minutes later he is back in his WebCom and till late into the night he works on the SOS message for the world. The last chance to prevent the unspeakable.

After a day of writing, Ramon prepares some food. He enjoys his daily soup when suddenly the mobile phone rings in his WebCom. Who can that be at this hour?

Good evening Ramon, says a shy voice on the other side.

Hello Mira, that is a surprise. It has been a while since we met.

All kinds of excuses and explanations follow.

Mira… You don't need to apologize… Yes, you can come over …No it is not too late... The soup is still hot.

Half an hour later, Mira enters the kitchen and Ramon immediately serves the soup with some homemade bread. While enjoying the late meal, she describes her odd experience with the Greys and with growing surprise, Ramon writes it all down.

So if I understand you well Mira, you have disturbed the code of the Grey ship and that effected the whole Grey block on the moon?

Well yes, at least that's what I think. It was as if the changes I made affected the whole Grey community linked with that ship. Even the golog wasn't able to reverse the changes I made and they had to leave the moon. The commands did no longer work and they were afraid of an intervention by the Sheyan. But to be honest Ramon, I really didn't know what I was doing. I think the Ancients helped me during this action. I know it sounds crazy but that's what happened. I don't know how to describe it another way. It all happened on a mental level. It was all so… so unimaginable for my normal way of thinking. To be really honest, I thought that I was going insane. That's one of the reasons that I didn't dare to tell you this strange happening. I was exhausted the day after. My colleagues thought that I came back from a party or something like that. I was that miserable. Jesus!

Ramon laughs as he hears everything Mira has to tell.

I understand your reaction, Mira. What a situation!

Indeed, Ramon. What a situation! It is all so crazy.

It is not easy to understand the logic on a mental level. Gradually we should get used to these weird mental happenings. But anyhow, I don't understand quantum mechanics either. But what happened afterwards? Did you have contact with Teimon?

Yes. I sent you two messages. You were on a music festival, weren't you? The second one was a message from Teimon.

Yes Mira. Sorry, but I had to get away from my computers for a few days.

You're right, Ramon. I should do that myself, but my damn job won't let me.

The festival was just great, Mira. I can tell you, it was an alien experience when I received your messages surrounded by electronic music. So, tell me something more about these messages. If I understand it well, the Sheyan used the telepathic moon beacon to get here.

That's what they told me. It was a surprise for them too, you know. First the Sheyan will go to the moon and then they will come to Earth.

It's almost too fantastic to believe that they are traveling to Earth right now. But okay, why not? And where will they land? It appears to me that they will land in the desert.

The landing place is a secret, Ramon. They won't run the risk of a Grey intervention while landing.

I can understand that, Mira. So afterwards, you didn't receive any other information?

No, they are underway. But the last weeks I have a constant pressure on my head. But it is not real contact. It is as if they want to protect me.

From the Greys?

I guess so. The Greys were seriously panicking after the code shift. From then on, the Greys were around me for days.

Mira! This is serious, you know. What are they doing?

Well, nothing in fact. How shall I describe it? I know they are there but I don't see them. I think they just keep an eye on me. They wanted to know why I was doing what I did. But they can't break into my mind to figure out if I am the one in contact with Teimon. That's the reason why they try to disturb me mentally.

Excuse me, Mira. What do you mean with mental disturbance?

Well, the Greys suggested me the most awful ideas and pictures of myself and everybody I know. They even ridiculed my pro bono work. Can you imagine? And that went on day after day since my intervention of their code. It was very exhausting to shield them off. If they want to break me, then they don't know

442

who they are dealing with. Those Grey bitches. Believe me Ramon, if I get my hands on one of these Greys, he will wish he never met me. Do you understand now why I didn't come earlier? I was too exhausted. But yesterday they stopped their surveillance. And so here I am.

That is a relief, Mira. Don't get me wrong. I think it is great what you have done. But please be careful with the Greys. For you are the only contact with the Sheyan.

I know, but I can't help it. I know that I have to stay away from the Greys. But it is not up to me. Suddenly they were there. The only thing I had to do is to protect my link with Teimon. Teimon warned me that this could happen.

So Teimon knows about it?

Oh yes, Ramon. If you want to fight an enemy, you have to face him one way or the other. But the Greys are no problem if you know what they are. It is just very exhausting, that's all.

The world will once praise you for that, Mira. Now I start to understand why you knew intuitively so many details of the code. You needed the information for this intervention. And to say that it all began with Isaak, remember? It is as if synchronicity is everywhere. But now what, Mira? Will the Sheyan really come to Earth?

That appears to be the case, Ramon.

I can't believe it. It is so exciting. But let's wait and see. Just imagine that they would suddenly show up in my kitchen. Ha, ha.

I hope they like your coffee, Ramon.

Both start to laugh loudly.

Yes well, let's wait until they land safely, Ramon. I'm sure they will inform me as soon as they have landed.

But Mira, have you any idea what they will do once they are here?

I guess they will eliminate the golog by altering his mother code. He doesn't stand a chance against the Sheyan. And when he is changed, the other Greys will change automatically. The golog knows that very well. But now I have to go, Ramon. I have to get up early.

Okay, Mira. Thanks for passing by. I'm glad that I have seen you alive and well. But beware of the Greys!

They had better beware of me, Ramon. I guess they will leave me alone now. As soon as Teimon contacts me, I will let you know. If that happens, everybody at work has to wait.

I will keep on working on the book, Mira. And I will listen to the interviews of the Jerry Pippin show. It is always fun to listen to his interviews. He has a good sense of humor. I have listened to almost all the interviews now.

And was there anything of importance for the book?

No, not really. But he discusses any topic. He talks to most authors in the field of ufology. Listening to all the interviews is a good way for me to learn more about the background of the authors.

Then I let you work, Ramon.

And in a hurry she returns home to spend some time with her animals. After the traditional waving, Ramon activates all the programs and wonders about the Sheyan. Are they really coming? That would change everything. We will have to wait and see. Quickly he makes some fresh coffee and with a full mug and some slices of cake, he sits down in his WebCom.

The TV screen turns to a grey noise, meaning that the vcr has done its work. Joy will have a serious job to see all the videos when she comes back from holiday. Before he starts writing, he activates the next interview file and Jerry Pippin introduces the next guest. Wesley Bateman.

Never heard of him, Ramon thinks. Bateman lives a life in retirement and it appears to be his first interview. While listening, he learns that Wesley is a mathematician and physicist and he has even a few patents related to nuclear fusion technology. That immediately catches Ramon's attention. He is also the man behind a lot of ideas used in the TV series Star Trek, warp speed for example. He spent a considerable part of his life studying the Cheops pyramid.

After the introduction, Ramon gets the shock of his life. Bateman starts to discuss signals of alien origin, received by SETI in 1995. Ramon is so surprised that he forgets everything and listens for hours to all the interviews on the Wesley Bateman page. Could this be the final proof that alien signals have been received? The story of Wesley is very bizarre. He starts with explaining that in 1995 a site was published on the web with the

444

name "The Contact Project". Curious as he is, Ramon immediately wants to find out if the site still exists and indeed, there it is. It strikes him as strange that the logo of the site is made with the font that was developed during the Apollo project. The site pretended to be an educational site for students, to test their skills in decoding messages. Nine encoded parts of a message were published. Because it was presented as a game, these messages were allegedly from space. Anybody could participate. Strange that this site was still active after twelve years! Nothing had changed. The site is as a fossil of the beginning of the internet, accessible to anybody and still waiting until somebody can decipher the code.

Wesley Bateman tells how he got in touch with this site in 1997. After some intense study, he came to the conclusion that the code was too complex for students. In time he became convinced that the code was a real alien message and not a game, invented by some computer geek. Wesley thought that the organization that received the alien messages was not able to translate the code. And in search for help, they had decided to put the code on the web as a kind of game, named The Tau Ceti Con Game. The site stated that the signals were coming from the direction of the star Tau Ceti in the Cetus constellation. Wesley argued that this was done in the hope that those interested would give clues to help them decode the meaning of the signals.

Ramon can't believe what he is hearing. The code of the star map, the starting point of everything, now almost a year ago, is published on the web! Already a year, he had surfed the web day in day out to find any trace of the signals and now he is looking at the code. It took him by surprise and to be sure he is not dreaming, he downloads everything and copies it all in case access is denied later on, for whatever reason. Quickly, he sends a message to Mira.

Mira... I have found the code of the signals on the web... Try to make time as soon as possible... Ramon.

The next day, Ramon is fully concentrating on the breakthrough of last night. He still can't believe it. He listens again to all the interviews of Bateman and reads all the documents carefully, to get an accurate picture of everything Wesley could extract from the code on the Contact Project site.

"The Contact Project" site was part of the site "Lunar Institute of Technology". But also this site was put to silence. Ramon could hardly believe that the receivers of the signals put them on the internet just like that. And that the site wasn't taken from the internet since Wesley made his study public, now one year ago, was even more puzzling. Even the list with the participants wasn't removed.

Strangely enough, the solution of the encoded messages was never published. If it was a game, you could expect that the creators of the site would put the solution on the web, just to satisfy the participants. But no, nothing like that happened.

Wesley had studied the code extensively from 1997 on. He wrote a script of everything he had discovered. It could be downloaded on the Jerry Pippin site for free. Wesley found significant relations between the encoded signals and the construction of the Cheops pyramid. But there were also specific physical formulae only recently known by science. Wesley concluded that there had to be a lot of hidden messages in the code, waiting to be discovered. But because the actually received signals were not published on the site, it was possible that mistakes were made while making a transcript of the signals. So, his conclusion was that the code could also be a warning or even information about a future landing of aliens. But he could only guess of course.

My dear Wesley, you are closer to the truth than you could ever know. Ramon is so glad that he has found this interview with Wesley Bateman. Finally, he knows one person who would definitely be interested in the book. Wesley Bateman is the man to break the code and to uncover the star map information in the code. He knows the code published on the Contact site like nobody else. Ramon tries for hours to find any relation between the code and the star map but he gave up. The Contact site

446

published the code in nine different parts. The site stated that the signals were also received in parts. 30 January, 2 February, 7 February, 17 February, 24 February, 1 March, 9 March, 14 March and 1 April 1995. But Wesley pointed out that the signals could have been received at an earlier date. One by one, Ramon starts to read the comments of the participants of this so called Tao Ceti game.

Booh, says Joy while she enters the WebCom.

Joy! You almost scared me.

They both start to laugh. Her brown skin, blue eyes and a relaxed smile on her face show that she had a real good time.

Joy, you make my day. Please, come in. Don't look at the mess here. I will make a fresh coffee with some cake.

Joy sees the pile of videos and while Ramon makes the coffee, she interrogates him about the latest developments in "The Days of Our Lives". With a full mug of hot coffee, they both take a seat in front of the screens of the WebCom. She tells him everything that happened on her holyday, while she plays her favorite games.

I am glad that you had a good time Joy, while I was working on the book.

Oh yes. How is the book?

Well, I see a light at the end of the tunnel, Joy.

And what is this?

She points to the printouts of the code, scattered all over the place.

What is this all about, Ramon? All these characters?

Oh, it is a game that I found on the web. It is a code that is still not deciphered.

Attentively, she looks at the code.

Maybe it is the source code of a website?

I really don't know, Joy. To me it is Chinese.

Well, if it hides a website, then the first and last four letters mean HTML.

Is that so? says Ramon surprised. How do you know?

It is always that way, Ramon. Don't you know that? I thought you knew everything.

Both have to laugh.

Sorry Joy, but I really don't know anything about those things.

I'm joking, Ramon. I don't know much about it either. I don't like computer science. Those exercises are so boring.

Ramon tells her about all the bands he saw at the music festival and when Joy goes home a few hours later, the evening falls.

Don't forget to bring me some tapes, Joy. I'm almost out of tapes.

I will do that, Ramon.

And while she drives away, the car of Mira comes around the corner. They both go inside and a new pot of coffee is made.

Sorry, Ramon. I couldn't come earlier. But since I found your message this morning, I have felt constant pressure on my head. I think Teimon wants contact.

That would be great, says Ramon while serving the coffee. Maybe he can explain us more about the code, published on the web.

So you really mean it, Ramon? Is the code really published on the web? How is that possible?

I couldn't believe it either, but I found a site that published a code way back in 1995. I'm not sure if it is the code of the Téry. But it definitely could be the case. Wait, I will take the prints. Maybe Teimon can help us out.

Ramon gives her the prints and explains her who Wesley Bateman is. Meanwhile Mira starts to study the encoded message.

Take your time, Mira. I get my writing materials.

As soon as Mira looks at the written code, the kitchen becomes illuminated by a purple light. The crystal skull appears in all its brightness and before she knows it, she is in contact with Teimon. She starts to read the document "The Rods of Amon Ra and The Tau Ceti Con Game", with all the details that Wesley could subtract from the code. As Ramon takes a seat, he sees that Mira is in her typical lucent trance and it is as if Teimon reads the script together with Mira. As she arrives on page four, the first part of the code, she looks up.

Ramon, this is not right according to Teimon.

1.517 **This code is not correctly transcribed. Meaning, it is not written right. The interruptions of the different parts are not in the right place.**

But it is the code they have sent? Ramon asks excited.

448

1.518 **It is indeed the code we have sent. But those who received the message haven't done their work properly.**

1.519 **Those who transcribed the signals into symbols have based the encoding on the duration of the parts of the signal and not on the frequency of the tones. This was not intentionally done but out of ignorance.**

But then, how must it be divided? Can Teimon say something about that, Mira?

1.520 **We based the code on words. Every part is a word. It is just our alphabet. But it is also the basis of our vocabulary.**

It is just their vocabulary? Ramon has to shake his head. Unbelievable!

Mira, can you ask Teimon to explain it a bit better.

1.521 **Their alphabet is made up of words. The same words can have a different meaning, depending on the frequency of the tone. The parts in this first message are the words and the frequency determines the meaning of the words.**

Wait a minute Mira. Not too quickly. So the first part of the code is the part with the different words of their alphabet?

1.522 **Indeed. The first part is the alphabet. So the first part is the basis to understand the rest of the code. The 81 tones are the basis of their language. You can compare it with Chinese. The Chinese also use a system in their language where the tone determines the meaning of the word.**

Okay Mira, I think I get it. And where does the star map starts?

1.523 **The second part contains the information to design the basis of the star map, the square of twelve by twelve. In the following parts, you find the information of the different maps.**

1.524 **But because of the wrong interpretation, some of Wesley's interpretations are also not accurate.**

That's understandable, Mira. But to be concrete, can you ask Teimon to give an example.

With full attention Mira starts to read the code from beginning to end, while Ramon wonders what the answer will be.

1.525 **Look Ramon. The code starts with GBGG. That's the first word. GBGG means Geya. And at the end of part nine, you see GXGG. This means Ter I, their planet.**

That's logical, Mira. The star map starts on Earth and it ends on

Ter I.

Ramon remembers what Joy said about the beginning and end of the code and laughs. Clever girl! So the first and last four symbols are the beginning and end of the star map.

Mira, can Teimon show us the right division of the first part?

Very focused she starts to divide the first line of the code.

1.526 **GBG   GBBG   GBBBG   GBBBBG   GBBBBBG GBBBBBBG   GBHBBHBG   GBBHBBBHBG GBHBBBHBBG**

Should be:

GBGG BBGGBBB GBBBBGG BBBBBGGBBBB BGGB HBBH BGGBBHBBBHBG GBHBBBHBBG

It should be like that, Ramon. And here starts the part of the square of the star map.

1.527 **The basis of the star map starts on this line, the line with all the B's.**

GBBBBBBBBBBBBBPQCACQPBBBBBBBBBBBBBG

That is indeed remarkable, Mira. These are two lines of twelve B's. It could definitely have something to do with the square of 12 by 12. But to me it is still a riddle how to translate this code in a way to construct the star map.

Can I see the drawings of the Caviglia tunnel, Ramon?

In a hurry Ramon opens the file with the marvelous drawings of the Cheops pyramid. With the prints Mira tries to explain what she means.

1.528 **Look Ramon. That is the first stone of the Caviglia tunnel. The first part of the code is related to this stone. And the second part of the code is related to the second stone, and so on.**

Okay Mira. I got it.

Sorry that I can't be clearer, Ramon. It is hard to translate what Teimon says.

Mira, you are doing just fine. I don't think that we have to translate the code completely because it will not be that simple, I guess.

Wait a minute, Ramon. Teimon is saying something.

1.529 **Originally, there was a cube shaped stone box present in the Cheops pyramid. If Wesley would know of this stone box, then he should compare the markings on the stone box** with the tones of the code. Then he would have a good blueprint of the basis of the code. The box should still be there. But it is not known by the outside world.

1.530 The stars on the star map all have the same tone in the signals. If you know the tone of stars, you have to check whether that tone is followed by a different tone. The different tone is the indication to which one of the 72 maps the star belongs.

Ramon is really happy with all the information. The Ancients thought of everything. They took care that the true meaning of the tunnels in the Cheops pyramid could be found, one way or the other. Who is interested in a stone cube box with a few markings? The Ancients must have known that whoever would enter the pyramids afterwards, would only be interested in gold and jewels. But a worthless stone cube box? That would be left alone. Although that cube box hides the most precious treasure: the key to unravel the real meaning of the shafts.

And the relation with the cube in the Chinese pyramid?

Oh, that's funny Ramon. Do you know what Teimon says?

Tell me, Mira.

1.531 With the help of the stone box, Wesley can also check whether the code is a deliberate fraud by leaving parts out or even by changing small parts. Just to prevent that somebody would have access to the complete code. Teimon sees that the code on the web is very similar to the code they have sent but that some parts have been changed or removed.

1.532 But with the map of the tunnels and the information that you have received over the year, it must be much easier to decode the message we sent. If Wesley would receive all the information of the signals and the coordinates of the tunnels, then he could discover the physics of the Neet.

The Neet? Never heard about that! What is it, Teimon?

1.533 The Neet is a part of space, which we use for interstellar travel. The star map surrounds the natural Neet space that connects our planet with Geya. It is like a tunnel in space where the natural forces are different.

1.534 In interstellar space, there are lots of these Neet tunnels between star systems. Like superconductivity, there is no resistance in the Neet tunnels. But the Neet tunnels are more

powerful. These space tunnels are created between two natural star gates. If two natural gates are open at the same moment, they create a Neet tunnel and with our technology, the Neet tunnel is accessible.

That is really fantastic, Mira. Now I start to understand. Did you know that Wesley spoke about a strange optical effect? He stated that once you leave the gravitational field of the sun and enter the interstellar space, starlight will become invisible. So you would enter a complete dark space, because light is only visible when you are inside the electro-magnetic field of the sun or any other star. So he was occupied with interstellar space and the conditions there. He also invented the warp speed for Star Trek. That idea proves that he is thinking of such phenomena as the Neet. Isn't that incredible?

But there is more, Ramon. Wait a minute.

1.535 **Wesley would better use a number system with 12 number than the decimal number system. The duodecimal system works much better to calculate physical phenomena.**

1.536 **But now I have to go back in trance. It is good that you found the code on the web. It will make you mentally stronger.**

1.537 **There is an important thing you have to know. This is not the only code we have sent. We sent three signals. Not one. Probably, the people who received the signals wanted to find support by publishing the first message. Maybe hoping that somebody would come up with interesting solutions in order to help them to decode the two other messages.**

What? But, then Steven Greer was right after all. He told about three messages that were received by Seti, Mira.

1.538 **See you soon on the blue planet Geya. We salute you.**

Ramon is really flabbergasted.

Give Teimon my regards, Mira.

The contact is broken, Ramon. Gradually she comes out of her trance.

Jesus! I am really exhausted. Have you got some more coffee, Ramon?

Of course, Mira.

In no time, Ramon makes two fresh hot mugs and gradually they can relax from all the excitement.

452

And don't tell me that this is all your imagination, Mira. We have found the code. Isn't this great!

Yes, Ramon, I can't believe it myself. I must accept that I am really in contact with an alien. But Ramon, does this mean that we will have alien visitors in a couple of weeks?

It looks that way, no?

Ramon starts to laugh loudly on seeing the face of Mira.

They can always land in my garden. There is enough room there. And I have plenty of rooms in my house. When did they say they will land?

They will reach the moon on 20 September and Earth on 27 September. Do you really think they will arrive?

Well what am I to think, Mira? I guess so. It is too crazy to believe but just wait and see. But please let me know when they are here. I guess Teimon will let you know when they have arrived.

You can be sure of that, Ramon. But now I have to go. You know, work!

Ramon waves when Mira leaves and quickly, he closes the WebCom to have a good night's sleep. The new moon is near and it is dark outside.

Unbelievable, says Ramon to himself. So at this moment, some aliens are flying in the direction of the Earth through the Neet tunnel. Relieved by the recent findings he can finally relax and quickly he falls asleep.

- 71 -
18/9/2007

At the next traffic light to the left, says the always friendly voice through the loudspeakers. The book was almost finished and a call from Rich was enough to convince Ramon to bring him a visit. He didn't tell anything about the possible landing of the Sheyan or the code found on the web. He wanted to surprise him with the book. They watched some movies of Stanley Kubrick and enjoyed a good wine.

I am glad that the book is almost finished, Ramon. I never thought that you could finish it in such a short time.

Neither did I, Rich. There is still a lot of work to get it right but I am glad that the basic writing of the book comes to an end. I hope I can start with the translation in a month or so.

I am really curious, Ramon.

So am I, Rich. It is still a surprise to me how it will end. That will keep me busy for some days. But I am glad that you showed me the movie 2001 A Space Odyssey. It is still a marvelous piece of art, isn't it?

Absolutely, Ramon. So you are sure that this was in fact the first official disclosure that alien civilizations really exist?

Absolutely, Rich, I don't doubt it for a minute. Because why was the greatest hyperrealist in the movie business suddenly that interested in alien life? Not for the money. That was the least of his problems. No, no, Rich. He must have been confronted with something in the beginning of the sixties, which triggered his interest related to the alien reality.

Well, now that I think about it, you could be right, Ramon. But you told me that Kubrick was probably the one that faked the moon footage?

Indeed, Rich. That was based on the documentary Dark Side of the Moon. But it made me think, Rich. Most people don't realize that if Kubrick made the fake footage, he not only had to fool the people of the world but also most people at NASA, who followed everything in real time.

That is hard to believe, Ramon. If he was behind such a fraud, then he really was a master of deception with a lot of guts.

Oh yes, Rich. He definitely was. You can compare him with Leonardo Da Vinci. Leonardo was the master of optical illusions and one of the first to use perspective in his drawings.

But how do you think that Kubrick did it, Ramon? How could he fool everybody?

I think that the first question you need to answer is: why? If he did it, then why has he done it? When I found the link between the two documentaries, I performed a thought experiment.

You mean the link between the documentary "The Dark Side of the Moon" and the documentary "Mirlo Rojo"?

Yes. It is all hypothetical, but it would make a lot of sense. Imagine that the person who died in the "The Dark Side of the Moon" documentary was the same person who delivered the
454

documents about the moon base of the "Mirlo Rojo" documentary.

You mean General Vernon Walters?

Indeed, Rich. The comments on the web about the documentary "The Dark Side of the Moon" call it a "mockumentary", meaning that it was just fiction or in other words, just a lot of nonsense. But fact is that Vernon died in the night after he had the last interview for the documentary "The Dark Side of the Moon". And that is very suspect, don't you think, especially if it was all just a joke.

That's an understatement, Ramon. It is definitely an extreme kind of coincidence.

So if he was indeed the same person, then that means that the footage of the moon base of the "Mirlo Rojo" documentary is real. At least, it is possible. Imagine that the footage was real, then that would be a good reason to punish General Vernon for breaking his vow of secrecy, no? Before somebody decides to give such an order, there must be a very good reason, don't you think?

Absolutely, Ramon. If he didn't die a natural death, he must have done something that was unforgivable. But it is all hypothetical, Ramon. You don't have real proof for that.

That's true, Rich. It is all hypothetical. But just imagine for a minute that it were true. That would mean that the existence of moon bases was known several years before Apollo 11 started its odyssey to the moon. And this brings us back to the "why". Why would Kubrick help faking the moon landing? He must have had a very good reason. And I really don't believe that he did it because some people feared that the images would be of bad quality. Or because they didn't have a camera to film on the moon, as was stated in the documentary. Come on, Rich. There were no problems to make pictures and footage in space. So why wouldn't they be able to shoot footage on the moon? That doesn't make sense. And secondly, the broadcast of the moonwalk was of a horrible quality anyhow.

You're right, Ramon. That couldn't be the reason. So you think that some of the participants in the documentary didn't know the real facts either?

I think so, Rich. I think they told what they knew, but they were in turn kept in the dark. They just had to arrange the deal with Kubrick. But however it went, Walters stated that he knew how and why the fake footage was made. He said that very clearly, when he asked to shut down the cameras. He even said that it would cost human lives when it would become public. And he was very serious about that. Next day he was indeed dead!

Indeed, Ramon. It could be that he knew what would happen when he would speak.

You take the words right out of my mouth, Rich.

Okay, Ramon. Suppose your reasoning is right, what will be the next step?

The next light to the right, says the voice of the GPS system.

Don't interfere, says Ramon, laughing. What I wanted to say, Rich… If I am on the right track, then the pictures of the moon base could be real. And then we arrive at the next stage of the reasoning. Kubrick became fascinated by alien life in 1964. So it could be that there were already rumors and speculations that ruins or alien settlements existed on the moon. Don't forget that project Blue Book dates back to 1955. The first hard evidence could be from the Ranger project. Ranger 8 made the first pictures of Mare Tranquillitatis in a resolution of 1.5 meter per pixel before impact in 1965 on 18 February. It was very close to the Apollo 11 site. If something had been seen on the pictures, then Kubrick could definitely be informed about that. And that was months before Kubrick started with the preparations of the movie 2001 A Space Odyssey.

That's right, Ramon.

So it could be that Kubrick made this movie not only for public relation purposes. If a select group of people was informed about the alien presence, then they surely had to answer the question how to confront the public with this knowledge.

It must be so, Ramon. Such a task could be compared to telling the people at the end of the middle ages that the Earth wasn't flat but round and that the Earth was turning around its axis and around the sun as well.

Rightly so, Rich. And this select group of people, I call them the Initiated, must have been puzzled about how to tell such a story to the people of the world, without stirring up social, political and religious conflicts.

456

That makes sense, Ramon. And you think that it is possible that for that reason, they decided to give Kubrick green light to make the movie 2001 A Space Odyssey?

Isn't that a logical deduction, Rich? Just think about it. The first scenes of the movie give a picture of the primates, living at the time of the dawn of the human evolution. But then, this primate comes into contact with an alien intelligence. Kubrick used a polished stone monolith as a representation of this alien intelligence. That was very clever because in this way, everybody could give his own interpretation of this intelligence, free from cultural projections. And then suddenly, the movie makes a jump of five million years to recent times. On the moon, the monolith is discovered, buried in the ground for five million years, which is as long ago as the human evolution lasted, suggesting that alien contact would be comparable with the dawn of the next step of human evolution. When I was watching the movie yesterday, everything became suddenly clear, when Dr. Heywood R. Floyd gave his speech on the moon base. Specifically when he told in very clear words why everything had to be kept secret for the public. That speech is so well written. There is not a word too many. I know the speech by heart, you know. It goes like this:

"Congratulations on your discovery, which may prove to be the most significant in the history of science. Now I know there have been some conflicting views regarding the need for complete security in this matter, more specifically, your (the people that work on the moon base) opposition to the cover story, created to give the impression of an epidemic at the base. I understand that beyond it being a matter of principle, many of you are troubled by the concern and anxiety this story of an epidemic might cause to your relatives and friends on earth. I completely sympathize with your negative views. I find this cover story personally embarrassing myself.

However, I accept the need for absolute security in this. And, I hope you will too. I am sure you're all aware of the extremely grave potential for cultural shock and social disorientation contained in this present situation if the facts were prematurely made public without adequate preparation and conditioning. Anyway, this is the view of the Council."

I would say "the people of the Council" are the Initiated, Rich.

I get it, Ramon.

A great speech, is it not? And Floyd ends it by saying:

"The purpose of my visit here is to gather additional facts and opinions on the situation and to prepare a report for the Council, recommending when and how the news should eventually be announced. If any of you would like to give me your views and opinions, in private if you like, I will be happy to include them in my report.

… [silence] …

Well, I think that's about it."

That's it, Rich. It sounds so real, having the two documentaries in the back of your mind.

It is indeed a remarkable speech, Ramon. It could well be the perfect method to make something public what had to be kept secret for the public. It is a perfect mix of reality and fiction. The message was indeed clear. Secrecy until the Initiated, whoever they are, knew how to bring the message to the public.

That's what I think too, Rich. The movie explains in a symbolic way that the discovery of an alien presence will be the beginning of a new period in history. The beginning of a new world-view and of a new attitude towards the place of humanity in the universe. But in essence, Kubrick made indeed a movie to disclose something that had to stay secret. By doing it this way, the movie brought the topic into the public domain. If Kubrick was informed about the existence of a moon base or some kind of alien presence on the moon and the Initiated wanted to use the Apollo to have a look there, then Kubrick knew what was at stake. It was out of the question that the base could be seen on live TV. At least, that makes it much more understandable why a man like Kubrick would ever want to participate to fake the live broadcast. There had to be a very good reason. And can you think of a better reason Rich? I can't.

You have a point, Ramon. Kubrick was too authentic to fool people. There had to be a very good reason why he did it. But how then did he do it, Ramon? He had to do it under the eyes of the NASA people. I guess most employees were also kept in the dark about that. How else could it be kept secret for so long.

That is the 2001 billion dollar question, Rich. How did he do it!

458

Don't forget. He was the grandmaster of camera technology. He was the best of his time. That was probably also the reason why he was chosen to work for the NASA and to prepare the broadcast of the moon landing as you can read in several articles. Do you remember how carefully the astronauts where prepared for the moon landing?

I remember it very well, Ramon. They used large models of the moon surface. They projected moving images in front of the capsule to give the astronauts a realistic impression of what they would see when they approached the moon.

I remember it very well too, Rich. They even made a model in actual size of the landing site, where the astronauts had to exercise every action they had to do in strict timing. So the whole period of the landing was scripted. And we must not forget that Kubrick had a lot of experience in making the movie 2001 A Space Odyssey. And after that, he had again a year to prepare for the moon landing. You have to admit that this movie is still outstanding and able to compete with all the special effects of recent movies.

My God, Ramon, it is too crazy to think about it. He was a master of deception. But how do you think he did it finally? How was it done? What was the trick?

The blue light posts of Ramon's village come in sight.

Next street to the right, says the GPS voice.

Well there are different options, Rich. I will explain in a minute how I think that Kubrick did it.

A few minutes later, both sit with a cup of coffee in front of the screens and Ramon shows Rich some footage of the real moon landing.

Do you see it, Rich?

Not really, Ramon. It is all so vague.

Look carefully, I play it again. Look how the astronaut walks in front of the flag. Look closely. Look! You can see the flag, even when the astronaut is walking in front of it.

Do you mean that they used double footage?

That could indeed be the case, Rich. The images of the moon are real. But the astronauts are almost like ghosts. You must not forget that Kubrick wasn't able to manipulate the footage, because it was a live broadcast. I remember that Chriet Titulaer made a remark on the quality of the footage. He said that it was because of the after-image being very strong, due to the extreme light of the sun. But that was not the case in the other moon landings. So it could very well be that we are looking at the real moon landscape but the astronauts could be faked. In the mean time, the real astronauts were able to do some archaeological research of the moon base. You must not forget that the whole scenario of the activities of the astronauts was known to the second. It wasn't that hard to use a few actors to do the same thing in a studio. And it is also very important to know that the shooting for the live broadcast was done with fixed cameras. To use the trick of the double footage, the cameras in the studio of Kubrick had to be placed on the same spot as on the moon.

But Ramon, then Kubrick had to have a special studio to make the fake footage.

Oh, yes. He could use the same studio that he used for the 2001 movie. The only thing he really needed was a blue room or something alike because he only had to film the astronauts. All the rest was on the moon footage. That was the essence of the trick. And because the pictures were in highly contrasted black and white, it was rather easy to show the two footages simultaneously.

Damn, Ramon. You could be right, you know. And everything looked real because the moon landscape was very real.

Exactly, Rich. Kubrick had to take into account that this footage must not be in contradiction with later missions to the moon. By the way, the landscape was very boring. The horizon was almost completely flat. There were no mountains. It was just a boring desert with a few craters, hardly visible, because everything was filmed from the ground. But it got even easier when they went inside the lunar module after a while to rest or sleep if possible. The camera could be stopped, once they were inside. Because there is no wind on the moon, they could then come out again to do some further investigations of the ruin. The trick of the double footage was that sometimes the astronauts could be real and other times they could be faked. In this way, it was hard to tell what was fact and what was fiction since the quality of the footage was bad anyhow.

But there was also constant contact with mission control, Ramon.

I thought about that too. The only way to solve that problem was if the footage was ready before the moonwalk. They had to have a very good timing to make no mistakes. But the script was very helpful to make that possible. But you're right, Rich. That's a puzzling thing. I don't think that there is one scene in the whole history of the movies that was rehearsed so often as this one. The astronauts had to know very well when they were visible and when not. It is of course possible that all the footage with the astronauts was faked. But in essence it was all rather simple. It was a question of timing. Nothing more than that. In essence, it was very simple and that's always the clue. Only a guy like Kubrick could come up with something like that.

Right you are, Ramon. But after all, it is even possible that the astronauts did the research of the base during the resting pause.

Even that is possible. I can be wrong you know. But if the footage were faked, I am convinced it happened with the trick of the double footage. Although, I must admit that my whole thought experiment stands or falls with the assumption that Vernon was the key figure in both documentaries. By the way, Rich, do you know that the first ten minutes of the movie 2001 A Space Odyssey were removed, after the premiere?

No, Ramon, I didn't know that.

I read it on Wikipedia. The removes scenes showed interviews with scientists, talking about their ideas about life in the universe. So Kubrick must have been very fascinated by the subject. I am sure he knew something that triggered him to become so involved in the subject. The question is of course, what did he know?

Both go on for a while until Rich looks at the time.

I have to go, Ramon. Thanks for the coffee and the cake.

Okay, Rich. It was my pleasure to relieve some steam yesterday. And the wine was excellent.

The pleasure was all mine, Ramon. Keep me informed about the book.

You will be the first to know when it is available, Rich.

Ramon waves his good friend goodbye while the GPS guide gives Rich directions. Back in front of his screens, Ramon opens the word processor and after a bit of daydreaming he starts to write the last chapters of the book. But he can't concentrate very well. The idea that the Sheyan will land on Earth is playing with his mind.

As he goes to sleep late at night, he sees the moon through the window. He realizes that it will be full moon tomorrow and it will be the 27/9/2007. What a funny date! Three times nine if you add up the numbers. And nine again if you add them all. Ramon learned something about numerology from Harish Johari. Those were the days, he thinks, those were the days. And already excited about what could happen tomorrow, he falls asleep.

- 72 -
27/9/2007

All day long Ramon tries to work on his book. There is no sign of Mira. The first phase of the book comes to a close. But Ramon is too nervous. Would the Sheyan land today on Earth? That was the only thing he could think about. He looks again at some of the footage of NASA. Especially the pictures of Secret Space were intriguing, showing footage of a kind of laser beam that seems to be shot at a UFO.

This footage was analyzed by David Serada and some of his findings can be found on YouTube. He stated that this beam was possibly shot from a place in Australia, where an American military base is located. Ury had already been working for years on a laser weapon. Could it be that this technology could be used for military purposes? Not only for enemy rockets because the laser can only be of use in a straight line. The horizon gets in the way. But to shoot on UFOs in space? That could be of course. Ramon knew rumors that this technology was already operational in the Star Wars project of President Reagan. To shoot down UFOs that move very fast with laser beams could be an alternative option.

If satellites could give the coordinates of a flying UFO to a ground station, then laser beams traveling with the speed of light would have a good chance to hit it. Especially the footage of the laser beam could mean that the military looks for weak spots in the Grey technology. That on itself was a positive thing. This technology could be of use when the information of Teimon

462

would change the secret strategic scenarios of the Initiated. These lasers could be a defense against the alien threat.

Hours go by and Ramon decides to go to the garden. It is cold for the time of the year, but the sun is shining.

Nuts lay on the ground, waiting to be saved from the wet weather. Ramon enjoys the fresh air and an hour later he goes back home with a bag full of nuts. To kill the time, he starts to make a nut cake. This traditional cake announces the coming of the winter months. He puts all the ingredients on the table. The nuts are mixed and the balance is used to do the measuring. As he shoves everything into the oven, Mira comes running into the kitchen, completely confused.

Ramon... I see fire! I think they have crashed!

Crashed? Are you sure Mira? Ramon is shocked.

What else could it be, Ramon? I saw a desert-like landscape, with very red sand. And then I saw a kind of light beam and then I saw fire, all around me.

Oh my God! I hope they haven't shot them down, Mira.

Shot them down? What do you mean, Ramon? Who would shoot them down? I have no idea what happened. I was so shocked by what I saw. That's why I came immediately.

Ramon is really mad while thinking back on the video footage.
Have you any idea if they are still alive, Mira?
I have no clue, Ramon. I see only fire.
I don't believe it! Those basta…

I will spare you what Ramon said next...
…

Acknowledgments

In the first place I would like to thank the humans of Ter I, Teimon, Aodin, the five others and Aryein, representative of the Ancients for their openness and patience.

I thank the twelve Tulkus here on earth, especially Merly and the Tibetan for revealing me hidden knowledge.

I especially thank the paranormal key persons Mira and Ury who trusted me to reveal this information.

I thank all my teachers, especially my Wise Teacher, for everything they taught me.

I thank everybody who helped me to put everything into words and who supported me to finish the task of writing the book.

I thank every person involved in bringing ufology and related topics into the open via the existing media. They put their good name and more on the line to spread the word.

Ramon.

www.ingramcontent.com/pod-product-compliance
Lightning Source LLC
Chambersburg PA
CBHW071340020726
47502CB00001B/191